Gerald Everett Jones's experience-based tale of Kenya's growth in a rapidly changing world is done with care and affection. Wonderfully entertaining, decorated with interesting facts, this tale acknowledges the hopes of past and present, along with warmth for the future. Virtual tourism which will make you long to share the experience yourself.

— EDGAR SCOTT, AUTHOR OF *418: I AM A TEAPOT*

HARRY HARAMBEE'S KENYAN SUNDOWNER

HARRY HARAMBEE'S KENYAN SUNDOWNER

A NOVEL

GERALD EVERETT JONES

LaPuerta
Books and Media
www.lapuerta.tv

Hardcover: 979-8-9860953-2-5; Paperback: 978-1-7359502-1-1

Kindle ISBN: 978-1-7359502-2-8 ASIN: B08ZV9ZPG6

EPUB ISBN: 978-1-7359502-3-5

Library of Congress Control Number: 2021904908

Cover and interior design by La Puerta Productions

Cover photo by TUBARONES PHOTOGRAPHY from Pexels

Author photos by Gabriella Muttone Photography, Hollywood and by Runkee Productions

PREFACE

Literary fiction should stand on its own. However, I have updated the text with this this brief note because so much has changed since the book's relatively recent release. My wife Georja Umano and I emigrated from our home in Southern California to Kenya in 2018. Our purpose was to pursue her goal of supporting wildlife conservation, especially the plight of endangered elephants. Kenya would seem to be on the forefront of these efforts, for two reasons: First, it is among the few countries on the continent that has outlawed trophy hunting and vigorously prosecutes poachers. Second, its Kenyan Wildlife Service is staffed with professionals who put some teeth into those policies.

At that time, during the first Trump administration, other government policies applying to immigration were becoming more restrictive. For example, a person with a tourist visa could not work in any capacity — even as a volunteer. Partially because Georja holds advance degrees in education, she found work teaching at a home for unwed mothers. These are impoverished young women who have been abused, raped, or abandoned. In the country's patriarchal society, they are outcasts. Although they live less than a day's drive from the nearest wildlife preserve, few have ever seen an elephant. And although this shelter was located in a resort town, none had eaten in a restaurant, and daily food rations often fell short of their needs.

Georja's classes in language arts also included lessons in environmental awareness and sustainability. The hope was that, if her students managed to return to their villages, they could help mitigate human-wildlife conflict: A new farm might dig a borehole (well) to provide water for consumption and irrigation — but perhaps with unintended consequences. Elephants can smell the water and may trample a corn crop on their way to it. Big cats may attack a herd of cattle. The community will likely dispatch local hunters to destroy the invaders. However, if they have been schooled in alternatives, prospects for both the beasts and the children can be brighter.

Georja and I had considered staying in Africa indefinitely. But at the outbreak of Covid, our situation there became a bit too "interesting." Nevertheless, we couldn't have known, having returned, that circumstances in the United States would become even more unsettling.

Since that time, Georja has founded the Elephant Matriarch Project (elephantmatriarch.org), a charitable organization that aims to further the work she did in Kenya.

Meanwhile, I have continued to write my own stories, as well as coach and edit the work of emerging authors. When we lived in Diani Beach, we had fiberoptic access to the Internet, so my own daily routine — then and now — has not been much different.

Like many novels that do not easily fit into a popular genre, this novel is something of a fictionalized memoir. As you would expect, some of Harry's experiences were mine, others I picked up from local gossip at the vegetable market, and a few are wild inventions, mostly to motivate the arguments and conflicts that propel drama.

I refuse to confess which episodes are true-to-life. I will admit that my neighbors in the market would assure me, "We are one," while also cautioning, "Corruption is the mother of Kenya."

I have since learned that the national motto, "Harambee," which originally meant *unity* is now synonymous with corruption. *Harambees* came to describe community gatherings. Those meetings morphed into town halls, then political fundraisers, and ultimately, unashamed solicitation.

Needless to say, I now view the world through Kenyan eyes.

Harry must ask himself whether he is to be a tourist or a citizen.

That is, indeed, the question.

- Gerald Everett Jones
Santa Monica, October 2025

PROLOGUE

*H*arry Gardner, who thought his given name "Harrison" much too formal, did not consider himself an immoral man. His shrink, if he still had one, would say he was on a therapeutic quest. The more generous of his peers in the golf-club locker room would say he was taking a much-deserved breather. But he had to admit, at least to himself, that his intention in going to East Africa was to engage in illicit activities, although he had only a vague idea of what those activities might involve.

CHAPTER 1

 s Harry sat at the bar in the Tiki Lounge in Diani Beach, just a short walk from the white sand, he wondered whether he'd been betrayed. Aldo was supposed to meet him here, and the fellow was more than an hour overdue. Granted that appointments in Kenya are more good intentions than hard deadlines, Aldo's client expected to get what he'd paid for. The trip package had been prepaid, as was customary, and so far all the bookings had been solid and the accommodations sumptuous. Harry doubted whether Aldo had absconded with any funds. But this was wary Harry's first venture offshore in a lifetime, and part of the deal was supposed to be Aldo's companionship and watchful guidance.

Harry would later learn that Aldo was in Mombasa meeting with an attorney, David Odiengo. Since Esther was in Mombasa as well, did they meet? Were they somehow working together? On what? And for whom? These became questions that nagged at him.

Esther, a local hottie, was an eligible widow who might be in her thirties, perhaps forty, and seemed to be captivated by Harry's charm, if not his looks. She would be too old for the younger men of this resort town, unless she was rich, which she apparently wasn't. But Harry was no prize when it came to physique. His body was thickset and pudgy, and he was losing his hair. He liked to think he had heart. He didn't think himself wealthy, either, but people here assumed he was. She'd taken to teasing him with the nickname "Harambee." Neither had told him what it meant, literally. Aldo had hinted it was complimentary. But now both of them liked to taunt him with it, usually accompanied by wide grins and chuckles. And Harry's affable, round face was now familiar enough around this little town that others were catching on, too, and they seemed just as amused. Good-naturedly, he hoped.

It wasn't until he was studying a banknote in this solitary moment at the bar when he saw *Harambee* emblazoned on the banner of the Kenyan coat of arms, just beneath two lions rampant guarding a tribal shield. Harry pulled out his phone and searched online for the definition, discovering that the national motto in Kiswahili means *We Pull Together,* or simply, *Unison.* Harry still didn't make the connection. He was aware that people on the street were likely to greet him as *Papa,* a respectful term for an older gentleman of any race, or *mzungu,* meaning *white man* or — if uttered with extra emphasis — meaning *crazy* (or *clueless* or worse) *white man.*

Harry Harambee would discover that, to some of his new friends, he would be *one of the boys* or *one of our boys* or *one of my boys who has our money.* Which is to say, *One for all and all for one.* Or, he feared, *You for us and all you have for all of us.*

Unity!

Had she taken advantage of him? Or was he exploiting her? Was he allowing himself to be manipulated, or was he asserting himself into her life?

But despite these troubling considerations, for once his life was interesting.

So, perhaps Aldo wasn't taking advantage, just trying to make Harry's life seem more worthwhile. That was what the fellow had promised.

And so here Harry was, killing time pleasantly at the Tiki. Waiting for Aldo. When Esther had taken off for Mombasa this morning, he'd mentioned he would be here in the evening. But it wasn't like they'd made a date. He'd only known her three days.

Harry was on his fourth gin-and-tonic, which the inexperienced adventurer might assume he was consuming to ward off malaria. True, malaria is serious and all too common in any part of equatorial Africa. But Harry knew, despite age-old claims by habitually soused Brits of the Raj in India, that the quinine dose in the tonic isn't nearly enough to have much medicinal effect. (If you consumed enough to knock out the disease, the toxicity would probably kill you.) What's more, malaria, while prevalent and widespread, is the word Kenyans use to describe everything from gut-wrenching influenza to the common cold. On a bus trip, a Kenyan-born white aristo told Harry that doctors encourage the locals to worry they have malaria whenever they have a cough or a fever or even the sniffles. They'd report to a clinic, and nine times out of ten they'd get an injection of distilled water and go home with an envelope containing two aspirin. The justification for this ruse was presumably to make sure that the relatively small proportion of patients who actually have the disease will bother to get treated. Harry wondered whether this canard was a benign public-health control measure or simply a racist myth to portray the descendants of indigenous tribes as gullible and easily controlled.

Where was Aldo? The sun had long since gone down and Harry was getting hungry. The Tiki specialized in marinated shrimp and calamari barbecued on skewers, and Harry was thinking a dozen of those and a few cold Tuskers would sit just right. He disliked eating alone, but he wasn't going to let his loyalty to Aldo deprive him of a good meal. And, should Aldo show up, Harry resolved he'd make the fellow pay this time, at least for his own dinner.

Just then, the loud put-put of an approaching boda boda cut out as the bike slid to a stop on the gravel of the car park. A passenger hopped off the back, and the driver sped off. As the newcomer stepped from the darkness into the warm light of the bar, Harry's reaction was a mixture of lust, disappointment, and alarm. It wasn't Aldo. It was Esther. And she was wearing a new, low-cut print dress with a matching turban, bright-red loop earrings and a necklace strung with giant beads of the same color, and designer heels. A smartly coordinated handbag hung on her forearm.

Her unblemished skin was almost as black as any Kenyan's Harry

5

had met. It wasn't until he'd ventured over to this side of the world that he realized how black African Americans *aren't*. Many, if not most, are some shade of coffee-and-cream, and, by one glimpse of them on television, any Kenyan could tell you their ancestry must be as much white as black. Indeed, indigenous Kenyans also tend to be suspicious of Arabs and Indians, whom they consider not white but *other*.

This morning Esther had appealed to Harry for money, explaining that her son and daughter needed textbooks for their advanced courses. These textbooks were not only expensive but also rare as hen's teeth, and the only bookstore authorized to sell them was in Mombasa. So she'd have to take a *matatu* to the ferry at Likoni and then into town and hope she'd be there in time before the precious books were sold out.

Harry had marched to the ATM next to the coffee shop where they'd had breakfast, withdrew a stack of crisp banknotes, and made sure to give her some extra for the transport and lunch in the city.

But why had he done this for her? She hadn't asked for it as a loan. She hadn't promised him anything in return. He'd complied cheerfully because nothing about this trip was going as planned and because she was gorgeous and because he *could*.

Esther and Aldo seemed to know each other, but Harry hadn't yet learned how. Maybe she could tell him why his friend was late. Or whether he was coming back at all.

WHEN HARRY BEGAN HIS ADVENTURE, as he still liked to think of it, he told himself he'd be a happy man if he only managed to dip his toes in the turquoise water of the Indian Ocean. He was too old and too unskilled and too cautious to surf. He was too impatient with children to help one build a sandcastle. He might consider snorkeling — that is, if the sea wasn't too choppy, if the boat operator seemed reputable and didn't gouge him on price, and if they gave him a mask that didn't leak.

It all started when the too-slick Aldo Barbieri, a friend of a friend, suggested a tour package for Harry. Barbieri had proposed they meet for a late breakfast at Barney's Beanery on the Santa Monica Promenade. Harry had met the guy at Vince Delgado's lawn party, one of those events Harry usually avoided. Vince came on like a pal and hosted poker nights. But at every opportunity he'd be hustling insurance annuities.

"What do you like to do?" Barbieri asked as he dunked a biscotti in his cappuccino and then snarfed it down.

"Simple enough. No expectations," Harry said. "Balmy weather and a beach. They're telling me I need to relax."

"Who is this *they?*" the Italian in a Calloway golf shirt and Ralph Lauren cardigan wanted to know.

"My daughter. Some friends. Vince, for one, which I guess is why he put us together." Then he added, lest he be accused of leaving her off his list of important persons, "Also, my wife."

"That's right," the faux-amiable fellow said and looked up. "My condolences. In our worst moments, we wish for them to be dead." He actually smiled. "And then they are. Life is so unfair."

"Forty years," Harry said and sighed. "You don't get over that in a day." Barbieri's humor might be lame and tasteless, but Harry couldn't deny its truth. His last years with Lucille hadn't been all that happy. They argued, she suffered. He never seriously wished for her to go. But he wanted the tension to ease. And he wanted her suffering to end. And then it had, more abruptly than he'd expected.

Lucille's passing was two years ago. The period since then could go down in his diary, if he'd kept one, on a page or two. Bored aimlessness. Amateurish golf with guys who wanted to sell him timeshares or reverse mortgages. Spurned invitations to bridge parties. More recently, offers from well-wishers to set him up on polite dates with lonely crones.

This first meeting with Aldo had occurred in August in the pre-pandemic year of 2019, typically a hot month in Southern California. But on this day the breeze off the ocean was downright chilly. Always cautious about temperature, Harry wore a windbreaker over his button-down shirt. Nevertheless, he ordered a cold beer, his summer drink, thinking it was a manful choice for a guy-meetup with the fellow he assumed would be his vacation planner.

7

"I do a lot of this, you know," Barbieri said as he took another look at the menu. "And I often go myself. Group rates, best places, safety, all of that. Not a worry in the world."

"I'm not good in groups," Harry said with a dismissive wave. "And I'm not one for small talk."

Barbieri quaffed his coffee. His skin was the color of his cappuccino and his curly hair was jet black. There were sharp lines in his face, possibly from habitually taking too much sun. Harry figured yachties looked like that. This Italian looked like a bookie — or Harry's notion of how a bookie might look. He didn't disapprove of gambling, but he disliked the little he'd done of it.

Harry feared he looked like a schlump. His skin was pale, and everything was beginning to sag. His moon-shaped face made him look fat, but he regarded himself as simply stocky with something of a belly. His chin was starting to go flaccid, and he was in serious danger of getting jowls. His lips looked thinner these days and colorless, and when his mouth was closed, the corners turned slightly downward, no matter what his mood. He refused to wear what was left of his hair in a combover and instead kept it short. He had to admit he was beginning to look like a dyspeptic old guy, even though he judged his mind was sharp as ever, and his digestion was still reliable.

When he looked in the mirror, he'd ceased to regard himself as handsome, if he'd ever been. The drooping of his facial features lent him a somewhat mournful expression. The best spin he could put on it was *sincere*. Indeed, he considered himself a man of his word, a straight shooter, an honest partner in any enterprise.

As he took a noisy sip, Barbieri raised an eyebrow, squinted, and asked, "You getting any?"

Harry hesitated while he wondered about the seriousness of the question. Then he muttered, "Nah."

"Since how long?"

Harry shrugged innocently. "Years."

"C'mon, Harry. Not one hooker? Blind date? Tinder? Not even a hand job in the front seat?"

Harry glanced quickly around at the guests at a nearby table. No heads had turned. They weren't being overheard, or, if they were, no one cared.

Lowering his voice, Harry replied, "I had a couple of dates that I realized were going nowhere from the first glance. But I didn't *want* those to go anywhere. And, yeah, nothing. Not once."

Barbieri teased, "You might as well be a monk, Harry!"

Again, apparently no one heard. Or cared.

"When Lucille was having one of her bad days, she even came right out and gave me permission. I mean, she didn't say 'Go do it,' but she did say if I did, she wouldn't blame me. But she made it clear she didn't want to know. Not that I would've shared."

"So, how do you know it still works?"

Harry smirked. This line of questioning was embarrassing. Especially from someone who wasn't a close friend. "How would anybody? A guy needs to do himself every now and then. You know, keep the prostate pliable."

"How about blue pills? You use those?"

"Tried them a few times before Lucille took a turn for the worse. The doctor gave me samples. Worked fine, maybe too well. I guess she didn't have fantasies about doing it to exhaustion with some young stud. She complained I took too long."

"Wow," Barbieri said. "You're wound up tighter than I thought."

"Is this discussion going somewhere? I mean, isn't this kind of personal when I don't know you at all? Vince Delgado said you were a standup guy, could get me a great price on a luxury tour package, and I wouldn't be sorry. I think I'm sorry already."

"Whoa! Peace!" Barbieri complained as his grin grew wider. "All this is very much to the point." Even though the people at the next table were in heated conversation themselves and would hardly have noticed, Barbieri was now the one to lower his voice when he added, "I arrange recreational encounters."

Harry was stunned. "I'm not asking for that."

"Your old pal Vince didn't tell you about Thailand last year?"

"He said he got an incredible deal on a couple of tailor-made suits. He rode on an elephant. And the high-rises in Bangkok go on forever, make Manhattan look like a kiddie park."

"Vince and his buddies had the time of their lives. I'm surprised he didn't brag. Maybe he thinks you're too uptight. By the way, we don't do the rides anymore. Animal cruelty. You wouldn't want to see what they have to do to get the elephants tame enough to put up with it."

"And what about those women? Or are they girls? Aren't they being victimized? Are they so happy to serve?"

Barbieri shook his head. Harry wasn't sure whether the fellow was indicating the option was no longer available or just not available for him. "I'm not suggesting Thailand for you. Okay, you didn't ask. But I don't have to guess that Vince knows what you need and figures he's doing you a favor."

"Do I look that desperate?"

"Harry, you're normal! Who was the guy who said that most men lead lives of quiet desperation? At your age and in your situation, that's a given. You'd have to be brain-dead not to still be thinking about it at least a hundred times a day. It's in the wiring, you know?"

"Okay, I'll admit to having fantasies. And I assume that's normal. But what you're talking about is immoral and I imagine totally illegal."

"Look, Harry. I'm a pro at what I do. Bottom line, I arrange once-in-a-lifetime experiences for people of high net worth. I'm in it for the money, sure. Also the lifestyle. Why not? But I will also tell you I have a knack. If what I'm talking about isn't your thing, I will get you whatever fires your rocket. Now I'm not talking about hookups. I'm no pimp. My business is tour packager, but actually it's more like *experience designer.*"

"I don't want this to sound mean, but some people might say you know how to spot a client's weaknesses, then exploit them."

You'd think the guy would be offended, but he just smiled. Barbieri held up a cautionary hand. "Let's back up a minute. Think of it this way. Say you're right here in the land of the free and the home of the brave. You're looking for a date, you spend some time scrolling and swiping headshots on your phone. You like this pretty face, you read her profile. Maybe her generous-sized chest is in the shot. She's not a kid, she's not perfect, so you figure she's for real, she might not object to having a fling with an older man. Thirtysomething? Forty? Maybe she's got a daddy thing. You reach out, she agrees, you meet for coffee or drinks. You hit it off, there's a chemistry, the date slides into dinner. Dinner slides into a passionate hookup on her couch. You stay the night. At breakfast, you guys decide you're into each other." He paused for effect, then challenged, "Could happen?"

"Yeah," Harry admitted. "I suppose. To some people."

"Okay, now let's say the circumstances are a little special. She tells you she's just lost her job. And she's losing her apartment, supposed to move out end of the week. You invite her to shack up with you at your place, just temporary, and she does. You know she can barely pay her way, so you buy the groceries, take her to dinners, and pay the bill. You even take her shopping and buy her some nice clothes. She's thrilled. You're thrilled you did something nice. It could get serious. Or not."

"It's special circumstances, all right. Is this the plot of some movie?"

"Stay with me here. You and your new squeeze are carrying on just fine. You're thinking this is happening really fast, but you won't be unhappy if it keeps going. Is she being exploited? I think not. Are you? She seems sincere. Then one morning — out of the blue — she informs you she has a boyfriend in Sacramento. She was trying to forget him with you, but she can't get him out of her mind. She likes you, but she realizes she still loves him. She makes a call, you put her on a bus, and you never see her again."

"This is a helluva hypothetical."

"It's a made-up story, for sure. But not at all impossible, you have to agree."

"Where are you going with this?"

"So, assume in this story neither of you is married. And you never offered money for her favors. And she never asked. Is what you did immoral?"

"If she wasn't coerced, I suppose not. I'm sure other women would say I'd taken advantage of her, but in that situation, if we were both into it with no expectations, I wouldn't call it exactly sinful."

"And not illegal?"

"Sure. No."

"Okay, Harry. What I described is how some tourists — mostly older Europeans and mostly white — of either sex — hook up with locals every day in Kenya. Understand, I'm not talking about anything that the authorities would describe as prostitution or child slavery. These are consenting adults. The men are usually middle-aged, maybe retired. They've got money, maybe not a lot, but enough. The women are twenty-, maybe thirtysomething. Many of them are single parents, either unmarried or abandoned by their husbands, and they may even have small children. The other way around, it's an older white woman, and the optics are different. She's the one with the money. And she's telling everyone who might care, including hotelkeepers and safari operators, the guy she's traveling with is her driver and her bodyguard. And he probably is, but he also happens to share her room. Or maybe he doesn't, if she cares how that looks."

Harry took a while to say, "I'm going to have to think about this."

To which Barbieri replied, "You're not obligated to hook up with anybody. As if anyone is going to force you to have a good time! Worst case, you'll stay in the best luxury lodges on the planet and eat spectacular food. And on safaris that will thrill you like nothing you've ever done, you'll see all the wild animals before they disappear from the Earth for good. Your driver will park you on the crest of a hill at sundown, set up a table and chairs, and get you cheerfully drunk on gin-and-tonic as you catch the breeze off the savannah, the herds come to the watering hole, and the sky turns pastel shades you never saw before. It's called a *sundowner*, and you could get seriously used to it."

Harry thought about it, then asked, "For how long?"

Barbieri said, "Two, three weeks?" And he stated a package price, airfare, lodging, meals, and all transfers included. "Mind you, a week of getting up before dawn and jostling around in a four-by-four all day is enough safari. I say we start at the beach. Indian Ocean. Relax first. You hook up, maybe we don't leave, even. Best not to plan too much in advance. See where it goes. And it will."

"Wow," Harry said. "Sure sounds like a deal. But, you don't know me. I'm a creature comforts kind of a guy. I'm Bilbo Baggins. I've spent most of my life editing and publishing history books. I'm not keen on taking risks. Why do you think I'd commit to this?"

Aldo lowered his voice and leaned forward. Harry couldn't tell whether this conspiratorial tone was the guy's standard sales close or whether he was really getting choked up. With characteristic Latin passion, he assured his new friend, "You'll do this, Harry, because there's a hole in your life. Not in your heart. I have a feeling you've got a big heart. You just need some practice sharing it." Then Barbieri grinned, resuming his casual enthusiasm. "Please, call me Aldo! We're buddies now. Like I say, once you get there, we don't have to stick to the program. And, believe me, I'll stick by you." Then he flashed a grin with a wink and added, "And you may not want to come back. Ever."

CHAPTER 2

*H*arry's daughter Nicole was not in favor of the idea, even though she'd encouraged her father to stop moping around and take an interest in something besides Lakers basketball. But Harry didn't exactly approve of her recent life choices, so he didn't feel bad about not giving her a vote. Nicole had been through a nasty divorce five years ago from a car salesman who bought more coke than he sold iron. Now she was living with an event promoter whose business had tanked when he was charged with a (presumably baseless) sexual harassment lawsuit, which was eventually dismissed, but the stink stuck. She seemed to fall for guys with big promises and meager assets. She was supporting this one by teaching English as a Second Language in evening classes downtown to Asians and Latinos who might have been just off the boat or, she feared, just out of a shipping container.

Harry informed her he was going for three weeks, and he only told her what Aldo had told him about the safari experience. He'd already resolved to himself that, if anyone asked, sighting wild animals was the main reason he was going.

"I don't see why you're going all that way," Nicole fussed. "You hate getting out of your comfort zone. You might try something less ambitious. There are those Alaskan cruises where you can see wolves and bears. Or those senior tours to Cozumel for dolphins and stingrays and sharks. And if you want to get primitive, you could do a week at Club Med in Cancun, then jump on a bus tour to Chichen Itza. The ruins are only a few hours away, and none of it is all that expensive. You can just as easily meet someone closer to home, and what about all those diseases over there? Africa is how many flights? How many hours on the plane? Do you even know whether the water is safe to drink?"

"No matter where you go, you stick to bottled water. But they are saying you'll have to buy it in glass. They want to ban plastic, I'm told."

"Oh," Nicole cooed in a mocking tone, "so you're thinking they've gone all progressive and green in Kenya?"

"Sounds like it," her father admitted. "I know they care a lot about wildlife conservation. They realize — no animals, no tourists. I've started to read up on it."

"Since when are you worried about wildlife? You used to tell me another ice age could be just as likely as global warming! It didn't sound like you thought we could do anything about either scenario."

"I admit, I'm not up on all the science. But the history intrigues me, especially the colonial period. Also, the way change seems to be accelerating over there. Technology. Even people who have very little money have a phone. It's their wallet and their checkbook. The app is called M-Pesa, and everybody uses it. They were doing that for years before we ever heard of banking with an app. Solar power, wind, geothermal — they're working on all of that. The Chinese are in there in a big way, building roads and bridges. We've pulled back, don't want to be seen as colonial oppressors."

There was a time, before Nicole's rebellious teens, that she shared her father's fascination with history. He recommended she read Balzac and Dickens. She turned him onto Harry Potter, and they read those books together. They played *Trivial Pursuit*.

"We can't afford foreign aid anymore, you mean. It's not like we don't have problems in the good old U-S-of-A." She shot him a look. "So, you're some authority on Africa these days?"

Nicole had dropped by unannounced. He'd phoned her to tell her he was going, and he hadn't expected to exchange goodbyes in person. He wasn't about to ask her for a ride to LAX. He preferred the promptness and dependability of a car service. He'd book a van with multiple passengers to save money. Now she was sitting on the edge of the bed in the master bedroom watching him fret over his clothes, and it occurred to him that the only time a female had ever sat there had been years ago when her mother was still ambulatory. Not that he hadn't wished otherwise since Lucille's passing, but he hadn't done anything to follow through on those fantasies.

Harry was rummaging through his sock drawer. Each pair was rolled up and folded in on itself, just as Lucille had trained him to do. He asked Nicole, "Do you think your guy would want any of these?" He was holding up Argyle woolens for her to inspect.

Harry was the kind of person who had a sock drawer and usually wished it was better arranged. Today he was working on the first draft of his packing. He'd be shipping a two-suiter ahead via Send My Bag to his first hotel and then bringing a duffel on the plane. The suitcase would hold his slacks and sport coat because Aldo said guests would sometimes have to dress for dinner at the upscale lodges. Into the duffel would go his safari clothes — cargo pants and shorts and light-weight short-sleeve shirts, ultralight rainwear, swim trunks, toiletries, and assorted gear, including chargers and voltage adapters, along with a pair of Celestron Nature DX binoculars he'd recently bought on Amazon. (He hoped he could sneak the duffel through as carry-on lest the binocs mysteriously disappear from his checked baggage.)

"His name is Courtney," Nicole said, "and you should donate those if you don't want them. Keep some homeless person's feet warm." Then she demanded, "What's going on here? Are you moving out? And what's up with Beto? I saw him on the way in — with his toolbox."

Beto Cruz was the handyman Harry trusted for all maintenance tasks around the rambling three-bedroom house in Rustic Canyon. Beto was about Harry's age and a semiretired building manager. The mild-mannered fellow didn't always complete work on schedule. Sometimes he underestimated the effort and ended up asking for considerably more money than he'd quoted. But Harry valued Beto's help because the guy could be counted on to give a reliable diagnosis of just about any household problem, from water intrusion to electrical faults to insect infestation. Even with the overages, Harry figured he wouldn't be paying for unnecessary work from opportunistic tradesmen. His confidence in Beto more than compensated for the fellow's less than consistent performance.

Perhaps best of all, Beto charged by the fee he quoted for the task and not by the hour. Good thing, because he liked to talk, and he'd spend time before and after his chores shooting the breeze with Harry about health problems, world affairs, and the rising cost of living. You might even say that these days Beto was Harry's only close friend. Nicole knew Beto well enough to suspect he was taking advantage of her father, but here was another of Harry's decisions in which he did not permit her to have a vote.

"That sounds like three questions," Harry said. "Where do you want me to start? I'm guessing you're taking a pass on the socks."

She huffed, "You're acting like you're not coming back. If that's the plan, I believe I have a right to know." Nicole gave off the vibe of not caring what her father did, but her question made her seem like a child who feared she was being left with a nasty babysitter.

Harry shrugged. "I can't say I have a plan. Beto is building storage cabinets for me in the garage. I'm putting the things I want to keep there."

"So you *are* coming back?"

"You asked the question. I never said I wasn't."

"But why do you have to go and squirrel everything away? It's not like you have all that much burglars would want to steal."

"I'm renting the place out. Furnished."

"For *three weeks?*"

"Yes. It'll help pay my expenses."

"You could have offered it to me! I could be your house sitter."

"You wouldn't have paid."

"Of course not!"

Now he gave *her* a look. "I don't know Courtney all that well — okay, I wasn't even sure of the name. I met him for less than an hour once, when we had drinks that time. Was it my birthday? But I'd question whether you two, once installed, would cheerfully move out. I mean, would I suddenly have semipermanent houseguests?"

"You could — in some alternate universe — move into a smaller place and gift the house to me. It's our family home, the house I grew up in."

"It still has a mortgage. And property taxes. Combined, that's a lot more than you pay in rent in Echo Park, I'd think. And there's upkeep, if for no other reason than to maintain the property value. Now, I wouldn't expect you to get married again, whether to that guy or anyone else. Lifestyle choices, they call it now. But you've got a paycheck for a gig that's only part-time, and is he bringing home anything?"

"You never seemed to care what I did before."

"Maybe you thought I didn't care because I didn't want to be telling you what to do. And then when I realized you might have wanted — no, needed — someone to give advice, it was too late."

"If you're going to take off for good, at least be honest about it."

The accusation was ironic, coming from her. Harry dearly wished she'd share more of her life with him, but he didn't know where to start. Or resume.

He could feel himself getting upset. "Okay, are you all spun up because I'm making life uncertain for you? *My* life is uncertain! I don't have a plan. I wasn't about to lay out all the options to you because I don't know what they are. Maybe this trip will help me focus. But if you're going to insist on having just the facts, let me put it this way: Whether I return or whether I stay over there and you only come to visit for my funeral, I'm renting this place out. I've found a property manager. Social Security isn't quite enough, and I need the income, whether I stay or go. If I do come back — which I was sincerely planning to do until you doubted it — I will probably take that smaller place. But understand — either way, you won't be living here — unless you can afford the rent or you offer me market price to buy it."

If she were a more vulnerable person, she might have cried. Instead, she just grew stiff.

"What if you don't come back because some terrorist cuts your head off?"

"Wow. You're not your mother's child. She had her opinions, but she always made it sound like hers were polite suggestions. Losing my life over there is not an eventuality I'd considered. Thanks for that." He could see she was ashamed she'd said it, but he realized he'd backed her into a corner. He said softly, "My lawyer has my will and a key to the safe deposit box at Bank of America."

"And is that where you've put your wedding band?"

"Thank you for noticing," he said sheepishly. "I suppose you can consider it a family heirloom. Or feel free to sell it after I'm gone."

She snapped, "Sure you won't be needing it again?"

"I don't know what traditions apply, but I have a feeling this kind of keepsake would be in poor taste to reuse. Your mother's rings are in the box, too. Those do get passed down, I believe. That is, if you were intending…"

She ignored the implied challenge. They'd both gotten in their digs. "How come I don't have a copy of the key?"

"Same reason I didn't spell out all the options from now until my end of life! I could change my mind. Realistically, from a financial standpoint, you'd probably be a bit better off if I were dead." Then he emphasized, *"Probably.* But don't go doing the math just yet."

"I don't know for sure you'd leave me anything," she said. "Not that I'd want the publishing company. I wouldn't want those headaches."

"Why not? We're not looking for new titles, and the backlist is selling. The catalog is on the website, the ordering and fulfillment are automated, and we've stopped accepting returns. It makes money while we sleep."

"I've told you before. I don't. Want. The job."

"No, I get that you don't. My parents — my father, particularly — would say the situation calls for self-reliance. Sadly, you didn't know him. But it won't come as news when I tell you he wasn't my favorite person. Maybe I'm just making the same mistakes he did. But I don't think it will make you a better person if you start thinking about how much you stand to inherit. If, God forbid, I have to go into assisted living one day, there might not be anything left by the time I'm finally gone. And don't trust me to shoot myself when I get the diagnosis to spare you the expense."

She sighed and looked away. "Why do I bother?"

"Maybe you think I didn't do right by your mother. I tried to be there, which is about all you can do in the end when they don't have a clue who you are. When my father died, my mother had him cremated and promptly took off with the maître d' from their favorite restaurant. Have I stood by you? Perhaps you'd say not enough. When and if I come back, maybe you'll have an answer."

She sulked. He turned her to face him and assured her, "The cell service isn't bad, even in the rural areas. Safaricom. All the hotels have Wi-Fi. Another thing I learned, everybody's using WhatsApp. So you could be hearing from me more than you want to. Electronic postcards. Stupid selfies. Pictures of my lavish dinners — hopefully, before I've eaten them." He looked at her squarely and said, "I'm sure you're not saying you don't want me to go."

"I'm not saying that. I just don't know where I stand."

"This is going to sound harsh. But the reason you don't know where you stand is because I'm worried about where you're standing. And who with. I've never told you what to do — or at least not since about the seventh grade. But if I'm out of the picture — however temporarily — maybe your choices will be clearer."

"It's only three weeks. Why am I thinking it's forever?"

"Because now you've got me thinking maybe it could be."

CHAPTER 3

*H*arry had thought making a trip to the consulate in Los Angeles would be a brief formality. Aldo had advised him not only to make sure his US passport was current — with at least a year left until expiration — but also to obtain his Kenyan visa in advance. The alternative would be to wait in a long line on arrival at Jomo Kenyatta International Airport, pay the ninety-day tourist-visa fee in cash, then wait another hour or more for his digital photo and fingerprints to be taken and duly recorded. Aldo warned that putting up with this bureaucratic process after a long, transcontinental flight would be needlessly wearying at the arrival time in the middle of the night. And the subsequent long ride from the airport to the arrival hotel in downtown Nairobi would be wearying enough.

The consulate was on the second floor of a low-rise office building in the Wilshire district that also housed the South Korean Business Liaison Office, as though all foreign interests starting with the letter *K* had been assigned to that location. The Kenyan office was modest and clean, with four guest chairs in a narrow waiting room, facing a Plexiglas security window, no receptionist, and an intercom to summon the officer on duty. A smiling portrait of the current President, Uhuru

Kenyatta, hung on the wall. Harry would later spot the same photo in every business he entered in Kenya.

After Harry buzzed to announce himself on the intercom, a female voice advised him to have a seat. After about ten minutes, an attractive young woman in business attire appeared at the window, let him in, and showed him into her tiny office. She invited him to sit and introduced herself as Ruth Ngigi, cultural attaché. She gave him an application form and a pen, explaining that he had the option of applying for a ninety-day tourist visa or a multiple-entry visa, available for an extra fee.

"And why would I want that?"

"If you're on business, you may need to come and go. If you simply plan a vacation and won't be coming and going, there is no need. But I should advise you that, if for any reason you decide to leave the East African Union — for a home emergency, say — you will require a reentry visa. Suppose you plan to stay past the initial ninety days of the tourist visa. In that case, you will need to either renew by visiting Immigration in Nairobi or be required to temporarily leave the East African Union, paying for a new tourist visa on your return. So, you see, arranging for a multiple-entry visa now preserves your options at modest additional expense."

Harry would learn that, given Kenyan protocols, paying the required fees online was easy enough, but obtaining a valid stamp from a breathing human bureaucrat would always need a major physical effort.

He decided to take her advice and paid the fee for the upgraded permit. She accepted it with a smile, took his signed application, then informed him that his application and his US passport would have to be forwarded to Nairobi for processing. He could return in two weeks to pick up his passport, stamped and signed with the visa authorization.

"You're sending my passport to Africa?" he asked incredulously.

She nodded. "By diplomatic pouch. I assure you, it's quite safe."

"Is there no one here who can use a stamp? I mean, this seems incredibly inefficient."

"Unfortunately, such authority is not vested in this office." Her smile persisted. "We are authorized only to receive applications and payments. You can understand, these regulations and procedures apply to all countries, not just the United States. And these days the sensitivities are quite high."

It didn't occur to him at the time, but the phrase about sensitivities would pop into his mind from time to time in the course of his adventures.

～

HARRY WAS JUST ABOUT to leave the reception area at the consulate when a tall African dressed nattily in a tailored silk suit and carrying a dark-suede briefcase strode in. His gleaming skin was the color of espresso, and the only hair on his head was on his frosty eyebrows, which nestled behind a pair of gold-plated wire-rims. He flashed a smile at Harry and asked, "Planning on traveling to Kenya?"

"Yeah," Harry replied, still heading for the door lest the guy be selling timeshares.

The fellow held up a hand to stop the older man and gestured for Harry to turn back. "If it's not an inconvenience, why don't you step into my office? I'm Consul General Antoine Wangari."

Harry gave his name in a low voice and dutifully followed Wangari through the door and into a paneled office at the end of the hallway. As the consul set his briefcase aside on the desk and hung up his coat, he beckoned formally for Harry to sit. As he took his place behind the desk and straightened a tie in tribal colors, he asked, "So, are you thinking of starting a business in our country?"

The question unnerved Harry. He wondered whether something he'd said to Ruth might have been misinterpreted, but he couldn't imagine what it was or how this Antoine would already know about it. "No, no," he shrugged. "Just a vacation. A few weeks."

Wangari smiled as he shot the cuffs of his immaculate white dress shirt. The cufflinks were gold and the size of half-dollars, and, although Harry didn't know much about timepieces, from the bulk of the gold watch on the fellow's wrist, he judged the sheer weight of the precious metal might be many times the value of the workmanship, however fine. "You'll be going on safari, of course," the consul prompted.

"Yes, my tour operator is handling it. I've never done anything like this."

"The finest accommodations in the world, I can assure you. White tablecloths, wait staff in black tie, and a sumptuous buffet a mile long! That's in the lodges, of course. But might you also be staying at any of the camps?"

It embarrassed Harry that he didn't know much about his itinerary. He wasn't sure how much safari he'd be able to endure, but Aldo had insisted he couldn't miss the opportunity. He didn't want to insult this diplomatic officer, so he said, "Yes, I believe so. Is there anything I should know? Special things to take?"

Again, the winning smile. "The camps are luxurious, as well. Also with white tablecloths! You'll think you're with Teddy Roosevelt and his entourage on a grand hunting trip! But of course all the shooting these days is with telephoto lenses. Kenya is at the forefront of wildlife conservation, you understand. But, advice? Let me think. Ah! I always advise our guests to take an American electrical plug-in strip. Everyone has so many devices these days. And we Kenyans rely on our cell phones, as well. You may be surprised how high-tech we are. But, you see, the power in the camps is solar. Very sustainable, you understand. No plastic water bottles allowed! The point I am making, you will want to charge your phone at night, of course. But there will be no power in your tent after lights out in the evening. There will be a community tent, which is also the location of the bar and the lounge, and there will be a tap on battery power where guests are invited to leave their phones until breakfast. However, in my experience, there are never enough outlets. So you plug in your strip, which will require one British-style adapter at the plug end for the tap. And then you and your traveling companions will have multiple American-style receptacles to accommodate your devices. Almost no first-time guests think of this."

"Thank you" was all Harry could think to say. "Anything else?"

"If I may be so frank," the Kenyan began, "a cushion for your bum." And he chuckled. "You see, the safari ride will likely be in an all-terrain four-by-four. A rugged Land Rover or Toyota Land Cruiser. You'll never get stuck in a ditch, but the ride is a bit stiff, and those bush tracks are bumpy. Some people jokingly call all that jostling a *Kenyan massage*. After a long day, you'll be glad of the extra padding."

"I hadn't thought of that," Harry confessed, and he marveled that his vacation plans merited such individual attention by the Kenyan government. The office must not be busy.

"Any other destinations?" Wangari asked.

"The beach. My planner tells me the South Coast on the Indian Ocean is marvelous."

"Best beaches in all of Africa! Very popular with European tourists. We don't get so many Americans. We do get people from upcountry on the weekends. Many luxurious venues, I assure you. You won't be disappointed. And the prices are wonderfully affordable." Then he added, in a lowered voice, "I particularly recommend Malindi. Beach-front resorts, nightclubs, and a casino. Tremendously popular with the Italians! You couldn't eat better in Rome!"

Harry would learn the story of Italians on the coast, but for now the consul's description wasn't engaging. Aldo hadn't mentioned this place, he was pretty sure. But he'd try to remember the name of the town so he could ask. He was sure they were booked into some specific places, but he also thought there was some room in the itinerary for flexibility.

Wangari leaned back and crossed his arms. "Are you sure you have no business agenda? Attracting enterprising people like yourself is part of my job."

"And why would I want to do that?" Once again, Harry worried that somehow Wangari had inside information on him. As if Nicole had phoned ahead to warn them that Harry had no intentions of ever coming back. He felt he was sufficiently paranoid about the US surveillance state, but he couldn't imagine the Kenyans would be so sophisticated as to know any more about him than he wrote on their forms.

"Or you might be ready to retire. Your pension will go a lot farther, you know. Kenya is a vibrant economy, growing faster than almost any developing country on the planet. Two trillion dollars in the next decade, they are saying. And we have land! Beautiful country-side. Ideal climate. There are the wildlife preserves, of course. Under government or tribal control, most of them. But there's plenty of room for new development — new cities, even! You should see Nairobi! Skyscrapers like New York! Superhighways, high-speed rail!"

"So, you're welcoming foreigners? And not just as tourists?"

"Certainly. Enterprising people like yourself. I don't know what you do, but you appear to be a well-off, mature man. A man of some experience. I'm sure you bring expertise. And, yes, I'll be honest. We need foreign capital. But here's a place not only to multiply your investment but also to ensure a comfortable lifestyle for the rest of your days. Now, I don't know your personal circumstances, but do you own your home in Southern California?"

"Yes," Harry admitted, careful to stop short of giving more information.

Wangari leaned forward, rested his dazzling cuffs again on the desk, lowered his voice, and offered, "For whatever you're paying in mortgage now, you can have a four-bedroom house in a gated compound with a pool and a full-time staff. You may choose to have a car, perhaps two. Or you may not want one. Just summon a private car and a driver whenever you want to go out. But in the seaside villages, people either walk or hail a tuk-tuk. At the beach, a dollar will take you anywhere in town."

"And setting up a business? What's involved?" Since the fellow seemed to be urging it on him, Harry thought he should at least find out.

"What manner of business, may I ask?"

"I don't have any plans. You could say I'm semiretired. I used to be in publishing." Harry still owned a small-press imprint that specialized in history books. His customers were mainly libraries, universities, and professional organizations. Taking any of that to Kenya was a new thought. But if it could be a tidy retirement plan, why not?

The consul offered a wan smile and said, "There is always a need for responsible journalism. Americans have no shortage of opinions. But you must appreciate that in the wide world one must be careful. You never know who is listening."

"I'm not a reporter," Harry insisted.

Wangari took a breath. "People may assume. To write anything, you must research, you must investigate. Just asking questions could bring suspicion."

"I'm not the curious type," Harry lied.

"I do think, in general, taking any kind of enterprise to Kenya is a potentially prosperous move. Despite what I've said, I would advise you to wait before filing an application. Get on the ground, look around, ask discreet questions. You will see soon enough how things are."

Wangari waved a hand to indicate it was all innocuous. "As to the application, when you are ready, it is straightforward. A simple form and fees. The form is online and it can be processed through this office. With the application, you state you have over a minimum net worth available for investment. And, I emphasize, anyone who owns a home in this fine city will more than meet that requirement. And the fees? A couple of thousand dollars, all in, even with some professional advice if you need it."

"Then what?"

"When you're approved, which takes about a month and almost no one gets turned down, you can get a work permit for a year showing yourself as your own employer. Very tidy. Very simple." Then Wangari asked, almost incidentally, "You're going on a tourist visa, am I right?"

"Yes," Harry said. "Multiple-entry, as Ruth advised. Not sure I'll need that, but I'm trying not to plan too far ahead these days."

"Very wise, and why should you, a man of comfortable means whose time is obviously his own?" He added, "I should tell you, so we're clear, on a tourist visa you are a visitor. You come, you spend money, you go back. If you wish to work — and, I must be very clear — if you want to even *volunteer* — you must have a valid work permit. I have to tell you that unless you are your own employer as I have described, it will be challenging these days to find an employer to sponsor you. Of course, if you're already employed by some international corporation or NGO, that's one way. I take it you are not?"

Harry shook his head.

"As I thought. But, Kenyan employers? They are required by the government to give preference to citizens unless the person is bringing expertise that can't be found in-country."

"Sounds like a strict system," Harry said.

"It's getting to be like this all over, not just in Kenya. Pushback against globalization, you might say. But that's why I bring up the idea of taking your own business there. Not much red tape, and you're the boss. Oh, and retiring? You can't do *that* on a tourist visa, either. There are much the same requirements if you intend to retire — you apply, demonstrate net worth, and pay the fees. It takes some time. You can't do it overnight." The man paused significantly, once again flashed his broad smile, and added, "Still, all things are possible in today's Kenya for a man of resources such as yourself."

The consul shoved his business card across the desk. It was decorated in the Kenyan national colors with its coat of arms.

"If you have questions, don't hesitate to call me on the cell number. If you decide you need a business advisor, I have colleagues in-country who will be pleased to offer guidance."

"I'll think about it," Harry said, intending for it to sound dismissive but not appreciating how much he would come to fret about Wangari's advice.

CHAPTER 4

*H*arry lived in a sprawling, white-clapboard ranch home nestled in the lush woodland richness of Rustic Canyon. It was built on a half-acre lot with a pool, a hot tub, and a redwood deck. He'd converted one of the three bedrooms into an office, another into an exercise room. There he had a set of weights, a wall-to-wall gym mat, and a fifty-inch television. He'd sold the treadmill Lucille had bought him years ago. He detested those devious machines with their tiny, embedded computers that insisted on controlling him while attempting to coach or entertain. These days, he used only the hand weights, or he'd lie on his back and meditate with earbuds to an app. Other times, he'd be in there catching a Lakers game or binge-watching some BBC mystery series on Netflix. He stared up at the screen while he reclined, his head propped up on a round foam exercise roller he rarely used for its intended purpose. He preferred the European cable episodes, not because of the whodunnit plots, which were just as unimaginative as their American counterparts but with less mayhem and gore. He loved the realism of plots set in locales where he'd never been. Istanbul. Tel Aviv. Singapore. The list of foreign countries he'd visited was exactly two — several times across the bridge to

Windsor in Canada to call on a printer when he lived in Detroit and once to a health spa in Mexico near Guadalajara with Lucille.

His preferred form of exercise was walking, which he'd do most days after his first cup of coffee at dawn. When he'd begun the routine, he'd intended to jog, but when he found out that walking took the same number of calories and heartbeats as running over the same distance, he was happy to slow the pace. Oh, yes, the fitness types talk about sustaining an elevated heart rate, but hadn't some of those Olympic sprinters fallen dead in their tracks?

His usual route was out his driveway, turning left down the hill to where the road traversed a little bridge across a creek at the canyon's low point. There he'd savor the swampy scent of the gurgling runoff water, mingled with the musty smell of logs rotting on the soggy bank. Then he'd climb the hill past the community center, where the rhythmic *ponk-ponk-ponk* signaled early birds were getting in a game of doubles tennis before heading into their offices, or overpaid private instructors were lobbing at retirees who stretched mightily to thwack at returns that went wild. Another half-mile down the road and making a turn to ascend a short block took him to the canyon crest and the prestigious addresses and stately homes along Amalfi Drive, named for a short, picturesque stretch along the western coast of Italy, another place Harry had vague intentions of going one day. But here he was in the Mediterranean climate of Southern California. So how much better could anyplace be?

As he started down Amalfi, he saw a familiar figure on the sidewalk up ahead. Even a hundred yards off, he knew it was Eleanor Amory dressed in a designer exercise suit, walking her Lab-mix Cudgel. He thought it an awful name for such a sweet dog, but Eleanor had once explained to him that Cud would be her protector against any and all attackers. She was of an age — about the same as Harry's, but he didn't dare ask — when petite stature and frailty might imply vulnerability, and this dog's mild manner disappeared the minute anyone — especially any man — got within his mistress's zone of avoidance, which Harry had learned from experience was about three feet.

Meeting up with Eleanor this morning was a lucky accident. He'd known she was a real-estate broker, and he'd already asked her to be his property manager for the duration of his trip. He realized that managers usually aren't needed to supervise short-term rentals. But he didn't know a neighbor — and he didn't trust Nicole — to deal with an emergency like a broken pipe or gas leak or electrical short. And this is earthquake country.

Eleanor had readily agreed, and she'd even offered not to charge him. He figured she was anticipating that, if he ever decided to sell, he'd give her the listing. And she wouldn't be wrong about that. Harry disliked making decisions, and he was doubly pleased when objectives converged like puzzle pieces fitting together. Perhaps that's why he was so willing to trust Aldo to make most of the decisions about the trip. So it suited him that he could rely on this lovely woman for those business tasks. Besides, he was happy to have any excuse to get to know her better.

Harry started to jog, wanting to give her the impression of being more vigorous. "Hey, Eleanor!" he called out as he got closer. Of course, she'd already seen him. (She might have even seen him come around the corner and noted his sluggardly pace.) Predictably, as Harry drew near, Cud started his low growl, and the woman automatically corrected the behavior, giving the leash a gentle tug, "Cud, shush!" The command had no effect but was issued to indicate to the gentleman that no harm was intended.

She looked up as Harry halted within an arm's length. He always thought she was movie-star gorgeous, but he didn't think he'd seen her in anything, and just as he was reluctant to inquire about her age, he'd never asked whether she'd worked as an actress. She had lustrous chest-nut-colored hair, which would have come from a bottle but applied by someone who knew what they were doing, with natural waves that framed her porcelain face. Her eyes were as dark as a gypsy's with an intelligent, penetrating clarity, and Harry was sure nothing escaped her attention.

And she seemed fit, which was another reason Harry wasn't at all sure about her age.

"Keeping to your routine, I see," she said approvingly. (They'd made their business deal the last time he'd met her this way on the street.)

Cud sat. He knew this conversation would take a while.

Harry was panting just from traversing the short distance. "Keeps me motivated when I can look forward to chatting with a lovely neighbor along the way." He wanted to tell her how captivating she looked or even come right out and declare he'd had a crush on her for years, but there was a line he wouldn't cross. He believed it was normal to lust after attractive people who live close by, to covet the beauties you see every day. His reluctance to express himself was complicated by his guilt. He'd been attracted to Eleanor even when Lucille was still alive. As his wife's health deteriorated, he blamed himself even more for those adulterous thoughts. On days he was willing to make allowances, he reasoned a therapist might advise him his secret affections arose from survival instinct. That is, Lucille's death, when it came, would feel like abandonment. Focusing on someone else would be a psychic defense for the ego. On days when Harry was inclined to be hard on himself, he feared he was actually looking forward to when Lucille would be gone. At the end, this fear was tempered by the excuse that he simply wished for an end to her suffering.

Today, as well, he wouldn't presume. After all this time, he didn't even know if Eleanor was married. Coming right out and asking her would be the same as declaring he was in the market, which he wasn't, especially now that he'd be leaving on his trip next week. What's more, his experience in the book business had refreshed his schoolboy history lessons. He recalled that the mature, war-weary President George Washington had warned against foreign entanglements. Harry planned to follow that advice, both at home and abroad.

He could have suggested coffee. He could have offered to walk with her, at least to the end of her block.

All these thoughts transpired in the short space of a few heartbeats, but it was enough of a pause for her to assume he wouldn't be forthcoming. So she asked, "How have you been?"

Harry never knew what to say to such everyday politeness. He hadn't been particularly depressed, but he couldn't claim honestly that he thought himself happy. Being in good health and experiencing only mildly annoying levels of pain should count as happiness. Odd that her innocent question brought such a flash of thoughts. He was worried about the trip. It would be unrealistic to think an excursion would redefine his notions of happiness at this time of life.

He forced a laugh and replied, "I breathe in and I breathe out. I put one foot in front of the other. It's been a winning formula so far!" Then he asked, "You?"

She gave him a polite smile and answered, "I have a glass of sparkling wine with dinner." She gave a prompting tug on Cud's leash, the dog came to attention, and she walked off in the direction of Harry's approach, saying, "Glad you're keeping fit, Harry. Stay well."

The mention of wine might have been a hint. It was more specific than anything he'd offered. But she didn't follow up with an invitation. Despite his wishing that she had, he didn't mind her not complicating his hopes just now.

Then he blurted out after her, "I'm leaving next week, you know!"

That stopped her, she turned around, and Cud promptly sat again. Harry walked back up to her as she was saying, "Ah, yes. We should plan to meet, and you can give me the keys and any instructions." He was a bit discouraged when she added dismissively, "Or you could just leave them in my mailbox."

He smiled and assured her, "I'll phone you and be sure to drop by. You gave me your business card, remember?"

He wondered whether she was also anticipating this opportunity to become better acquainted. She didn't seem at all concerned about the logistics. It might have been professional politeness when she said, "How wonderful for you! I took my daughter there two years ago. Will you be on safari?"

"Yes. Kenya. We stay a while at the beach first, but then I'm sure we've booked some game drives."

"We?"

"This fellow Aldo Barbieri. Friend of a friend. A tour packager, a pro." He chuckled, "Someone who hopefully can steer me away from the tourist traps."

Provocatively, she asked, "No one else in your group?" Then she shook her head. "No matter. You'll never be bored."

He realized she was asking whether he had a girlfriend. He assumed she knew he was alone now.

"I believe we're meeting up with some Europeans," he said. "Other clients of Aldo's. I don't really have many details. Perhaps I'm too trusting."

"I'd say send me a postcard, but no one does that anymore. Maybe put some remarkable videos on Facebook. Are you on Facebook? It's the main way Delia and I stay in touch these days." Harry made a mental note that he'd have to give Eleanor contact information for Nicole. He thought it best his daughter should not have a set of house keys, though.

He used social media rarely, but Nicole occasionally sent him text messages and posted pictures of her food. He was happy Eleanor had just encouraged him to friend her. Now he'd be able to check out her personal information discreetly, including photos of friends and family, husband or boyfriend, if there was such a person in her life.

"You'll never forget when you smell Africa for the first time," she said.

"Smell?"

"In Kenya, you're in the tropics, in the heat and the funk and all that teeming life. When you're out in the wild, it smells like a horse barn. It's glorious. Some people say it smells like home — our ancient, our very ancient, home. You know, when our ancestors lived in trees in the Rift Valley?"

He had trouble imagining himself living in a tree. Or her either. He might be going for a wilderness experience, but he wouldn't want to live there. He didn't envy the animals their freedom. He guessed they lived in fear much of the time.

"Any advice?" he asked.

"Let the credit card companies know where you're going. Don't carry a lot of cash, but carry some — say, enough to pay for dinner if they refuse your perfectly good credit card, which some will try to do to save the commission. But hoard small bills — it will seem like you need to tip someone every time you turn around. Leave all your jewelry at home. Buy yourself a plastic watch. Wouldn't hurt to have a spare phone, but don't pack it in your luggage, or it's sure to go missing."

This woman was obviously practical, used to managing her own affairs. Lucille had been good with details. Harry was usually content to take direction unless he had strong opinions.

"Be careful, though," she added.

"Oh?"

She laughed, "You might not want to come back!"

"You're not the first person to say that."

"If things get any crazier here, I may just sell the house and come join you. You'd think things would be on a downturn, but the market is still strong for property."

She was telling him it was her decision, implying she was either widowed or divorced, and, considering the value of homes in this neighborhood, decidedly well off.

He had no realistic hope of it, but he couldn't help thinking at that moment that she could be *his* reason — to come back.

"Three weeks may be more than enough," he told her. "We'll have that glass of wine and I'll tell you all about it."

"Don't hurry back on my account. Not that I won't want to see you. But don't be planning too far ahead until you take it all in." She hesitated, then added, "And, Harry? Be careful who you trust. It's a different culture."

He hadn't intended to hit on her. Was that what he was doing? Until now, he'd been thinking about her as a wayside attraction. He had to admit, his thoughts of her had been pure fantasy all along. He didn't ask her to explain her parting comment. He didn't want to keep her and figured he'd learn soon enough.

But in the space of a few more heartbeats, here they were talking about real-estate transactions and lifestyle changes and futures decided by each other's intentions.

It wasn't until he was home and turning his attention to packing for the trip that he realized she might be planning on inviting herself into his life.

CHAPTER 5

The flight on Turkish Airlines from Los Angeles International to Istanbul Havalimani would take thirteen hours, longer than Harry remembered he'd ever had his ass in a chair at one sitting. Throughout his career, he'd worked in an office, mostly in front of computers since the eighties, but he'd always made it a habit of getting up and walking around, even going off on errands if he got tired or bored. Now he feared his hemorrhoids would start to itch, and that would be no way to start a vacation. Still, he was happy they weren't flying directly to Nairobi, which would have meant no less than twenty-two hours in the air.

At no point did Harry want to fret the details of their itinerary. That's how Aldo was earning his fee. But occasionally Harry would give himself permission to ask out of curiosity, if for no other reason than to be ready for whatever came next, such as choosing wardrobe items for the prevailing climate or setting his watch for the local time zone.

It wasn't until they were comfortably installed in the first row of Business Class that Harry ventured to ask, "So, why Istanbul?"

The plane was still on the ground, but a flight attendant was already hovering over them, a patient smile on her face. The name on the badge pinned to her chest was Zehra. She was petite and pretty, with dark eyes and Mediterranean skin. Her bright-red uniform was topped with a cap that covered most of her dark hair, which was pulled back into a bun. A Muslim hijab was notably lacking, replaced with a colorful scarf tied around her neck. It struck Harry for the first time that, for the next few weeks, he might be regarded as the clueless white person in a throng of multicolored ethnicities who were speaking in incomprehensible languages and eagerly offering spicy food that was sure to irritate his stomach lining.

"Order your drink first," Aldo commanded Harry. Then to Zehra he said, "Bombay gin and bitters, on the rocks with a twist." Then, back to Harry, "Go ahead. Drinks don't cost you a cent more."

"Oh, uh, red wine," Harry told her. "Dry, if you have it."

Pleased she could accommodate, she asked him, "Pinot noir, Chianti, Cabernet, or Malbec?"

Harry looked to Aldo. Aldo grimaced as though the choice of anything not Italian would be a personal insult, and commanded, "Chianti, *senza domande!*" And, beaming at her, he laughed too heartily.

"Piacere," she responded demurely and retreated behind a bulkhead.

Aldo gestured to indicate their comfortable surroundings. "For one thing, Turkish always promotes me to Business Class. There is no First, so this is the premium treatment. I'm a million-miler, so it's a free upgrade for me and a companion. You paid Coach for both, if you don't know. Second, if you fly direct to Nairobi, you arrive stressed and exhausted, even if they pamper you the whole way. Besides, I like flying Turkish, and Istanbul is the same time zone as Kenya. We're booked into a luxury hotel in Sultanahmet — the tourist quarter — sights to see, great food, nightclubs, shopping. We will take a couple of days, recharge our batteries, then on to East Africa."

"You don't do anything without a reason," Harry observed.

Aldo chuckled. "Not at my age, no. And I don't take chances with paying clients. You don't travel much, I think?"

"Not that I didn't want to," Harry sighed. "But by the time I was ready to quit working twelve-hour days, my wife fell ill. She was always the adventurous one. Then, when she passed, I kept promising myself I'd make plans, but I never took the next step. I guess I needed someone like you to point me in a direction." Then he asked, "Do you speak Turkish?"

"Harry, you can get by in English most places in the world these days. Or you wave some money and point."

It was a night flight, takeoff at 6:30 p.m., and they'd be arriving about the same time in the evening in Istanbul. Once they were in the air, they'd get a four-course dinner, after which they could watch movies, read, or sleep. The convenience of the night flight, Aldo explained, was that almost everyone would want to sleep. But no one would mind at all if you kept drinking the free booze until you passed out. He liked to do it that way.

Harry was an experienced drinker, but he accepted that Aldo might set a stiff pace. He wouldn't try to keep up with the fellow, but the prospect of settling into a quiet buzz was appealing.

~

THEY'D BEEN in the air about ten hours. By the time Harry finished the baklava dessert, he'd had four glasses of wine. Two had been his limit, at least when Lucille was making the rules at home. Then at Aldo's urging, he'd accepted a Courvoisier VSOP cognac from Zehra.

It finally occurred to Harry that the discomfort in his bladder could not be ignored. Aldo was snoring, his head nodding on his chest and bobbing slightly with each rhythmic breath. Harry hated to disturb him, but he decided he couldn't wait any longer. Getting up and edging past Aldo in the aisle seat was awkward even with the extra legroom in this cabin, but Harry moved slowly and gently and finally navigated his bulk into the aisle without waking his companion. The cabin lights had been turned down to allow the passengers to sleep, and Zehra was nowhere to be seen. The lavatory was just steps away, but the effort it took to get there surprised Harry. He felt light-headed, and he was gasping. He knew he'd had more booze than he usually consumed in a week. When he threw the latch on the door from the inside, the courtesy light seemed unusually bright. He relieved himself standing up, taking care with his aim lest the slight swaying of the plane throw his stream onto the floor. It took him a while. He understood enough about the effect of aging on the prostate gland to know that his flow was restricted and that this symptom, in itself, was not particularly ominous.

He didn't worry all that much about growing old, but he worried some. The grim thought occurred that he should enjoy this trip as much as possible while he still had the chance.

He shook it a couple of times, remembering from his childhood that more shakes than necessary to clear the bore was considered by some prudes to be a sin of self-abuse.

He struggled with the zipper of his pants, turned to unlatch the door, stepped out, his knees buckled, and he fainted dead away onto the carpet.

MOMENTS LATER, Harry regained consciousness as he lay on his back, stretched out on the floor of the galley. A sandy-haired young man in a jogging suit was hovering over him as he knelt to pump the bulb on a blood-pressure monitor. Harry could feel the sleeve of the device growing tight on his arm. There was a clear plastic mask covering his nose, and its tube extended to a green compressed-gas tank attached to the bulkhead. Harry took a deep breath and felt his head clear as the oxygen filled his lungs. The hit from the pure gas was bracing.

Aldo and Zehra were standing nearby, speaking to each other in low tones. Four people were about all you could fit in there.

"Ah, you're awake!" the young man said to him softly. "You passed out. Too much to drink, maybe? No worries, we check you."

"This man is a doctor," Aldo turned from Zehra to announce. "Doctors Without Borders. Lucky he's riding with us."

"Lars Karlsson, MD, at your service. Johns Hopkins." His smile seemed sincere. His English was crisp and confident, the accent Scandinavian. He asked Harry, "Did you hit your head? Anything hurt? Injuries from the fall?"

Harry shook his head slowly. He didn't know whether he was

allowed to talk with the mask on. Now he noticed wires emerging from his unbuttoned shirt and attached to a little screen that was charting his heartbeat.

Karlsson held up a familiar pill bottle. "You take these? Your friend got them from your carry-on."

Harry nodded.

The doctor squinted at the label. "One hundred milligrams, once a day. Not a particularly high dose. For blood pressure. Do you remember what your numbers were before your doctor prescribed these?"

Harry's reply was muffled but understandable: "One fifty over ninety?" The doctor grinned again, sharing the amusement of his patient's garbled speech but indicating he understood.

"You take in the morning?"

Harry nodded.

"How long ago did you take?"

"Ah, this morning," Harry replied, getting annoyed he couldn't speak clearly.

"This morning, Los Angeles time? Or just now?"

"Back home," Harry told him.

"Any chest pain? Discomfort anywhere?"

Harry shook his head again.

Karlsson gestured with the bottle. "These can cause dizziness. Maybe not usually, but you drink, you're tired, it's not unusual. It's because for a moment your blood pressure is too low. Can't get enough blood up to your brain." Then he shrugged and smiled, "You black out, you fall down. But falling down solves the problem. Once you're horizontal, the blood rushes back to the brain right away. The worry is you could hit your head on the way down. And that's serious. So you have to be careful, know what I mean?"

Harry nodded.

Zehra spoke up, "Mr. Gardner, don't try to get up. We have just another hour before landing, and we'll work around you." She giggled, "I promise not to step on your tummy!"

Aldo was quick to add, "No emergency landing. Lars says you're going to be fine."

Karlsson said, "Get checked out before you continue your journey. I would say, though, that it might be a good idea to split the dose. Fifty milligrams in the morning and fifty in the evening. Even things out. You've stabilized quite nicely here, so I don't think there's any cause for worry." Then he smiled too broadly and said, "But, you know, a man of your age…"

Until now, Harry had not thought of himself as a man of a certain age. But getting urgent care from a doctor on a plane might be a sign, a milestone. If he didn't apply himself to having a good time on this trip, he might not have other chances.

Karlsson gave Harry a pat on the chest and got to his feet. Then he turned to Aldo, and Harry could hear him say softly, "Possibly a trans-ischemic attack, but I doubt it. If it were so, you'd expect he'd be disoriented, confused. But he's fully present. Just get him looked at. Keep an eye on him. Can't be too careful." Then he asked, "What is your eventual destination?"

"Kenya."

The doctor's expression changed. Aldo picked up on it and asked, "Nothing is going on, is there? Ebola? Dengue fever?"

Karlsson's grin did not seem as sincere now, and he replied dismissively, "No. Congo is still a bit risky, but you should be fine in Kenya. I'm on my way to a posting in Rwanda." He hesitated before he went on, "Skin lesions, you get a scratch, you wash, apply antibiotic cream, and have it seen if there are any signs of infection. It's the tropics. Snakebite, it's rare, but watch where you tread. If it should happen, try to get a picture of the thing before it gets away. Hospitals won't necessarily stock the antivenom. And pray you never come across a mamba." He smiled, perhaps too broadly. "And, of course, you'd want to be careful about HIV anywhere."

Aldo followed up with, "Did you ever live there?"

Karlsson turned away, gathered up his medical bag, and was slipping out of the galley when he replied over his shoulder, "Yes. Yes, I did."

He didn't give the impression it was a fond memory.

CHAPTER 6

*I*stanbul Halvalimani was the most modern airport Harry had ever seen. Aldo told him it handles more international connecting flights than London Heathrow. He explained, "They were still building it when they had the Mediterranean Games and then the World Cup a few years back. Then they lost out on hosting the 2020 Summer Olympics. They'd have spiffed the place up some more for that."

During the taxi ride into town, Harry was quick to decline Aldo's offer to take him to a hospital or even to an urgent-care clinic. "I'm sure Dr. Karlsson was right about the medication and the dizziness," Harry explained. "I remember my doctor warned me about it, and he cautioned me about the alcohol, too. I'll be more careful. Please don't fret about me." Then he was quick to add, "And don't — whatever you do — *don't* start mothering me."

Aldo laughed, "Harry, my friend, I doubt you have ever been blind, stinking drunk. I *have*. Many times. And will no doubt do so again. Perhaps in your company. Yes, it's my job to look out for you, but I expect you'll be doing as much for me. I hope you don't mind."

It was Harry's turn to laugh. "I don't know any languages, but I expect I can manage to get us a cab, and I'm still strong enough to throw you into it."

Aldo smiled. "You're going to enjoy this trip, I assure you. It might even change your life, but I'm not foolish enough to make such promises. And I expect you will get along famously with the friends we're meeting."

"Who? How many?" Aldo had told him there would be other guests in their party when they got to the first safari lodge, but he hadn't provided any details.

He chuckled, "Some in the group will be what we call *voluntourists.*"

"Volunteer tourists?"

"They donate their labor to causes. But they'll get stopped when they find out they need a work visa just to do *that.* Then maybe they'll join our safaris. As well, we will have some crazy Europeans. Most of them, regular clients by now. Satisfied customers, time on their hands. And we'll meet up with some expats and also some Kenyan-born whites. Brits, Belgians, Germans. Some of *them* are truly crazy. *Kenyan cowboys,* the locals call them."

"Cowboys?"

"I don't know why. Maybe because in the bush they'll be wearing broad-brimmed canvas safari hats and chukka boots with no socks. At the beach, flip-flops and ball caps. But always those loud-colored, tropical shirts and khaki shorts. It's like a uniform. You see them at the bar and they're gulping Tuskers all day long. These guys, many of them, they've retired to Kenya. Maybe they're on government pensions from the EU. They stretch their money, live like kings, and act like bums most of the time."

"What's Tusker's?"

"Tusker is the Kenyan beer. Big, brown bottle. If it's beer and you order anything else, I'm not with you. They see you with a Heineken and you might as well wear a sign it's your first day in-country. The Tusker slogan is *Bia yangu, Nchi yangu.* My beer, my country, in Kiswahili. But the one I like better because it's so true is, 'Helping white men dance since 1922!'"

Harry sighed, "I can't drink enough beer to get drunk. I'd be peeing all the time. And, drunk or sober, you're not going to get me to dance."

Aldo smiled. "I won't be the one to try!" Then he muttered, "But remember you said that. I wouldn't be making any bets if I were you."

Their hotel in the Sultanahmet district was the Golden Horn, an elegantly renovated nineteenth-century building. The place must have been a regular stopover for Aldo because they gave him the Ataturk Suite on the fourth floor, and Harry knew they weren't paying top dollar. One flight up was the roof-terrace restaurant, which afforded a panoramic view of the Bosporus and included a lavish buffet breakfast. Harry was impressed with the sumptuous surroundings. It wasn't the Ritz, but it was more luxurious than most places he'd ever stayed.

The décor was traditional Turkish — overstuffed chairs and sofas, wood paneling, and ornate rugs and tapestries, with arrays of multicolored light fixtures dangling from molded ceilings.

Aldo had booked two nights, and it was comfortable to share the large room. Harry was relieved there were two beds. He wouldn't have to worry if the fellow tossed and turned, and he judged he could endure Aldo's soft snoring. But he wondered why they were taking their time in this city, and not just overnight. Aldo explained that flying east is particularly stressful on the body's sleep cycle. Whether or not you get any sleep on the plane, about midday the next afternoon you'll be overcome with exhaustion. If you were on a tour and walking around, you'd be suffering. If you were on a bus, you'd be fast asleep, and you'd miss everything because you wouldn't want to get off for sightseeing. He advised that the best thing would be to sit down to old-fashioned British high tea around four in the afternoon. Have strong, black tea and a bite but not a full meal. Avoid sugar, tempting as it will be with all those cakes and trifles on the serving cart. Eat like little old ladies — nibble at tiny cucumber sandwiches or smoked salmon. Resist the urge to take a nap, and stay up until local bedtime, the later the better. Have a late dinner, substantial but not too heavy. Take in a nightclub perhaps, but don't drink too much, if at all. Set your alarm or ask for a wake-up call at six the next morning. Help yourself to the buffet and jolt your system fully awake with a few shot-sized cups of syrupy Turkish coffee. Hold to this routine, and after a couple of days your internal clock will be blissfully reset. Then when they journeyed on to Africa, they'd be flying due south along the meridian, more or less within the same time zone.

All as if to say, *Stick with Aldo. He knows how to travel.*

They'd arrived at the hotel in the early evening, unpacked, showered briefly, and set off again on a walkabout as the sun was going down. Aldo sat Harry down at a tea shop near the Blue Mosque, then didn't linger but popped off "to see a friend." Harry didn't require an explanation, and when he'd finished his tea and a cup of the ubiquitous lentil soup, he took Aldo's suggestion and strolled over to the mosque for a tour.

Removing his shoes as instructed and entering via the side door, he stepped into an enormous, seemingly empty sanctuary. The ceiling was easily three, maybe four, stories above his head. On the floor, not a stick of furniture, just an unobstructed expanse of carpet. An array of incandescent bulbs was suspended from above by wires and provided the only lighting in the place other than the waning daylight shining in from the small windows that ringed the cupolas of the domed roof and stained glass around the perimeter of the ground floor.

Harry's background was Catholic, although he wasn't at all observant these days. It was remarkable to him, then, that in a place of worship there wasn't a single religious portrait or statue. The walls, pillars, and ceiling were covered with intricate geometric designs, executed in meticulously inlaid tile. He remembered then that Muslims take literally God's commandment against worshipping graven images. To Harry, the lack of beneficent visages of saints gave the place a cold, alien atmosphere. To the faithful, he expected, the absence of human warmth was intended to turn their thoughts toward Heaven.

There was no call to prayer at this time of day, and only a few other tourists besides Harry lingered in the mosque, standing in silence, staring up at the cavernous ceiling and marveling at the hollow echo of even the slightest shuffling sounds and the occasional sniff or clearing of a throat.

It didn't take long for Harry to feel uncomfortable just standing in that space. On his exit, he retrieved his shoes and found Aldo waiting for him out front. Beside him was a diminutive, old fellow wearing a skullcap and tunic. He was bending Aldo's ear with what sounded like nonstop pleading in Italian.

On seeing Harry, Aldo turned to the little fellow and dismissed him with a shoving motion and a deprecating smile. The man backed reluctantly away but then doubled back and came right up to Harry.

"Please, sir," the fellow said in English. "I try to tell your friend. My cousin give you excellent price on carpets. The best. We ship all over the world, no problem. You don't regret, ever. Also you want fine coat, best leather, no plastic, I can find. Also briefcase, luggage. Anything you want. I take you. Please, come. Deep discount, every-thing. Small cash fee for my trouble only."

Aldo waved him off, this time with a grimace, and the fellow slunk away.

"How did he know I'm American?" Harry asked his friend.

"First off, even though he could see we're together, you hardly look Italian. They see a tourist, they start with English. When he came up to me, I told him to get lost in my language, and that's when he gives me the whole pitch like he's some *paisano.*"

"I guess I have to work on my sales resistance."

"In this part of town, they're all over the place, especially this time of day. But of course, when you travel, you have to realize, any locals you meet, they're thinking their next meal is in your pocket. Most of the time, they're not out to rob you. But if you lack for anything, it's their job to find out what that is — and get it for you."

"So, it's the old saying, don't buy a rug from this guy."

"Not at all. Somewhere probably close by, he does have a cousin, the guy does sell rugs, and they will give you a good deal. And, what-ever else you need, he has a cousin who sells it. You have it shipped home and it will actually show up. Now, if you get the story about the little children with the hands so tiny they can make the tiniest knots for the most intricate designs, and with the finest textiles, and that's why the high price, you might pay a lot more than you should."

Neither of them was ready for dinner, so Aldo led Harry to a nightclub, Glitz & Glamour, on a back street, within walking distance.

THE CLUB WAS PREDICTABLY dark and smoky. Harry was relieved that the American rock coverage coming through the audio system wasn't too loud. He expected it was early in the evening for clubbing, but there was a fair-sized crowd, mostly men in suit and tie, some in running togs with team shirts and ball caps worn backward. Attractive women, all in evening dress, sat with groups of men at some of the tables. Other men sat in pairs and seemed to be conversing intently.

No sooner had the bouncer-host showed them to a private table than Aldo jumped back up, saying, "Order me a brandy and soda. I gotta see a man about a rug."

Harry assumed his friend was off to the restroom, but when Aldo had been gone ten minutes, he began to suspect he was off on another errand. Making dates with connections was not something you'd expect a tour guide to be doing.

That's when two lookers in low-cut gowns sidled over. The taller one wearing bright-orange lipstick cooed in accented English, "I'm Azra, and my friend here is Miray. Do you mind if we join you?"

That's when it dawned on Harry that Aldo's errand might have been for the purpose of setting them up with dates. But Harry wasn't sure he was ready for any heavy action this early in the game. When Harry smiled back but didn't answer, both girls slipped into the booth beside him, each snuggling up to his haunches on either side.

As she pushed up against him, Azra asked, "What do you say to a chilled bottle of champagne?" and the same officious waiter in black tie and fez who'd already delivered the first round of drinks was quick to show up. Assuming Aldo would be stepping back any minute and that this was all part of some orchestrated plan, Harry muttered, "Sure, why not?"

Having taken care of business, Azra politely asked his name, and he told her. She asked where he was from, he answered California, and soon the cork was popped and the wine poured into four flutes with the bottle nestled in a bucket of ice at tableside.

Both women were wearing perfume, the same label, he thought, and the musky scent was so strong Harry feared he might grow dizzy again. Still, as he sipped the sparkling wine, the earthiness of their bodies, the close contact, and Azra's sultry voice (Miray hadn't said anything so far) were rousing his anticipation for the mission of the trip. And making him think that Aldo knew what he was doing, that his guide would make sure Harry would thoroughly enjoy himself, without much effort or a moment's worry.

That's when, from out of nowhere, here was Aldo standing at the edge of the table and looking very much annoyed, if not downright angry. Ignoring the women, he pointed at the bottle and asked Harry, "Did you order that?"

Harry replied sheepishly, "Yeah, I guess I did. Say hi to Azra and Miray."

Aldo beckoned brusquely to them, "Come on, get up. My friend is new in town. He doesn't know the game, and you two *get lost!*"

Azra wasn't about to get up and cast a cautioning glance to Miray to make sure she was staying. She told Aldo sweetly, "We're having a party." She patted the seat beside her. "Now, why don't you be a love and sit down?"

But Aldo winced and growled back, "Get *up!* I'm a friend of Boris, and I do not expect to see a bill for this!"

And more quickly than Harry thought possible, the women got up and were gone.

Then Aldo sat back down and downed his brandy and soda in three big gulps. Then he said breathlessly, "Harry, my friend, I'm sorry. I need to be straight with you about some things."

"You didn't send them over?" Harry asked innocently. "What could it hurt?"

Keeping his voice down, Aldo told him, "Those girls are not hookers. At least, that's not their job in this establishment. They're bar girls. They spot a tourist or a businessman, especially a guy in a nice suit,

48

and they invite themselves over and talk him into buying a bottle of champagne."

Aldo pointed to the bottle in the bucket. "A wine bottle holds five glasses. You notice, on the table here, we have four glasses. So as of now, there's one glass left in the bottle. It goes down easy. It's good stuff — not all *that* good — but good enough. So the girls chat you up, maybe put a hand on your thigh. You're feeling just fine, so why not have another bottle? After three or four rounds, two girls and one or two guys, you've gone through maybe *four* bottles."

He leaned in so close Harry could smell the brandy on his breath. "You get ready to leave, and you're gonna get a bill for *fourteen thousand* lira. That's two thousand bucks — five hundred a bottle! Plus tip, plus service charge."

"That's outrageous! How can they get away with that?"

Aldo gestured toward the bouncer and shot him an obsequious smile. "You see the guy who showed us in? He has a pal, just as big as him. You say you don't pay, they take you out back. Maybe they don't beat you, but they know how to scare you pretty good."

"Wow," Harry sighed. "Good thing you know this Boris."

Aldo laughed. "I didn't go to meet anyone. I had some upset in the restroom. Sorry."

"There's no Boris?"

Aldo shrugged. "Of course, there's some Boris somewhere. The whole town is owned by the Russian mob! Lucky guess!"

Aldo coached Harry to leave a hundred dollars US on the table and slip the bouncer another hundred on the way out.

This was Harry's first lesson in corruption.

CHAPTER 7

*O*n their arrival in-country, after just one restful night at a hotel in Nairobi, Aldo informed Harry that they'd be boarding a regional airline at Wilson Airport, bound for the gigantic seaport city of Mombasa on the eastern coast. He professed to have urgent business there that couldn't wait, and he explained that, after all, the little resort town of Diani Beach to the south was to be their ultimate destination anyway. That's where a guy could indulge his every inclination with, as the fellow quipped, "zero adverse consequences."

But soon after he and Aldo arrived in Diani, it took Harry exactly two encounters with young working girls to convince him he did not crave their company.

They'd checked into the Kusi Lodge on a Sunday morning. Aldo had booked them separate bungalows and advised him that entertaining locals in his room would be perfectly okay. (Reception wanted a name, but you could offer it the next day, no ID needed.) Aldo warned, "Of course, you get more than a few in there, you guys get drunk and play loud music into the night, and you'll hear from the manager." Aldo grinned and added, "But that's not your style, I think?"

"I'm glad we're not bunking together," Harry told him. "I got a sample of your snoring, and, yeah, I suppose we'll want our privacy if we have dates. Isn't that the point of the whole thing?"

Somewhat to Harry's surprise, Aldo offered no counsel in those matters. "Look, Harry, I don't pimp for my clients. Under any circumstances. I tell you what's possible here, how a man can enjoy himself all kinds of ways. No details. No procedure. I don't make introductions, I don't even tell you where to go. Many times I tell you where *not* to go. But, you realize, in this town you can't take two steps without some woman offers herself."

Aldo claimed he had errands to run, so he suggested Harry start his adventure by taking a stroll down the beach. He could begin here at the seaside resort and walk south. "There is a café in town where expats and tourists hang out. Kokko's. You turn right off the beach about half a mile down." And he added, "Beachboys are mostly panhandlers. Ignore them. No conversation, just keep moving. They also offer boat rides, hang gliding, diving lessons. You want to do any of that, we book with guys I know. Safer, and you don't pay so much. So, relax! Take a look around. Have a beer or five."

Harry changed into the obligatory floral shirt, khaki cargo shorts, and sandals. He was proud of his new straw hat. He sunburned too easily.

The white-sand beach was broad and strewn with seaweed in some places. Out past the foaming breakers, the water was glistening and turquoise. The sky was bright, azure blue with just a few wispy clouds. Aldo had told him that it's shallow water to almost a mile out, where there is a long coral reef that follows the coastline. The reef moderates the energy of incoming waves and also provides a natural barrier that keeps sharks away from swimmers in the shallows.

Out past the reef he could see some of the small motorboats that offered the excursions the beachboys were peddling. A few white families were in the water, along with some mixed couples. Remarkable to Harry, it was the women who were white and older. In some cases, considerably older.

As Aldo had predicted, no sooner had Harry set out than a young black woman strode up in back of him, overtook his stride, looked over her shoulder at him, and asked, "Why are you walking alone?"

She turned all the way around to face him, blocking his progress. He must have looked bewildered when he asked her, "Isn't it safe?"

He assumed the area near the hotel would be monitored and guarded, but he didn't see anyone around but the bathers. He figured most if not all of them were guests of the hotel.

She grinned broadly and explained, "Why, Papa, it's safer if I walk with you. I tell the beach boys to stay away!"

And she took his arm. She was wearing a thong bikini with a see-through, panty-length robe. She might have been in her late teens, and she was gorgeous — lithe and slender, with ample curves.

Now that she'd taken hold of him, the only thing he could think to say was "Why not?"

As they walked, perhaps predictably if he had thought about it, she wanted to know where he was from, where he was staying and for how long, was he married or did he have a girlfriend, what did he like to do at the beach, and did he know the best places to eat.

The only specific information he gave was "Los Angeles," to which she only remarked, "Oh?" And he declined to provide more than yes-or-no answers to the rest. He wasn't about to tell a stranger where he was staying.

She said, "I live here a long time. I tell you all the best places to go. And then for my help, maybe we stop at Havana, and you buy me coffee."

Havana Bar and Grill was located directly across the beach road from Kokko's. Harry would soon learn that mzungus frequented the café for breakfast and meetups, and much the same crowd, mostly male, hit the bar at Havana to do some serious drinking in the evenings and scope out the local talent.

She said her name was Monique. As Harry sipped a couple of beers, she downed four margaritas and made quick work of a plate of roast chicken and chips.

As she got increasingly tipsy, she giggled more than she talked. And her conversation was limited to variations of the same questions she'd already asked him. He tried to sound pleasant, but he was no more forthcoming with his answers than he'd been before, and he doubted whether she cared.

Finally, after she'd finished her food and drained her last drink, she looked up at him and asked, "So, do you want to have a party with me? You know, private?"

It wasn't that Harry had expected anything different, but the tawdriness of the situation, despite this woman's obvious allure, turned him off. Somehow, he'd imagined these girls would have more personality, some imagination. He didn't demand intellect, but he wanted to somehow be captivated. It had been decades since he'd been on anything like a date, but it occurred to him now that he was thinking like some prude who would never consider jumping into bed on a first date.

But, he had to admit, the prospect of somehow getting to know this or any hooker better seemed ridiculous.

He signaled to the barkeeper, an attractive woman in a halter top about the same age as his companion, then handed her four thousand-shilling banknotes and told her to keep the change. Seeing him dole out the cash so readily, Monique broke out in a smile, no doubt anticipating he'd be making her evening more than worthwhile.

He hadn't asked for her price, and he was too embarrassed to find out now. Instead, he folded five more bills and slipped them discreetly into her hand. He said quietly, "I'm going to have an early night. If you work for somebody, tell him we did it anyway. You can tell him I said you're a dream come true."

With that, he slipped off the barstool, marched across the street without looking back, took a seat at the counter at Kokko's, and finally ordered that coffee. Monique must have been too stunned to call out after him.

HARRY's second brush with adventure turned out to be more serious. By the time he finished his coffee at the café, the sun was starting to set. He realized he hadn't had lunch. Monique's plate of greasy food hadn't tempted him, and he hadn't even bothered to look at the grill menu. Normally, he'd expect to meet up with Aldo for dinner, but they hadn't made plans. He decided he'd be true to the fib he'd told

Monique. He'd have a sandwich here, get a tuk-tuk back to the hotel (best not to walk alone after dark, Aldo had told him), and make it an early night.

He'd finished his light evening meal of fried tomato-and-cheese sandwich, washed down with two Tuskers. It was still early, but he was getting drowsy. He strode out of Kokko's intending to flag a tuk-tuk on the beach road for the ride back to Kusi.

But as he emerged from the café, a female voice called to him from somewhere up above, "Papa! Papa! You like massage?"

He looked up to see a handsome woman in a cocktail dress, who might not yet be thirty, leaning over the railing on the mezzanine of the building next door. That floor housed an art-supply store and a hair salon.

"Oh," Harry called back. "Not tonight. I just ate! Can't have you leaning on me when my stomach is full! Do you work at the salon?"

"Yes," she smiled. "This is my place. I'm Stella! We do everything to make you relaxed and even more handsome! And you *are* a handsome man, Papa."

"Why, thank you. You're very attractive yourself."

"Not tonight, no. That's not what I am suggesting. What I'm saying, I can take your booking now. You tell me what time in the morning, and I give you an hour myself, more if you like."

Harry thought a moment. He had some idea what he was getting into. His experience with massage was limited to treating repetitive injuries from golf, but this suggestion of therapy for relaxation was coming at just the right time. It was odd to think on his first day in this beach town that stressing about having a good time would be getting him down. But it was. In a way, he wished that Aldo would orchestrate all of it, but he understood why, for the more intimate services, he'd have to fend for himself.

"Sure," he replied. "Why not?" He felt brave. He was in control. He'd been able to turn Monique down, hadn't he? He resolved to take things at his own pace, one step at a time. There was no reason to let anyone make him feel uncomfortable. If all he ever accomplished was dipping his toes in the turquoise water, he would have fulfilled his dream. He was already most of the way there, halfway around the world! (He was stunned he hadn't slipped off his sandals and waded in on his way over here. But he'd been too distracted by Monique's attentions.) Still, it felt odd — and, he had to admit, uncomfortable — to be in a place where there seemed to be no rules, where a guy might have to work at *not* getting into trouble.

"Delighted!" she exclaimed. "How about nine o'clock? And don't you go filling up your tummy first thing. You can have a full-portion English breakfast after!"

"It's a date, then."

"*Karibu,* Papa! Stella will make you a happy man!" Then she added, "Two thousand shillings, my dear. Cash, no cards. ATM right here. And bring some extra. Maybe you want a manicure."

"Okay. But call me Harry. *Papa* makes me feel old."

"Oh, but it's how we show respect, you know!" And she laughed. "Or you let Stella color your hair! Take off ten, twenty years, then no one call you Papa!"

"It's Harry. Or Mr. Gardner, if you don't mind."

"My pleasure, Mr. Harry. Nine, and don't be late!"

To SAY that the massage Stella gave him was uneventful would be honest enough. But, for Harry, it was a turning point. It was obvious from her skilled touch that she knew what she was doing. She'd either been professionally trained or had studied under someone who had. She knew her anatomy, could trace the paths of musculature and the routes of congestion. She kneaded his glutes like twin mounds of bread dough, dug into the painful points between his shoulder blades with her knuckles, and plowed furrows in his back with her elbows. She found the pressure points on his scalp and on the soles of his feet that magically triggered the immediate release of tension in other places. He was getting his money's worth.

Aldo had cautioned him that, where special favors were concerned, you don't get if you don't ask. The women learned to be careful. It would be unusual for a white man to be an undercover cop, even less likely for an American. But anyone could file a complaint, and everyone was paranoid these days. So no one except perhaps the girls calling out from doorways will offer. Just offering is a crime. So is asking, which is why a cop won't do it. That would be entrapment (not that they are all so scrupulous).

However, during this first time with Stella, Harry could tell she was being cautious. When she worked on his thighs, applying pressure with her thumbs and she worked upward from his knees to his groin, she came close to the nerve endings that might excite him to erection, but not quite. Was it a tease, or was she simply being competent and careful?

Harry wasn't about to ask, and he wasn't sure what he wanted. They didn't speak the whole time, and that was fine with him. After all, what did he have to say to her? Smalltalk would distract him from enjoying her touch, and sharing his emotions with her like she was some shrink was out of the question, hardly appropriate. He allowed himself to enjoy what she did, but as the session progressed, and particularly as she began to work on his upper thighs, he became increasingly uneasy.

He was like a little boy who didn't know how to swim, wading into the shallow end of the pool for the first time. He wanted to have fun like the older kids seemed to be doing, but his fear was more powerful than his anticipation of joy. And, in the case of her touching him, there was the added guilt that he'd be asking her to break some moral code, show him she was one of those women the locals called *nasty girls*.

As she was working on him, he remembered Leonard Cohen's sarcastic remark that you have to be a man to appreciate why it feels so good to be treated like a piece of meat. And that was a fair description of his feelings now. Here was a transaction, purely physical, performed with skill and care — even with compassion — but ultimately giving satisfaction that lasts no longer than the sensation of touch itself.

He didn't ask her to do more, and she didn't. She didn't even act as if anything further was available or expected.

But as he was getting ready to go, she did something that surprised him. She helped him get dressed. She buttoned his shirt, zipped his pants, buckled his belt, slipped on his socks and shoes, and deftly tied his shoelaces. And then she kissed him sweetly on the cheek.

The gesture was kind and intimate but not necessarily sexy. Once again, he felt like that little kid in the pool.

He tipped her generously, as he had done for Monique, as though he'd received the full treatment and then some. As he left, Stella gave him the business card for the salon, and she wrote her mobile number on the back.

But he doubted he'd ever have the desire or the courage to call.

So, after two potentially intimate encounters with attractive and presumably available women in this freewheeling community, Harry was beginning to expect that his exploits on his vacation would hardly be sordid enough as locker-room stories — provided he stuck to the truth.

The next day, he met Esther at the supermarket.

CHAPTER 8

On the third day of his visit to this beach town, Harry met Esther Mwemba in the checkout line of the Chandarana store. He and Aldo were on a morning errand scrounging liquor and snacks for their hotel rooms. Aldo was still browsing the wine selections. He drank wine like it was water, but he insisted it be Italian or at worst French and never, unless there was absolutely no choice, South African. (*"Troppo forte,"* he would say with a sneer.)

She was buying milk and bread. She spoke first, looked down at the items in Harry's cart and quipped, "I hope that's not breakfast."

Harry smiled and shot back, "I don't have anyone to tell me what not to do. Besides, I think there's soccer tonight. Excuse me, *football.* It's a lot cheaper than room service when we're watching TV."

She laughed and said, "Honey, the only TV that gets the movies and the games is going to be in the lounge. And there it's definitely not bring-your-own. And the one in your room? Channel One only. Clips from today's speeches in the National Assembly and some gospel choir! You only flip that on so you can fall asleep."

He was struck by how pretty she was. And how relaxed. It was uncharacteristically brave of him to come back with, "You got a better idea?"

And she proposed they meet at the café across the street in an hour. (It wasn't even time for lunch yet.)

"And how about my friend?" Harry asked, indicating Aldo, whom they could see was still browsing and squinting at the labels on wine bottles.

She looked amused. *"He's* a friend of yours?"

"Aldo Barbieri. Do you know him?"

"I see him around," she said evasively. "No, let's have some time to ourselves if you don't mind being seen alone with me."

So in a short while the two of them met for coffee at Kokko's. And they had coffee, even though the place had a full bar. She mostly listened as, not knowing what else to say, he told her the unremarkable story of their trip so far, omitting his brushes with two young women.

No sooner had she taken the last sip of her coffee than she announced she was off to work. Harry was disappointed at the abruptness of her departure. And at the realization he wouldn't be spending the day with her. But the fact that she had some job, which she neglected to describe, heartened him. It suggested she wasn't some hustler.

He didn't see her at all the next day. Or the day after. He didn't see much of Aldo either. Harry wandered around the town, peeked in the shops, swam in the hotel pool, and indulged himself in local cuisine and more than his usual quota of booze.

There was a small bookshop next to the market. Harry spent some time scanning the titles. Predictably, the new paperbacks were tourist guides. The used stock was mostly popular beach reads abandoned by departed tourists and expats. Many in English, quite a few in German, and a scattering of other European languages. Harry found a well-thumbed copy of *The Constant Gardener,* which he had read when it first came out. He bought it, thinking now that he was a Gardner in Kenya, a rereading might hold messages for him.

As the scope of his wanderings increased, he got used to hailing a tuk-tuk from the almost continuous streams speeding in both directions down the beach road. The meager two-stroke engines of these three-wheeled vehicles were annoyingly loud and reeked of petrol fumes, especially when the car was old or in poor repair, as most of them were. And even on smooth roads, the vibration could be bone-jarring. Harry was tempted to plug his ears, but most of the drivers were eager to chat. He was happy to engage in these exchanges as he and his new friend shouted to be heard above the engine noise. A ride from one end of town to the other typically took a few minutes. Harry learned not to overpay at the mzungu-tourist rate, but he always made sure to add some extra, which he found made it easier to flag the fellow down the next time.

The tuk-tuk drivers, of course, wanted to know where he was from and where he was staying. They'd hand him business cards or write down their phone numbers so he could call whenever he wanted to be picked. (He learned that Kenyans say *picked* instead of *picked up*.) They wanted to know who else was in his party. But the drivers didn't ask Harry personal questions, presumably out of courtesy to wary visitors. However, they were eager to share stories about their own wives and girlfriends, the children they were working to put through school, and their current health challenges, which they typically blamed on malaria no matter what the symptoms. Surprising to Harry at first, but not at all in his later travels, was the tendency of the locals to complain about government corruption, which they assumed to be pervasive and permanent. The general opinion was that their news media feared to present the whole truth, and therefore gossip was the most reliable form of information. Hence, their eagerness to talk, especially to anyone who might have news of the wider world.

They complained about the cost of food, especially restaurant meals. (Harry knew it was a fraction of what he paid at home.)

They complained about other ethnicities. But never in his presence about whites, except to joke about mzungus. Sometimes bitterly about other tribes, Indians, and Arabs.

They talked about Kenyan national politics — who was in, who was out, what families were destined to rule forever.

They talked about the persistent prevalence of HIV, even though government clinics offered treatment. The rumor was one in four were infected.

They gave him advice on tourist sites, including the beach and the ancient ruins of the mosque at the mouth of the Kongo river, no more than a half-hour up the road.

They gave him history lessons about the abuses of the colonial period, the Mau Mau uprising that climaxed in Independence and the birth of the new nation, and — amazingly, to Harry — the heritage of the slave trade in Zanzibar, dating back thousands of years and run back then, not by whites, but by seafaring Arabs.

And after Harry had ridden with the same drivers more than once, he sensed they were so free with him that they regarded him as more expat than tourist. It was his first inkling he might enjoy staying.

Harry occasionally got a lift from Aldo's driver Joseph, who worked the coast as a taxi driver when he wasn't taking them on tour. And from some of Joseph's stories, Harry began to appreciate that the fear of being exploited wasn't necessarily a black-on-white racial thing. Kenyans, he'd been told several times over from any driver who got onto the subject of fair dealing, like nothing better than to game each other, especially when it comes to a member of one tribe taking clever advantage of a rival. The citizenry comprises forty-three tribes, each with its own language quite distinct from the common Kiswahili. While they might not hate each other as of old, there is still mistrust. Most of the politicians, bureaucrats, and wealthy families are Kikuyu. These days, the opposition party is led by a Luo — or, translated into the Brit-speak of the old colonialists — these factions are the counterparts of monied Tories and rebellious Laborites.

Joseph, who was a member of the Luo tribe and a proud retiree from Kenyan military service, advised Harry never to buy a used car from either a Kikuyu or an Indian. The man warned him, "You buy it in fine condition on a Monday, it's running very okay, but they tell you they want to clean it up, and you can collect it on a Wednesday. When you return, the oil pump and the distributor and the battery and all kinds of other parts will have been replaced with substandard crap that will be *funga* on your way home!"

Funga! An all-purpose word meaning *empty, gone, closed,* or *failed.*

So many things in Kenya are, they say. Ask anyone!

And here was what Eleanor must have meant about being careful whom you trust.

In at least one tangible respect, which proved to be far from minor, Aldo's sage advice had spared Harry from the torture of mosquito bites. When they'd first arrived in this beach town, Aldo suggested lunch at Nomad's, The Sands luxury resort restaurant. It was Sunday in the waning weeks of the tourist season in September, and the bar was hosting a farmer's market. Aldo directed Harry to one of the tables, where a local expat couple, who introduced themselves as Nellie and Sid, were selling homemade soaps, lotions, and artisan bread. Aldo quickly browsed their offerings and then held a vial of golden liquid up to his client's nose. "Buy this! You won't regret it, and you will thank Aldo for the rest of your life! Rub on your ankles and wrists after a shower and — magic! — mosquitos hate you!"

Nellie, who was white-haired and wizened from the sun, explained her concoction was a mixture of coconut and lemongrass oils — along with her secret herbs. She admitted that the lemongrass was the repellant, but she cautioned that just buying it in the store and rubbing it on could irritate the skin almost as much as a bite. Harry paid the thousand shillings (ten bucks) and forever afterward counted it a wise investment. The potion seemed to work, and he guessed it was nontoxic, which most commercial repellants aren't. (Harry would soon learn that price was dear, by local standards. But a week later, when he ran out and tried to mix his own, his product was far from satisfactory, and now he'd have to ask around to reconnect with Nellie.)

At Harry's favorite watering hole, the open-air Tiki bar (and what place wasn't open-air in this part of the world?) the insects were always a nuisance. The slow-flying black mosquitos that hovered especially around the damp bases of beverage fridges were not the worry. Nor were the seasonal termites, even if they can be almost the size of butterflies. You could see those and shoo and swat them. But the tiny no-see-ums could be chewing you up, and you wouldn't know it until the middle of the night when you'd wake up scratching the welts in a fury.

~

ON THE EVENING of the second day after Harry had met Esther, and with still no sight of her, he happened on Aldo at the Kusi hotel bar. The fellow was dressed nattily in a business suit, but Harry didn't inquire as to the nature of his friend's business. Perhaps he should have. Aldo seemed preoccupied, then declared, "Harry Harambee! Good name for you." Harry didn't catch the reference then, didn't ask what it meant, didn't think it at all important. The Italian went on jovially, "Have you had enough of this beach town? Want to go on safari? The rest of my group crapped out. Funga! So we can stay here as long as you like, or we can explore the countryside, stalk wild animals instead of scoping buns in bikinis!"

"I don't know," Harry mused. Trying not to sound too eager, he asked, "But what about Esther?"

Aldo looked only mildly surprised. "Esther? Pretty lady. You got a thing for her? She's a widow, you know."

Harry hesitated before he replied, "Let's just say I thought there was some mutual attraction."

"Tell you what," Aldo said. "I have to go to Mombasa tomorrow, and I'll be gone most of the day. Did you get her phone?"

"Yeah," Harry said, embarrassed to admit he hadn't called the number.

"So, why don't you call her and make a date for breakfast? And if it looks like it's going anywhere, you can tell me all about it at dinner. We can meet at Tiki after my errands."

Esther agreed to meet Harry for breakfast, and it was all smiles and chit-chat. He noted she was dressed in a no-nonsense, dark-blue pantsuit with a plain white blouse. Simple, understated jewelry — one pearl in each earlobe and a small strand around her neck. He assumed they weren't real.

He mostly told her about himself — his marriage and loss of his wife, his uncommunicative daughter, his uneventful semiretirement, and his reluctant decision to make this trip. She told him almost nothing about herself. He admitted he'd heard from Aldo she was widowed. She did confirm this coyly, muttering she'd already been married twice. She claimed she was unattached and added she had two teenage children in boarding school in Nairobi.

He asked her what she thought of Aldo. All she would say was she was sure he was in good hands.

Harry did most of the talking because he was nervous. He wanted to keep up the chatter, and he was embarrassed to ask her for personal information. This was dating. Not a sport he knew how to play. From the few details she'd shared, she seemed reserved on those topics. He didn't want to press. He regaled her with stories he'd heard from the tuk-tuk drivers. He kept it light and pleasant. And they found themselves laughing, not least because of their delight in being together.

And then she asked him for money. Not in exchange for anything she promised he'd get but simply because she needed it — *that day.* Oddly, he reflected later, he hadn't given it much thought. The woman's request was sincere. She'd given a plausible reason, needing to help her kids. If he'd been here on vacation with Lucille, she'd probably have loaned it to the woman as an act of sisterhood.

So he withdrew cash from the machine next door and handed it to her there in front of the bank. He asked her about her plans for the day. She shrugged off the question and explained she'd be all day in Mombasa. He mentioned he'd be dining with his friend Aldo that night at the Tiki Lounge, just up the beach road from his hotel. Then she jumped into one of the waiting tuk-tuks in the car park and sped off.

MOMENTS AFTER ESTHER had left him and he was still at the curb in front of the bank, he saw Aldo emerge from a building across the street, which from its sign and the vehicles parked around it appeared to be the offices of a safari-tour operator. Aldo was conversing heatedly, with his trademark Italian gestures, to a middle-aged man with a logo on his golf shirt.

Harry caught Aldo's eye, waved, and crossed over.

Aldo's conversation ended abruptly. He shook the other fellow's hand firmly and turned to flash his salesman's grin at Harry.

"*Ciao,* Harambee!"

"Is that Kenyan for 'Harry'?"

Aldo chuckled and patted his client on the back. "Let's just say, a guy with a big heart! How did it go with the lady?"

"I thought you were going to Mombasa today."

"I am. Joseph will be fetching me in about twenty minutes." Then he insisted, "I asked you a question."

At the outset of this trip, after he'd bought-in to Aldo's plan, Harry hadn't intended to be so hesitant about intimacy. But, in his mind, he'd just made an investment and a commitment, albeit for reasons not explicitly expressed. So he came right out and asked Aldo whether he thought it would be safe to go to bed with Esther. Perhaps Harry should have noticed that, as before when he'd mentioned her, Aldo hadn't looked surprised. The fellow said frankly that it would always be wise to ask a woman to get a blood test first, and even then to use a prophylactic. But that's when Aldo mysteriously advised Harry that he was sure Esther was not a hooker. She was a familiar face in the village, he said, and on previous occasions he'd never seen her with a mzungu tourist. Aldo then ushered Harry across the street to the walk-in medical clinic and had him take a chair in the waiting area while he stepped back into the doctor's consulting room.

Aldo emerged after a few minutes smiling broadly, took Harry by the arm, and led him outside. "No worries!" he said confidentially. "Of course, the doc won't share her records or any details, but he knows her. And for a small consideration he tells me you need not be concerned."

Harry would later wonder what, if any, information Aldo and the doctor had exchanged.

Harry shared that he'd told Esther he'd be at Tiki this evening, although they hadn't made a date. Aldo agreed to meet him there at six for dinner.

Harry didn't tell Aldo about the "loan" he'd given her.

THE MOST REMARKABLE event of that day was Harry's encounter with a young man he passed as he was walking back to the Kusi from town. Harry had browsed in a shop that sold children's toys and sporting goods, mostly for visiting beachgoers. He thought perhaps he might buy a mask with a snorkel. He'd wade out some distance and crouch down in waist-high water to catch sight of underwater fauna and flora. He wasn't ready to take a boat trip, and he had no use for swim fins. But it didn't take him long in the shop to realize this errand was just another time-waster. He'd go to all that bother and probably wouldn't be able to see anything.

The fellow was walking toward him, carrying a bundle of sticks on his head. His clothes were dirty and tattered, and he wore no shoes. Seeing Harry approach, he offered a big smile, laid the bundle at his feet, and held up his hand in greeting.

"Papa, where are you from?"

The path here was narrow, and Harry didn't feel right shoving the man aside.

Harry stopped, noting there were other people around, mostly vendors at their roadside stalls. He didn't feel unsafe, but he didn't want to linger.

"I'm from Los Angeles," he replied.

"Ah, Hollywood! Tell me, who is your favorite actor?"

The man was so amiable, Harry guessed exchanging pleasantries with him might be as enjoyable as chatting up those tuk-tuk drivers. He knew that the most popular American actor of all time with international audiences was Charles Bronson. Mostly because action-adventure movies with revenge themes entertain even if translated poorly. But Bronson was long gone, so he picked a star the fellow might know and suggested, "Clint Eastwood?"

The man laughed heartily as he announced, *"High Plains Drifter! For a Few Dollars More! The Good, the Bad and the* Very *Ugly!"* And he laughed some more.

"You've seen all of those?"

"Oh, yes, Papa. Many times. We have DVD. My children enjoy." He shrugged and his smile dropped. "I have many, you see."

"It looks like you have a job," Harry observed, indicating the bundle of sticks. He added the universal gesture of goodwill, "What is your name?"

"I am Peter! I am the rock, and I am my own boss!" he declared. "I gather the dead branches. If I cut from the trees, this is forbidden, and I will be arrested. Not so much wood around. Others are doing the same. I take this wood to the cooks at the restaurants. They buy for their cooking fires."

"I'm Harry. I'm sure you work hard," Harry told him, not knowing what else to say.

"May I ask, sir, do you walk here in the mornings?"

"Usually, yes."

"Papa, I must ask you a small favor."

Here came the appeal for money. So far, Harry hadn't seen any girls or women of any age begging. Apparently, in Kenya, even the breadwinners who panhandled were men.

But this beggar stunned Harry by reaching into his pants pocket and pulling out two hundred-shilling notes. He didn't push them on Harry but pointed toward a firepit by the side of the road, then explained, "These street people, they sell a bag of rice for two hundred. But it is a very small bag. Not enough for my family and I fear I am being cheated. But at the market, I am told, for two hundred, the bags are many times this size."

"You may be right. I know a loaf of bread is eighty, so I'd think two hundred could buy a lot of rice. Sure, ask at the market."

He looked down, spreading his hands to indicate his appearance. "Papa, they don't allow such as me in the market." Now he offered the cash, saying, "So, please buy. You go, and I wait for you here. Or, if it is not convenient for you to go now, take the money, you go tomorrow, and I see you here, same time."

Harry was both ashamed that he'd feared he would be robbed and annoyed he was being played, although by a man whose intentions seemed not only honorable but scrupulously honest.

Harry gently pushed the fellow's hand away and said, "You can keep your money. When I'm in the store tomorrow, I'll find the rice. A big bag. I'll see you here on the way back. You won't have to pay me, but, you understand, I'm only visiting, so I can't be doing this for you every day."

The man grinned and, realizing Harry might not wish to shake his filthy hand, offered a salute, pocketed his money, picked up the wood, and walked on.

～

So here Harry was that evening at the bar in the Tiki, waiting for the overdue Aldo, then stunned by Esther's grand entrance wearing clothes she must surely have purchased that day with his money.

Harry tried to stroll casually over from the bar to join her after she'd seated herself at a corner table with a settee. He'd drawn the obvious conclusion that she was wearing his money, but he wasn't about to call her on it just yet. Now his suspicions were growing. For all he knew, he wasn't the only guy she'd hit up before she'd set out for town. But he feared asking her would give her an opening to walk him triumphantly down some rogues' gallery, which was a gloomy corridor less painful for him to imagine than to confront in reality. He calculated she was in her mid to late thirties. Yes, this morning she'd told him she'd had two husbands so far, each of them long since departed for reasons he wouldn't care to guess. He didn't want to know those stories either. And the assortment of gentlemen who had escorted her during the intervening years would be a long row of frozen wax figures behind the glass of some rogues' gallery.

It wasn't as if Harry were paying for her services. True, he was captivated by her, and he admitted it. He didn't figure her for a tease. He still didn't know much about her personal life, but the attention he felt coming from her seemed sincere. And she didn't flirt, didn't hint, didn't pout. When she'd asked him for the money, her reason was a statement of fact — even though now he knew it wasn't the whole truth.

Now he wondered why he had given it to her so freely. But what else did he have to do with his money? Save it for Nicole to inherit so she could lavish it on her next boyfriend?

As Harry joined Esther at a table, he fussed to himself not only that she may have played him but also that his presumptive protector Aldo was still a no-show. Harry wondered whether Esther knew where Aldo might have gone and whom he might be with. She must know him somehow from his previous visits, and there were certain people everyone seemed to know — like the doctor at the walk-in clinic, the druggist at the no-questions-asked pharmacy, the proprietor of the open-air vegetable stand in front of the supermarket, and the only hairstylist in town who seemed to know anything about coloring Caucasian hair.

Harry groaned for effect and said, "I was going to have Aldo pick up the check as payback for being late. But we'd better go ahead and order."

His irritation with her was rising. As he took a place on the settee beside her, she already had her drink. He assumed it was Bombay gin on the rocks, which he judged to be uncharacteristically unladylike. He and Aldo had drunk with a few men who took gin neat, as well as with some Brits who did the same with whiskey, which they spelled *whisky* and mistakenly meant Scotch, not bourbon. Harry's gin-and-tonic, which he still carried but needed a stiff refill, was a choice mainly to quench the thirst on a hot day. He'd admit to a fondness at more pensive times for what Americans call *sipping whiskey*, which had to be from either Tennessee or Kentucky. He'd found a cheap Kenyan knock-off brand of "blended whisky," which is what he had stashed back in the room.

He'd think a woman would be more conscientious about staying sober while her male companions descended by gulps into progressive stages of foolishness. She should have her booze with fruit juice or soda, that would be more like the norm.

So far, she didn't seem at all inebriated, but she seemed much more relaxed than she had been this morning, as if a day on a shopping spree in the designer boutiques had made her downright chatty. Granted, enduring the transit across the channel in the ferry would have been tedious — involving as much as two hours' wait for one of two boats depending on the time of day — and all the more annoying when you're wedged into a minibus with a dozen or more sweaty strangers. She'd obviously had time to shower and dab on some strong patchouli scent — and to touch up her nails and eyeliner — before getting dolled up in her purchases to meet up with Harry at the Tiki.

"So, do you know what's become of Aldo?" Harry asked her.

She shrugged and actually giggled. "I thought he was with you," she said, "letting young things chase you in the surf."

"He was supposed to meet me at six. You'd expect him to at least send a text. But nothing."

"Did you fellows have plans? I mean, you know, other than…?"

"Not especially."

"Then why are you worried? Maybe he's got a girl stashed someplace, one you don't know about."

"I don't know about any. He doesn't talk about women, but he knows every hangout up and down the coast and all the angles on anything you could ever want to buy or rent. I know the guy hardly at all, but I'm in this situation where I don't have any choice but to trust every word he tells me. He could be working all kinds of angles, and I'd never know."

But all she wanted to know was "And what does he say about me?"

It wasn't helping Harry's mood that the waitress seemed to be ignoring him as he waved his empty glass at her.

"Do you mind?" he asked Esther as he grabbed her glass and took a gulp.

It was water.

Now she knew that he knew she wasn't drinking. Was she Muslim? Or just intending to feign drunkenness while he lost all sense of reason and judgment?

Now it was Harry's turn to choose his words carefully. "Right off, he said you aren't a hooker."

From her now, a sarcastic grin. "I don't know how he would know. It's not like I've ever seen him in church." She took another sip, then looked Harry in the eye for the first time since he'd sat down, and added, "But, about that, he's right."

Harry finally got his drink. Rather than setting it on the table, the waitress put it into his hand with a knowing smile, which he interpreted to mean she'd observed his wobbly behavior and was slowing the rounds to pace him.

Harry chugged half of it and sighed. Maybe he'd been misjudging everyone. He had to finally ask his dinner date, "Did you manage to get the textbooks?"

She pursed her lips, downcast again. "Actually, no," she said softly. "Out of stock, more coming from Nairobi, but they won't say when. So I have to tell Charles and Yvonne they must find someone to share with, maybe for the whole term."

"And the money burned a hole in your pocket?" He tried to make it sound like good-natured teasing, but she was almost certain to take it as scolding.

She pretended not to understand.

"It's a saying," Harry said. "Meaning, you couldn't wait to spend it?"

She looked annoyed, neither angry nor apologetic. "You want to call it a loan, suit yourself. Just don't press me about when I expect to have it because, honestly, I don't know. I asked you for the money because I really needed it, and I guessed you would have it. Did you think you were buying something with it?"

He ignored the question because he wasn't sure of the answer. Instead, he teased, "Aldo says the ones in the silk dresses — and particularly with the designer eyeglass frames, shoes, and handbags — *they're* probably hookers."

"How about in sportswear with running shoes? You would think she's somebody's wife. Maybe if she climbs into an SUV, you know they've got kids. But — if it's just a pretty dress? Cotton print? No accessories? It will be the only one she owns. She bought it used from a street vendor. That's how we buy most of our clothes. Me, I don't need glasses. I could see that stupid grin on your face from across the street."

Now he wasn't sure whether she was teasing or scolding.

She surprised him by reaching across the table to touch his hand. The preliminaries were over. Her mood had shifted. She was being sincere, and she must have thought he wasn't too drunk to see it. In a hushed voice, she said, "I bought this outfit for a reason. Yes, I wanted to impress you, to please you. But not just that. I'm invited to tea tomorrow." Then she added, "You might say it's a job interview. It was a question of whether I should look professional or... desirable. I know this person, and considering the audience, I decided it's important for me to look pretty. And not poor."

That's when Harry realized her choice wasn't just for him, the urgent need was never for textbooks, and her play, whatever it turned out to be, must involve much more than a new dress.

"What's the job?"

"I'm a bookkeeper. And this would be a step up."

"And the client is some horny old guy?"

She smiled. "I see you understand business." Then she offered, "I'd like you to go with me. Victor Skebelsky is a force of nature, and you should meet him."

During dinner, she chattered about her teenage children and her pride in their achievements at school. She was sure that the meticulous Charles was destined to be an honorable public official. The querulous Yvonne could be the tough-minded barrister who would have his back. Harry described his differences with Nicole about her life choices, but he hoped his complaints were tinged with affection.

The only further information Esther would share about Skebelsky was that some people called him the meanest man in town.

CHAPTER 9

*H*arry'd had about as much as he could drink and still be marginally functional. As he was settling the bill, Esther strode out into the car park and hailed a passing tuk-tuk. He climbed in after her, and they rode a short way up the beach road to his lodgings in a private bungalow at the Kusi Lodge Beach Resort.

Harry had assumed, wrongly, that Esther would fall into bed with him. She'd shown no reluctance to return with him to his room. But regarding her as simply one of the local pickups was a mistake, one he was sharp enough to correct before he might have embarrassed himself.

She declined his offer of the anonymous brown liquor served neat. He judged he should cut himself off as well, and they sat primly on his couch. He hardly remembered what they talked about. He insisted he liked the dress and the accessories she'd picked, and he liked the way she looked in it. He thought she'd make a nice impression, rather like a fine lady dressed for a society function. They didn't talk about this Victor fellow, and Harry didn't fret about her suggestion to go along. He was mildly surprised that she wanted him to accompany her to the meeting, but if the guy was such a rascal, perhaps she was just being cautious. Considering the effort she'd gone to, she must think it was an important opportunity for her, and he finally admitted he was glad he could help.

She spoke softly, smiled, and giggled. He tried to make his voice sound tender.

When the time was long past that he should have embraced her and attempted a kiss, she took the initiative and bestowed a wet one on his cheek. That broke the ice, and what followed was a half-hour of kissing and caressing. Also contrary to Harry's expectations, they didn't carry on like horny teenagers. Their touching was more like old lovers getting reacquainted after a long separation. She kept giggling and smiling, and he kept forcing his voice into what he thought were lower, manful tones. They both kept their clothes on.

Finally, she pushed away slightly and informed him she had to go, explaining she had to work in the morning. He offered to escort her to a taxi out front or even ride home with her, but she said it would be best if they weren't seen at this hour together in the lobby. She assured him she'd be perfectly safe, she knew all the tuk-tuk and boda-boda drivers personally, and she would be comfortably home after only a short ride for a small fraction of what the hotel taximan would charge him.

They shared a languorous kiss at his door, with no words of either love or lust. She assured him she'd see him tomorrow, and before he could ask how they'd manage that, she was retreating across the pool deck and disappearing into a passageway of the main building that bypassed reception.

He was far from being disappointed. This was not the adventure he'd been anticipating. But he was sure, without knowing exactly how or why, that it was the beginning of *some kind* of adventure.

WHEN HARRY AWOKE the morning after his make-out session with Esther on the couch, for a moment he was surprised to find himself alone. It had been years since he'd kept to one side of a double bed, but here he was hunched over a stack of pillows on the far edge as if he'd expected Esther would be beside him. But he was sure he hadn't been so drunk as to entirely forget a liaison, and her side of the bed wasn't mussed. The room did smell faintly of her patchouli perfume. He remembered she'd gone home. Now that he was sober, he recalled fragments of their conversation. But he still wasn't sure whether she had a boyfriend.

Harry didn't know who Skebelsky was, he had never even heard the name. Last night at dinner, when he'd asked Esther for an explanation, all she would say was "This man can make you rich. Hear him out."

Harry had never aspired to great wealth, and given the prospects of his small publishing business, he never imagined it was possible. Two weeks remained in the itinerary Aldo had set for their vacation in Kenya, and Harry had assumed they'd be returning to the US as planned. Granted — Nicole, Eleanor, Aldo, that consul Antoine, and even Esther — each of them had separately teased him about staying on as if they'd all held a meeting and agreed he'd want to retire here or perhaps start some sideline business to keep himself occupied. Antoine had hinted strongly that setting up a business was to be preferred to declaring full-time retirement because it would give him more options about how to spend his time and how he could derive the income to subsidize a lavish lifestyle here, where expenses were so much less.

In the end, simply being comfortable in a beautiful place for the rest of his years was all Harry aspired to. He hadn't grasped all the details Antoine had given him about applying for a business license, but he doubted he'd be able to tolerate the risks. He liked living in Santa Monica well enough, with its moderate climate and upscale amenities, but living expenses in Los Angeles, as well as taxes in California, were getting burdensome. If he stayed there, his quality of life was in danger of decreasing from comfortable to merely getting by. He appreciated that he was lucky to have these options, that so many people his age were already struggling financially.

And then, there was the basic consideration of how he felt about Esther. On this trip and perhaps until the end of his days, he hadn't expected to give his heart to anyone again. Although Aldo had made life on safari sound both exciting and luxurious, they hadn't yet spent a day in the bush.

And not being someone who'd been all that interested in stalking wildlife, Harry had meekly gone along with the revised plan. From Aldo's allusions to his secretive business dealings, Harry had surmised that asking questions could implicate him needlessly in nefarious activities. After all, to possess an insider's knowledge of the seedier side of his trade, as well as to be savvy about all manner of deal-making in the Third World, Aldo had to be a friend of, if not partnered with, influential persons who, even if they weren't criminals, operated in the gray muck of underground economies.

Harry's initial flirtations with younger women here at the beach had been satisfying for only the briefest moments, and then ultimately disappointing. At his age, hookups without companionship — and, he had to admit, without affection — seemed pointless, even annoying.

He began to think of the money he'd given Esther as a wager, a bet that his future would be markedly different from his past. It was the first time in his life he'd been so reckless. Oh, he'd donated to the occasional charity. But here he was trusting that he either wasn't being played — or that he *was* and wouldn't regret a moment of it.

So. Esther wanted him to meet this guy Victor. Okay, no doubt some kind of scam was in the offing. But here he was becoming adjusted to a culture where scamming is assumed by the citizenry at large to be the daily routine of both business and government — and, more often than not — the engine of the most intimate personal relationships. Brothers supported brothers and then tricked them on alternate days. Young people employed in the cities dutifully sent chunks of their paychecks home to their families in tribal villages, only later to spam friends and family on WhatsApp, citing personal crises that might or might not exist or that needed urgent attention for reasons other than those given. Malaria or HIV? School tuition or a police citation?

～

ESTHER HAD PROMISED she'd meet him sometime today, and it was all he could think about. He showered quickly, dressed in freshly laundered shorts and a golf shirt, and trundled out across the lawn and into the hotel dining room, where a lavish buffet breakfast could be expected.

And there, sitting at a four-top table, was Esther, dressed in a practical blue pantsuit and a white blouse, sipping coffee demurely across from Aldo, who looked much the international entrepreneur in a tailored linen suit and designer silk tie.

Seeing Harry approach, Aldo decorously pushed his chair back, stood up, and extended a warm hand in greeting, almost as if they were meeting for the first time on a business matter.

"Harry Harambee!" he exclaimed as he gave a knowing wink in Esther's direction and added, "our distinguished guest, our benefactor, our good friend!"

Taking a seat next to Esther and gesturing to the waiter for coffee, Harry mumbled, "Okay, what did I do to deserve all this admiration? Or what am I *gonna* do?" And then, confronting Aldo, who having sat was ostentatiously shooting his starched cuffs, "And where have *you* been?"

"New suit, do you like?"

"Stunning," Harry said, underwhelmed as he gulped his coffee black.

"An Indian tailor in Nyali. You text him your measurements and it's done in two days. You couldn't do better on Savile Row, not even in Hong Kong. Maybe you want one, maybe two, Harry? The price is beyond belief!"

Harry looked up and said tiredly, "That can't be why you went to Mombasa." And after another gulp he finally turned to Esther and tried on a smile. "And a beautiful good morning to you, my dear."

She smiled back, and to Harry it seemed genuine. "Harambee, you know we both love you."

Harry frowned. "You guys are a team now? Since when do you know each other?"

Aldo lowered his voice, "The time has come, Harry, as they say in a friendly game of chance, to lay our cards on the table."

Harry knew this moment would come, had even hoped for it. But now he wasn't so sure he wanted the answers.

Aldo went on, "Esther and I are colleagues. But we are not, how you say, *in cahoots?* It is no coincidence you and I stay at this fine hotel. It's because dear Esther here works in the business office. I book my tour packages here, and she always gives me the best price. But it is a coincidence for sure you pick her out of the grocery store! And even bigger nice surprise she says you like each other so very much! And I must add before I say more that you should count yourself a lucky man to enjoy her attentions. This is a very classy lady. It was not my plan that you'd have a relationship with such a fine person. I expected you would have some innocent flings, some young, forgettable dates. And, as you've already expressed to me, you have had opportunities here, but you find these tiresome. You are a man of sophisticated taste — and, I will go so far as to say — an honorable man." He turned to Esther to prompt her with, "And I believe Esther sees this in you, as I do."

"Yes," she said submissively as she beamed at Harry. "Our Harry is a lovely person, a generous spirit. A gentleman. As you can imagine, we don't see so many like you."

Harry wasn't at all drunk, but having only sipped his morning coffee, his head wasn't yet clear. He responded with unusual frankness when he said, "Why do I get the feeling I'm being kissed before I get screwed?" It came out nastier than it should've.

"Come now, Harry," Aldo laughed. "We can be serious now. Esther tells me she has broached the idea of introducing you to Victor Skebelsky."

"Yeah, 'the meanest man in town,' according to her."

Aldo laughed again. "Esther loves to tease. I'm sure you appreciate that by now. You'll see, Victor is a pussycat. No, he is a lion! Sure, he has claws, but you will win his respect."

To Aldo, Harry asked, "So, you know this guy, as well?"

With a glance to Esther, Aldo rested a hand on Harry's bare arm. The mask of his smile dropped. He looked earnestly at the American and said, "Harry, when I proposed the tour, my motive was to make my usual cut on the package. Now the Frog foot-doctors are funga, and I am a big loser. *Così è andata.* It's normal, I also do some side business along the way. Innocuous, as they say. Pocket money." He leaned forward and added, "But I have a suspicion. Do you believe in destiny, fate, higher power, Harambee? I know now that meeting Victor is why I brought you to Kenya."

CHAPTER 10

*D*iani Beach Road, the two-lane tarmac through town, extends southward to the border with Tanzania, a distance of about thirty miles. On the way, after about four miles is the village of Galu, where the beach is pristine, and new real-estate developments proceed by fits and starts. Construction on a shopping mall, two condominium complexes, and a luxury hotel had halted when bank funds dried up because of the most recent economic downturn. Farther on is Mzambweni, a larger town and home to one of the area's major hospitals.

After the threesome had finished breakfast at the Kusi Lodge, Joseph was waiting for them in a private sedan in the circular drive of the hotel. Joseph's pride was his reconditioned and only slightly battered white Toyota Camry. It had right-hand drive suited to the British-system Kenyan roadways. As Harry got in the back seat after Esther, he noticed for the first time that the windshield of the car lacked the usual stickers for a taxi license and insurance certificates. By now, he'd been in enough vehicles to know that taxis usually displayed lots of them. When Harry asked, Joseph explained that, if a policeman were to stop them on the road, lack of the required documentation might cost them a hefty cash bribe. And if he couldn't convince the officer this was a private car and not a taxi service, he might be arrested, and his passengers might or might not be allowed to continue their journey without further difficulties.

Joseph smiled deferentially and then started the car. A disembodied female voice immediately scolded something in Japanese. Aldo, who was seated in front, turned back to explain, "So many automobiles here are imported from Japan. Right-hand drive like here. She is telling you to buckle your seat belt!"

None of them bothered, and the dashboard display lit up with Japanese characters. (Not wearing seat belts would be another way to incur a fine from the police if they were stopped.)

Joseph chuckled and pronounced, "It's an excellent car! And the air conditioning is fully operational! You will enjoy, and it will be my pleasure to serve you."

Then, suddenly, Harry felt sick. Esther saw his distress, took his arm, and asked, "Are you okay? Too much to drink last night?"

He was so ashamed! The alcohol had fogged his memory, and he'd been too preoccupied with all the recent excitement to focus on routine chores. He muttered morosely, "I promised to buy Peter a bag of rice."

He explained the problem to Aldo, who smirked but wasn't critical. He instructed Joseph to drop them at Skebelsky's first, then run back to Chandarana, purchase the rice, and cruise the road to find the needy fellow and hand it over with their good wishes.

Joseph added, "You realize, boss, you will now be seeing that guy every day of your visit."

Harry worried Joseph had called him *boss*, but he would learn that Kenyans use it commonly instead of *sir*, ignoring its possible origins in the colonial era.

Harry looked over to study Esther's face. Would she now have confirmation he was a clueless sucker, a suitable victim for her schemes? Or would she be touched that Harry Harambee had proved true to his name?

~

VICTOR SKEBELSKY'S place was about halfway to Galu, the property located off an unmarked hard-right turn onto a dirt track. Although the tarmac of the beach road was in fair condition with only the occasional speed bump or pothole, the dirt road was barely passable. It was deeply rutted from the rains and strewn with rocks, some as large as footballs.

The car bumped along slowly as Joseph navigated, steering continually to avoid the worst of it, the ride jostling the passengers as severely as Consul Wangari had warned Harry those safari treks would be. Harry wondered whether the car's shock absorbers could withstand such rugged use. He asked Aldo, "If this guy's so rich, why doesn't he fix the road?"

Aldo told them, "You will notice, all over Kenya and even in Nairobi, you may find nicely paved main roads, but the driveways leading up to even grand houses are in such terrible condition. As they say in America, it's not a bug, it's a feature. Think about it. If thieves show up at your home and manage to load your stuff into their truck or car, they won't be making a fast getaway!"

The track took a sharp turn at a long masonry wall that stretched more than a hundred yards to the south. As is typical of compounds where invisible security is too expensive, the wall was topped with razor wire and broken glass.

At an iron gate, Joseph sounded the horn, and an *askari* stepped out from the guard shack. He was dressed in the badged paramilitary uniform and beret of a commercial security service and wore the characteristic red-plaid blanket of a Maasai warrior across his shoulders. The fellow carried no firearm. A baton-sized stick, or *rungu* club, tipped with a knob the size of a fist, dangled at his side.

Joseph rolled his window down and said something in Kiswahili to the guard, who nodded curly without expression and promptly opened the gate.

On hearing the sound of the gate opening, two large Alsatians on the other side of the wall began to bark ferociously.

Once inside the gate, the car ride smoothed out immediately. The track was neatly bricked and richly landscaped. The dogs quieted, somehow realizing the entrance was authorized, and they simply trotted alongside the car.

The compound was huge — Harry figured it must extend for many acres — densely covered with a lush, leafy canopy of old-growth, deciduous trees. Permanently shaded from the sun, the grounds were cool and dark.

On the way to the main house, they passed a swimming pool, two tennis courts, and a crushed-granite bocce pitch. All of these amenities appeared to be immaculately maintained, but no one was using them.

Joseph pulled the car into a circular drive in front of a massive colonial-era home. Two stories, white stucco walls, and a traditional Swahili thatched roof. A Spanish-style fountain adorned the landscaped area at the center of the drive. It was planted with manicured blooming bushes ringed by mosaic-tiled stonework, but the fountain was dry.

Joseph jumped out and opened the car doors for his passengers. The two dogs sniffed the new guests and then bounded away.

An aging mzungu with silver hair emerged to stand regally with his hands in his pants pockets at the top of the steps of the house. He wore a floral silk shirt, white ducks, and deck shoes without socks. As he smiled in greeting, his sunburnt face broke into a thousand lines.

"Welcome!" he croaked. "Call me Vic."

Aldo smoothed and buttoned his suit jacket as he waved a hand to introduce, "The lovely Esther Mwemba, whom you know, and our dear friend from Los Angeles, Harry Gardner."

Skebelsky chuckled and extended a hand as Harry climbed the steps toward him. Broad smile, gleaming white teeth, so perfect they might all be dentures or implants. The man cooed, "Would this be the famous Harry Harambee I've heard so much about?"

Suspicious as Harry was under the circumstances, he resolved to be good-natured. He shook the fellow's hand and replied, "That's what they call me." Then he added, "I'm not quite sure yet why."

CHAPTER 11

*S*kebelsky invited them in to sit on chintz-covered couches in an open-air veranda. Like most living rooms in this part of the world, it had no glass windows or screens, with stucco archways supporting the traditional, thatched roof of closely knitted palm fronds. The colonial furniture was heavy and dark, milled from the dense Kenyan hardwoods of yesteryear, the rare kinds no one is allowed to harvest anymore. As there might be in the parlor of any Victorian home the world over, besides couches and ottomans, here was a breakfront full of Wedgwood and Spode china, as well as a sideboard with silver service and ice bucket. The Indian hammered-brass coffee table rested on a pair of (now also illegal to buy) enormous elephant tusks.

As Harry glanced around the room, he was suddenly alarmed to spot a good-sized snake entwined around a trellis under one of the arches. He looked over at Aldo and pointed to the creature. Aldo looked around to see it but didn't seem concerned. Victor saw the exchange, chuckled, and explained, "It's getting to the be the heat of the day, but if you were here in the cool of the early morning, you'd see monkeys in the trees, munching on the blossoms. They hate snakes. This one's rubber, and the monkeys stay clear, even when there's food on the table. Beats chasing the little buggers all over the grounds with a slingshot!"

Richard, a tall, graying houseman in a white-coated uniform, appeared carrying a silver tray with teacups and a pot in a quilted cozy. After he poured the tea, he retreated into the house and returned with the tray filled with crackers, cheese, grapes, and sliced apples.

In perfect English that had some flavor of accent, their host pronounced, "I know it's almost time for lunch, but please excuse our scant repast. We had something of a plumbing mishap this morning, and Richard did not have time to do his usual marketing."

The fellow's breathing was labored, and he wheezed repeatedly as he spoke.

"Are you British?" Harry asked. "Your speech is distinguished, but I can't place the accent."

"Ah," Victor chuckled. "I suppose one would say it's Etonian. I was born in Poland, then they shipped me off to boarding school in England. No sooner was I graduated than my parents had moved to Jo-burg, and I was carted off to there, so I fear there's a bit of South African mixed in. But I've been a Kenyan for dogs' years now."

"Victor is well known in the town," Aldo explained to Harry. "A regular at the Rotary Club, and you'll see him breakfasting some mornings at Kokko's. And he's been a supporter of local causes, but he'll tell you about all that."

Victor coughed and shrugged, "No memsahib, sadly. The dears can't abide me, nor I them. I've a bit of a crust, you see. My father built this compound, years before Independence, and we are extremely fortunate the bloody wogs haven't torn it all down." He took a sip of tea and winced, not because it was hot but perhaps because he'd have preferred something stronger. Then he waved an arm in an expansive gesture as if to include the entire compound and said, "Five houses on the property, you see, and not one of them occupied — save for where we're sitting — at present. Oh, Richard and I could do the weekend vacationers, but what a *bother* — and for *pennies?* Bloody taxes will eat this white man alive, I'll tell you for nothing."

Aldo chimed in again, this time to Victor, "Harry has been in town just a week, getting settled. He is taking some time off, enjoying the beach life, and, if I may say so, thinking about life's advantages on the South Coast."

Victor nodded sagely, as if this was the way all supplicants found their way to him. He turned to Esther and asked, "And, my dear, we see one another so infrequently. May I ask, how is your father?"

Esther looked embarrassed for a moment, set her teacup down, and replied, "He's undergoing cancer treatments. In Nairobi. You probably haven't heard."

Victor sighed, "Alas, no, I'm sorry. He's getting the best, I hope?"

"He's well fixed," she said curtly. "And responding, so they say."

The old man was wracked with a fit of coughing and wheezing. He pulled an inhaler from his pants pocket and took a hit.

With a deep gasp of relief, he turned to Harry to explain, "Esther's father and mine were colleagues, very close. Samuel, her dear father, was a member of the legislature. This was all before Independence. My father conducted his cement contracting business with the British administrators. Very tight, you see, all wired, as everything was back then," he said with a wink. "Then, of course, after sixty-three, all bets were off. Lucky we still have our heads!" He set his own cup down, deciding he'd had enough of the awful tea, and muttered for Harry's benefit, "Made a friend of Esther, have you? Well done. Smart fellow."

Aldo took the initiative to suggest, "Perhaps you could tell Harry some of your plans."

Skebelsky cleared his throat with difficulty and sat up, but what came out was still the croak of a lifelong chain-smoker. "Mr. Gardner, Aldo tells me you run a publishing company. College textbooks."

Harry clarified, "A small press, yes. History books, academic market."

"So! You're both an educator and a businessman!"

"My degree was in political science. But I think I can safely say I've forgotten just about everything I learned in school. The business management I picked up the hard way. Negotiating contracts with airheads and trying to meet payroll. The business still operates but barely. It's time for me to accept that I'm out of it."

Skebelsky nodded enthusiastically. Harry could only guess what pleased him so much. The fellow gasped again and announced, "I, too, am a student of history! What do you know of the history of East Africa? And particularly the South Coast here."

"Not much a all," Harry admitted.

"All the land along the coast was, until recent times, the property of the Sultan of Zanzibar. The Arabs, you know, were the original slave traders, going back more than a thousand years, way before the Europeans showed up. By way of the Arabs, there were black slaves in many of the wealthy houses of India and China centuries before any got shipped over to the Americas. Later, it was the bloody Portuguese. Kiswahili was an ancient language of Bantu people on the coast, the traders, and the sailors, and spoken everywhere the waters of the Indian Ocean touched. Anyhow, even after the Brits drove out the Portuguese and grabbed Kenya as a colony, they didn't give a tinker's damn for the coast — except of course for the port of Mombasa. In the early twentieth century, they built the railroad from Mombasa to Nairobi, which was just a kind of depot, and they built it up as the capital city it is today. They wanted to pull wealth out of Uganda and the Congo, ship it up the Suez, suck on that teat forever. Rape Africa — they were all keen to do it. But all along, they ceded control of the coast to the Sultan. Today, even though Kenya is an English-speaking country where most people are Christian, here on the coast, it's still mostly Muslim, with strong Swahili traditions. For the most part, the Christians who live here are upcountry Kenyans who came to work in the hotels. And they've intermarried with the locals. We have a very tolerant little community, let me tell you. Because we all worship the same god — the white tourist's money!"

Victor had to take a moment to catch his breath again, and he gestured to the houseman, who was standing quietly in the doorway. "Richard, fetch my medicine, there's a good fellow."

Richard had a silver hip flask at the ready, which he handed to his employer, who uncapped it and took a long pull.

"Ah!" he exclaimed, "Bloody kerosene, but it does the trick." Richard was waiting for the man to hand the flask back, but Victor tucked it into the cushion of his chair. The houseman resumed his attentive post, and their host continued, "After Independence, the Sultan had to give up the land here and turned it over to the rebel

Kenyan government. The top politicians kept it for their families. I mean, the bloody Queen owns half of England, there's the model! Why should the top wogs be any different? A few politicians still own most of it today. But this little piece of paradise is titled to *my* family, and so far that deed has held up."

Harry could see that Victor was tiring, and he doubted the interview could go much longer.

Victor went on, fascinated by his own lecture, "As a tourist destination, for whatever reason, Diani has attracted vacationers from Germany. Up the coast, in Malindi, it's been Italians. But a curious thing has happened. Many Europeans have decided to establish residence here and, recently, some South Africans who are finding home uncomfortable. We also have plenty of missionaries. Why, nobody seems to know, but the government persists in giving them special status on immigration, long after the colonialists have been kicked out." He chortled, "Our politicians seem to like Christians. Any denomination will do! Maybe it's just to stave off the bloody Arabs. No one can abide *them*, never have."

Victor's eyes were watering with the strain, and he cast his gaze at Harry. "Bear with me, dear boy. This history lesson has a point. Because and an odd thing has happened — and scholars have studied this — these Europeans have seen the poor living conditions here — especially the lack of community services because of government neglect — and they've set up charities to step in. Saving Africa, whatever that means to the donors, is still a thriving industry!

"You have only to look around this town! The local schools, especially the decent ones, are private and run by philanthropies. Likewise medical clinics and hospitals, along with wildlife conservation and environmental cleanup.

"The result?" Skebelsky clapped his thigh, wheezed, and cackled with delight. "Besides tourism, philanthropy is the biggest business in Diani! And did you hear me say the government *doesn't care* about the coast? Now they care *even less* about us because they have no incentive to provide the services the citizens would expect from the public purse!"

Harry glanced over at Esther, who had her head down. Aldo sat, looking attentive, his hands folded respectfully in his lap. "That's not right," Harry muttered.

Skebelsky slapped his thigh again and shouted, "Not right? I call it *opportunity,* man!" And the exertion threw him into another brief coughing fit.

"I don't follow," Harry said. "It seems like a new kind of colonialism. Wouldn't the people want more control of their own communities?"

"Oh, they mistrust us Europeans. But they *despise* the crooked politicians in the government more! They'd much rather make peace with us than those fat-cat land-grabbers in Nairobi. Fact is, they all think they can twist us around their little fingers!"

"So, what's the opportunity?" Harry asked. As he had expected all along, he guessed the purpose of the visit was to propose some kind of investment.

Victor leaned toward Harry and rested his hands on both knees. "Because, my fine friend, the stars have aligned. The government — and the banks and all the commercial nabobs — are about to get *very interested* in the South Coast — *finally.* Tourism has been off for years, and then the last economic downturn all but killed it. Some years back, Muslim terrorists came in from Somalia, and there were pirates off the coast. American and European tourists stayed home, afraid they'd get their heads lopped off. The United States had a presence here, they called it 'development assistance,' and then their government had cutbacks. In recent rainy seasons, too much fell on Nairobi and flushed great gobs of sewage into the river and then onto the beaches of Malindi, and most of the Italians held their noses and disappeared."

Later, Aldo would offer the opinion that it was the Kenyan autocrats who chased the Italian Mafiosi out of Malindi. Because they refused to share.

Victor continued, "The wealthy political families not only control the land here, but they also own many of the hotels. So if tourism is off, so is tourist income and hotel taxes. And despite all that charitable help, demand for health and community services from the locals is skyrocketing, and it threatens to be a huge drain on government funds."

He took a deep breath. His guests knew here was the payoff and the pitch.

"Here's what they plan to do. The overland transportation from Mombasa down to Diani has always been awful. There's only the ferry at Likoni because the government refused to build a bridge even after the Japanese gave them money for it. The revenue from those boats going back and forth with cars and trucks and thousands of pedestrians every day is a huge cash-cow for somebody. But it's a bloody bottleneck, slows commerce. So — here's major improvement number one — they're finishing the Ukunda Road, a modern highway to bypass the ferry, and major shipments of goods can finally get here efficiently.

"Improvement number two — is the so-called floating bridge at Likoni to link the island with the south. It's finally built, designed in sections to open and close to let the big ships pass in and out of the harbor. There's some question whether opening an hour before each ship requires access will ever permit the thing to be closed so the vehicles can cross, but there you are, and it's soon to be a thing. This new bridge is narrow, for foot traffic only. But they're planning a bigger one for cars and trucks. Someday, but don't hold your breath.

"Major improvement number three, the Ukunda Airstrip, the runway in Diani that serves regional aircraft, will be built up as an international airport. Construction is underway, and they're already moving locals out of their homes. Visitors won't even have to connect through Nairobi or Mombasa. You'll be able to fly direct from New York, London, Amsterdam, Istanbul, Addis Ababa, Johannesburg, or Doha — and put down scarcely a few kilometers from here.

"All this by way of saying, we're sitting on land that — perhaps a decade from now — will be worth many more times than its market value now. Think of it — The Ritz Carlton Diani!"

"You're very fortunate," Harry observed, then added, "or at least your heirs will be."

It was an obvious question why someone so old and in such poor health should be so far-sighted. More than how much they expected him to kick in, this aspect of the pitch had Harry puzzled.

"However, I must be honest," Victor said with an almost apologetic smile. "I can't afford the taxes now, let alone down the road. They're closing in on me like a cackle of hyenas, and there isn't much time. Bloody politicians want to grab what's mine! But I've devised a scheme, not just to hold onto the land, but to profit enormously while we wait for the new South Coast tourist economy to emerge."

Harry shot Aldo a confused look and said, "I may not be your man, but this is all sounding like an honest business deal."

Victor chuckled, wiped his lips with the back of his hand, and said, "Oh, mate, is it ever not!"

The excitement brought on another coughing fit, and Victor seemed overcome by a bout of weakness. He was holding the inhaler in his hand but couldn't move it up to his face. Richard was at his side in an instant, grabbed the inhaler, and administered a dose.

The houseman looked up and told them, "Mr. Victor appreciates your visit, and he invites you to come again. In the meanwhile, I believe Mr. Odiengo will be in touch, should you care to know more."

They were about to climb back into the car with Joseph when Richard emerged from the main house and offered to give them a tour of the grounds. As Victor had described, there were four other houses on the property, all of colonial design, each of them with three or more bedrooms. Richard said most of them were furnished, but he didn't offer to take the visitors inside. Beneath the shady canopy of trees, the gardens were copiously planted and well maintained. Each of the houses was situated on its own plot of an acre or more.

But there were no vehicles parked on the driveways and no one visible in or around the buildings.

CHAPTER 12

*H*arry had worked himself into a fury. He hadn't been this angry in a long time. It was the afternoon of their visit to Skebelsky's, and they were back in his bungalow at Kusi Lodge. Harry had sent Esther home, wherever that was (he resolved to find out), telling her he and Aldo needed to have a serious talk.

Harry couldn't help yelling, "So, you brought me all the way to Africa to involve me in some investment scheme?"

Aldo was comfortably seated on their patio as he sipped a glass of wine. Harry was pacing in front of him, too nervous to sit or to drink.

The Italian replied calmly, "Not at all, Harry. Perhaps you notice, no one has asked you for money."

"Esther managed to dispose of a chunk of cash yesterday. It was all I could get out of the ATM at one go. Four hundred dollars!"

Aldo held up a hand in mock defense as if to fend off a blow. "Hold on! What transpires between you and the ladies is your affair, or whatever you wish to call your friendship with her. If Esther is working for anyone, it's for *you.*" Then he asked in that conspiratorial tone of his, "Tell me, Harry. Are you falling in love with her?"

"You know that wasn't my plan," Harry said cautiously. "And I'm not sure that's what I'm feeling. Years ago, Lucille and I went crazy.

But toward the end, it was two old people smiling at each other across the room. Grand passion is fleeting, also blinding. But I do see something in her eyes. Reminds me of my grandmother who, I have to say, was the first great love of my life." Then he asked, "What about her? What do you think Esther wants?"

Aldo sighed, "She's an accountant. So she's more like you than me. I can tell you she's honest. And she will never try to hurt you. But is that love?" And he chuckled, "Not in Rome!"

Harry had to admit, his feelings toward Esther were confused. He was stunned she'd spent his money on getting all dolled up, but the way she looked in that dress took his breath away. Would she have lovely ways of showing her gratitude? Harry didn't want to think of it as a transaction, but he wondered what if anything she planned to offer him. He protested, "You said she isn't a working girl."

Aldo gulped the wine. "She's not. At least, not as far as I know. From what I can see, you got lucky with a local widow of a certain age who is in serious need of a man friend. You might think I set you up because she is not a stranger to me, but this is not the case."

"So she *is* a widow?"

"I've never seen her with a guy, tourist or local. And she hasn't said. I suggest you come right out and ask her."

"Whose idea was it to introduce me to Skebelsky?"

Aldo seemed proud of himself when he said, "I confess, it was mine."

Harry couldn't believe the two weren't somehow conspiring against him. "But *she* suggested it to me before you showed up at the Tiki!"

"Earlier in the day, I had asked her in confidence whether she thought you'd be open to considering something more ambitious. She wouldn't mind it if you stuck around, that much is obvious. I did this both because I knew she is also acquainted with Victor — everyone in this town knows him by name and reputation — and because I believe, in a short time, she has gained your confidence."

"She said he's the meanest man in town."

Aldo winced. "An exaggeration, of course. Now, if you mean *mean* as in being tight with a shilling, I'm sure she is correct." Then he muttered, "And he doesn't have the sweetest disposition, true enough."

"And where were *you* yesterday?"

Aldo did not seem the least bit guilty. "I was meeting with Odiengo, Victor's lawyer. He has an office in Mombasa."

"You were talking with Victor's lawyer — *behind my back?* Before you'd proposed anything to *me?*"

"Slow down, Harambee. I have business with Skebelsky and Odiengo whether or not you are involved. It's a recent idea to include you, now that it seems you might be interested. You're more than capable, I was the first to notice. But it was not my first thought when I offered you the tour package. You know I had booked us on safari, and we were supposed to meet up with other guests. I make a profit. It's a living." Then, he muttered, "Although not so profitable now, it appears. The others were a group of podiatrists from Marseilles. I had intended to inform you — they got *cold feet* — *get it?* They will forfeit their deposit, but that doesn't help our plans. We will decide, you and I, safari or no safari. Meanwhile, it seemed to me that you like it here more than a little. We've been here at the beach just a week, and you couldn't be more settled in if it had been a month!"

"It's not like there's a lot to do around here." It amazed Harry that this wasn't a complaint.

Aldo laughed. "Besides get drunk, eat good food, and make love? I see how you are with Esther. The bar girls do not amuse you. Are you telling me you want to go snorkeling all of a sudden? Windsurfing? How about a thrilling crab hunt? You are a serious man, Harry, and I respect that about you. When your friends back home tell you they worry you won't come back, they have sensed something. I know this also. I don't think you will want to go back."

"Aren't we getting ahead of ourselves?"

"Ahead, behind, at our age we are wherever we find ourselves. What I'm saying is, I see cleverness in Skebelsky's plan. And I believe I want a part in it myself, whether you're in or out."

"But what's the plan? Other than to hit me and possibly others up for the money to pay his taxes. I assume he wants me to buy one of his houses."

"It's much more sophisticated than that, I assure you. And it might not end up costing you *anything*, nor me. That's the beauty of it."

"Excuse me, this is sounding like a con job. How can I profit from this scheme of Skebelsky's if it costs me nothing?"

"Hear me out. I don't know the finer points. That's for Odiengo to explain. And I must warn you, that fellow is not yet on your side. I believe Victor would have laid it all out if our meeting hadn't been cut short." He'd drunk most of the bottle himself, but he poured Harry what was left into another glass and gestured for him to sit. "Come, help me finish this. It's an excellent Sangiovese! Those Italians in Malindi, the supermarket shelves are stocked with the good stuff because of them! And it's cheaper than Chianti because the other mzungus don't know what it is! I mean to look for the Montepulciano next time."

Harry sat and drank. "Come on, Aldo. It's time you were straight with me."

Aldo held up a hand of caution. The gesture was getting to be a habit with him. "I insist you get the details straight from Odiengo. I think I understand, but I don't want to get it wrong. It's a legal matter." He drained what was left in his glass and then said, "But the essence of it is, Victor wants to start a charity. There are already enough schools and hospitals, he says. This will be a rehabilitation clinic, and the houses on his property will be the facilities — meeting and classrooms, dormitories, and recreational areas."

"Okay, he's going to need money. A lot of it, I'd guess."

Aldo smiled. "But not from you! Or from me! He told us, and this was the reason for the history lesson — besides tourism, the biggest business in Diani is philanthropy."

"So where do I come in?"

"Do you know how to write a business plan?"

Harry was afraid to say yes. "I've done it once or twice. Not the most fun I've ever had."

"I figured as much. What we need are what Odiengo calls *pro forma* statements. Mostly for government filings. Donors don't need the details, but if I ever line up anyone you'd call a *sponsor*, they look it over just like it's an investment. The return isn't profits but results." Aldo spread his hands wide, all generosity. "And, most important, you're a responsible businessman who has never done any business with Victor. So you, Harambee, will sign all the paperwork. You will be the director of this fine new facility!"

"And why would I do this? What would I get?"

"Besides the satisfaction of shaping the future of this great country? Besides helping underserved human beings? You will have a salary and use of one of the houses. I think you might even have your choice!" As Aldo groped beneath the table for another bottle to open, he chortled, "Or, perhaps it will be Esther who will be picking the house?"

Harry thought a moment. "And why doesn't Victor want to head up the project himself?"

"For one thing, he's not well-liked in the town. For another, people think of him as an old-school, colonial Brit, even though his heritage is Eastern European. The fact that he speaks with a South African accent doesn't help. Kenyans resent those whites even more. On the other hand, as for Americans, they liked Clinton, and they love Obama. They'd like to see some of the old foreign aid come back. And you — you have a college degree, you have business experience, and you run a publishing house. You're obviously an educated, credible fellow."

"I'm still not sure this passes the smell test," Harry said. "Skebelsky looks to be in his eighties, and he's in terrible health. I'm no doctor, but I'd guess COPD, late stage. He was telling us how there's going to be a real-estate boom here on the coast with the new airport — but that's years away. It's likely he won't live that long. Why go to all this bother when he could sell out and check himself into some comfortable rest home?"

Aldo smiled. "Is that what you'd do in his situation?"

"No. No, I wouldn't." Harry thought a moment, then answered, "I'd find something to keep my mind occupied. That is, as long as I have a mind." And he drank.

Aldo offered, "Perhaps the old fellow doesn't think he'll live forever, but he probably hopes he'll make it a lot longer than he will."

"Or maybe he's thinking long-term after all," Harry insisted. "Okay, he says he's not married, but maybe he's got women or offspring he needs to take care of. Do you know who they might be? This is an awfully ambitious project to take on just to dodge taxes for a few years. I'm guessing, but you'd think he could borrow against some business asset for the tax money, then at worst it would be a debt for his investors or his estate to settle. None of that new resort development is going to happen overnight. And the longer he sits on that land, the more it will be worth."

"He's a crafty fellow," Aldo said. "But so, I'm pleased to note, are you, my friend."

"What about Esther? How much of this does she know? You said it was your idea to involve me, but it seems like she was awfully quick to agree."

Aldo looked wistful. "I think perhaps you would do best to find out how well she knows Skebelsky."

CHAPTER 13

avid Odiengo was a portly, fastidious man with a congenial, round face, thick-frame glasses, and a careworn expression. His gray suit didn't fit him all that well. It was probably off-the-rack from Carrefour in the nearest available extra-large size. His white shirt was starched and clean, with bold stripes, and there were no spots on his rep tie. His leather briefcase was severely battered and might have been a holdover from his college days. That is, he was dressed suitably for the role of working-class barrister who is engaged primarily in matters of filings for governmental compliance, one whose fees were modest and who, as a consequence, worked much too hard.

He sat with Harry and Aldo in Kokko's café, at the long table by a window usually reserved for club and team meetings. They were thus out of earshot of the breakfasters on the patio and the few solo regulars seated at the bar. Behind them on the wall was plastered a giant Mercator map of the world. Harry wondered how many world-saving plans of missionaries and the perennial, do-gooder voluntourists had been discussed at this auspicious table.

Aldo was dressed in one of his fine suits, Harry in beachwear. He wasn't intending to insult this lawyer, but Harry hoped his casual appearance would help him feign disinterest, signaling a lack of commitment that would encourage compelling argument. Thus, their outward appearance might give the impression that Aldo was inclined to join the club and Harry was still deciding.

In a low voice, Odiengo explained, "What Mr. Skebelsky proposes is not the typical NGO — nongovernmental organization. This is the way charities sponsored by foreign entities are typically set up. No, what we're considering is called a *CBO* — a community-based organization. Such an entity may be privately held, but it is licensed and partly subsidized by the Kenyan government. As a result, to achieve this support, the entity must be broadly focused on its public mission and nonsectarian policies and practices. You can appreciate, such an organization might be seen to have more legitimacy — more *credibility* — than charities imported here by foreigners."

Harry asked, "This subsidy, might it be in the form of reduced property taxes?" He suspected getting out from under those taxes was Skebelsky's primary motivation.

Odiengo smiled, "Quite right. Possibly no property taxes whatever at the outset, plus a modest annual allowance for staff salaries and essentials like food and medicine for the client residents."

"That doesn't sound like enough to keep the doors open," Harry observed.

"Your assumption is correct," Odiengo said. "Victor will lease the land and buildings to the CBO for a nominal rent. He may decide to stay on in the main house. A considerable portion of the clinic's budget must be defrayed by philanthropy. It will be necessary to set up a new foundation or seek partnerships with existing charities and donor networks. In recent years, the European Union has been particularly helpful to these types of initiatives."

"And Aldo is telling me you guys want me to serve as director?"

"Quite right, again," the lawyer smiled. "The CBO must be incorporated with a board of directors. We propose you, Mr. Gardner, as chairman and managing director. Victor prefers to remain an anonymous benefactor. I will have a seat on the board, and as a Kenyan national, this will very probably facilitate the approval of our endeavor." Then the lawyer added meaningfully, "Victor must be seen to be unconcerned with operational decisions and responsibilities. You and I will have joint signature authority on the bank accounts."

This was a surprise and sounded ominous. Harry looked over at Aldo, who was being uncharacteristically quiet. "And, as for Aldo, what plans do you have for him?"

"In his profession as an international tour operator, Mr. Barbieri has influential friends in many parts of the world. In the language of philanthropy, these persons might be categorized as 'high-net-worth donors.' Mr. Barbieri may also sit on the board, and his primary responsibility will be fundraising." Harry remembered Aldo's use of the phrase. The salesman must always think the money in his prospect's pocket is already his.

Aldo was quick to add, "My compensation is to be a straight percentage of the funds I bring in."

"Yes," Odiengo said, "that is the customary arrangement."

"And who are these patients? Or should I say, clients?" Harry asked.

Odiengo sighed and explained, "Private service organizations in Kenya often have a two-tiered system, although ideally to the community the distinctions should not be apparent. But some clients pay, some don't. And those tiers apply to all aspects of the program. Some pay not only for their treatment but also for their lodging, prepared hot meals in the cafeteria, visits to the infirmary, perhaps even clothing. Then, some attend on a full stipend, either from our organization or from the government. But these days, as you can imagine, public funds are extremely tight, if nonexistent. So, particularly in the beginning as we strive to demonstrate our value to the authorities, it will be up to us to support the needy of the local community."

Aldo added, "Let's be honest. The ones who pay will be mostly white."

Odiengo smiled again and corrected, "Properly speaking, they are middle-class. The town has prosperous Kikuyu, Indian, and Arabic families, as well. These tend to be government officials or business owners. The point is, if it is a quality facility of sufficient standard, we will get referrals from the private caregivers as well as from the public agencies. For the most part, the alternatives are either underfunded government centers or church-affiliated programs, which require religious instruction that to some families may be objectionable."

"What happens next?" Harry asked.

"We draw up a formal plan and submit it with the necessary paperwork to Kwale County. While I'm steering it through the process, we're drawing up plans for converting the property to a campus. There will be a fair amount of renovation and construction work, including upgrades of electricity and plumbing, followed by acquisition of furniture and equipment. Beds for the dormitories and furniture for the treatment and meeting rooms, for example. For all of that, we'll need budgets and then bids from contractors. And then management of the implementation."

Harry asked, "And how long do you expect all this to take?"

Odiengo replied, "With luck, about a year."

Aldo asked, "I don't imagine you need me in-country the whole time. How about Harry? Do you need him to be here?"

Odiengo answered directly to Harry, "Mr. Gardner, you would need to be present for court filings as we get started. Aldo tells me you can work with me on the business plan. Mission statement, objectives, staffing plan, notional cash flow, balance sheet, use of funds — straightforward, all preliminary. Much of this is best done in Nairobi. You'll also have to apply for your work permit and residency status, and I can of course support you in those efforts. There are some fees, but those are minor. I can interview and qualify bidders if you aren't available. Then I'd say you needn't be on the ground until we begin the contracting work."

"So, what at this point do you need from me?" Harry asked. "So far, this all seems so informal."

Odiengo took a half-inch-thick sheaf of papers from his briefcase and laid it on the table in front of Harry. The cover page bore the title *HARAMBEE REHABILITATION AND RECOVERY CENTER CORPORATE CHARTER AND PRELIMINARY PLAN OF WORK.* The lawyer tapped the cover page with a fat finger and pronounced, "I assure you this document is not informal at all. But the business plan at this point is only a stack of empty templates. Consider it carefully, sir, but you will find a place for your most worthy and elegant signature on the last page. But even once the plan is done, I should caution you to refrain from signing. Technically, I'm an interested party. From this point onward, I shouldn't be advising you. If you decide to proceed, I will arrange a meeting for you in Nairobi with Mr. Skebelsky's corporate attorneys. They will be handling the formalities of extending offers to you, Mr. Barbieri, and Mrs. Mwemba."

CHAPTER 14

*W*hen they were done with Odiengo, Aldo excused himself to browse for booze at Chandarana again, and Harry phoned Esther. He said he wanted to see where she lived. She didn't seem concerned or surprised.

Skebelsky's proposal and Aldo's apparent role in the fellow's scheme had caused Harry to shift his attitude from layback tourist to wary expat. He had too many questions, and just how Esther figured into all of it was still a big one. All this mystery was getting annoying. Perhaps she wasn't holding anything back. Perhaps she knew as little about plans for the project as he did. Or perhaps she and Aldo had been plotting with Skebelsky for a while now, even before Aldo had proposed this trip, lying in wait like ticks on a tree to drop down on a passing traveler and suck his blood.

"Give me two hours to prepare, and I'll give you tea," she said. "I have chores and I must tidy up." She gave him the name of a house in the Ukunda village, which is where most of the working folk of Diani lived.

Harry lingered in the café, ordered a Tusker, and set to the task of reading the Harambee project charter. There was a lot of pro forma and legalese, but from what he could tell, the document set out in formal terms just what Odiengo had described to them. As the lawyer had told him, the business plan, including the financial statements, was still mostly blank. There were also blank pages where the CVs of Harry and Aldo were to be inserted. Odiengo's background had been included, and it showed him to be a graduate of a Catholic boarding school in Nairobi. He'd earned a BA from Strathmore University and his JD from the School of Law of Jomo Kenyatta University of Agriculture and Technology. He'd been in private practice in Mombasa for fifteen years. On paper, anyway, the fellow looked legit — and hardly wealthy.

Although Skebelsky's involvement was to be invisible to the public, it had to be stated for purposes of the project plan. The background provided for him was sketchy, perhaps deliberately so. It gave vital statistics, places of residence (including, as he had stated, Warsaw, London, and Johannesburg), and UK citizenship. He was designated as a local property owner and community benefactor, intending to lease his compound south of Diani to the CBO for the nominal sum of Ksh2,000 per year (twenty bucks), renewable. His commitment to the town was evidenced by his longstanding memberships in the Rotary Club and the South Coast Residents' Association. According to the writeup, his fondest wish was to give back to the community that had welcomed and nurtured his family for four decades.

The clinic's mission was stated as follows:

The Harambee Rehabilitation and Recovery Center aims to support and sustain the recuperative needs of community members, young and old, who must cope with noncriminal behavioral challenges as we focus on developing the individual's integrity, responsibility, sustainability, and a sense of purpose for the greater good.

Bound into the packet was Harry's application for a one-year work permit. Besides the information that would also appear on his CV in the project charter, there were a lot of blank spaces and checkboxes. He could see that completing all the forms would require much more effort than simply signing his name.

Oddly, it seemed to him, one requirement for the work permit was for him to specify the names of five Kenyans he would be training during the permit year to replace him. If the government were serious about enforcing that provision, perhaps this wasn't such a permanent position after all.

～

THE TUK-TUK DRIVER knew the street and the house. Harry didn't feel safe on a boda boda, and taking a taxi for a distance of a couple of miles seemed extravagant. Joseph was off with Aldo somewhere and unavailable. It wasn't that Harry couldn't afford the fare. He just didn't want to be seen arriving at her house like some aristo colonialist riding in the back seat of a chauffeured sedan.

All the roads off the highway were dirt but far more passable than the track leading up to Skebelsky's. Matatus and service vehicles needed to use these roads routinely, and obstacles would serve no purpose. There was a wall, but its stone was ancient, there was no razor wire, and the masonry enclosed the entire neighborhood rather than a single grand residence.

The house was built of mortared, rough-hewn sandstone blocks with a corrugated tin roof. There was a small car park of loose dirt, overrun with squawking chickens, squealing preschool children, and a mangy dog who barked excitedly at everything that moved. There were no vehicles.

Summoned by the sound of the retreating tuk-tuk, Esther stepped out into the shade under the awning of the small porch. She had on a simple, blue-cotton shift with a food-stained apron fastened around her waist. Her dark hair was done up in a kerchief. Her face looked clean and fresh-scrubbed, without a trace of makeup.

To Harry, she seemed remarkably pretty in her plainness, a different person, a softer soul. She smiled broadly and thrust out her arms to draw him to her.

"So now you get to see where the help live, my dear." She hugged him lightly and kissed him on the cheek.

He said softly into her ear, "Thank you for inviting me. I had to see."

She pulled away in mock scorn. "Had to see what, exactly?"

He said simply, "What your life is like when you're not dressed for dinner in town."

Hinting at her purchasing that dress was a bit of a dig, but she ignored it. She took him by the hand, saying, "Come on in. I hope you're hungry. It's a modest meal, but as hearty as you want it to be."

The inside of the house reminded Harry of his great-grandmother's farmhouse in South Dakota. It had the basics and little else: A wooden table with oilcloth cover and four folding chairs, none of them matching. On a wall shelf, a small flat-screen TV and a clock radio. A propane cooktop with two burners. A vintage-model fridge that emitted a constant chugging noise. Pots and pans strewn around a dripping sink and the damp warmth of cooking smells.

Standing over the cooktop was another woman about Esther's age, who looked briefly back over her shoulder to smile at him.

A couch with sagging cushions was covered with two floral-patterned bedsheets. And, on it, a young woman who was nursing an infant sat next to a white-haired woman who might have been about Harry's age.

Esther gestured toward the women, who nodded silently in turn. "My mother Naomi and my cousin Vera and her son Kendrick." Indicating the cook, she added, "And my sister Alice." And to them, "This is my new friend Harry I told you about. He's visiting from Los Angeles."

Harry muttered, "Ladies. Thank you for inviting me into your home." Naomi shoved closer to Vera on the couch, making room for him to sit, and she patted the cushion next to her. Harry smiled and sat. He'd have preferred a place at the table, but he imagined not accepting the woman's invitation to sit might seem rude.

From their attentiveness watching Alice load up their plates, Harry guessed they were all eager for lunch. Esther served them in turn, beginning with Harry, then her mother. They ate with the plates balanced on their laps, with cups of drinking water set at their feet on the wood floor. Harry had heard that Ethiopians ate with their fingers, but he'd never had a meal with Kenyans other than in the tourist restaurants. So he was relieved they'd all been given forks, not just him.

The fare was beans, rice, and cooked greens, accompanied by a small stack of hot chapati bread, which was freshly made. The beans were spicy, the rice peppered, and the greens had been sauteed in oil with diced onion and tomato.

Esther sat facing them at the table and picked at her food. Alice never sat but ate from a plate perched on the kitchen counter as she did the washing up.

Harry had worried about making conversation, but everyone seemed shy and so busy eating that no one spoke. Between mouthfuls they'd look up at him and smile pleasantly. It occurred to him they might speak mostly if not entirely Kiswahili or their tribal language at home.

After they'd cleaned their plates and Alice collected them, she returned with a teapot and a tray of mugs, setting them in front of Esther on the table. Esther beckoned Harry to sit with her there. Naomi and Vera rose silently from the couch, Vera lifted the baby and straightened her dress, and the mother gave Harry a demure smile and said softly, *"Karibu sana."* They retreated into a back room, which he guessed was the only bedroom.

Esther poured tea for him, which had been steeped in the local fashion with hot milk, while Alice continued her chores at the sink.

Esther finally spoke, her voice scarcely above a whisper, "I expect you know, the nasty girls have much finer houses." And she giggled.

Chastised, Harry sipped meekly and replied, "And cars and fine wardrobes, not just a nice dress or two. Or so I'm told."

"Don't forget the designer sunglasses. I don't have those, either. I do own some pretty beads, but no jewels."

He said, "I'm sorry if I gave you the impression I'm the suspicious sort, worried about being ripped off, whatever. Taken advantage of." He realized she might think he was talking about the dress, but he was much more concerned about this murky proposal for the clinic. He continued, "This scheme of Skebelsky's was a total surprise, and now I find out Aldo has been planning it with Odiengo for some time. He's even admitting it's the real reason he brought me to Kenya. Sure, he admits he knew about it long before this trip. And he's insisting I'm not some kind of target. He suspects I'll want to set up residence here — I never told him that, mind you. But I suppose when expats see the quality of life, the relaxed way of doing things, and then they do the math on the living expenses — they realize there are few places on Earth where they could do better."

"Is that how you feel now?" She looked amused as she sipped her tea demurely. She knew she was charming him, had known she had that ability all along.

"I suppose I seem like the ideal candidate. Widowed, retired, no strong ties at home. Oh, yes, I told you I have a grown daughter. But she doesn't seem to crave my company these days, so going back to visit her a couple of times a year might be all of me she can stand." Then he added, "Aldo knows I have money, but not how much. He also knows I ran a publishing company, which I suppose in some way could make me seem like an educator, but what we're planning is more like a clinic than a school. What do I know about these people we want to serve or what they might need?"

Esther asked, almost as a tease, "You have no strong ties? Not one woman who eagerly awaits your return?"

This woman was too canny. Harry had to smile. He said, "There is one neighbor lady. She expects to share a glass of wine with me and hear safari stories. I know her name, but that's about all. Oh, and she's watching my house while I'm gone."

"Is she pretty?"

Harry smirked and replied, "Oh, yes." Then he was quick to add, "Not nearly as pretty as you, and I mean that in all sincerity."

She sighed, "You don't know much more about me, and I can see it's making you nervous. I don't go around telling everyone the story of my life."

"We've only known each other a short time."

She smiled and sipped her tea. "And did you expect it would only be for a short time? That's how it usually goes around here. Not with me, mind you, but the way people behave with the mzungus who come and go. The way most of them act, getting serious is a risk. Something you might catch despite your precautions. Like a disease."

"Frankly, based on how Aldo described it, I expected to have brief, passionate encounters with willing young adult women who would do almost anything I asked for money or a hot meal and then disappear."

"And?"

"And it only took one session on a massage table in a barbershop to convince me that's not how I want to live, even for a short time."

"They say all those girls in the hair salons are nasty, but I wouldn't know. People have to make a living. Also the girls in the bars, and especially the discos."

"But you and I have been seen together in the bar of the Kusi Lodge. Also at the Tiki."

"At the hotel, I sometimes have a much-needed drink after work. And I don't waste money having more than one. I do the accounts in the back office there. My boss is not an easy man to please." She added, "Although I will admit that encountering a mzungu guest who might be willing to pay for dinner would not be the farthest thought from my mind."

Then he finally asked, "So, how do you know Aldo?"

"It's part of my job to do the quotations for the tour operators. He always books with us when he's in town, and I give him the most favorable discount." She smiled, "And then he gives me a bit extra, I can admit to you. We've been doing business for some time. He's here several times a year, usually on the way to or from a safari lodge upcountry." She thought for a moment, then said, "He has bought me dinner on occasion. He hit on me the first time, I discouraged him, and he never tried again. And he's never tried to set me up with one of his clients. Some of the Europeans he travels with can be rather crude." She took a breath, shot him a sincere look, and added, "I assure you our meeting was not his doing."

"So, are you going to tell me more about you? You must be good at doing the math, that's one new piece of information." He teased, "You're the calculating type!"

"I can do my sums and a bit more," she said. "I can tell when things don't add up. If they're trying to hide something, I'll see it. The owners of the Kusi are a second-generation family from India. The grandfather lives in London now, and his eldest son is my boss. He's manager of the hotel." She set her cup down and asked him, "More tea?"

"I don't know. How long is your story?"

She smiled again, "Short. Short and sad. Nothing they'd make a movie about, that's sure."

"I do want to hear. As much as you're willing to share." He nodded in the direction of the bedroom. "Are there any men in the household?"

"No," she said flatly. "We are a family, and you could also say a little commune of independent women. My parents were divorced when Vera and I were in our teens, and my mother did not remarry. They no longer communicate. He sends small gifts of money to the children on their birthdays and at Christmas. He has taken another wife, and they live in Nairobi. That's where we grew up and I earned my accounting certificate before my father cut us off. As you heard me tell Victor, my father is being treated for stomach cancer. My husband was a policeman, and his first posting brought us here to the coast. He died four years ago." She nodded toward her sister, who was still busy in the kitchen. "Alice has a new boyfriend, but she won't tell us anything. I think he's this punk who rides a motorcycle, takes on passengers, and makes his booze money snatching shopping bags from tourists as he whizzes by. He's also very good-looking."

Alice finally turned to them briefly to tell Harry, "She knows *nothing*. For all she knows, I could have a rich mzungu in Mombasa!"

Esther teased back with, "Then why do you never have a shilling, my girl?"

Alice laughed and resumed her scrubbing, "I'm saving up for my wedding dress! I'll captivate a rich Indian, and we'll be married on the beach in a grand ceremony attended by a thousand of our closest friends."

Esther warned, "If he's Indian, you'll be Muslim or Hindu one day, and either way you'll never please his mother — if she even allows it to happen!"

"You're just jealous," Alice huffed. "I'm sure this gentleman is very honorable. But does he know there are almost no Americans in Diani? He won't want to stay. The Germans will snub him, and so will the British."

Esther ignored her sister and told Harry, "Vera's husband is a ranger with the wildlife service, and he's posted to a camp in Tsavo

East. He gets a month leave, usually during rainy season, and he sends money home. But hardly enough. She worries he has other responsibilities."

Harry wouldn't mind cornering Alice and posing her a few questions. But he was more concerned about getting to know Esther. He asked her, "Your husband, was he killed in the line of duty?"

She smirked. "We never got a full explanation. Like all government employees, police must go where they are assigned. Often, it's far from their home village, perhaps hundreds of miles away. My Malcolm was posted near the Kwale County courthouses and prison in Kilifi, which is up the coast, not terribly far. But he did not usually stay with us here. He'd be gone weeks at a time, sometimes months. Then, that last time, he went missing. He was on assignment and he didn't come back. He wasn't the best at letting me know what he was doing or even whether he was safe, but he'd check in every week, send me a text on a Friday night, that kind of thing. He always wanted to know the kids' grades, for example. He'd send money home, and he was pretty good about that. They get paid just once a month, so at times things were thin. If the children needed medicine or a visit to the clinic, for example, I'd text him and he'd borrow from one of his colleagues. Fortunately, when the children were older and placed in boarding school, I got this good-paying job. We now get his small pension, as well."

"Surely the department gave you some details about what happened to him."

"They sent me a letter by regular post. With the Posta the way it is, that could take a week or more — or a piece of mail might not ever show up. That's how concerned they were. They called it an *incident* and the cause was a gunshot wound. Understand, in this country there are not many firearms. Even the traffic officer who stops you on the road may not have one. Wildlife rangers carry rifles, and the policemen who apprehend criminals also have weapons. The army, of course, is well equipped, but you'll not see them much around here unless there's been some recent terrorist activity. But whether Malcolm was cleaning his gun or someone had it out for him, perhaps even some drunken colleague, I have no idea. They returned his body to the mortuary in Ukunda. I wanted to see it, see his wounds, which might have told me something, but they wouldn't let me. And they said the autopsy report was for the police only. They advised against my viewing the body because it had not been refrigerated in transit and it would be horrible to see. The casket was sealed, and when I insisted it was my right, they refused to show me."

"Might he have taken his own life? They'd have trouble admitting to that, I suppose. And that might be why they wouldn't let you see."

"Malcolm? He was an egoist. Also something of a gossip. Bribes are the order of the day. It's normal. It's routine. But perhaps he couldn't keep his mouth shut. Telling tales can be hazardous to your health."

"I'm sorry." Harry wasn't sure what more to say. "It must have been difficult — must *be* difficult."

She shrugged, "We get by. We're optimistic people of faith. My children are doing well in boarding school, and so far my salary at the hotel is enough. And Alice has a new job at a nail salon. She'll do pedicures."

Alice grumbled, "She won't let me do massage."

Esther shot back, "Ha! You know it's Kenyan men who don't want their women doing massage." And then, to Harry, "Again, the mystery boyfriend."

"You said you're people of faith? When I realized last night you were drinking water and not gin, I wondered if you might be Muslim."

She laughed. "Many if not most here are, but not my family. In a small town like this, the best way to get the gossip about your neighbors is to go to church. Our tribe is Kikuyu, and we attend the Pentecostal services. The working people don't have much time to hang out in bars. Our church teaches it's sinful to drink or smoke. Obviously, not everyone pays attention these days. You know I don't mind a drink. The nasty girls smoke, I suppose to show they can. Are you a Christian?"

Harry muttered, "Lapsed Catholic, I'm afraid. Bar attendance fairly faithful, though." Then he asked, "I was confused about the way Skebelsky's plan was presented to me —"

Esther put a finger to her lips and announced, "Alice, Harry and I are going to take our chairs out on the porch to catch a breeze. I'd say you've earned a nap on the couch if you'd like."

Alice wiped her hands, took off her apron, and pushed past them on her way out the front door, saying with a smirk, "I'm done anyway. I have a date with my thieving boyfriend." And she giggled as she hurried out the door and onto the road to hail a boda boda.

The others were still in the bedroom, but Harry realized why it would be best to take their conversation outside. The children who were playing in the yard had gone, along with the dog. They must not have been from this household. Without the kids to chase them, the chickens had calmed down, and many of them had gone to roost in a small henhouse back by the stone wall. A lone rooster strutted about as if keeping watch.

Seeing Harry study the chickens, Esther told him, "We gave you a modest but wholesome meal. For breakfast we have ugali, that's corn cake, and greens. On Friday evenings, we try to have chicken, when we can."

"What about beef?" Harry asked. "I see the young boys on the road herding cows and goats."

"A head of cattle will fetch about four hundred dollars at market. The meat goes to the hotels and the rich people in the cities. Maasai ranchers count their wealth in head of cattle and number of children. Most Kenyans would rather sell their animals than eat them."

"Do you kill your chickens or do you sell them?"

"For a dinner, I must kill one," she said. "Mother taught me to wring their scrawny little necks. You learn to do it quickly, but the chore is in the plucking."

Harry finally got to ask the main question that had brought him here: "You were the one who suggested I meet Victor, but later Aldo told me it was his idea he was trying out on you. We met with the lawyer Odiengo this morning, and I believe I understand the extent of Aldo's involvement so far. He's thinking he will get generous commissions on fundraising. I have no trouble believing that's his motivation. He knows people, and he's certainly a salesman. And it could be a lot of money. But I'm unclear how much you know of the plan. And, for that matter, how well you know Skebelsky."

Her brow furrowed as she took a deep breath. It was obvious she didn't like the man. And Harry guessed she'd be reluctant to speak too harshly of their new benefactor. "I know him by reputation, of course. It's a small town, and gossip often tells us what the newspapers won't or can't. He has investments locally. A hardware store and an auto repair shop, I believe. I know him mostly from the Rotary Club. I attend their monthly dinner meetings with Balvan Patel, my boss. Skebelsky has lots of opinions, voices them loudly, but rarely backs any of his suggestions with actions — or money. It's the usual issues of beach cleanup — plastic bottles and bags everywhere, despite the bans — electrical outages, streetlights that somehow don't work whenever there are thieves about, potholes on the beach road."

"And what does he know about you? Are you on speaking terms?"

"As you heard in our meeting, he knew my father, and they did business years ago. We were a prosperous family once, before Independence took Papa's privileges away and he deserted Mother. When I was growing up, Victor was a frequent and welcome guest at our dinner table. Now I greet him when I see him in town. That's the extent of our friendship these days."

"You called him a mean man."

"Yes, he's mean-spirited. More so when he's drinking. For you, he was acting tame, but you'd have to see him in a fit of anger, as I have at some of those meetings, to get past his politeness. There are good reasons he has no wife."

"I have to press you on this question: How, if at all, are you involved in his plans for the rehab center?"

"The first I knew of it was from Aldo yesterday, in the morning at the hotel, before he left for Mombasa. I had spent the night at home and returned ready for work in my business clothes. When I came to take my coffee, he invited me to join him at breakfast. I knew nothing of this until he asked me whether I thought you'd be willing to meet with Victor." She took a deep breath, smiled sweetly, and said, "Victor and all of them at the Rotary know of my position with the Patels. And Aldo sees how close you and I seem to have become in a short time. Aldo told me they want you to be the director, accountable to the board and their lawyer, and I will keep the books. Yours is a new face in town, and this way Victor and his reputation could hide in the background. No one likes him. For all anyone knows, the recovery program is your idea, something you brought to us. People will assume Victor is renting his place out to the clinic because he needs the money. Which is *almost* true. And they may naturally assume the source of these funds is you and your well-meaning American friends. As for me, I believe I have a reputation for competence, and I wouldn't mind at all giving my notice to Balvan."

"Does Balvan know you're getting too friendly with a guest? You're awfully secretive. I hadn't even noticed you work there."

She shrugged. "I'm careful how I come and go. They call it the back office, and it really is in back. When the guests settle their bills, they deal with the cashier. They rarely see me unless the barman is giving me a coffee, and Balvan keeps to himself in a private office. Some days he's not there at all. He'd rather hang out with his friends in Bamburi. He owns apartments there."

Harry hadn't been introduced to the hotel manager, wouldn't know him if he saw him. But he realized it might be a good idea to be discreet if he and Aldo were to stay there any length of time. Then he asked her, "Have you seen the project charter? Does it look legitimate to you? Is it just that you want to get away from the job at the hotel, or are you attracted to this idea?"

"Balvan trusts me, and he should. But about the charter, Victor's lawyer hasn't shown me the paperwork yet. I'm sure they want a commitment from you before they decide to go forward. Hiring me will not be complicated. But — legitimate? Do you mean in the British legal sense or the Kenyan street reality? Understand, in this country, indeed throughout Africa, charities are a business — suction pumps for foreign money. They render valuable services, no doubt — but the government and the citizens see them mainly as job creators. They employ people who are performing public services that the government would otherwise have to pay for. And to the people at large, there's no dishonor in running a charity, no matter what cause you are promoting. You can be an expat director or manager and sit at some bar all day downing Tuskers, but if you're employing Kenyans, they think you must be doing God's work."

"You say it's normal, but something in your tone tells me you have reservations."

"It's always wise to be cautious about entering any new venture. And especially when you don't know your partners all that well."

"How will we know?"

"If there are irregularities and they persist, you can bet some politically powerful people are getting their cut to look the other way."

"This possibility doesn't concern you?"

"If they try to hide something, I will find it. I can't help it. I was trained to follow the pennies. And I know all the ways to hide them. Perhaps they don't appreciate this. Perhaps to them I'm simply someone who knows how to use a spreadsheet. But, you ask, what would I be afraid of? I told you, my husband was a gossip. On Friday nights, when we were treating ourselves to chicken at the bar and grill, those glasses of water he was chugging down were straight gin. A few of those and he'd chatter on before he'd pass out. That's how I learned of whatever misbehavior he was involved in, most of it petty corruption. But, as I say, maybe he met his demise by shooting off his mouth to the wrong people. I don't worry that I will be caught up in some illegal schemes and not know. But I fear that, if I ever find something, I won't be able to keep myself from telling someone about it. I don't pretend to be a saint, but, as I say, there are some things I won't do."

Harry invited her to dinner in town, but she begged off, saying she had to put in a full day at the office tomorrow and needed some rest. He thanked her for the meal, stressed that he'd enjoyed every bite of it, and commented that he was impressed with how the women supported each other. She phoned a tuk-tuk driver she knew, negotiated the fare in advance, and had Harry picked at her gate.

Still alone on the porch, they exchanged a tender kiss goodbye, and she promised to phone him the next day when she got off work.

Harry now had many more questions for Aldo, which he hoped to pose over dinner that night.

He had a lot to think about.

∽

As HARRY STRODE through the lobby of the Kusi on the way to his bungalow, he found Aldo sitting alone, having a Sambuca Romano at the bar. The Italian had on the same distinguished tailored suit he'd worn to Victor's. He looked tired.

"More meetings with attorneys?" Harry asked him.

"Not all of my business concerns you. If you don't mind, I will have a sandwich here and turn in early." He knocked back the rest of the liquor. "And have you also enjoyed a productive day?"

Harry took a seat, signaled to the barman, and ordered his usual whiskey. "I'll skip the sandwich and try the Italian joint up the road. I'd go for the gnocchi, my favorite, but it's too heavy. Perhaps crabmeat ravioli and a salad. I paid a visit to Esther's house, met her family, and they stuffed me with beans at lunch."

"I have not had the pleasure," Aldo said. "Nice place?"

"A one-bedroom, working-class home in the village. Four adult women and a newborn under one roof. A yard full of chickens. So, you're right. If she were turning tricks, she'd be living a lot better."

"She is the accountant here at the hotel. Did she tell you?"

Harry nodded and took a long pull on his drink. "I pretty much got the short version of her life story. After lunch, she and I had a private conversation on her porch, and she told me what she knows of Victor and his plans for the clinic. She says she hasn't seen the charter, just knows you guys expect her to keep the books and report to me as director." He gave Aldo a sincere look and added, "I think she is okay, she is what she appears to be. Honest, hard-working woman. Smart. Head of household. Lived through some challenges. Loves her kids."

Aldo smiled and observed, "And maybe a bit lonely."

Harry tried to make it sound like teasing when he asked, "You sure you didn't set me up?"

"For romance or for a business deal?" Aldo seemed annoyed. "Neither one, I told you. I won't find you women."

"Right. I book a haircut. Or a pedicure. Or a massage."

"You see? No instructions from me and you know your way around already."

"Enough to know I'd just as soon avoid those young girls."

"Ah, not to your taste? You are a man of refinement. You see, I knew that about you. That's why I also knew that you are not a man to go crazy-stupid on vacation, recharge your batteries, and go back to some boring job. I knew you would want to stay! That's why I know you are the man for Skebelsky. You will be the face of his organization. He will be generous. You will make a nice life here."

"How do you know he's not crooked?"

"Crooked? What does that mean in this part of the world? Victor is a businessman. Smart. Years of experience. A white Kenyan from an old family of settlers, connected in Nairobi all the way to the top. A rich man who can make any kind of trouble go away. You can't do that everywhere. This is what *privilege* really means — in any country." Then he asked the two pressing questions, "So what about this deal? And what about Esther? I'm telling you, you can't take forever to decide."

"What's next if we follow Victor's plan?"

"You want to get serious? We go to Nairobi. File papers, set up accounts. No more vacation."

"And I hope we can find ways to enjoy ourselves."

"Sure, sure. Normally, it's a short flight. Businesspeople commute every day. But instead I will hire Joseph to drive us. It's a long day trip. But if we travel by car, we will pass through Tsavo National Park. We can stay a night, do that safari. Take two days if you like."

"Can we take Esther?"

Aldo shrugged. "Your money, Harry."

CHAPTER 15

*L*ater that evening in his bungalow, Harry showered and dressed for dinner. It wasn't that his clothes needed to be more formal. He just liked the idea of sitting down to a meal in a fresh shirt.

Even though he'd intended to dine alone as he'd told Aldo, he phoned Esther. After all, he had to tell her about the trip to Nairobi, and he needed her answer to the important question of whether she wanted to go.

When she came on the line, he heard loud noises in the background. She obviously wasn't at home. She must be in a bar or perhaps a busy store.

"What's all that noise? Where are you?" he wanted to know.

"Oh," she said. "I'm out with Alice. I must get to know this boyfriend of hers before it becomes serious. If he pays for dinner, it will be a good sign. But I'm not optimistic."

"I was hoping you'd reconsider having dinner with me. We need to talk."

She laughed. "Even more than we did today?"

"Aldo is telling me, if I want to follow through with Victor's plan, he and I must go to Nairobi to take care of business. I'm not at all decided on the plan for the project, but I agreed to go — you know, as a way of finding out — and we're leaving by car before dawn in the morning. We'll stop in a game park and go on that safari. I was hoping you'd want to come."

"Harry, I can't go," she said firmly. "And you shouldn't either."

"But I thought you were encouraging me."

"I haven't said the plan is a bad idea — for either of us. I don't know enough, and neither do you. But, as for me, I have a job, and I can't take leave. I'm perfectly willing to quit at the proper time, but things are far from set."

"I understand it's asking too much for you to take off, but why don't you want me to go?"

She took a breath. "If you go, you will be committing yourself. Oh, perhaps you're not signing anything, but you're signing on nonetheless. Whatever you find out will be decisive. If it is discouraging, I worry you will fly home and I will never see you again. But if you decide to continue, you may realize it's more comfortable in Nairobi. Or you may meet someone, realize we're just a fling and there are more qualified people for this work than me. You see, we haven't been together long enough. We have affection, but we don't yet have trust."

He sighed. He really wished she'd join him. For dinner, for the trip.

"I'm really glad you had me over today. It was a privilege to meet your family. And we needed that honest talk. I do feel I can trust you. I'm not saying I've made up my mind about the venture, but I won't really feel comfortable about it until Aldo and I dig into the details. That's why I agreed to go."

"You say you'll be leaving before sunrise, and that's before I get to the office. But I'll be up. Call me before you go."

She sounded convinced he'd be going, even though he guessed she was still hoping he and Aldo would decide to wait.

In the brief pause before she ended the call, he caught the sounds of laughter and the clinking of glasses and tableware.

～

HARRY WALKED BACK through hotel reception intending to get one of the porters to hail him a tuk-tuk. As he strode out of the lobby, he found Joseph leaning against his car at the curb.

"Where are you going, Papa? I give you a lift, no charge!"

Harry replied, "I'm just going up the road to that Italian place for dinner. Shouldn't you be home getting some sleep before the long drive tomorrow?"

"Sure, sure. I'm just going off my shift now. But I must stop at the car rental agency to pick the van for our excursion tomorrow. I want you fellows to be comfortable and have room for our refreshments and your cases."

After they were in the car, Joseph leaned back to say, "May I tell you something? I know a better place for your dinner."

Harry thought it best to trust Joseph, who knew even more about local haunts than Aldo did. "As long as it's not far," Harry agreed. "I'm growing tired already, and I haven't packed."

"Very close by," Joseph assured him as he pulled the car out of the drive and headed south along the beach road. "I'll be taking you to the famous Ali Barbour's Cave. It's a high-class place for tourists and grand celebrations. When you settle and find yourself a new wife, you will be taking her there for your wedding anniversaries!"

"Joseph, you are so far ahead of the game, I don't know what to say. Is that what you predict for me?"

He laughed. "I don't give advice on such matters, boss. What I am saying is that the mzungus who decide to stay, they marry. You take this fellow who built the restaurant, George Barbour. His family came from England when he was a boy, and they farmed in Kitale. He made his fortune, then he makes a new life here at the beach. Played rugby, coached teams, raced cars. He also founded Forty Thieves Beach Bar. Everybody knows that place. All-you-can-eat buffet on Sundays with a live band. You go there, you meet your neighbors whether you like them or not!"

"Maybe I'll see him in the restaurant tonight. I'll let him buy me a drink."

Joseph laughed again. "Oh, he may be there. His ghost! He's

passed on. When the sea breeze passes through, perhaps you hear him sing! I'm sure his heart is in that place."

They were hardly past Kokko's and Chandarana when Joseph signaled a left and turned onto a dirt track in the direction of the beach. It was a short ride over the rocks and ruts, and the car came to a stop in a large, unpaved car park. Off to the left was the marquee of Forty Thieves, where an askari wrapped in a traditional Maasai *shuka,* a red-plaid blanket, sat listlessly under the lit sign.

Joseph pointed instead to the right, where the cliffside entry to Ali Barbour's was marked. "The boss, he also likes this place very much. He brings his tourist clients on the last night of their stay in Diani, gives them a grand going away party before they fly home. Okay, it's *your* last night for a while, so he owes you a good drink, I think."

"No," Harry said as he got out. "Aldo told me he'd be staying in tonight."

Another laugh from Joseph. "Oh, but I've just come from dropping him here! Mr. Barbieri dressed for a party, but he has no guests! Maybe he meets his pals from the Rotary? You tell him Joseph says you're invited!"

Harry mumbled, "Or, could be he wants to drink alone. There are times when a man needs to do that."

"Sure, sure," Joseph said affably. "Just remember, if you boys get drunk, don't go walking, don't take any taxi. I told you, I go to pick the van now. You tell Aldo, call my colleague Mordy. He will pick you. I'm phoning him now, and if the boss fails to call, I tell Mordy to come anyway at midnight."

Joseph got out and led Harry across the car park to the top of the stone stairway that led down into the restaurant. The driver grinned broadly as he shook Harry's hand. "Tomorrow, we go! I bring coffee and some bitings for your breakfast, then you curl up in the van for a long nap, and before you know it, we are in Tsavo, and we get in a game drive before sundown!"

Harry nodded and smiled gratefully, bewildered that Joseph must have innocently assumed Aldo would welcome his joining whatever private party was underway.

The descent down the stone steps wasn't long, just twenty feet or so to the bare floor of the grotto. But the air down there was notice-ably cooler, with the faint musty odor of a cavern. The walls of the restaurant were the naked rock, lit every few feet with the golden glow of shaded incandescent fixtures. The low, luxurious lighting reminded Harry of the nightclub atmosphere of that bar in Istanbul. He could hear the low buzz of conversation, the clinking of silver on china, and the subtle melody of piped-in jazz. The atmosphere was seductive, and Harry could appreciate why Joseph had implied it was a meeting place for lovers. You wouldn't hold a kids' birthday party here. Perhaps a send-off on the occasion of your favorite boss's retirement.

Or, yes, that wedding anniversary. Harry wondered at the speci-ficity of Joseph's suggestion. If the fellow regularly served Aldo and his guests at the Kusi, perhaps he knew Esther well. They hadn't exchanged words when he'd taken them to visit Skebelsky. But it was a small town. Harry hadn't so far worried that people had seen him in Esther's company. But he did wonder whether anyone thought of him as some new benefactor, the fine fellow who would defy his midlife crisis, come to stay, and marry Esther, adopting first a new family and then perhaps the entire community.

The entry passageway was narrow, just a few feet across, then opening on a wider but still cozy space, with a long, profusely stocked wet bar on the right. There Harry was met by a pretty hostess, who confirmed that Mr. Barbieri *and his guest* had already been seated. Her expression betrayed a mildly perplexed look, which told Harry he wasn't expected. She led him inside, where, at the end of the bar and a few steps lower, the space opened up to a dining area.

The most striking feature of the place was its roof — or, rather, lack of one. The grotto was open to the sky and a canopy of stars. The effect was dazzling. The night was clear and calm, but Harry could imagine the effect of Joseph's prophecy about what eerie sounds even a slight wind might inspire here.

Nearly every table was occupied, and, as he scanned the faces of the diners, Harry realized why the hostess might be confused. Against the far wall in an intimate corner sat Aldo and Esther at a table for two. If he were to join them, they'd all have to move.

They hadn't seen him. Aldo was gesturing in his usual expressive way with his hands as she studied the earnest expression on his face.

He was painting a picture for her.

Harry halted and gestured to the hostess, "It's okay. My friends aren't expecting me. I'll just have a light meal at the bar."

She smiled submissively, apparently relieved she needn't disturb the other guests. Harry took a seat at the end of the bar farthest from the dining room. There, in the shadows, he could still see Aldo and Esther, but he told himself he was no shameless stalker. He could also turn away and engage in conversation with the barman, a frail young man who later gave his name as Collins and confided he was a medical student with romantic issues of his own.

Harry ordered a double bourbon. In the moment, he fully intended to get stinking drunk. Both of his friends had obviously lied to him. And finding out that they were meeting privately inspired in Harry all kinds of paranoia. Were they closer to each other than they'd let on? Were they plotting against him? Was the Skebelsky deal a trap they were conspiring to set for him?

He glanced over at them. There was a bottle of wine chilling in a bucket stand beside their table. They were taking their time, and they weren't expecting anyone else. Just then, Harry saw Aldo reach across the table to take Esther's hand. She pulled it away, but the impassive expression on her face showed neither shyness nor annoyance.

Harry decided he wouldn't confront them, and he didn't have the patience to wait them out.

He tossed back his drink, got up, thanked Collins, paid and tipped him generously, and made his way back up the stairs. Perhaps concerned his premature departure might mean he was somehow upset with the service, the hostess followed him up. He turned back and waved her off with a smile, then beckoned to the Maasai, who escorted him to a waiting tuk-tuk, which he directed to the restaurant where he'd intended to dine all along. Alone.

~

AFTER HARRY'S solitary dinner at Leonardo's, he returned to his bungalow with a tummy bulging even more than usual, stuffed full of pasta. He'd polished off most of a bottle of chianti by himself, and he'd made sure to follow Aldo's advice to tell the waiter, "Not too much sauce!" which was the Italian's main complaint about working-class restaurants in the States that smothered the plate with so much red gravy you couldn't even tell the shape of the pasta underneath. Considering his starchy lunch at Esther's, Harry had resolved to eat only salad for the next two days, but he knew in the morning he'd crave a generous stack of pancakes, slathered with butter, drenched in real maple syrup. If he could still summon some willpower, maybe he'd skip the bacon.

He hoped a preoccupation with his diet would force out thoughts of Esther. He had no reason to expect her loyalty. He scarcely knew her. And he'd known from the first day he met Aldo that the fellow was slick. Harry was realistic enough to expect that both of them were pursuing their self-interests. And he should think of his own. Now that he harbored these suspicions, he'd be even more skeptical of Skebelsky's scheme (if it wasn't really, in fact, Aldo's). But if he were going to protect his own self-interest, continuing with the plan to go to Nairobi should be the best way to get to the truth of the matter. Just because Aldo and Esther might be colluding didn't mean Harry should pass up the deal. It was just a reason to ask more questions and proceed with caution. He was enough of a fatalist to think that his life path had brought him here for a reason. He preferred to think he might finally find some purpose for this late phase of his otherwise unremarkable life.

After all, things were happening, and he was at the center of them. He wasn't the driver of events, not yet anyway. But he was the focus, and it was a new feeling, a new reason to get up in the morning. Whether he was a victim or the recipient of gifts, it was too early to tell.

He resolved to ask Aldo for his version of events first. They'd have plenty of time to talk on the trip. Then, depending on the credibility of that story, he might call Esther. Or, simply try to forget her.

As he thought about packing for tomorrow, his stomach was

uncomfortably full. He'd overeaten in an effort to suppress his anger. He'd noticed that young Kenyan men seemed universally slender, and some prosperous middle-aged men were what you'd call stout. None he'd seen were downright fat. But even early on in his adventure, he knew it would be all too easy to put on a few pounds chowing down all this rich restaurant food, especially the lavish buffets in the resorts. Ordinarily, he'd indulge himself on vacation and then be more careful once he'd returned home. But now he had to wonder whether Esther would appreciate a pudgier Harry. (And here he was, even now, measuring his behavior in relation to what she might think of him.) He wasn't expecting he'd be hooking up with her indefinitely, but if they did undertake this Harambee clinic thing, they'd be seeing a lot of each other. And it was obvious that both Victor and Aldo thought having her around would be an inducement for Harry's eager participation.

Was she the bait or the prize?

And, of course, they were right to assume he'd be attracted to her. She seemed sincere, and, until this evening, Harry thought he'd dispelled suspicions that she might be a fortune hunter. He felt he knew just enough about her now to get a sense of what she wanted from life, even if he was not entirely sure what she wanted from him. Or what *they* wanted from him.

Could there be an innocent reason for their meeting in the cave? And for keeping it a secret from him?

It was only nine o'clock, but Harry was already feeling drowsy. He wanted to turn in soon. Aldo had warned him to get a wake-up call because they'd be setting out with Joseph before dawn the next morning. His packing took less than a half-hour. He simply wadded his things into a two-suiter, the duffel, and his carryon. He vowed to stay up a little longer so he could place calls when it would be breakfast hour in Los Angeles. First he phoned Nicole on WhatsApp, but she didn't answer, so he texted her:

Change in plans. Please call when you get this.

Esther was not the only relationship he could anticipate. Next he tried Eleanor, and she answered right away. "Hello, Harry! Where are you?"

"I'm having a wonderful time in Diani Beach, but we're driving to Nairobi in the morning. I think we'll finally get a game drive tomorrow afternoon. We'll be stopping at a lodge in the national park."

"That would be you and your friend, the tour guide?"

"Yes," he replied. "His European group canceled, and it's just the two of us. So we're free to kind of make it all up as we go along. Aldo takes care of the bookings, and I'm enjoying not having to plan too far ahead."

"I was thinking it would be such a shame for you to spend the whole time at the beach. Unless, of course, you've made new friends." She didn't wait for him to take the hint, and then her voice took on a tone of concern, "I'm glad you called. There's been what you might call a development."

"How so?" He hadn't read anything about an earthquake. And if the water heater had ruptured, she'd have called him right away.

"The couple who rented your place are nice and all, but they had a change in plans. They're both private-duty nurses, here on assignment with UCLA, and their plans changed. Her training program got canceled, and he was transferred to San Diego. They know they will be forfeiting their deposit, but they were wondering if you'd prorate the rental fee. They've already moved out, you see. They paid the full three weeks in advance, and I told them it's customary to forfeit that, too, since they couldn't give notice. But it's not like these are vacationers who just decided to go somewhere else. I didn't say that you'd be flexible, but I did promise I would ask."

"You know it's not so much about the money. I just wanted to keep the place occupied. How difficult would it be to get someone else in there?"

She answered lightly, "I could post it on Airbnb. We might get lucky, find someone who wants a week."

"That's just it," Harry said. "We could do longer. Turns out I have some business to take care of here, and I won't be coming home when I'd planned. That's why we're headed to Nairobi. Oh, I don't mean I'm here to stay, but as of now, I've had to postpone my return flight indefinitely. In fact, I believe I could be quite flexible on the timing. So if you find someone who wants a month or two, give it to them. When we know their end date, I'll book my flight. And, even if they want longer, don't say no right away, and we can talk about it."

"Oh, my," she said. "We were joking about your liking it so much you'd stay. It sounds like whenever you do come back, you might be putting your house up."

"Eleanor, as of now, I'm at least fifty-fifty on that. When I find out more about this business opportunity here, maybe I'll be able to decide."

She hesitated, then said sweetly, "Be sure to think of me."

He told her to go ahead and refund some of the rental fee, which he left to her judgment to calculate. They exchanged pleasantries, she promised to follow up on rebooking the place, and they ended the call.

It wasn't until Harry was getting lost in the fog of sleep that he wondered what she'd meant by *think of her.* Was it only the real-estate listing she wanted?

CHAPTER 16

The van Joseph rented was a Toyota Nomad, which had ample room for passengers and cargo space. He explained that it wasn't a safari vehicle — which would have to be a true four-by-four — but he'd chosen comfort over ruggedness, and he explained that tourist cars weren't permitted to go off-track in the bush. The weather recently had been hot and dry, but extra caution would have been in order during rainy season when getting stuck in the mud far from base camp would be more than just a minor annoyance.

From the outset, it was clear that Joseph considered himself an authority on everything from tourist venues and accommodations to wildlife identification, habitats, and behavior. He was dutiful and quiet as they made their way out of Diani. Harry accepted a coffee from the thermos and kept deliberately to himself, not having to entirely feign grogginess. He'd decided he wasn't going to confront Aldo right away. When Aldo tried to make small talk, he asked whether his friend had enjoyed the crab ravioli last night, and Harry supplied the details of his experience at Leonardo's, failing to mention that he'd first had that drink in the grotto.

Even though Harry had promised to call Esther before they set out, he decided to wait. He wanted to confront Aldo first, but he'd pick his time to do it.

Harry got his cue when they were well underway and Joseph spoke up, "Harry! Could you find nothing to your liking at Ali Barbour's? I was sure you fellows would have a grand time!"

Off Aldo's puzzled look, Harry had to explain, "Joseph picked me from the hotel and assumed you'd want me to join your party in the cave. But I saw you were there with Esther and I left. I was going to ask you what it was all about. She'd told me a fib, said she was having dinner with her sister Alice. So I thought maybe you'd offer to tell me before I came right out and asked what you guys are really up to."

Aldo looked genuinely apologetic, but by now Harry knew that being genuine was not necessarily one of the fellow's strongest character traits. The Italian hesitated as if needing to word his response carefully, then said, "I told you I was retiring early, and that was my plan. But then she called me and wanted to meet. I offered to bring you, but she said no. She was firm about that. I suggested the place, which I do like very much, especially for going-away dinners. I'm sorry to disappoint. It was not my intention."

"What did she want to say that I couldn't hear?"

Aldo gave an embarrassed shrug. "She wanted to talk me out of taking you to Nairobi."

Harry mulled this, then said, "It didn't look like a business meeting. I thought I saw you try to take her hand. I couldn't hear anything you said. I was across the room at the bar. But I could tell you were getting emotional. And you looked very much like a couple."

"Harry! I'm Italian! Passionate! I express myself!"

"Passionate how? About what, exactly?"

"I told her how this plan of Victor's helps you! It helps her! You are happy when you're together. I see it. She *knows* it."

Harry admitted, "I phoned her before she met up with you last night. And she did warn me off our trip to Nairobi. I wasn't sure exactly why."

"Esther is a practical person. People who are good with numbers are this way. She might like the deal, but she doesn't trust Skebelsky."

"You told me the only way to get to the heart of this thing is to make this trip. That's why I agreed to go. Yes, I'd just as soon stay with her and kick back at the beach. But you're acting like there's some kind of urgency. I'm trusting you, which until last night seemed safe enough."

Aldo took a breath. "I must admit I had to persuade Victor you are the man for this. He doesn't know you. He is a careful businessman. But the other guys he has in mind, I tell you, they're creeps, local whites, Kenyan cowboys who haven't held a job in years. You are an honorable man. An educated man. I've said this more than once."

Harry wanted to believe Aldo. But if this new enterprise was not entirely legit, the value of Harry's honesty would be more to provide cover than virtue. He really wanted to know, "Were you and Esther ever a couple? Are you now?"

"I told you. And she told you, I believe. We are colleagues. Okay, maybe we played kissy-face sometime, a long time ago. But we have been doing business for years. And it's not the first time I've bought her a meal. And, as I do, she likes a glass of wine. There's no harm in enjoying a friend's company! I'm sure you agree." Aldo reached over and put a hand on Harry's shoulder. He flashed a smile and said, "She cares about you. Otherwise, she wouldn't have bothered." Then he added, "Harry, are we still friends? Are you going to trust me?"

Harry tried to keep it light when he put on a kind smile and said, "Like you say, we'll find out more in Nairobi."

HARRY GREW quiet and gulped more coffee as he surveyed the landscape. Perhaps hoping to relieve the tension he'd inadvertently created but also to regale his listeners, Joseph added his narration to the journey.

After they'd been northbound along the coast for about an hour, they entered the outskirts of Mombasa and wended their way through surface streets toward the embarkation point for the car ferry at Likoni. The city is both a natural deep-water port and an island. On the north side, modern bridges connect it to the upscale suburbs of Nyali and Bamburi on the mainland. But here on the south, the only way to cross without taking the long way around through backroads is to queue up for the ferry.

It was now just after daylight, and there were about twenty cars and trucks in front of them in twin lanes waiting to board. As they sat there, a huge container ship passed slowly through the channel. Two ferryboats were crossing at the same time, one headed away and one coming toward them, and Harry thought the tanker passed uncomfortably close to the approaching boat they were waiting to board.

"Whoa!" Harry exclaimed. "Wasn't that a close call?"

"These crews deal with it all the time," Joseph said. "The boats must share the waterway. Years back, the Japanese gave the Kenyan government grant money to build a bridge here. They didn't want their ships running into us! But, what happened? Our President diverted the money. No bridge, no explanation. When people ask him, he just say, 'It is our time to feed!'" Joseph sighed and added, "Ah, corruption is the mother of Kenya!"

It was not the first time Harry had heard it said. He knew that corrupt regime was history by now, but the powerful family still owned large tracts of land in the country, and rumors persisted that the politician's son would be next in line for executive office.

From the time they joined the queue, it took them an hour to get across a distance of less than half a mile.

HARRY CATALOGED the sights along the way, and he began to form conclusions he would appreciate more fully later in his experience of the country. His mood had turned from uneasy to blue because of his lingering suspicions about Aldo and Esther, along with a vague apprehension about the advisability of the Skebelsky venture and the reasons for this trip.

TO TAKE the road from Mombasa to Nairobi is to journey through time. The ancient seaport has been there for at least two millennia, but just a century ago, the capital city was little more than a wide place on the trek, a depot for British caravans bound for the mines and forests of the interior.

In recent years, a project sponsored by the Chinese government rebuilt a rail line that parallels the highway for its full length. It moves freight and passengers, although trains run much less frequently or reliably than they might. As collateral for the multibillion-dollar program, the Kenyan government granted a lien on the port of Mombasa. If the Kenyans default, control of the port is likely to be in dispute for a very long time.

There is a single highway connecting the port on the Indian Ocean on the east to the nation's principal city in the forested central highlands. Over most of its span, the highway is two-lane, and passing and dodging slow-moving commercial transport vehicles is a national sport. Closer to Nairobi, it becomes a four-lane superhighway. But at the outset, as you leave Mombasa, the driver of a passenger car faces serious challenges in a multiplicity of hazards, and passengers who gawk out the windows will think they are in a war zone. As the highway emerges from the city center, the way is strewn with rocks and ruts, concrete construction barriers seemingly placed haphazardly, and parked heavy earthmoving equipment. Many kilometers of roadway are under reconstruction — and have been for years. Work crews may be in evidence, but they seem to only stab at the piles of earth and rubble with picks and shovels. Most of the hydraulic equipment sits idle. The roadway is lined with the crudely built shops, hotels, and bars of yesteryear — many of which have sat only partially demolished for much too long. Most of those businesses remain desperately open, even though the portions of their structures that verged on the shoulder have been torn down.

Business continues among the rubble and piles of litter, including huge mounds of plastic bottles accumulated long before disposable containers were discouraged.

Years ago, the highway commission declared its intention to widen the roadway and ordered property owners to comply with new setbacks on short notice. And then bickering and lawsuits stalled everything. And as construction activities slowed down or stopped and equipment sat idle, critical components and even some vehicle tires disappeared overnight, and petrol was drained from the tanks.

One might ask innocently, *Who benefits?*

Who, Harry wondered, derives the revenue from the ferryboat tickets? Despite official obstruction and legal challenges, the bridges at Likoni have been in the works for years. Commercial access to and the economic viability of the South Coast's resort towns could be significantly improved. But might those vested interests continue to oppose any construction?

Harry would come to appreciate that Kenyans are both resourceful and clever. So, incompetence is never a sufficient explanation for why things don't get done.

CHAPTER 17

*D*espite having downed three cups of Joseph's coffee, Harry dozed for the next hour of the trip. He awoke when he felt the van come to a stop with a jolt. He opened his eyes to see a Kenyan policeman standing beside the driver's-side window.

They were on a rural stretch of highway. There were no roadside attractions in sight, just a nearly treeless expanse of savannah. Looking past the policeman, Harry could see other officers standing in the road and on the shoulder. Several tire shredders, metal rails studded with spikes that will puncture the rubber, were laid across the highway as roadblocks. Not having chase vehicles, this is how Kenyan cops summon cars and trucks onto the shoulder for inspection.

Joseph rolled the window down and spoke with the officer in Kiswahili. He then handed over papers, which the officer scanned as he frowned. The man started to yell at Joseph, who replied in a courteous, measured tone. The officer grunted in disgust as he handed the documents back.

Then, in a quick motion, the policeman reached over to grasp the rear passenger door handle. Aldo was sitting on that side. The officer yanked open the unlocked door and brusquely motioned for Aldo to move over. He then jumped in, sat down, and slammed the door closed.

"We are now proceeding to the station!" the officer announced in English.

"Is there a problem, sir?" Aldo asked.

The officer huffed, "This driver of yours cannot present a taxi license. I will charge him at the police station, where if you gentlemen wish to proceed on your journey, you may summon a taxi or board a matatu. I presume you are bound for Nairobi?"

"Nairobi, yes," Aldo replied. "But this is an unfortunate misunderstanding! This is my houseman Joseph, and this is a private car. He drives me everywhere I go."

The policeman turned to Aldo and sneered, "We are sitting in a rented vehicle. How is it you do not have your own car? You've hired this man as your driver for the day, I think. And therefore he is operating as a commercial chauffeur without the proper permit." He gestured to Joseph, "We will proceed to the station!"

Joseph cast a fearful look back at Aldo but didn't start the car.

Aldo pasted on his best smile and explained with stunning rapidity, "We are on a business trip. I travel upcountry regularly from my office in Mombasa. Frankly, I am surprised we have not met on this road before! My Range Rover is in the shop today in Nyali. An impressive paint job — British Racing Green! I am no doubt being overcharged, as usual, for modest bodywork from a mishap in a car park. And then there is the expense of this rental! But these are no concerns of yours, sir. I apologize for troubling you, officer. I know you have more urgent matters to attend to. These Somali terrorists, for example! Our business is pressing and urgent. In fact, we have an afternoon appointment with the commissioner, and if we dally here, I fear we will be late. While Joseph is innocent of these things you say, if perhaps there is a fine we would post at the station, might we pay it now and go on our way?"

The officer hesitated, and his frown deepened. "The fine for operating without a taxi license is fifty-thousand shillings. And a week in jail." Then he added, "If you have the cash, perhaps the jail time could be waived."

Aldo pulled a wad of US hundred-dollar bills from his pants pocket, counted out five of them, and handed them to the policeman.

The officer held back a smile as he folded the bills and tucked them into the waistband of his pants.

He hopped out of the vehicle, and before he closed the door on Aldo, he pointed to Joseph and cautioned, "If I see him again, with or without you, in similar circumstances, I am running him in!"

He slammed the door shut, and Joseph promptly eased back onto the highway from the shoulder and sped off.

As Aldo counted the bills he had left, he muttered, "I'm surprised the bastard didn't demand all of it!"

Joseph called back, "Sorry, boss. He refused to accept my explanation."

"No matter, Joseph," Aldo said. "One look at us, and he knew we had money. There was nothing you could say."

"How much did he get?" Joseph asked.

"I gave him fifty-thousand. Five-hundred dollars!"

"So sorry, boss" was all Joseph could say.

"Is this… normal?" Harry asked.

"Yes and no," Aldo replied with a dismissive shrug. "If Joseph had been driving by himself and in a beat-up car, the fellow might have asked, 'Can you spare something for my tea?'" And the bribe might be, say, ten bucks. It's all about how much he can scare you and how much he thinks you can afford to pay."

"Has this happened to you before?" Harry asked.

"Oh, from time to time. This one was a nasty hit. You see, to begin with, it's illegal for him to get into the car without making an arrest. And, yes, there could be a fine at the station, but that takes paperwork and a couple of hours out of his day, all said and done. This was an out-and-out cash bribe. He didn't even take Joseph's name for the record, you notice."

"You said it," Harry told Joseph. "Corruption is the mother of Kenya. But I thought it was mostly crooked bureaucrats."

Aldo laughed. "You know what's really silly? Those crooked bureaucrats were tired of getting complaints about police corruption. Of course, bribes are totally illegal, both to give and to take, but there was no enforcement. So what do you suppose they've done about it?"

"Some kind of crackdown?" Harry assumed.

"No," Aldo said. "Did you notice what the officer did with the money I gave him?"

"I thought he tucked it under his belt. That seemed odd."

Aldo kept laughing. "The brilliant way they chose to deal with police corruption was to issue new uniforms with *no pockets!*"

Joseph added, "But they are silent on the subject of Jockey shorts!" And he laughed, too.

HARRY'S BLADDER had been uncomfortable for a half-hour before he requested a pee break. Then it was ten more minutes on a barren stretch of road before Joseph could pull into a rest stop. This place was a densely stocked curio shop where there was no charge to use the latrine out back. Access to the toilets required traversing rows of long tables in the shop laden with hardwood carvings, mostly of wildlife.

The latrine was a ceramic-tiled pit, which was disgustingly dirty and reeked. Harry resolved that the next time he needed to stop, he'd ask them to just pull over to the side of the road, as he'd seen others do on the highway. On one end of the pit was a one-person-sized closet with no door. It had a hole in the floor. If that need arose, Harry hoped he could hold it until they arrived at a hotel. In place of toilet paper, there was a partially shredded magazine lying in a puddle on the floor.

On the way in, he'd seen a sign, "Internet Café," which turned out to be a kitchen table with a single chair and a darkened computer screen. Harry tipped the attendant a hundred shillings to obtain the Wi-Fi password so he could finally phone Esther via WhatsApp.

He expected she'd be at her desk in the office, and he got her on the first ring.

"Harry, have you arrived in Nairobi so soon? I expected your call this morning, but perhaps it was too early. Did you sleep well?"

"Well enough," Harry said. "We're at a rest stop somewhere near Voi. Aldo says we're stopping overnight at a safari camp."

"So, you are finally acting like a tourist. May you enjoy." She said it without enthusiasm as if reading from a briefing book on hospitality.

"Esther," Harry said with a sigh, "I happened to see you and Aldo at the restaurant last night. It looked like a private conversation, and I decided not to stay. But you told me you were meeting Alice, so it seems you're not being honest with me."

"What did Aldo tell you? I suppose you asked him."

"Oh, I asked. But I want to hear your side of it first."

"Am I being interrogated? Are you comparing our stories?"

"It didn't look like a business meeting. It's a romantic spot, somewhere you and I could have gone on my last night."

"He suggested it. All I wanted was coffee."

"You shared a bottle of wine, I believe."

"Why should I be rude? Why should I not enjoy myself? Yes, he gave me dinner. I don't say no to anyone's food. Why do you care?"

"I haven't abandoned you. You know why I agreed to take this trip."

"You say it's to investigate. But there is a strong possibility you will be pulled in. And before you know how far, you may not be able to get out."

"So is that what you two were talking about?"

"Where you are concerned, yes."

"What else?" Aldo hadn't mentioned any other purpose for the meeting.

"Look, Harry. Not everything is about you." She took a breath as if she wanted to say something else, but she didn't.

"Don't you want me to do this deal? Or, at least, find out more?"

"Harry, I have work to do. Nothing I say is going to change things. Try to enjoy your vacation."

"Wait!" he exclaimed, lest she hang up. "Do you trust Aldo? Should I?"

"So far, I trust Aldo to do business and keep his word. More than that, I cannot say. What do *you* think of him?"

Harry sighed. "You're right. He's kept his word. And I know it's been only a short time, but I'd thought you and I were learning to trust each other."

She said softly, "You are a good man, Harry." Then she added, "That's why I worry. Don't take this wrong, but you're not clever enough to be bad."

"And how about you?" he asked her.

She found the question disconcerting. "How about what?"

"My dear Esther, are *you* clever enough to be bad?"

There was a catch in her voice when she replied, "As I told you, I'm clever enough to know bad behavior when I see it."

"You consider yourself an honest person, then?"

"Of course. It's my job. As I believe I've explained."

Harry had been suppressing his annoyance, and now he let himself sound less than tender. "Yes, you did explain — eventually — why you bought the dress. And I believe it was your intention all along to buy the books. But when you found you had those extra banknotes in your pocket, they were easily spent. You had a good reason, as it turned out. And perhaps I wouldn't have understood it if you'd shared it with me when you asked for the money. But even then, when we'd known each other scarcely an hour, I'd have probably given it to you if you'd just said you wanted to make such a gorgeous entrance at dinner."

"I believe I've thanked you for the dress, and I thank you now for the lovely compliment. You do understand, Harambee. You're scolding me now, but I know you do understand. You knew nothing about the meeting with Victor then — or how important it would be — for both of us."

"But here's what has me bothered — upset, really — and I'll just have to come out and say it."

"I'm listening," she said meekly.

"Your story about the books and the dress, we can call that an excuse. A fib, maybe. But when I called you last evening, *you lied.* And it wasn't just an excuse, saying something like, 'I'm sorry, I'm meeting a friend.' That would have been the truth, and I didn't need to know more. You wouldn't have to say you were meeting Aldo — although he wasn't straight with me either. You two do business, and it doesn't concern me. I don't have a right to pry into your deals. But you told me you were with Alice, and you had a readymade story about why."

"Aldo told you, and I've told you, that I went behind your back because I think it's too soon for you to go rushing off to Nairobi."

"And I appreciate your concern. I'm flattered. It makes me think you care as much about me as you do about the new job. And, who knows, we got to know each other so fast, maybe you worry I can forget you just as quickly."

"I want you to be sure about what you're doing. With Victor. With Aldo. With me."

"Fair enough. But that's not what has me upset."

"Aldo is a salesman. You know he doesn't always give all the facts. He is sincere, though. He wants what's best for you. For us. And with me, you can be sure, I know how to do my sums."

"Oh, really? Because it's been my experience that people who are honest by nature — people who can't help but tell the truth — they're terrible liars. You do it too easily, my dear."

She gasped. It was a stomach punch. She responded curtly, "Text me when you arrive safely in camp. And get some pictures on your game drive." And she ended the call.

Harry caught sight of Aldo, who had helped himself to a bottle of Coke Zero at the refreshment stand. He beckoned in the direction of the van, where Joseph stood expectantly, but Harry pointed to the interior of the shop, indicating he wanted to have a look around.

Near the old-fashioned cash register, there was an assortment of ladies' beadwork on racks, but Harry was in no mood to go buying more gifts for Esther. And he didn't want to buy her some trinket. A jewelry shop in Nairobi would be the place to find something, provided his mood had changed by then.

Had he gone too far? Now he wished he had a recording of every word they'd exchanged at dinner. And — if they truly hadn't been talking only about him — what else did they have to argue about?

He might pick up something for Nicole. He wasn't sure he was going back anytime soon, but he knew he'd be returning at some point. And he couldn't go empty-handed. It wasn't about the expense or the value of the thing, whatever it was. It would be that he'd thought of her, made some effort to please her. In a way, he didn't really care whether his daughter would like the gift. There was a strong possibility she wouldn't, no matter what he got her. He just didn't want to carry the guilt he would feel if she thought he'd deliberately ignored her.

He regarded wildlife icons as tourist trinkets, even though some art dealers in the States marked up this stuff shamelessly. He suspected that people who bought these carvings would have their favorite animals, as children had their favorite toys, but he had no idea what Nicole's might be. You'd think an elephant would be a safe bet. He found them there in all sizes, from smaller than your hand to as large as a suitcase, carved in teak, with white tusks. Seeing the tusks made him pause. He knew that, years ago, those carvings would have been real ivory, banned from sale now to discourage poaching. But so, he thought, were most hardwoods, including teak. At the very least, the hardwood forests were endangered. Surely the tusks would be plastic. But he didn't want to take a chance. Would the US Customs officials arrest him or simply confiscate the item? Even more than he didn't want to be irresponsible, he dreaded the hassle and the shame.

His eye was drawn to a cluster of statuettes of tall, lanky women. Some carried baskets or buckets of water on their heads. On this trip Harry had seen locals do that as they trudged along the side of the road.

A short, smiling fellow came up to him, announcing, "Karibu! My name is Kumar. I will be privileged to serve you. Please let me know if you have any questions."

Harry asked him, "Are these carvings real ivory?"

"Of course not! I assure you, totally legal. The whole shop! No worries for you. *Hacuna matata!*"

Harry's gaze flitted back to one of the female figurines, which was two feet tall.

"Ah!" Kumar exclaimed, reaching over to pick it up and fondling it as he came closer. "The Maasai are tall, don't you see? Basketball players and runners, the very best, you see! Where, may I ask, are you from, sir?"

"Los Angeles," Harry replied.

The fellow chuckled and shook the figure enthusiastically, "Go Lakers! Very fine. I'm a fan of cricket, myself. My family came from Mumbai, one generation back." He caressed the statue as if Harry might have the same pleasure if it became his. "She is carrying water, don't you see?"

"Yes, I've seen them do that," Harry offered.

"Oh, and you might say it is an injustice! It's only the women!"

"What do you mean?"

"The Voi River runs through this region. No worries. The water must be boiled. This is a small bother. But farther into the bush, some years we have drought for months. Kenya Wildlife Service brings water in tanker trucks to fill waterholes for the animals. Elephants come, even the big cats! But no one is bringing water for the people! So the women set out from the villages at dawn, and they may hike twenty kilometers to the nearest spring or borehole. Then they hike back those same-same twenty clicks — with forty kilos of water in a bucket balanced on their heads! And they do this every day, while their husbands sit in the cafés sipping sweet tea and gossiping like magpies! Some of those chaps have motorbikes, and you would think they could go, but instead they are making money taking passengers and goods to market. Do they bring that money home? You might wonder."

"I recall some charities collecting money to drill and make wells."

"*Boreholes,* we call them. Yes. You see, you mustn't put a borehole just anywhere. If it's only a hand-pump for the people, okay. But some of these well-meaning outfits also make a watering hole for the animals. Okay, one might think, all very fine. The animals will come and drink. But the problem is, you've now disrupted the migration route. And the new path, of which you are unaware, will likely be through some farmer's cornfield! If the elephants trample those crops, they will be hunted down and killed! And if the elephants don't poop the seeds of what they eat in the right places, there will be no forest in the future!"

"Thank you for the information," Harry said. "I guess I have a lot to learn."

Kumar gestured with the item and asked, "Cash or credit card? If you have cash, I make you the very best price."

143

"How much?"

"Three thousand shillings with the card. If you have cash, twenty-eight fifty."

Harry wasn't a bargainer (perhaps not clever enough, in Esther's estimation?), but he had learned to ask, "Is that the best you can do?"

Kumar smiled sheepishly, "Twenty-five hundred, cash. And at that price, it is sadly all for the boss. Please add some small money for myself if you would be so kind."

Harry paid the fellow in cash, got the receipt, and then handed him two hundred.

Back in the car, Aldo caught sight of Harry's purchase and remarked approvingly, "Harry, you finally begin to behave like a tourist!"

"It's for my daughter," Harry explained, sliding into his seat. "Is this teak? I've heard it's endangered."

Joseph glanced back at it and remarked, "A lot of teak is inky black." This gleaming wood was a deep, rich, reddish-brown. "Mahogany," he judged. "Also endangered in Kenya. This material, if it's legal, is perhaps imported from Congo."

As Joseph started the car, Aldo checked his watch. "It is just past three o'clock. We'll be at the camp in a half-hour, and we'll have time for a short game drive before sundown." Then he asked, "Harry, that was a long phone call. Everything okay back in the States?"

"Nicole and I have yet to hook up," Harry said. "I guess I'll count myself lucky if we exchange a few texts. Maybe a picture of some unusual bird." He was less offhand when he said, "No, Aldo, that conversation was with Esther. I was scolding her for fibbing to me. We all have some way to go before we're a team."

Aldo simply nodded. Then he asked, "What do you most want to see, Harry?"

Most tourists want to see the Big Five — water buffalo, rhinoceros, leopard, elephant, and lion. In Aldo's experience, the women and children wanted to see elephants. The men and boys were eager to track lions. He expected Harry would name an animal. Giraffe, maybe. Or that bird, for Nicole.

"I confess I don't know much at all about wildlife," he said. "I suppose it will be an experience just to see how they behave when they're not in cages."

Harry meant it as an offhand, innocent remark. But that's just what he saw. It changed the way he would later see the rest of the world. And his place in it.

CHAPTER 18

The lessons of life in its raw natural state were incremental and enduring for Harry. Less than an hour after they'd checked in at Satao Camp inside Tsavo East National Wildlife Reserve, Aldo and his party were navigating the tracks of the park, guided by Joseph, looking for telltale signs of the Big Five.

It didn't take long for Harry to understand that going on safari could feel much like visiting a movie set, which he'd done a few times before in Los Angeles. There's an unreality about it. This is real life, but some happenings are so unusual you doubt the evidence of your senses. Most of the time, you watch, and you wait. Nothing and no one around you seem to be moving. They are waiting, too, but few (except the director, perhaps not even the tour guide) know what to expect. Suddenly, at the periphery of your vision, people (or animals) come together and cluster around something that happens very rapidly. If you're not on the lookout, paying close attention, you will miss it. Then the scene goes back to stasis.

You soon realize that much of the day will be downright boring. You live for the delight of anticipation, then the rare thrills.

Soldiers and sailors in war zones report much the same scenario —

long periods of boredom interspersed with brief episodes of threat and abject panic.

No matter what the day held, Joseph promised that, before they returned to camp, they'd park on an overlook for a sundowner, after which he'd set a table and break out the picnic basket and the gin. "It's a grand tradition," he told them. "You'll live like the rich white *bwanas* of a bygone age!"

Joseph went on to explain that most of the time here in the bush, prey animals lead an uneventful existence. They wander about, flee alarming sounds and smells that might signal nothing, and, whenever undisturbed, eat the vegetation constantly. Then there are those brief moments of terror — a brief chase, the attack, and then one of your own, perhaps you, are being eaten alive. Moments later, in the space of a few heartbeats, your surviving relatives run off a safe distance and go back to chewing grass.

The first lesson for Harry was small and subtle and yet profound. It changed the way he looked at the world every time he stepped outside.

Joseph stopped the van abruptly, pointed upward to the northwest, and announced, "There is a kite, a large raptor, high up in the tree over there. Do you see it?"

Harry had removed his Celestron binoculars from his backpack and trained them on the spot Joseph had indicated. It took him a couple of minutes panning around and adjusting focus before he had the bird in sight. And, indeed, the ominous raptor was perched high atop a baobab tree, scouring the ground with its sharp vision for any movement that might suggest the opportunity for a quick meal.

"Amazing," Harry said, handing the binoculars to Aldo. "How did you see that from way over here?"

Joseph responded with his favorite question, "May I tell you something?"

"We're listening, Joseph. Until the sun goes down and I get that drink, you are the sole authority in this car," Harry assured him.

"Well," the driver sighed, "it's like this. When you look up at these trees, do you notice which way the wind is blowing, and how much?"

Indeed, the leaves were being disturbed by a slight breeze from the west, and the tops of the trees were bent and swaying in the same direction.

Joseph went on, "Now notice where the hawk is. I stopped the car because I saw a disturbance in that tree. The leaves and the branches were agitated, but not in the same manner as in the other trees. The bird, which I had not seen, was moving. It must have been preening or hopping to another branch. When you see such a disturbance, even so small, something that doesn't fit the pattern around it, an animal is sure to be causing it. You look for the source of the motion, and you will spot the beast."

How many times had Harry looked up on his walks and failed to notice the presence of squirrels or birds or monkeys? Such a basic skill, essential to our ancestor hunters, was of seemingly little practical use now, except for the observant human to sense the activity and acknowledge the community of surrounding life forms.

There followed a predictable period of no action and lethargy. Aldo reached into the ice chest and helped himself to a chilled cocktail in a can. Consuming liquor inside a moving vehicle was prohibited on the public highway, but here in the bush there were no rules. Harry wanted to stay alert and didn't drink, but he was nevertheless feeling drowsy as the heat of the afternoon peaked.

Harry learned from Joseph, who was narrating to his guest almost nonstop whenever he wasn't on the phone to his colleagues. There are three types of giraffe. One of them — the Maasai — lives here, identified by their distinctive body markings of jagged spots. Oddly, they eat mainly thorns as their long necks enable them to munch on the tops of acacia trees. Their tongues are tough as shoe leather with a surface rough as sandpaper. Giraffes appear calm as they stride elegantly across the wooded grassland, and, for the most part, they probably are. That's because predators, including the big cats, are wary of them. An adult giraffe can defend itself and the young ones by swinging its head in a powerful downward arc, dealing a single, lethal body blow to the attacker.

There are two types of gazelles, Thomson's and Grant's, both named for nineteenth-century British naturalists as if the poor little creatures had been anonymous for eons because Adam had skipped over them in the Garden of Eden. Like their relatives the antelope, the impala, and the lesser kudu, gazelles roam in close-knit, all-girl herds ruled by a single, dominant male. The other boys keep their distance until one of them feels strong enough or foolish enough to challenge the boss. When they fight, the loser either dies or runs off, now destined to be enfeebled prey for big cats and hyenas. Joseph had explained how you could tell these two types of gazelle apart. It had something to do with the markings on their tails, but Harry forgot the distinction as soon as he'd heard it.

Joseph cautioned, "You are not to get out of the van — except for an urgent rest stop, of course. Going on foot is generally not permitted in the preserve. For example, if you come upon a herd of water buffalo, they will stare at you. The look is cold. It's hostile. Move on quickly, and don't stare back. They don't like people at all, and they could charge. They could even overturn this vehicle if they got mad. For the death blow, when you've fallen to the ground, they will hook their horns beneath you, flip you over with a twist of the head, and gore you in the stomach."

"What did we ever do to them?" Harry asked, not expecting an answer.

But Joseph was serious. "It's the legacy of the hunters, man," he said. "If you are walking with a ranger and they approach, just the sound of cocking the rifle will send them away. I have also heard stories of hunting parties. The buffalo move off, but later in the day they circle around, find their way to the hunters' camp, and trample everything! They may look big and stupid, but they are sneaky and wise!"

The vivid image Harry took away from this afternoon's expedition came an hour later, just before sunset. This is the time of day when predators are most active. It's also the time when tour guides do their best to orchestrate a stunning climax to the safari experience. The goal could be sighting a herd of elephants clustered around a waterhole or spotting a pride of big cats. To share this impressive finale, the tour guides in various vehicles patrolling the park confer continuously on their phones. Any of them spotting an opportunity will notify the others. But too many vehicles converging on the same spot can spoil the experience. If the park is crowded, guides will exchange information in their tribal language to confound rival operators who have brought tourists from upcountry and don't know the likely spots.

Joseph received a call that got him visibly excited. He announced, "Just ahead, to the east, very soon, you will see something, I am telling you!"

He pointed to the horizon, where a herd of wildebeest was stampeding away at full gallop. If they were the objective, Harry didn't see how the car could keep up with them, especially as they got farther from the track.

But after less than half a mile, Joseph stopped short on the side of the road, pulling up behind three other vehicles. Telephoto camera lenses protruded from open windows, and passengers with binoculars stood on the seats in the open cabs to get a better look.

About twenty yards from the observers' vantage point, three cheetahs were gnawing on a bloody carcass, their muzzles smeared with gore as they chomped down hard to crack bone.

The carcass was a small animal. It might have been a dog or a hyena.

But it was a wildebeest. A calf. And it was squealing!

This sight was gruesome enough, but when Harry took his eyes off of it for a second and caught a glance of the wider scene, the full horror of the situation struck him. Just a few steps away from the attackers and their prey stood the calf's mother. She was frozen, transfixed by shock and sorrow, as she stared at her baby's suffering.

The frightened herd had deserted them. Perhaps the calf was a straggler and she'd gone back for him.

Was it mindless instinct or undying devotion that kept her rooted in place? Perhaps at first she had brayed in agony, but now she had no voice left.

Harry felt a sudden chill as he realized, *If she can't force herself to flee, she will be their next meal!*

"Joseph, amazing! Well done!" Aldo exclaimed as he gawked. He was snapping pictures with his phone. "Harry! Quick, get a video of this!"

But the American muttered, "You know, I'm getting hungry. Let's skip the sundowner and head back to camp." Aldo looked surprised, and Harry added, "And if you guys have no objections, why don't we press on to Nairobi first thing? I've seen enough."

CHAPTER 19

$\mathcal{T}$he incident of the cheetahs and the wildebeests gave Harry an insight on the justification offered by the politician, "It is our turn to feed." He knew that Kenyans would understand, as perhaps others might not, that their leader was citing the laws of nature, not the morality of humans. There can be nothing evil in the cheetah's need to sustain itself. Nor could the mother's painful dilemma be avoided.

What is needed is necessary, the politician seemed to say.

The citizens could understand, but they might not forgive.

What brought all this up for Harry was the nagging question of whether Skebelsky's scheme was right or wrong. Right or wrong for the community? Right or wrong for the disadvantaged people they intended to serve? Right or wrong for Harry Gardner?

Perhaps framing it as right or wrong was mistaken, even naïve.

And underlying this consideration was whether Harry should be undertaking this trip to Nairobi at all, which Aldo and Victor — and, yes, Esther — would interpret as stepping willingly into the plan.

These thoughts occurred to Harry as he stuffed himself with a full English breakfast at dawn on the patio of Satao Camp. The tables were set on a fenced deck under a thatched roof and adjacent to the bar. Fifty yards past the railing where Harry sat was the resort's artificial watering hole, which was about the size of the fishpond on his grandfather's farm. This morning a herd of elephants had come, a dozen females and two babies. This, Harry had learned from Joseph, was the basic family unit, led by a matriarch, the oldest and wisest. The bulls generally keep apart except when tolerated by the cranky old dame when the females are in *musth,* the hormone that triggers mating season.

"Predators usually don't attack at the watering holes," Joseph had explained. Perhaps there was something like morality among the beasts after all. At least there would be no bloody scene to spoil Harry's appetite.

Aldo was sipping coffee as he studied his phone. Joseph usually didn't join them for meals. The driver had already been up for a couple of hours and out on errands in the nearby town of Voi to refill petrol and stock up on provisions.

"How goes it in the world?" Harry asked Aldo.

"Oh, the Pope has made another liberal change in doctrine." Aldo smiled. "Maybe Italy is becoming more permissive, more like the United States. But then, the US is becoming more divided, like Italy under Berlusconi, I think."

"And Kenya's becoming more high-tech and developed, like Silicon Valley and Singapore. All while the US and Italy grow more openly corrupt, more like Kenya."

"Harry, have you been to Singapore?"

Harry answered, "Nah, but I've seen a couple of movies. That hotel with the twin towers and the garden connecting them on top? They wouldn't dare do that in LA. Don't they have earthquakes in that part of the world?"

"I don't know. But tropical storms, for sure. You're right. Maybe that skyscraper is a disaster waiting to happen. There's another crazy-big pair of towers in Kuala Lumpur." Aldo shot Harry an apologetic look, "I should be trying to cheer you out of your dark mood. You never saw anything like yesterday?"

"It's not that I'm squeamish. It just caught me in a mood. You don't want to see sausage made, that kind of thing. I suppose I was thinking of safari as entertainment, and it's not. Or it shouldn't be."

Aldo gestured with his phone, saying, "I also have emails from my colleagues at the booking agency. I have another party, and I must go to Milan to collect them on Thursday. Schoolteachers, mixed couples. But this means I can only spend three days with you in Nairobi. I can get you started, set up the meetings. Then you will be on your own for a while."

"As long as you lay it all out for me. You know I know nothing about the next steps."

"I trust you to follow through. It's not complicated. Just time-consuming." Then he asked, "But where is your enthusiasm?"

Harry didn't respond.

Aldo went on, "Tell me now. If you're so worried, we don't have to go through with any of it. I don't know enough about the plan to like it or hate it. But perhaps you want Joseph to take us back to Diani. I can just as easily fly from Mombasa."

Harry shrugged. "We've come this far. Maybe I'm not enthusiastic. Yet. But I'm still curious."

"What about Esther?" Aldo asked. "Since I'll be gone, perhaps you will want her to join you."

"I'm not sure we're still talking. When I phoned her yesterday, she didn't disagree with your story about your meeting. I haven't forgiven her quite yet, and maybe she won't give me the opportunity." He hesitated, then added, "Let's go on. If it looks like the clinic is a bad idea, there's no reason for her to come."

Aldo looked concerned, but then he chuckled, "Harry, if there is no deal, there's every reason for the two of you to take some time in Nairobi! What else would you do? Go home? You did not enjoy the safari, I believe. You are a man of too much feeling. You can't just enjoy it as a show. And, at the beach, you refuse to just go crazy with some women. Instead, you're getting in deep. Maybe this is the only way for you. When are you going to start enjoying yourself?"

Harry had no answer. But then his phone rang and he got up and walked away.

~

"What is it, Dad," Nicole asked right away. "Are you okay? It's late here, and I'm exhausted, just going to bed. So I can't take time to chat, but I want to make sure it's nothing serious."

"I just wanted to let you know I won't be coming back for a while."

She was not at all surprised. Or pleased. "So, it's what I thought. You're going to stay."

"For a time. I don't know how long. Not yet. There's a business opportunity I'm looking into."

"I thought you were retired! How is it you need more stress in your life?" Then she returned to her familiar theme, "And what about the house?"

"It's an opportunity, it sounds interesting, and I can't say more until I know more. I'm on my way to Nairobi now for meetings. As for the house, I gave Eleanor Amory your contact information, and she has yours. The renters had to move out early, and she'll be finding someone else."

"It doesn't sound like anything has changed," she said finally.

"No, I suppose not."

Nicole yawned as she said, "So, Dad. Stay well. And try to have fun. But it's not sounding like you will."

CHAPTER 20

*T*he rest of the car trip, from Voi to Nairobi, was uneventful (no more encounters with cops, for example). Harry slept most of the way. They arrived downtown at midday, where Aldo checked them into the Sarova Stanley, a renovated luxury hotel with a famous history of hosting diplomats and movie stars. After unpacking in their elegant shared suite, Aldo said he needed to use the computer in the hotel conference center to straighten out a snarl of bookings for the party of schoolteachers he would meet. Joseph, who had family in Thika, announced he'd be staying there and promised to be on call to support their errands in the city.

Before leaving the suite, Aldo excused himself from an agenda he'd set for Harry's evening. Instructions included meeting a woman, Veronica Lindbrook, in the exclusive 1902 Club Lounge promptly at six. Aldo's explanation was "She's in the United Nations diplomatic corps somehow, a friend of a friend. So, be on your best behavior. These are the kinds of friends we're going to need. She knows her way around philanthropy, I think."

Harry demanded, "Why is it when I feel clueless about what's next, you disappear?"

"You're the director," Aldo insisted. "I know a little more about the business deal than you do now, but about all the rest, I'm just as clueless as you are. If you don't have the answers, tell it the way you *want* it to be. You may be guessing, but you won't be lying."

"What can I tell her?" Harry had few facts and felt he needed a brief. "Wouldn't there be legal consequences if I just make it all up?"

"Tell yourself, whatever is in the plan, it's already a done deal. As far as she knows, you are *already* the director! No one can say otherwise. We're in town to meet backers. You can tell her we're going to break ground for the clinic any day now. We're preparing the news releases and a celebrity cookout on the beach. Date to be announced." He grinned. "And if you fancy her, invite her!"

"And what do we want from her?"

Aldo shrugged. "Her good opinion? Names of influential people she knows?"

That afternoon, Harry amused himself by swimming in the indoor pool on the second floor, followed by several strong gin-and-tonics at the bar. The colonial heritage of the place was obvious from the legendary names on its directory of meeting rooms: Churchill, Baden Powell, Patterson, Huxley, Hemingway, Batian, Lenana, and Baker. Lore included the proud fact that the Exchange Bar where Harry was getting pleasantly pissed had once been the site of the national stock exchange.

Most of the other guests were men. The whites wore golf shirts, and the blacks were in suits and ties. There were a few Chinese and some Indians, also in suits.

Harry knew that repressing his resentment over being abandoned by Aldo tempted him to drink more. He also told himself he should be keeping a clear head since he knew this woman not at all but might ultimately care very much whether he'd be making a good impression.

He had too much time to kill at the bar, and he was too upset. He downed three drinks, one short of his quota of irresponsibility, before he toddled unsteadily off to the appointment.

ALTHOUGH THE 1920 Club Lounge was an exclusive perk for returning guests, the uniformed attendant must have been sufficiently impressed with Ms. Lindbrook's appearance to accept her story that a guest with privileges had invited her. She was already seated in a richly upholstered chair at a small private table in the mahogany-paneled room and sipping her white wine when Harry entered. Aldo had briefed him that the hotel had a strict dress code — either formalwear or "smart casual." So Harry wore his everyday Beverly Hills outfit of golf shirt, pleated gabardine slacks, and herringbone sport coat. He wore his one pair of black leather slip-ons, having shined them as well as he could by buffing them with one of the knee-length socks he wore with them.

Hers was a severe look. Perhaps not quite middle-aged, she wore a modestly cut black cocktail dress with pearls. Her hair was done back in a businesslike bun. Her makeup and lipstick were carefully applied but understated. Her eyebrows were either shaved or nonexistent, sketched in archly with light strokes of kohl.

Instead of a purse, she carried a designer brief bag, which she'd laid beside her on the table.

Fair-haired with only the finest of facial wrinkles, she gave the impression of a younger and prettier Margaret Thatcher.

No introductions were necessary. They were the only diners in the place. The intimate room offered "complimentary evening city sundowners" from six to eight, meaning snacks and limitless drinks.

Harry decided he'd permit himself just one more, consumed slowly. Perhaps, if she was pleasant company, he'd invite her to dinner in the Thorn Tree Café, where tables were clustered about an ancient acacia tree in a courtyard.

Already a little unsteady on his feet, he was relieved to sit down. She didn't get up. She took his hand languidly and gave him the barest smile as she quipped, "Mr. Gardner, I presume?" Her accent was British. This could have been her attempt at dry wit, the greeting being on-the-nose appropriate to the setting, using the same terse words with which the American journalist Henry Stanley had greeted the reclusive British explorer David Livingstone in 1871 in the Congo after an arduous two-year search. Harry knew enough of the story to get the joke. He wondered why the founders of the hotel would choose to honor Stanley rather than Livingstone. Was it meant to encourage travelers rather than meddlesome white settlers?

"It's Harry, Ms. Lindbrook. And my pleasure," he said as he sat and signaled right away to the attendant he needed a drink.

A meager half-bottle of Chardonnay, still half full, had been set to chill for her in a bucket on the table. Perhaps she thought that sharing would send the wrong message.

"Please, it's Veronica. I hope you don't mind I've begun to indulge," she apologized as she took a discreet sip. "It's been a challenging day."

Her glass seemed almost full, as well. So she was lying about boozing, but Harry didn't fault her for it.

"Not at all," Harry smiled as he muttered "Boodles and tonic" to the waiter. To her, he added, "I confess I began a couple of hours ago. We drove up from Diani rather than flew. I'm not sure I'd make that choice again. Rough roads and rougher scenery. I need something with tonic to ease the pain."

"Bloody metrics!" she fumed, taking her cue from nothing Harry had said, except perhaps his frustrations. She sipped again and then pouted, "Can you imagine Albert Schweitzer with a clipboard counting snotty noses? These days, we all stare at our screens until we're bleary-eyed. Some of us miss the fieldwork, but the younger ones couldn't find their way to the field with their GPS!"

Harry commiserated, "As a tourist, the annoyances for me are mostly temporary."

She muttered, "Oh, you'll get into the muck soon enough." Then she laughed. "Aldo told me you stopped in Voi. I take it you haven't been on safari before?"

"No. We got in a short one, possibly to be my last. I don't know which was worse, the boredom or the carnage."

"Oh, my," she said. "Not the naturalist, I see. I haven't done much of it myself, I admit. Not for lack of interest, but no time. Not a minute! Bloody Zoom meetings!"

The waiter brought Harry's drink and a tray of canapes, smiled, and retreated.

"Rough day, you said?" Harry asked, taking any cue for meaningless conversation.

"I'm a bureaucrat," she confessed. "I trained as a barrister, but these days it seems all I do is read reports. Then I write reports summarizing those reports. Then a program manager or a committee chair clips a note on top and passes the thing to some brahmin at the funding source. If the donor is pleased, there are bum-pats and drinks all around. But if they're unhappy, we must find a head or two to lop off as we make our apologies and confess our shortcomings. Accompanied, of course, with our heartfelt pleas for more money to fix whatever it was we botched."

Harry smiled and teased her, "And what is there to report?"

"Oh, the monied interests are still winning. And the people — and the animals, poor dears — are losing. The land is developing, the resources are dwindling, and the pollution is too pervasive and too expensive to mitigate. And the climate crisis? *Dear God!* I don't know why anyone pays my salary to keep telling them these things."

Harry decided his attempt at making polite conversation was not improving her mood. He might as well get right down to it, finding out whatever the purpose of this meeting was. The wine would do more than he could to ease her discomfort. His hunger was raging, especially after sloshing down so many drinks with only a few handfuls of nuts at the bar. And in this club, from the look of the place settings, a robust dinner must not be included in the sundowner presentation. So he resolved to have a polite drink with this prim, moody lady and excuse himself to a more substantial, solitary repast. Maybe later he'd find cricket on the TV and miraculously it would start to make sense.

"Aldo tells me you might want to learn more about plans for The Harambee Rehabilitation and Recovery Center," he said.

She smiled. "If your purpose is to improve lives and employ Kenyans, that's highly commendable. I hope you'll be hiring plenty of women."

"Certainly," Harry said, taking a long pull that drained half his glass. "Why ever not?"

"Women are only beginning to have any influence at all in Kenyan policymaking. And that's generally the case all over Africa. I believe you know I work for the UN. We have ongoing programs to get women involved in political parties. We sponsor their candidacies, from local office all the way to legislatures, and we monitor the elections if the old farts in power will let us."

"Is that so hard? I'm sure I've seen female politicians on the news."

"Oh, there are some. And there will be more. But, to give you an example, just a few years ago, Coca-Cola planned a management training program — not just for women but deliberately *including* them — at the bottling plant in Nyeri. And on the first day of the program, all the men — and I mean *every last one* — walked out in protest!" She sipped the rest of her wine, and before Harry could reach for the bottle, the waiter was at her side and refilling her glass. She added as she sipped again, "Cultural change takes time, of course. Generations!"

"Of course," Harry agreed, sure it was the truth and that agreeing would cost him nothing.

"I want to stress to you," she said, reaching across the table to take his hand. Her hands looked older than her face. He noticed there were no rings on her fingers. She went on, "I emphasize the importance of getting off to the *right start*. I've been at this for twenty years — I hope I don't look that old! — and I see heaps of well-meaning initiatives. It's a truism of Western culture that Africa somehow *needs to be fixed*. And in many ways, it *does*. What society on Earth doesn't need some level of reform? I mean, I haven't visited the States in an age, but I can hardly bear to see the news anymore! The land of the free? *Give me a break,* I believe is the expression. But of course we have Brexit and our own versions of self-destruction, mass hysteria, and stupidity. We British aren't trying to run the world anymore, thank goodness. That's *your* job now! And we advise, of course. The privilege of seniority and centuries of arrogant policies." She toasted with a smile, "Lessons learned, what?"

"Oh, I quite agree," Harry said. Her hand hadn't moved from resting on his. What little wine she'd already had was making her more talkative, and a flush had come to her high cheekbones.

He didn't pull his hand back. He wasn't uncomfortable, just a bit confused. He wondered how long it had been since she'd been entertained. If she was on Aldo's radar, he must know more about her than just her job description at whatever agency. It occurred to Harry this could be another trap, that his encounter with Esther might be only the first in a series.

She gave his hand an advisory pat, saying, "Now, Aldo didn't have a chance to share much with me. But what I want to *stress* — and I mean stress very *sincerely* — is the importance of *M and E*. Does your proposal include a management plan with metrics?"

"The management plan is still formative, I would say," Harry fudged. These terms were new to him, and he was pretty sure the documents he'd seen didn't mention any such thing.

"Then I suspect you have no idea what I'm talking about," she said. "I don't mean to be impolite, and I'm sure you are very professional, but many people — I'd even say *most* people — who show up here with proposals for new charities and NGOs haven't the faintest idea what I'm talking about."

"I used to run a publishing company," Harry said. "I confess that *M and E* is not a term in our business, that I know of."

"Are you retired now? I suppose it's your wife who's gotten you involved in philanthropy."

The only explanation Harry gave was "I'm on my own these days. I came to Kenya as a tourist, but Aldo had other ideas."

She was going to say something but stopped herself. She helped herself to a canape, patted her lips with a linen napkin, and this time her sip of wine was more of a gulp. "Monitoring and evaluation," she announced as if beginning a slide presentation. "The process of monitoring generates metrics. I complain, but as I say, it's mostly what we do these days. Milestones and measurements. And only from metrics — and I mean data gathered *in the field* — can one have the basis for meaningful evaluation. M and E. I must tell you, it's UN gospel these days. The notion is, without metrics, you have no idea what you're achieving — or even what you're meant to achieve!"

"That sounds very scientific," Harry said, perhaps implying to her it could be *worthwhile* but thinking to himself it would be *too much work.*

"Donors will want to see your criteria for success. A key metric, for example, will be *ROI.*"

"Now there's a term I know about. Return on investment. But we're to be a nonprofit. I expect we'll operate at a loss, year after year. Surely our donors won't expect to be repaid."

"All the more need for some metric by which you will judge success! For x dollars in donations, what is the expected result y? What will the money I give you achieve? How far will it go? How can I brag to my bridge club I've made a difference in the world? How many beds will you have? How many clients can you treat as residents? As outpatients? How much will you improve client outcomes? What percentage of clients will become self-supporting? How many responsible citizens will you return to the community, and what will be their roles? And will you just turn them out, or will you track their progress through the years after they've left your care?"

"I expect we'll learn as we go from our clients — what they expect, what the community needs."

"You won't raise much money that way. It's very competitive these days. And — even if you have specific objectives — those criteria might not be good guidance or good policy."

Harry offered, "Perhaps you have one of your management plans we could use as a template?"

"I'll do better than that. I can consult with you, help you write an effective plan. A plan that will get you both funding and credibility."

Now Harry thought he understood the purpose of the meeting — or, at least, *her* purpose.

"I'm sure we'd welcome your contribution, Veronica." He didn't expect she'd be donating her services, but it was too soon to ask her to quote her fee. Maybe they did need her help. This was a new dimension, the kind of thing he and Aldo had come here to learn.

She kept her hand in place and gave his a few more emphatic pats as she spoke. "Let me give you an example of metrics — use and misuse. A classic example from years ago, program goals were set to reduce the rate of mortality in children by age five. They'd do that by various methods, including improving nutrition and healthcare. And, after years of diligent effort and masses of money spent, they succeeded. Many more children in Africa now survive until they're old enough to attend school."

"But are you going to say that's somehow a problem?"

"It is. When you consider *unintended consequences.* Many parents struggle to keep their kids in school, even though the public ones are now free. There are expenses for textbooks and uniforms. And for the dropouts, there are few job programs. So now you have a whole generation — a healthy-baby boom — of teenage children who have nothing productive to do. And especially in poor areas in countries like Nigeria or Somalia, along come the jihadists, who offer the boys a job and regular pay. These kids aren't fanatics when they're recruited. They just want to eat and be able to send some money home." Then she added, "And then they kidnap the girls to serve the boys. You've heard of Boko Haram?"

"Only from the headlines," Harry admitted.

"So — is it mainly children that your clinic will aim to support?"

"In the beginning, our intention is to serve young adults from Kwale County. Many are poor, no longer in school, and possibly unemployed, but I don't think the circumstances you describe are typical. The initial focus will be on alcoholism, drug abuse, and anger management."

"There has been significant terrorist activity in Somalia, and at times some incursions and incidents on the South Coast of Kenya. Al-Shabaab, in your backyard. And offshore, the Somali pirates threaten the oil tankers and container ships. The French navy claims they have it under control, but let's not count too much on the French. You're aware of this?"

"As I say, I've seen some news reports, but I'm not familiar."

She stared at him, and she gripped his hand firmly. "Understand, by the time you open your doors, the situation could be different. Very possibly, worse. Kenya might not seem so volatile today, but things could change. Rapidly."

Her earnest look held steady as she reached under the table with her free hand and rested it on Harry's inner thigh.

She curled her fingers to caress him as she cooed softly, "You really do need me inside your tent."

After he'd drained his second drink, he excused himself to the restroom, attempting to navigate a steady course, where he phoned Aldo and asked for a call back in five minutes. Seated again at the table, when he received the call, he winced as he said into the phone, "Okay, you've got me chasing rockets again!" He ended the call and told her, "I'm sorry. Aldo says he's set another meeting for tonight. I'd hoped we could spend more time, but I really must go. You needn't hurry off, and if you'd like more than the hors d'oeuvres, it's on us." He took her business card and promised to be in touch.

The look she gave him was impassive. She'd been turned down before.

Before he left, he conferred privately with the attendant to make sure that if the lady wanted a meal, it would be charged, along with a generous tip, to his room.

Harry took the elevator down to the Thai Chi Restaurant. At a table almost out of sight in the back, he indulged himself in a solitary five-course dinner washed down with a potful of strong, black oolong souchong tea. He didn't bother to invite Aldo to join him. His head was hardly clear, but he wanted time to think.

He was beginning to realize that, in this culture, being a mature white guy who is presumed to have money might be a job in itself. Nairobi would be an education, for sure.

He'd intended to phone Esther after dinner, and he hadn't yet sent a promised text. If he were to call now, he feared he wouldn't sound coherent, and, particularly if she was still vexed, he thought it better to confront her with a clear head.

He wondered if, as a bookkeeper, she knew anything about M&E.

CHAPTER 21

The next morning was a portentous meeting at the pinnacle of Kenyan commerce, in a conference room on the twenty-sixth floor of one of the three Anniversary Towers in downtown Nairobi. The office was a little more than a half-mile from the Stanley.

It was a fine, temperate, sunny morning. Harry proposed they stretch their legs and walk over from the hotel. Aldo agreed after hiring a security guard from the lobby to accompany them. "They don't call Nairobi *Nye-robbery* for nothing," he grumbled.

Evans, the strapping guard who told them he was retired from the Kenyan Rangers, advised them as they set off, "Beware of teenage boys walking in pairs and women who look pregnant and beg."

The conversation effectively dispelled Harry's fine mood. He wondered again why he'd bothered to make the trip. But then, he had no intention of settling in this city.

He still hadn't called to check in with Esther. He resolved to do it later in the day when he could find some time alone.

The morning traffic along the route to the skyscraper was grid-locked with taxis, trucks, motorcycles, and bicycles. Aldo estimated that if they'd taken a cab, they might need an hour to get where they were going.

～

AFTER THEY'D PRESENTED their credentials to a formally courteous, uniformed fellow at reception, a high-speed Otis elevator whisked them silently to the top of the building. When the doors swished open, Harry and Aldo stepped directly into a plush-carpeted meeting room that took up the entire floor. A young woman with Asian features and a pasted smile broad as a grimace greeted them. Her blazer was the same uniform they'd seen in reception. A crest on the breast pocket showed a pair of rampant lions, not quite identical to the country's emblem.

"I'm Melissa Chen," she began as she beckoned them in. "Mr. Singh will be joining you shortly. Meanwhile, may I offer you coffee or tea or bottled water, sparkling or still?"

Their first sight of the room was so impressive they both ignored the question. Directly in front of them was a polished black-marble conference table the length of two cars. The room was surrounded on three sides by floor-to-ceiling tinted glass, with a panoramic view of the city, extending from the windmill farm on the Ngong Hills in the west to the plains of the Athi River in the east.

Even more remarkable than the sumptuous appointments was the collection of artifacts, which gave the space the look of an exhibition rather than a place of business. Against the wall was a human-sized, four-armed statue of the elephant goddess Ganesh, swathed in floral garlands with her trunk auspiciously upraised. On the opposite end of the same wall, near the elevator, a leopard skin with a permanently snarling, stuffed head was hung, flanked by a pair of enormous mounted rhino heads. In front of them stood three figures of inexplicably smiling male humans in safari dress. Beside them stood a pair of elephant tusks, about five-feet tall, curving inward to form an arch on either side of the elevator doors.

On the wall adjacent to the table was mounted a pair of big-bore, vintage Rigby Mauser rifles — elephant guns.

The sight of the wax men was even more disconcerting than the ostentatious decorations. It took a moment to realize they weren't live guests. Melissa was hardly surprised by the astonished look of her visitors and explained, "Gentlemen, you'll be joined in spirit by Teddy Roosevelt, a younger Winston Churchill, and Ernest Hemingway. You will learn, Mr. Singh is a passionate student of history."

Aldo ordered them both bottles of still water, and they took seats at the conference table. After Melissa fetched the water from an ornately carved sideboard, she disappeared down the elevator.

Harry ran his hand over the leather of his chair. "What do you suppose this is? Don't tell me it's elephant hide." He shuddered and exclaimed to Aldo, "This place is so politically incorrect, I don't know where to start! Who is this Singh? Some kind of rich maniac?"

Harry's back was to the elevator, and he hadn't heard the doors open.

"A humble student of history," Bryce Dinesh Singh assured them as he glided over. "As well as, more suitable to your purposes, an attorney expert in corporate law, taxation, international trade, and nongovernmental initiatives."

He took a seat at the head of the table and laid a bound document, a file folder, a writing tablet, and a Montblanc fountain pen in front of him. Harry recognized the logo on the cover and assumed the document was the draft business plan of the Harambee clinic.

Already on the table were yellow pads and disposable ballpoint pens for his clients.

Harry collected his thoughts as he took a couple of greedy gulps from his water bottle. He really wanted to know what kind of person they'd be dealing with and, from the look of the extravagant surroundings, how they were going to afford his fees.

Indicating the furniture, Harry said, "If I'm not mistaken, these chairs are upholstered in elephant hide."

Singh gave a benign smile. He was elegantly dressed in a three-piece, pin-striped, worsted gray suit, dazzling white shirt, and paisley silk tie. "These chairs are from the offices of the British East India Company, early twentieth century. Everything you see is antique, with historical significance. Most of these things would be impossible, many illegal, to buy now."

"Not prohibited to own?" Aldo asked.

Singh's smile became a mischievous grin when he said, "We don't make it a practice to entertain members of law enforcement in our offices. We typically meet them in their humble digs. Or in court."

Harry didn't like this guy. Implicit in the surroundings was a defiance of sensible norms. Arrogance! Gesturing toward the religious statue, he said, "I thought Hindus worshipped elephants. And cows."

"Quite true," Singh admitted. Then he added, "My family has been Anglican for two generations."

Harry became even more uneasy. "I mean, the way this place is decorated, I'd think some of your guests would be offended, insulted even. There's hardly an object in this room that isn't an obvious reminder of the shameful traditions of the colonial era."

"That we respect our forebears and remember their history does not mean that we strive to repeat their mistakes," Singh said. He leaned back, folded his hands on his vest, and observed, "Mr. Gardner, I believe at one time history books were your stock in trade."

"That's right," Harry said cautiously, "among other subjects." It occurred to him Singh had already done background checks on his guests.

"I won't waste your time with small talk, sir," Singh said abruptly. "Your past profession is very much to the point of our business today. You formed a publishing enterprise, did you not?"

"Yes," Harry replied. "LightSpeed Press. Incorporated in California in 1985."

"Excellent," Singh said as he uncapped his pen to make a note. "And is it still in operation? No winding up or plans to do so?"

"Still selling the backlist," Harry answered. "To university libraries mostly."

"Excellent, as I say," Singh pronounced. "Then, I can see a clear way forward."

"What does my business have to do with anything? I understand educational publishing plays well on my CV, but I was told I wouldn't be required to invest anything of my own in the project."

Singh took a reluctant breath. "As I see it, yes, the plan is that your involvement shouldn't cost you anything. You are sure to benefit substantially. But, as you must appreciate, the way things are presented on paper and what exists in the real world may be quite different. In fact, those distinctions are *my* stock in trade, you might say."

Aldo said, "Now I am confused. Victor never said anything about either of us putting money in, and I didn't see anything in the plan about that."

"Quite right," Singh assured him. "It is, at the risk of oversimplifying, a matter of paperwork. There are two considerations here. First, Victor Skebelsky is donating the land and the facilities — or, to be precise, renting it to the clinic for a nominal amount. And, as I'm sure you surmised from your meeting with him, his motivation is to retain title to his property and also to avoid taxes. The draft plan proposes you, Mr. Gardner, as director of the facility and Mr. Barbieri as chief financial officer, responsible in practice for fundraising. Qualified professionals will obviously have to be hired." Singh shot Harry a hard look and said, "No one is thinking of you in the capacity of medical director, for example. You are a qualified business manager. With a track record."

Harry nodded.

"That's what we understood," Aldo agreed.

"But, you see," Singh went on, "for Mr. Skebelsky to make a donation, there must be some existing entity to receive the gift. He can't be seen to be gifting it to himself or even to an entity he owns. And he can't be seen to be your employer. He's not hiring either of you. Or, at least, the venture shouldn't be set up that way."

Aldo naturally wanted to know, "So who's going to pay to get this going?"

Singh stroked his pen thoughtfully. "Oh, the seed money is not the barrier, I think. Whether it comes indirectly from Victor or from colleagues or third parties, we need not concern ourselves with this just now. However, the *second* challenge is that, by law in Kenya, a new service organization such as this cannot be certified until it actually has been in operation. So that means not only property, plant, and equipment brought into compliance, but also fully staffed and with clients in residence." Singh shot a look to each of them in turn and added, "So with site preparation and staffing, it will be at least a year, probably more like two, before Mr. Barbieri will have a licensed institution he can brag about to donors. And advertise to paying clients of affluent families, which you will need to attract to offset the cost of stipends for the others."

"How do we create that out of nothing without funding?" Harry asked.

And Aldo's question was "What about the government?"

"The national and the county governments will be granting tax breaks. No cash. They consider that hugely generous. The clinic isn't their project."

Harry sighed. "Then I don't understand how we can get from here to there."

"These challenges are how I earn my fees," Singh told them. "And that's why I believe your publishing company can be a suitable vehicle. I should emphasize, you won't be giving up ownership or pledging assets to anyone but yourself."

Harry said, "Why am I thinking I won't be liking this much?"

"Hear me out," Singh said. "No matter how we do it, you will both need work permits to stay in Kenya. By far the simplest, quickest, and least expensive way to do this will be for you, Harry, to register LightSpeed as a Kenyan enterprise. Then LightSpeed gives you both employment contracts here. This way, you're not appealing to some local company or charity to hire you. You're not displacing Kenyans in the employment market. In fact, you're showing you're serious about creating jobs."

Harry mused, "You do make it sound like little more than paper-work. But I assume there are fees."

"Yes, of course," the attorney said. "But nominal. No more than you would spend for a retirement visa." Then he added, "There is the requirement for you to prove company assets. The equivalent of a hundred-thousand US."

"Yes," Harry replied. "The consul in Los Angeles told me the same. It's part of the business-registration application. He said if I simply showed I own a house with or without a mortgage in Los Angeles, it would probably be enough."

"But perhaps he didn't tell you the rest of the story," Singh said. "When your application is approved, those funds must be deposited in a Kenyan bank. And to facilitate the approval, at least one Kenyan on your board should have signature authority on the account."

"Ouch!" Harry said. "No, the fellow didn't share that little detail."

"If you don't wish to risk your own funds, there are private investors here who will loan you the money, short-term." Singh chuckled. "And I do mean short. A matter of days, presumably. You see, the government licensing officials verify the deposit, but they don't seem particularly concerned with withdrawals. Theoretically, you can take the money back out as soon as you are notified your application has been approved."

"Sounds too easy," Harry said.

"You're right to be cautious," Singh told him. "The short-term interest rate will be exceptionally high, compounded daily. If you put it in and promptly take it out and repay, the transaction will seem reasonable. But if there is any delay between the application and the approval — and in Kenya bureaucratic delays are to be expected — the charges could become exorbitant. So my advice would be to use your own funds, choose a reputable bank, and be careful whom you trust with the checkbook."

"Okay," Harry said. "That might not be an investment per se, but it's putting a hundred grand at risk!"

"Quite true," Singh agreed. "And there is one other element of strategy you might consider. LightSpeed is a private company, is it not?"

"Yes," Harry told him. "An LLC. When I formed it, my wife, my daughter, and my accountant were on the board. Now, it's me, myself, and I."

"You might consider taking LightSpeed public in the United States. Then form a nonprofit subsidiary. This will enable your domestic donors to make tax-deductible contributions. Presumably, many of Aldo's prospects will be American citizens."

Aldo nodded.

"Then, also," Singh continued, "you might consider transferring some of your personal assets to the new corporate entity. Make it look more viable, pump up the balance sheet. Mr. Gardner, you mention you own your home there. If you stay in Kenya and you decide to sell it, perhaps you set the proceeds aside for your retirement fund. Put the cash in an offshore account, if you wish. This way, you'll be sure to live comfortably no matter how this clinic venture goes. But if you have other assets, such a stock portfolio, perhaps you transfer those to LightSpeed."

"I don't have much of that," Harry admitted. "However, there are shares of a venture my old business partner started. You know, software that was supposed to work magic. They gave me a chunk of their startup equity instead of paying me for several years when I advised them. I even threw in money from time to time when they were struggling so they could meet payroll. The company is still in operation, still privately held, but I doubt those shares are worth much."

"The market value of the stock might not be as important as the fact that your entity has contingent assets from diverse sources. As with the other considerations, these strategic moves shouldn't cost you anything. You'll have legal fees for the incorporation, but you can bundle that with estate planning, which I'd think you should be doing anyway. And you won't be giving anything away — not to Victor, not to Aldo, not to the Kenyan government."

"But who's paying your fees?" Aldo asked. "Victor told me to meet with you, but you're already very far along. You've spent some time thinking about this."

Singh looked amused. "Remember I said that Victor can't be *seen* to be your employer. But he has had our firm on retainer since my father started it. Neither of you will ever see a bill from us."

Yes, it sounded like free lunch. But for the first time since he'd read the proposal, Harry was intrigued. Victor Skebelsky must have his own good reasons for making this happen, and he knew he couldn't do it alone. It wasn't so much a question of whether Harry was qualified, but whether he was willing.

CHAPTER 22

When they returned to the hotel after their meeting with Singh, Harry sent a message to Esther, but they didn't connect. (Back then, Safaricom didn't provide voicemail.) He wanted to tell her what they'd learned and get her reactions, but he hadn't yet sorted out whether they were destined to be business partners or lovers or both. He didn't feel as though he owed her an apology, but he knew she didn't think she was in the wrong. And she'd be too proud to call him, even if she did.

While Aldo conferred with persons unknown via phone, Harry went back to the room for his second refreshing shower of the day, as if a purifying cleanse was necessary after being in a room with all that murdered wildlife.

Harry lunched with Aldo where they'd had breakfast at the Thorn Tree Café. As Harry joined his friend at the table, Aldo pointed to the tree and quipped, "You see the notes pinned to the tree? The story is, in the colonial period, travelers left mail there for each other. These days, they are saying people still use it, but it may just be the hotel staff preserving the curiosity for tourists."

"Aldo, you're just full of tourist trivia. No doubt our future donors will open their fat wallets or part their legs as you regale them with such fascinating lore." Then, gesturing to the waitress, he added, "I need a drink. A bloody stiff one." And to her, "Double Jack Daniels with a splash of soda. On the rocks — er, with a *handful* of ice."

"So, what do you think of Singh?" Aldo asked, quaffing from a glass of Valpolicella that had been poured from a full bottle on the table.

"Does the guy sincerely want to be British, or is he just mocking the colonialists he's cheerfully fleecing?"

"Could be he thinks he's a Yank," Aldo chuckled. "I heard he went to Dartmouth, then Yale Law, then Wharton."

"Yikes," Harry said. "They'll be making him an ambassador, and he'll be in Washington scolding us for shrinking back from the Russians and the Chinese!"

"Seriously," Aldo began. "What do you think of the plan?"

"Who doesn't love mountains of free lunch?" Harry harumphed and gulped the brown liquor. "Except somehow I'll be the guy signing the checks. But it won't cost me anything. Alternative math, is it?"

"The signers will be you and Odiengo or some other Kenyan they put on our board," Aldo said. "As I understand it, your deposit will be there for the sake of the business application, but I don't see why operating funds couldn't be in a separate account. They've said all along they don't expect you to spend your own money on the project."

"In theory, no one touches what's mine," Harry said. "But it's what they call an exposure. The guy could drain the account, run off, and we'd spend five years in rigged courts pleading that we didn't blow the money ourselves and then chase him away."

"So I guess it had better be Esther," Aldo said softly. And he wasn't kidding.

Harry took a moment to take this in. "It wasn't in the plan to make her an officer. Is this a new thought?"

"I confess I didn't think carefully about the requirement for the board member until today. But, we have to ask, who's a citizen we can trust? Not Skebelsky."

"But wouldn't he insist? Could he be anonymous and still have a bank card?"

"I told you this morning, Harry. Get it through your head, you're the director. And now, based on what Singh is saying, it will be your company. You are giving Victor what he wants — what he desperately *needs,* so he says. Who else that he knows can bring him such a handy solution? And if you believe this Indian about keeping it all separate, you have every right to tell Skebelsky to stay out. And soon we'll be raising our own money. Do we pay him back? Perhaps, perhaps not. Doesn't our help have a price? Okay, he pulls strings, we listen. He gives advice, sure, but I don't think he signs checks. If we find out he demands control, we walk away." Aldo added, and it seemed in all sincerity, "Harry, you get to decide. I've always thought this was a good deal."

"Let me hear you say exactly why," Harry said.

"From my viewpoint, it's simple. I make a generous commission on what I expect to be very big donations. As for you, you get to plug a new, worthwhile purpose into your life. But — let's be practical only: You have a way of living like a rich man, on a grand estate, with Esther at your side. Not to mention the thankful blessings of the good citizens of Kwale County. You'll be a prominent citizen, admired and respected. And deservedly so!"

Let the record show Harry didn't actually say yes. He finished his drink and beckoned for another. Then he asked, "So, Mr. Tour Guide, what's next? Do we spend the next week filling out forms?"

Aldo gave Harry the look of a parent bestowing a child's first bicycle. "Mind your drinking and get your nap this afternoon. Tonight, we go to a party!"

CHAPTER 23

*M*ore than fifty guests milled about the grassy courtyard of Matbronze Gallery. It was just after sunset, and the outdoor dining area had been strung with festive lights. Harry could see that the partygoers included many more whites than blacks, most if not all of them middle-aged or older, all in cocktail dress, except for a few silver-haired white males who dared to wear their leisure suits with running shoes. All of the black men were in sharply tailored business suits. The women wore colorful print dresses or evening gowns, most with deliberately gaudy African craft jewelry.

Wait staff hustled among them carrying trays of drinks and canapes. The help were noticeably younger men and women, perhaps college students with part-time jobs, in monogrammed red golf shirts and black slacks.

The occasion was a fundraiser for the Elephant March, which was all Aldo had told Harry about the purpose of the evening. Harry didn't have trouble guessing why Aldo would want to network with local philanthropists, but he was amused to think that elephants should do a fine job of marching on their own without human sponsorship. He promised himself to keep an open mind.

Matbronze is set in the lush forest of Karen, a bedroom community on the north edge of Nairobi. The suburb is named for Karen Blixen, whose coffee plantation covered the area in colonial times. The commercial gallery sells fine art, featuring bronze wildlife sculpture and hardwood carvings, as well as paintings and graphics. The shadowed, looming figure of an elephant — three times normal size — on the footpath approach from the car park would be fearsome in the dark were it not for its obviously unreal electrified eyes, which glow in a garish sequence of iridescent colors.

"You wouldn't know you were in the big city," Aldo commented to Harry as he sipped his gin. "The expats and the diplomats live around here. Also, fat politicians. Five-bedroom homes with swimming pools in gated compounds. New shopping centers with designer stores. Several private schools and universities are here, as well. A person could do a lot worse."

Aldo had on one of his Italian silk suits, accented with a paisley pocket-handkerchief to match his tie. Harry wore his sport coat with dark slacks and an open-neck white shirt. He wished he'd brought better shoes. He felt underdressed.

"You sound awfully interested," Harry observed. "Like you're some real-estate rep and now you're going to pitch me some property."

Aldo grinned broadly, "Harambee, you're getting wise to all my tricks! Yes, I've been thinking if we're going to be in town any length of time, we'll need a base of operations. You might not have noticed as we came in on the highway that we passed Wilson Airport. It's ten minutes by car from this spot. That's the regional hub, handling everything from bush planes to small jets. If you want to fly anywhere in-country, you can get cheap flights from there. You could fly from Wilson to Ukunda and commute to Diani, for example. A direct flight is an hour and a half in a Cessna, a hundred bucks."

"You're not proposing I buy one of those huge houses, I hope."

"No, but the hotel is getting dear, and we should be able to rent a guest house. We'll have a houseman and a cook. We'll keep Joseph on as our driver. We might have to venture downtown occasionally for meetings, but it's only about an hour each way if we avoid rush hours."

"What about that pitch about my not having to invest any money?"

"Harry, no matter what you choose to do in Kenya, if you're going to stay here, you will have living expenses. Now, since we're actively pursuing this venture, perhaps some or all of those expenses will be write-offs for you. When the project is funded, you might even be able to pay yourself back. Think of it this way — if we're tourists, all we can do is spend your money. But if we're businessmen, someone someday will pay our way!"

Harry surveyed the crowd. They were gathered in clusters as they held their drinks and gossiped among their friends and neighbors. He guessed the people in the huddles were no strangers to one another. "So, are these your high-net-worth donors? Are they why you want to move out here?"

Aldo took another refreshing gulp to drain his glass. After Harry's overindulgence the last two days, he was nursing a Tusker. Aldo grinned and said, "It's my job, after all!" And he toddled off to the bar for a refill.

Harry wasn't inclined to mingle. If Aldo knew any of these people, he wasn't making introductions. So Harry decided to wander into the gallery to have a look around.

The main exhibition room was about four times the size of a residential living room, with a high roof. Richly upholstered easy chairs were placed alongside pedestals that held sculptures of every size, from miniatures of elephants and rhinos to full-size big cats, even a crocodile. The walls were hung with original paintings, numbered prints and drawings, and photography.

It was all impressive stuff, attractively and dramatically lit, with wildlife themes. No matter which artist, the animals were depicted as elegant and noble. Predation, carnage, and victimization were not among the themes.

A small, engraved plaque stood alongside each piece. The prices would have been upmarket even in Palm Springs.

Harry was drawn to a spot-lit nook with a display that seemed out of place, looking more like housewares laid out in a department store. As he drew close, he realized these were open steamer trunks tricked out as picnic kits — replicas of the lavish sundowner gear of yesteryear — including place settings with plates and saucers, flasks, cups, and goblets in either stainless steel or Sterling silver. He wondered whether these were curios one might display in a home or practical items to be stored at the ready in the back of an aristo couple's Land Rover. Considering the prices, these might be collectibles after all.

He'd been alone in the gallery. As he stepped out onto a veranda, he saw more sculptures lined up along the outer wall. He was arrested by the sight of a bronze cobra, raised up ready to strike, its hood flared, with its head balanced almost four feet above the ground.

As he marveled at the creature, a voice came up behind him. "I don't know about you, but it's not something I'd want in my house," he heard Veronica say.

He turned to see her decked out in a decidedly unbusinesslike miniskirt with sheer hose, designer pumps, and blouse with a scoop neckline that bared a showy amount of cleavage. She was dressed like a young cougar on the prowl, and he was surprised how well she brought it off. Her blonde hair was done up in a fashionable twist, and her application of makeup for after-dark was not at all understated, including bright-red, wet-look lip gloss.

"You could put it on your porch to scare away the monkeys," Harry said, trying not to act surprised to see her. "It's a trick I learned from Victor Skebelksy."

"Ah, Harry," she cooed. "You're catching on."

He didn't recognize the perfume. He'd gotten used to Esther's patchouli. This one would have competed. It was both floral and musky, and he figured it was something expensive.

A wave of desire swept over him. His lust swelled at the memory of her hand on his leg. His usual reluctance dissolved when he realized the only objections to be overcome now would be his own.

CHAPTER 24

*H*arry awoke in an enormous bed. He didn't realize there was a size larger than a king. He was naked, swathed in silk sheets, and Veronica's perfume still hung in the air. But she was no longer on her side of the bed.

His clothes were folded neatly on the chair of her dressing table. The sun shone brightly through the French doors of the bedroom, so he figured it was midmorning already. He'd slept solidly. The doors opened to a balcony, beyond that a manicured garden bordered by a tall hedgerow. If there were other houses nearby, they were tucked away and hidden in the lush foliage.

He heard the clatter of pantry sounds coming from downstairs. Her voice called up, "Are you awake, luv? Harry!"

"Yeah, wow," he called back. "I guess it's late."

"Coffee or tea with your breakfast, dear?"

"Uh, coffee," he grunted as he sat up and donned a plush bathrobe that she'd set on the edge of the bed for him. There was also a pair of men's slippers on the carpet, but they were too small for him.

He intended to shower and then dress, when she emerged from a stairwell carrying a steaming tray. She was wearing a dressing gown with fuzzy slippers, and her hair was tied up in back with a simple scarf. The party face and the makeup she'd worn the previous evening had been scrubbed off, leaving porcelain skin with a slight blush, elegant and even aristocratic in its plainness.

"I intend to spoil you," she said as she set the tray down on a café table. "Come, sit." And she laughed, adding, "We need to keep the boy's strength up, after all!"

She arranged loaded plates and cups and coffee pot on the table, set the tray aside, sat, and beckoned to him to join her.

As he sat, he muttered sheepishly, "I wasn't so drunk that I don't remember what we did. What you did."

The plates were Haviland. The silver was vintage Elkington. The linen napkins were embroidered with her initials.

"Don't give me all the credit," she said as she poured his coffee from a Stieff carafe. "You were very much involved, as I recall."

She'd been both generous and meticulous, practiced and yet tender. He wasn't making a conquest. He was being entertained.

"Some say married men are boring," she said as she sipped. "But faithfulness is admirable. Steady on. Yes, bad boys are more exciting, but they're mostly arseholes, and they make the most annoying companions after the shine wears off."

Harry gulped his coffee black and said, "I believe I told you. My wife has been gone two years now. You know, passed on."

"Yes," she said. "I do remember. But what I'm trying to say is, I can tell you're not an adventurer. You were lovely, don't get me wrong, but a woman can tell when a man has a set way of doing things."

She'd made him wear a condom, and he hadn't objected. She had a supply of them in the drawer of the bedside table. There was a new pack of six, and they'd used two. She had a lovely way of getting him aroused, and then she did the putting on in a languid ceremony.

"I guess I'm kind of an average guy in that department," he said.

She giggled. "No, my dear. I'm trying to tell you how exceptional you are!"

"Do I say thanks? I mean, yes, thanks. You've been very kind. A nice surprise. Maybe that just sounds lame. But you're not at all the prim businesswoman I thought you were. You're kind of exceptional yourself. I can truly say I've never known anyone like you."

"I believe I know what you're trying to say. You have a good heart, and whatever might transpire between us, you would make a good friend." She encouraged him to eat. "You must have an appetite." And she giggled again.

"A full English breakfast. Oh, my." And he tucked in.

"Does it taste all right?"

"Of course! Wonderful! So nice of you to go to the trouble."

"Everything on your plate is vegan. Soy scrambled eggs, sausage patties made with pea protein, cashew cheese, and baked beans without a hint of lard. If you start eating this way, your cholesterol count will drop, and so will your blood pressure."

He took another bite of the sausage and savored it. "It's a bit less greasy, but the texture and the spices are exactly the same as good, old-fashioned pork. No piggies killed, and maybe Harry slims down!"

"It's difficult to find vegan food in Kenya," she said. "They're all such meat-eaters here. But it's catching on, and all over the world. Healthy and sustainable. They're mad for it in Europe these days."

"Do you get back often?"

She sighed. "I don't have much reason to go anymore. My parents are gone. They built this estate back in the fifties. Daddy was an importer. I had a sister, also gone. She and her husband were missionaries, and they both succumbed to dengue fever in Nigeria a few years ago. Their son lives in London, and we don't speak. He's taken up with a gang of white supremacists. They seem to hate Jews and Muslims equally. And he thinks I'm wasting my time on Africans. Fortunately for my professional reputation, we don't share the same surname, or I couldn't show my face anywhere, especially here." Then she asked, "What about you? Family back home? Anyone over here you fancy?"

"I have a daughter, and we don't communicate well. Nothing like the problem with your nephew, but I'm sure she thinks I'm wasting time and money over here. And she has trouble with relationships, but I know better than to try to give her advice."

"So, except for Aldo, you're all alone?"

Harry took a moment, then said, "Aldo pitched this trip as adult misbehavior, and I went along. But the working girls and the amateur fortune hunters, they scare me. So I've avoided them. I have made the friendship of a Kenyan woman, a widow with two teenage children. She's a bookkeeper in Diani, supports two sisters and an elderly mother. I wouldn't say it's a romantic relationship, but then again, I wouldn't say it isn't. Maybe we just don't know what it is quite yet. She and Aldo have done business for years, they say. She helps him put together his tour packages. And she's been mentioned as key personnel for this clinic project that Victor Skebelsky is sponsoring."

"I suppose she's pretty. You seem quite taken with her."

"Veronica, forgive me if I'm being too frank, if not just rude. Considering. You are so lovely and so incredibly kind. And here I am going on about Esther. I really don't know where any of this is going, and it's probably my fault that I seem to be just letting things happen to me. I should know what I want, be more decisive."

"No," she said cautiously, "you've jumped onto a new timeline. That's the thrill of traveling, the adventure of discovery — new places, new people, new roles, new sense of self. I admit I'm jealous — oh, not necessarily of this Esther of yours — but of this opportunity for you. Neither of us is young, but here you are starting out like some kid just out of school! It should be thrilling, and it sounds as if you're open to all of it."

"So far, I haven't learned how to say no, if that's what you mean."

She shrugged. "Be open, and be watchful, that's all." Her face became serious, and she added, "But I must tell you something."

Not expecting her answers to be true, he teased, "You're married? You're the kept woman of some powerful politician?"

"Not at all," she said. "Aldo told me you'd be at the party. I intended to seek you out. I had *not* intended to bring you home. But I had planned to take you aside. There are some things you should know."

"About you? About Aldo?"

"No, about Skebelksy. I hadn't heard of him until Aldo told me of your project. But I did some research. Proprietary databases and some backchannels. One of my duties is to conduct background checks, including financial and criminal investigations, for our personnel department. Skebelsky has been a player in this country for a very long time."

"Yes," Harry said, "he said as much. He said he used to supply concrete for government civil engineering projects. Back before Independence. I guess it was a game of good old boys. Colonial capitalism."

"He's still in that business. Or, that's *one* of his. Only now it's the Chinese who have the construction contracts, and his firm is a major supplier. For the concrete mix, they dredge sand from the beach. From the *public* beach. Oh, it's a stretch where there isn't any tourism these days, and it's strewn with trash, but it's not private land. It's controlled by one of the political families. They don't own the sand, but they control the access and the use, so perhaps it amounts to the same thing. Even without the dredging, beach erosion is a problem, so that's a sin of the first rank. Some environmental and citizens' groups have complained, but no one with influence is listening."

"So when Victor pays for the sand, I'm guessing that money doesn't go into the public trust."

"Of course not. But then also, there's an even greater sin. The Chinese use the concrete to build public works — highways, bridges, parking structures, whatever. And these are government projects funded by public money. They're building the new Kenya! But the dirty secret is that the beach sand itself is dirty — it's saturated with sea salt. Some salt in the concrete mix is all right, makes the stuff dry quicker. But this amount contaminates the material so much that it doesn't bond properly as it sets. So whatever you build with it will begin to crumble eventually. By the time the structure fails, perhaps the cause and the culprits won't be obvious. But the repairs will require another government contract and more concrete — from, who else, your ever-ready supplier, Victor!"

Harry had eaten hungrily as he listened to her description. He had to admit, if most vegan food was this good, maybe he should consider being more careful with his diet.

"So, are you warning me off Skebelsky? Off the project?"

"No," she said, leaning forward intently and, once again, taking his hand in that intimate way. "Not at all. Keep an open mind. Be watchful. I'm sure you don't intend for this clinic of yours to be a medical facility. There's too much oversight. The licensing and the standards would be much too demanding. But you could do a halfway house, a behavioral counseling center. You'll need trained social workers, but you won't be administering drugs or practicing psychiatry. There's a need for this, I'm sure of it. It's the kind of help for people who've fallen betwixt and between. They are too dysfunctional for school, not sick enough for the hospital or prison. These are neglected people, many of them young. Not necessarily the ones who tried and failed, but those who don't even yet know how to try! There's no place in the government budgets for them, I can tell you."

"But if Victor is crooked, won't it all be a mistake?"

"Victor is corrupt, and so is the system. If you can use his money to do something good, something worthwhile, something no one else will bother to do, who will stand in your way?"

"You're a pragmatist!" he exclaimed and meant it as a compliment.

"As that cynical Frenchman Albert Camus said, sometimes you have to get your hands dirty."

"I believe the translation is more like, you have to thrust your hands into the *merde.*"

"Just so," she laughed. Then she asked, "Esther, the bookkeeper. Is she a sincere person?"

"She seems responsible. Genuine. Mostly, she wants a better job, and we can probably give it to her."

"Does she have a Kenyan boyfriend?"

"No mention, no evidence. Not that I've inquired."

"Bookkeepers tend to be no-nonsense people. Honest even, up to a point. But you should watch your back with her, too."

"I suppose I'm not going to like this."

"The old story in Kenya, particularly in the tourist spots, is the old white gentleman takes a local girlfriend, one thing leads to another, and sooner or later they're married and build a grand house. He may be retired, or he may have a stake in a business. Either way, he's prosperous. He becomes an active member of the community. They like him all the more because the woman is one of them. Then, one way or another, natural causes or accident, he dies. The wife gets it all, and in a very short time, the boyfriend who's been waiting in the background all along moves right in. And if the mzungu has heirs from his previous wives, they promptly contest the estate. The battle may drag on for years, but the Kenyan courts will favor the new wife. You can bet on it, especially if she's had any children by him."

"Wait, are you saying if he doesn't die before she loses her patience, she may have him killed?"

"Harry, you won't read about it in the newspapers, but I've heard this kind of gossip more than once. And in a country where the press is intimidated if not totally controlled, gossip *is* the news."

CHAPTER 25

$\mathcal{H}$arry met up with Aldo back in their suite at the hotel. The Italian was packing his bags for his flight to Rome. Aldo teased Harry about going home with Veronica, and he shot back, "You know, I've been paranoid about your motives all along. But now I'm thinking maybe you're just a professional matchmaker. Did you set me up for a second time?"

"Of course I set you up with this Lindbrook lady! But it was to get her advice, penetrate her network. The other kind of penetration was not in the plan. I hope, for our sake, you did okay!"

Harry shrugged. "It's like she's two people. This prim lawyer in the daylight and a lioness by night. She didn't seem to mind that I couldn't keep up with her. She knows about Esther, and, at the very least, she's now a friend. I like her, and I'd even go so far as to say I think I trust her."

"Have you spoken with Esther?"

"No," Harry said. "One of us owes the other an apology, and I'm not sure which. Besides, there's such a thing as too much information, plus I don't want to get into the habit of checking in every day. If you're worried I'll take off with Veronica, don't. She wants a consulting contract. I don't think she's shopping for a relationship. At least, not with me."

"They say she knows everybody, and as you can tell from last night, the rich expats and settlers in Nairobi are a very small club. She's smart enough not to head up any of the charities, but she'll be at all the parties."

"Inherited wealth. You should see her place. I'm sure she doesn't need a job." Then he added, "She ran a background check on Victor. He's a bigger crook than we thought. Or, than I thought."

"Isn't it the same the world over? Behind every great fortune, there is a great crime? What does she say he's done?"

"Contaminated concrete supplied to government civil engineering contractors. Mixed from salt-saturated sand stolen from public beaches. The usual gang of thieves getting payoffs all around."

"So, is she warning us off of him? Telling us not to go near?"

"Nope. She applauds us for trying to turn his dirty money to righteous purposes."

"*Trying?* Is that how she put it?"

"I didn't pursue it with her, but I suspect she thinks there's a strong chance we won't succeed. Or worse, get so caught up in the corruption we'll lose our way."

"If this scam does go back all the way to when Victor was in business with Samuel, you might ask Esther what she knows about it."

"Did you know Samuel?" was Harry's question.

"I met him a couple of times, years ago, when he was still talking to Esther and visited her. He's a crusty fellow, like Victor. The two of them together must have been a horror to anyone who crossed them."

Aldo was ready to leave. He was taking just one bag, and he didn't call a porter to carry it down. "Harambee, you know I'm in it for the money. I don't think anything we're planning to do is illegal. You, you'll have to decide not just whether you'll go through with this, but also what's in it for you. I suppose you don't know yet."

They shook hands warmly. It was Aldo who reached out first. Then he added, "You will be getting a call from a real-estate lady in the morning. Pauline Ochieng. She has some houses to show you in Karen. Joseph will be at your service. I have an early flight to Rome."

Harry had a dip in the pool at the Stanley, two drinks at the bar, and returned to the room for a nap that lasted almost through the night. He was wide-eyed at two in the morning, beset by wee-hour anxieties, fearing that this Kenyan adventure was a huge mistake.

CHAPTER 26

The knock on Harry's hotel room door was insistent. Three sharp raps in quick succession.

Assuming it was an impatient housekeeper, Harry called back groggily from the bed, "Come back later?"

Esther's angry voice shot back, "Harambee, if you don't open the door *this instant*, there won't *be* any *later!*"

That got his eyes open. Clad only in his shorts, he shuffled over to the door and opened it.

She was standing there in a jumpsuit with a colorful neck scarf and holding an overnight bag. There were beads of sweat on her forehead.

"Just what was in your fool head?" she demanded.

Harry fumfered, "I guess Aldo must've —"

Shoving past him, she took one bold step in and turned back.

She asked breathlessly, "So, have you showered since you went home with that albino prune?"

He didn't know whether to be shocked or amused. "Hmm, am I still beating my wife? Yes, I have showered recently would be an answer to part of your question." Then, walking toward the bathroom, he said over his shoulder, "I'm sorry, but I didn't know you cared. I mean, *this much.*"

She dropped her bag, lunged at him, grabbed him by the shoulders, turned him around, put both palms on his chest, shoved him hard until he fell on his back onto the bed, jumped on him, and shut him up with a pressured kiss.

An hour later, the only thing lacking in their love life was breakfast.

~

HARRY OFFERED to have breakfast sent up, with champagne. But as she checked her phone, she told him, "You'll have your coffee soon enough. There's just time to meet Charles and Yvonne before school."

So, he surmised with pleasure and relief, she must be intending to draw him closer, in more ways than just intimacy.

They dressed quickly, and Harry was impressed to find Joseph waiting for them in the rented van at the curb. Aldo must've offered the fellow's services to her already. So, without asking, Harry figured Aldo already knew she was in town, further evidence that the Italian had alerted her to Harry's dalliance with Veronica.

He didn't ask Esther about Aldo, not just yet. He felt closer to her, even though his head was still spinning from the suddenness of her rush of emotion, but he still wasn't entirely sure he trusted her. He certainly wanted to.

And she hadn't asked him about Veronica. Not yet.

Joseph drove them to Hillcrest School in Karen. Harry gratefully got his brace-up coffee black from the driver's thermos before they even got to the superhighway.

"Hillcrest!" Joseph exclaimed gleefully. "They must be fine students. Expensive place!"

"They're both on scholarship," Esther was quick to add.

"Do they know we're coming?" Harry asked her.

"I shot them a text this morning," she said. "I've told them I plan to be changing jobs, coming to work for you. I haven't said you and I are anything more. Not that I'd hide it, but perhaps now is not the time."

Harry grinned, "True enough, as of yesterday. Today's another story. Maybe I don't need to say it, but I'm glad you decided to make the trip."

"I was hoping you'd feel that way," she smiled back. Then she muttered, "And I hope you will feel the same later."

What did *that* mean? He chose not to ask. Why ruin the sunny, morning-after mood? Later, whenever that would be, he might understand, and then he could decide whether to be upset.

It was rush hour, but they were headed out of downtown, against traffic, and the trip to Karen took just twenty minutes. Along the north side of the route for about a mile stretched the rooftops of Kibera, the world's largest slum, which Joseph in his role as tour guide felt obliged to identify, along with the fact that it houses some half-million souls, many of whom work in the kitchens and laundries of the posh hotels. To the south, he indicated Wilson Airport, as if to remind Harry this would be his point of embarkation for future routine flights to Diani.

Harry couldn't help asking Esther, "If this school is so upscale, how come you had to search for textbooks in Mombasa?"

The incident remained a sore point, the wound minor in the scheme of things, and he a willing participant, but it had festered, despite her explanations.

"How come you had to go home with Veronica?" she shot back.

He didn't answer right away, then he admitted, "You deserve an answer, but I don't know what to say. I wasn't so sure about you, she was sure she wanted a thing with me, but it turns out we won't be a thing. She didn't want more than an amusement, and I probably disappointed her."

Esther's brow furrowed as she feigned shock. "Disappointed! How?"

"She hinted I was too conventional, set in my ways, and not nearly inventive enough."

"Oh, my," Esther mocked. "My dear, there's nothing at all wrong with conventional as long as it's diligent and persistent!"

"Perhaps I wasn't inspired enough. With her."

"I should hope not! Granted, I was tired when I arrived, but you wore me out, Papa."

"Glad to oblige. But I believe, as long as we're being honest, there's still an open question on the floor."

She looked only slightly annoyed. "The kids are a year apart. Charles is in Hillcrest Secondary, and Yvonne goes to Hillcrest Prep. He needs physics, and she needs biology. The science books sell out quickly in Nairobi. Those are updated with new editions almost every year, so the used copies are not quite good enough. And they cost a lot, whether new or used. When there's a new one, they sell out quickly in Nairobi. There are academic-track schools in Mombasa, as well, particularly in Nyali, but the demand for the books is not so great." She sniffed. "I was taking a chance I'd find them there."

"Okay, okay," Harry said. "Sorry."

"You are the man for the job," she quipped. "Inquiring minds need to know."

They pulled up to the school gate. After a vehicle inspection by two askaris, they were waved through. Esther saw her children standing dutifully, dressed in their uniform blazers and holding their knapsacks, on the verge of the car park. Joseph pulled up at the curb. She jumped out, hugged them both to her at the same time as she bestowed motherly kisses, and beckoned for them to climb with her back inside the van.

Both children seemed less enthusiastic than she was, presumably because they didn't want to be coddled in full view of their friends. But they didn't act like rebellious teens, didn't grimace or push back.

Charles got in front next to Joseph, and Yvonne sat on a rear bench seat next to Esther and facing Harry.

As he first caught sight of them and Esther was getting out of the car, for a moment Harry thought these were two other students, perhaps comrades of her kids she'd recognized. Charles' skin color was more white than black, what in America used to be called *yellow* in the black community. His short-cropped curly hair was blond, as were his eyebrows. He was tall and lanky. Yvonne's skin was nut-brown but noticeably lighter than her mother's, and her hair was raven-black and straight. Her features looked more Indian than tribal Kenyan. He judged she was almost as pretty as her mother, and it amused him to think they'd quibble over *almost*.

As they settled, Esther announced, "Kids, this is Harry Gardner, the man I've told you so much about. Harry, you finally get to meet Charles and Yvonne."

"Pleased to know you, sir," Charles said with deliberate courtesy.

"Yeah, you're American?" Yvonne asked him.

"Yes, from LA," Harry said and laughed. "Hollywood-adjacent, you might say. It's my first time in Kenya, in Africa really, and your mother has been helping me understand things."

"Do you know any stars?" Yvonne asked. Her tone might have been sarcastic, but her sweet demeanor, betrayed by a wink of her dimples, made it seem more like polite teasing.

"Vonnie!" Charles rebuked her, and she giggled. Then he asked earnestly, "Do you know anyone at Jet Propulsion Labs?"

Harry answered, "I know some members of the Santa Monica City Council. That's about it when it comes to anyone you could call a celebrity. Sorry."

"I'm going to apply to Caltech," Charles announced.

"In your dreams," Yvonne muttered. "Like I'm going to Juilliard?"

To Harry, Esther explained quickly, "They have only minutes before class, so we're lucky we caught them." And to them, "You are both looking so well. I promise not to worry so much, but you know I do. Harry here is the generous fellow who offered to sponsor your science textbooks, and I'm sorry to say I haven't been successful finding them."

"Oh, we'll manage," Charles said. "That course is a gut, believe it or not. It's all algebra. They don't use calculus in any of the models because they know just about everybody would flunk." And Yvonne added, "It's very okay, Mom. Really. Charles would teach the class if they let him! And biology is a snore. The teacher has us memorizing names of body parts. I bet he was a med-school dropout."

Esther dug into her purse for two envelopes and handed one to each child. "Some money for expenses until I get to see you again. I'm sorry it has to be so brief. But, traffic, you know. I'm just in for the day, and we have appointments."

"Sure," they said simultaneously as they grabbed their cash and jumped out, calling, "Bye, sir! Bye!"

Harry took a breath and shot a look, eyebrows raised, to Esther.

She shrugged. "You could've asked me for their pictures. You didn't. In fact, I would say you showed no interest at all."

"I didn't think it was any of my business," Harry said. "Until now."

He waited for her to speak, but she raised a finger to her lips and asked the driver, "Joseph, perhaps you'd like to take a minute, step out, and have a smoke?"

"I'm trying to quit, Mum, as I believe you have encouraged. But I don't mind a breath of air." And he got out.

When the door was closed, Esther told Harry, "I've known Joseph for years, and I have no secrets from him, but I'm sure we need a moment."

Harry realized she wouldn't be surprised by anything he had to say. But he began carefully, "They're attractive, apparently well-behaved, and, to hear them tell it, excellent students." Then he added, "I expect you're going to tell me next that they're not the policeman's children."

"That's right. He was Luo. Almost as dark as me."

There was a reason she'd arranged this meeting, and it wasn't just because her being in town was a chance to check in with her kids. She hadn't prepared Harry, and she'd wanted to judge his reaction. He wanted to keep thinking of her as a sincere and honest person, even though he still wanted to know more about what had been going on between her and Aldo. But here she was, dropping her mask, risking that he cared enough about her to forgive her for any indiscretions, past or present. He still had his doubts about her, but he knew whatever transpired between them in the next few minutes would color all of his decisions going forward, and, so, hers.

He decided he might as well come right out with it: "And now you're going to tell me their father is Victor Skebelsky."

She smiled demurely, "I'm impressed, Harry. You jumped to the right conclusion more quickly than I expected. If you want to say I was keeping it from you, I admit I was. Very few people know, and I want to keep it that way. Aldo knows, of course. That's another thing I haven't been completely forthcoming about. He and I were together for a time, you see, after Victor and before Malcolm. He's been my best and closest friend. We've always looked out for each other." She stopped talking to study Harry's reaction.

Harry returned her frank stare. He was more curious than upset.

She continued, "If you feel I've betrayed you, you're right, of course. And now that you know, you may wish to have no more to do with me. Perhaps no more to do with the deal. I wouldn't blame you. But I hope you don't blame Aldo. He wants everyone to do well. It's in his nature. Oh, it may seem he hustles his clients, but everyone gets good value. In your case, he wanted more for you. He still does."

"I wondered about you and Aldo, but I admit I accepted the business relationship story."

"All true," she said. "Every word of it. But what I want to know is, what made you guess my mzungu husband was Victor?"

"My suspicions didn't have anything to do with you. Or that you mentioned you've been married twice. I didn't think it mattered, then I simply forgot. Like I neglected to ask about old boyfriends or to see photos of the children, I suppose. I assumed the answers didn't affect me. But what did nag at me — for more selfish reasons — was Victor's purpose for doing this deal. There have to be easier ways for him to meet his tax bills. And he's too old and too sick to see such a grand scheme play out. He's behaving like a brahmin who's worried about his legacy — like a British lord of the manor who needs to keep his estate intact. For his heirs."

"The kids know who he is. But we were a second family for him. He had another wife in Germany. They were childless. Then she died. Her family was well-off. I expect he got her money, which, of course, he hardly needed. I left him when the kids were three and four. He gave me some, not considerable, but I didn't expect anything more. He'd been abusive, especially when he drank, and I just wanted it to end. And, yes, it was Aldo who helped me through all that. He and I were together for a year, but he was always coming and going like he does now, and we decided it wouldn't work. He has some other responsibilities he may tell you about. After Aldo, I settled down with Malcolm, and he is the only father Charles and Yvonne remember. In many ways, he was a dear man. Foolish, but dear."

"You loved him."

"Yes," she said simply.

"And what about Victor all this time?"

"He traveled more than Aldo did, and that was a lot. Back and forth to Europe. To other women, maybe. I never knew. He didn't dote on the kids, but for the past few years, he wants to see them at Christmas and on their birthdays." She shook her head. "He's nice enough now. He forces himself to be sober and seem kind. They don't know what to make of him."

"And how does he treat *you* now?"

"Like some secretary he fired years ago."

"And you have no feelings for him?"

"Are you kidding? It used to be red-hot hatred. What about you? Will you be seeing more of the proper British lady?"

"I told you, what she wanted she got. Or as much as I could give. In that department, we're done. But she wants to consult on the project. I believe that's why she approached us in the first place."

"Hmm," she mused. "I'll be keeping an eye on her! As for Victor, now that I see what he's trying to do, it's like I have some piece of valuable property he wants. I don't intend to cheat him because, one, I don't think I'm slick enough to do that, and two, I still value my opinion of myself. The kids use Malcolm's last name, Mwemba, as I do. I'm wondering whether, after this deal is done, he'll want them to be Skebelskys. I don't know how they'd feel about that. As for me, if it came with a trust fund, I'd shut up and tell them to get on with life." Then she asked, "How about you? Is it too soon to ask? Do you want to tell Joseph to turn around and take you back to the hotel? I can get a matatu. You don't owe me anything."

Here was her ask. She made it sound offhand, but they both knew that the person who spoke next would be giving power to the other.

"This is a lot to take in, of course," Harry replied carefully. "About you and me, we have something together, and I want to hold on to that if we can. About what you're calling the deal, I still don't know. It keeps getting more complicated. Are you still saying this was Victor's scheme and you've only recently learned of it?"

"Yes," she said. "I had no idea. I thought we were all done with him. I thought we might see him as a family a few more times, and then he'd be dead and buried. No tears."

"And Aldo? I can't say I'm surprised to find out you two have a history, but what about now? He obviously told you about my hookup with Veronica, and since he set you up with Joseph today, does he know what you intended to do, where we are now, what you've told me?"

"Yes to all of it," she said frankly.

Harry told her, "Our plan as of late yesterday was to go to Langata Link this morning to meet a real-estate agent about renting a house in Karen."

"Yes," she said. "He expects Joseph to take us there now. It's just minutes away."

"So, have you known more about our plans than I do?"

She hesitated, then said, "Not from Aldo. All I can say is, he always is who he seems to be."

"From time to time, he sneaks away. He says he has other business. I worry about what else he might be doing."

She smiled meekly, "I know him well. He has his reasons, which would be for him to tell you. But there's nothing you should be concerned about."

"You say you know more about the plan, but not from Aldo? You really have me confused."

"I'm sorry. A lot has happened in the last two days. I have much more to tell you, but it will be news to Aldo, as well. So I'll share everything I know with both of you, very shortly, at Langata."

CHAPTER 27

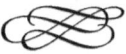

*L*angata Link is a boutique shopping and office complex nestled in the lush greenery of Karen, off Langata Road, in proximity to upscale residential areas, including Hardy and Bogani Estates. The place serves as a support hub for expat residents by providing services such as a real-estate brokerage, a merchants' bank, a currency exchange, a courier drop, a wildlife NGO station, and a government immigration liaison office. There is also a vegan tearoom with an artisan gift shop in front that's a magnet for tourists.

Harry and Esther found Aldo waiting for them, seated in the garden courtyard. Whatever she'd told him must have made him delay his flight to Rome. At this hour of the morning, they had the luxuriant space to themselves. Birds were singing in the overhanging trees, and a profusion of flowers sprouted from the manicured lawn. There was a light breeze, with no traffic noise. Joseph was taking his usual nap in the van.

As they sat down on the cast-iron lawn chairs, Harry's face flushed, and he teased Aldo, "It must've been you who ratted me out, buddy."

Aldo replied earnestly, "I'm sorry. You know I am one to keep a confidence. Especially about matters of the heart. But this time was the exception, I swear. What we're doing is too important. Esther is one of us now. Veronica is an outsider, and I'm assuming she will stay that way."

"So you sounded the alarm?" Harry asked Aldo. "And you expected Esther to come running?"

Aldo looked over at her fondly, saying, "I didn't know what she'd do. But I like that she came." And to Harry, he added, "And I'm pleased you've met Charles and Yvonne. It was the right time for you to find out."

Harry admitted, "I feel as though you're both finally taking me into your confidence. And I believe I understand why it's taken some time to bring me in. But Esther says you have more to tell me about your personal situation."

She interjected, "I've told him about what we've been to each other, but I haven't shared anything about your other responsibilities."

Aldo demurred and simply said, "My concerns should be no concern of yours, either of you, and I'll explain. But first, Esther, I want to hear your news. You told me it wasn't just your passion for Harry that's brought you here so suddenly."

From the looks on the men's faces, neither of them could guess what she was about to say.

"The game has changed," she announced. "Victor came to see me."

Aldo was the one to look perplexed. "I don't know why he didn't just phone me," he said. "We haven't even given you an offer of employment yet. In fact, we're just starting to create the organization. That's why Harry and I met with Singh." And, to Harry, he explained, "I briefed her on the substance of our meeting with the lawyer."

She went on, "Victor showed up at my house! He pulled up in that old Mercedes of his. Richard was in the driver's seat, and he stayed in the car. It was the heat of the afternoon, I was taking a nap, and somehow he must've known I was at home and not at work. I'd given Balvan an excuse, you see. I had one of those headaches, and the Panadol wouldn't touch it."

"So what did he want? Is it what really sent you here?" Harry asked.

She gave him a hard look. "You know what sent me here. I had to save you from the clutches of the wicked witch!" More seriously, she asked Aldo, "Do you think this means I'm loyal? Do I have to prove I care as much about you both as I do about my own children?" She didn't wait for an answer. "Testing me is what Victor wanted, as well. I had to prove whether I'm in or out. He's taking a gamble, trusting me with this message. He was all in a panic, and I thought he was on something. He was chattering away like a monkey who's spotted a snake."

"It's not like him," Aldo offered. "I'd guess he didn't want to say whatever it was on the phone, and he wanted to make sure you were serious before he told you whatever he came to say. Which was...?"

Esther explained, "Suddenly, he's in a big hurry. He needs to move funds fast. He has personal wealth socked away in Switzerland, but both the US and the EU regulators are all over those banks these days. He doesn't like the idea of transferring it here, but for now he believes he has no choice. On paper, it will be a trust fund for the benefit of the project. We can draw on it for our seed money. But I don't want to imagine what he'd do if we, let's say, managed it badly."

Harry asked, "Who is *we*? Why doesn't he just go and do it? He's exposing himself by telling you — and by involving us!"

"Because," she explained, "the account is to be in *your* name, Harry. I'm to keep the books and make sure you don't steal it! If you are still in the game, you open an account here in Nairobi. I send him the account information by courier — no email, no text — and he has the bankers in Zurich take care of transferring the funds."

"How much are we talking about?" Aldo finally asked.

"Five hundred million shillings, five million dollars," she said without hesitation.

"How do they do that, legally?" Harry asked. "Don't amounts like that throw up red flags everywhere?"

She replied, "He has people who know how. I don't. They say there are ways to do it with Bitcoin. Maybe with offshore accounts?"

"Wow," Aldo said.

"Wow," Harry mumbled.

"Wow, indeed," Esther said.

Aldo said, "It might not be all his liquid assets, but it's a chunk."

"It raises the stakes of this game to a whole new level," Harry said. "I'm beginning to think this was never some small-scale project to avoid taxes. I can only guess what the stakes are for him, but it's probably something more like avoiding prosecution." Then he said to Esther, "Veronica told me there are rumors from way back that one of the schemes Victor and your father worked was selling concrete to government contractors for public projects. Concrete with sand dredged from local beaches and contaminated with salt. Defective material. Things would fall apart way too soon. Did you ever hear anything about this?"

"She's right, it was a rumor," Esther admitted. "Never proved. I mean, if all the players were corrupt, who would ever bother to investigate?"

Harry pressed her, "She says it's still going on, that Victor is engaged in the same business, now with the Chinese."

Aldo put in, "Until today and this news about the funds, I'd have said none of this should concern us. There's no telling how many schemes Victor has going. It's almost business as usual in Kenya. Our project would be separate, raising its own money. The only asset coming from him would have been his land and those houses." He shrugged. "But now?"

Harry said, "If someone follows the money, it will be a short trip to us. I told you, Veronica is offering to consult. She claims to be an expert in monitoring and evaluation. And she insists that generating results by the numbers is the expected thing for any organization trying to raise money internationally. If fundraising is still the plan, we're going to need that kind of help. But how do we avoid being associated with him if we're leaving paper trails all over the place?"

"Oh," Esther sighed, "M and E is an old story with Africans. We think of them as spies. They are always looking over your shoulder, and their job descriptions give them license to poke around."

"What's the harm?" Harry asked. "If we're talking about legitimate charities, what can they learn that they're not supposed to know? I believe she's talking about reporting results to management and our donors, not auditing our funding sources."

"Charities are like political parties," Esther said. "They are careful to account for how they spend their money. But don't ask them where it came from."

"So, is everything a scam?" Harry asked her.

"It's safer to assume so, yes," she answered. "But if there's good work getting done, does it matter? If we're saving children or wildlife or the environment? When we're pleading with rich foreigners to help save the world, are we going to ask how they got their money? I think not."

"When we met with Singh, we assumed Skebelsky would be paying the legal, accounting, and filing fees," Harry explained. "They are still saying I don't have to invest my own money, but then there's this requirement to keep a stash of my own in a Kenyan bank for the sake of appearances — and for purposes of the business application and my visa."

"Now you'll have all the money you need to get it going," Esther said.

Aldo asked, "What do we do now? More than ever, it's your decision to make, Harry. As for me, I'll still be raising money for a charitable organization."

Harry replied, "Needless to say, I don't like the idea of being in business with Victor. And even though it would be riskier for me, I'd almost rather sell my house in LA and finance the startup myself, never touch Victor's money. But if money comes to us as donations, there may not be a problem. I'm sure there are all kinds of ways of setting up a trust. It depends on how it's set up. I'll need legal counsel of my own, independent advice. There's a lot to think about. Why are we doing this? Shouldn't Victor's fortune do something to make some lives worth living? Shouldn't I finally do something worthwhile?" He added, "What about you, Esther? Now I know why you'd do this for the kids, but what about for yourself?"

She answered, "I want a good-paying job and a boss who treats me with respect."

Harry turned to Aldo, "I'll have to get some guidance on this, but it seems as though, if Victor tries to give us orders, especially if he asks us to do anything suspicious, he'll bring the whole thing crashing down."

Aldo agreed, "He has to appear to be arms-length from his money — and from us."

Harry smiled and said to Esther, "We might owe Victor, but your boss would have to be me."

She took a deep breath. "Harambee, if you asked me, I'd suck the venom from a snake."

He didn't have to wonder how she came up with the image.

CHAPTER 28

*P*auline Ochieng emerged from her real-estate office as if on cue, summoned by an imaginary stage manager. Their appointment had been for ten that morning, and they'd arrived early. She must have seen their animated conversation in the courtyard from her window and wisely assumed they needed to settle matters among themselves before they saw her.

She marched over to them with officious strides. She was a large woman dressed in a twinset with pearls and heels. She gave the impression hers would be the most powerful voice in the church choir.

She flashed a huge grin as she exclaimed, "My, my, Mr. Barbieri! Who are these charming people you've brought me today? I believe it is the appointed time."

Aldo stood and took her hand. Harry was struck that his friend seemed more formally courteous than usual. "My dear Mrs. Ochieng, I've brought my friends Esther and Harry. Esther is a businesswoman from Diani, and Harry is a quiet American who has fallen in love with your country."

"Delighted," she said as she shook their hands in turn and sat. And, focusing intently on Harry, she held her smile as she asked, "And, may I ask, if it's not too forward, are you two a couple?"

She didn't mean Harry and Aldo.

Harry shot a look to Aldo and answered cautiously, "The three of us are colleagues in a potential philanthropic venture in Diani. But we must necessarily be in Nairobi much of the time, especially in the early phases. So we've come to you hoping to find a furnished place in Karen with at least three bedrooms that we can use as a base of operations as well as a residence."

Esther piped up vehemently, "And, yes, we're a couple."

There was a short, embarrassed pause as the others didn't know what to make of her outburst. Then Harry started to chuckle, and they all laughed.

Pauline was forthright, teasing him, "Have you not yet proposed, sir?"

Harry smiled back and replied, "One reason I came to Kenya was I thought the pace here would be more relaxed. Don't rush me!"

Esther muttered to her slyly, "He just doesn't know when he's caught."

And they laughed again. Harry didn't mind her joke at all, and he was gratified by her willfulness, but in the same moment he realized that what she was saying also applied to his commitment not only to her but to the whole Harambee project. For him, as of now, there was no turning back.

Pauline grew serious as she asked Esther, "I take it you are a Kenyan citizen, my dear?"

"Sure," Esther said.

"But not you fellows?"

The men shook their heads.

Pauline explained, "That's all very well and as may be. Esther, it might be wise as we embark on our shopping to say to these landlords that you will want this home for you and your extended family. These fellows are your advisors. You see, the rates will be lower for locals, for one thing, and for another, our community is sufficiently sexist to assume that women need men to make their decisions for them. From a legal standpoint, your name can be on the lease with one or both of the men as cosigners."

Now Aldo spoke, "It's Harry who pays all the bills, at least for now."

"I'm a widow," Esther added. "And, yes, I have an extended family, but I won't be bringing them here."

Pauline went on, "Many of the fine homes in Karen are built on estate plans. An estate is a named development, gated and guarded. Within the estate are family compounds of several houses, owned by an individual, usually the head of a family or an investor. The compounds are also gated, with their own askaris. Probably also there will be an electric fence around each property, with masonry wall enclosures. No one will mind if you have a dog or even several large dogs, and if they bark ferociously at the slightest disturbance, the neighbors will regard it as a benefit and not complain. These fine homes may have four or five bedrooms. This is because wealthy Kenyans and expatriates tend to live with their extended families and guests. So I doubt you will have trouble finding a place with enough space for your bedrooms and offices. However, your wanting furnished, that is another story. There will be not so many of those properties. Or, if there is furniture, it will be old colonial and not likely to your taste."

"We'll live like royalty!" Aldo exclaimed.

Harry wasn't so enthusiastic. "Price range?" he asked. He feared this woman was assuming his pockets were deep and she intended to mine them.

But Pauline quoted a ballpark figure in dollars that was hardly a third of what Harry could get for renting his house in Rustic Canyon.

She could see the look of surprise on his face, and from experience she knew it wasn't because he thought the number was out of the question. She emphasized, "And for that, you will have the services of the staff on the compound, including gardening and maintenance. Laundry services, firewood, and propane for the stove will be extras but simply added to your monthly bill. You will want to hire your own houseman and a cook."

"Firewood?" Harry asked.

Pauline shrugged and said, "Many of the homes, even of more recent construction, have no central heating. After all, you only need it a few months of the year. So mornings you build a fire in the fireplace, or you have your houseman do it before you rise, and you wear a sweater."

It was November of 2019. Harry's initial three-month tourist visa would soon need to be renewed. He already knew enough about Kenya to know that here, south of the equator, the seasons were reversed. What he regarded as the summer months were winter here.

"How cold does it get?" he asked.

Pauline laughed, "We still have our cool days now. Colder than you would experience at the coast, for sure. Maybe five degrees centigrade. I believe that's about forty Fahrenheit. In old tribal traditions, they called this part of upcountry *the cold place*. And often, when it's cold, it's also rainy season. Sudden storms roll in on a sunny day that drench the ground and disappear in a couple of hours. Not a good time to be on the roads."

They agreed to depart right away on a house-hunting trip. Aldo suggested that Joseph drive them all in the van.

As they made their way from the courtyard into the car park, they passed through an alcove with bulletin boards on either side. Here's where expats could post notices, but most of the space was taken up with photos of houses for sale or rent.

And whom should they find there pinning up a new notice but Veronica Lindbrook. She was dressed all in white, with a sportive shirt, slacks, and sneakers appropriate for tennis or lawn bowling. Her large, floppy straw hat set off the rich-settler look.

She seemed intent on her posting and didn't turn to notice them until they came up beside her. She turned to greet them cheerily. "Aldo! *Harry!*"

The polite smile still stuck on her face as she glared at Esther. "And, my dear?"

In Kenya, *my dear* is usually a term of genuine affection. But not always.

"Esther Mwemba," Esther answered softly, offering her hand.

Veronica took it limply, then quickly let go. The smile dropped. "Ah, yes. Harry speaks highly of you."

With extreme restraint, Esther said simply, "He speaks also of you." The omission of how well was a vicious dagger thrust.

Veronica was unperturbed and asked Harry, "Do all of you have business in Karen today?"

"We're house-hunting," Harry stated and left it at that. His failure to explain the *we* and the *why* was also pointedly curt, if not rude.

"Oh!" Veronica remarked, "I was just posting a notice for my friend Jonathan. He has a house to let in Bomas."

Pauline interjected, "Jonathan McAdie?" And she added, "I'm Pauline Ochieng. My real-estate brokerage is just here."

"Ah," Veronica reacted, caught up. But she had her business card at the ready and handed it promptly to Pauline. "If you would be so kind," she said. "Do you know Jon? He didn't mention a broker. To tell you the truth, I'm not sure how serious he is. He's putting out feelers, perhaps. It's an old colonial, three bedrooms. It was his mother's place, and she passed away last year. It's fully furnished, but it's been empty. I don't think he's been ready, if you know what I mean. Emotionally. If he was planning to list it, I'm sure he'd have come to you."

Pauline huffed, "I see him in the bank now and again. In many ways, it's a small town, as you know." A branch of the I&M commercial bank was located in the same complex, just steps away.

"All right," Veronica said, "if you want to have a look, you needn't go through me. I've written Jon's number on the back of the card. However, he isn't well these days, and if you have trouble reaching him, give me a call. I could drop 'round and see what's what, pave the way."

"As you wish," Pauline said as she stepped on, cueing the rest of them to follow. The way she said it, she might have wanted to rip the card up on the spot, but she didn't.

Veronica called after, "Lovely to see you, Harry!"

THE HOUSE-HUNTING, which continued until just after sundown, was tedious, frustrating, and disappointing. They all appreciated that finding the ideal place in a day was ambitious. But they wanted to involve Aldo in the choice, and today would be his last day in Nairobi before his business trip to Europe. Pauline again emphasized the inventory was limited because they wanted the place to be furnished. But she was quick to add that furniture rental wasn't readily available or was ridiculously overpriced. She said they might do better buying locally crafted pieces and reselling them at the end of the lease term. Imported items would not only cost dearly but also would take forever to ship and clear customs. They'd be waiting months.

They looked at a couple of grand houses that had been empty for years and were dark, gloomy, and drafty. Although they might not be staying out the full year of the lease, depending on how their business preparations went, they all agreed they might as well be comfortable. They wanted something more like home than a hotel room. Even so, Harry thought both of the places were practical enough, having sufficient space, and Aldo probably would have agreed if they'd discussed it. But Esther put her foot down. The appliances were so old as to be hopeless, and the vintage furniture, even if rips and cracks were repaired, was disgusting.

One of those houses had four bedrooms, the other five. Pauline knew her market. She knew these clients might not stay out the year, but she didn't so much as hint this to the housekeepers who showed them around. None of the landlords were in evidence, and Harry got the impression that many if not all of them lived abroad. In one case, they were told the landlady was an Indian widow who lived in London. In another, the owner was an Arab gentleman retired from the consular corps and living in Egypt. But it was Pauline who shared these facts from her own research. The housekeepers talked not at all of their employers.

There was a cute bungalow with two bedrooms and a loft that was currently occupied. An American diplomatic family was moving to their next posting, and their four primary-aged, hyperactive children had almost trashed the place. No less than a dozen pairs of muddy sports shoes in various sizes were strewn around the side entry door by the pantry. It was the housekeeper who showed them around, and she insisted vehemently that she'd oversee prompt repainting and cleanup to make the place ready. But Esther hated the vibe, adding that the lawn area was so small there would be no place for her kitchen garden. Besides, waiting on tradesmen to do the renovation could be another cause of frustrating delays.

Pauline also showed them a newly built condominium townhouse, located next to a new office park. The unit was all glass surrounded by concrete and steel, and lavishly furnished in industrial-modern with top-of-the-line amenities because it was the only showcase model. A pretty, young saleswoman in a crisp, blue suit carried a portfolio of glossy brochures as she showed them around. This model unit was the only part of the project that was finished. But the developer was anxious to sell or rent this one, even before the scheduled public open-ing, presumably to help cash flow. The fourth bedroom had been outfitted as an executive office, decorated on a safari theme, and Harry had no trouble visualizing himself tending to the woes of the world from behind its expansive desk. But the road inside the complex was still severely rutted from the ongoing construction, and amenities such as the pool and the community room were still in the blueprint stage. Harry guessed the perpetual noise of construction would be madden-ing. He could have wished otherwise because, besides the snobby office and brand-new upscale appliances, it was the only house they'd been offered that had a four-season heating and cooling system.

As dusk came on, Aldo informed the others that he'd be catching his rebooked flight to Rome later that night. Harry and Esther agreed they'd meet Pauline for coffee the next morning to continue their search. Then Joseph dropped Pauline at her office at Langata Link. Not far from there, Esther got off at the Galleria shopping center, where she planned to meet up with Charles and Yvonne at the pizza parlor.

As she was getting got out, Esther gave Harry a sweet kiss and a tender pat on the cheek. "Is the white lady following you around?" she cooed. "At least, now she knows what she's up against."

"It's only you," Harry assured her, "from here on out. Until you get tired of me."

She laughed and called back just before she walked away, "Oh, Harambee, I'll be tiring you out before I ever get tired of you!"

Aldo climbed into the passenger seat beside Harry so they could talk as Joseph navigated the superhighway to Jomo Kenyatta International. The airport is on the other side of the sprawling city — which during this rush hour would require at least a two-hour drive.

Harry didn't want to be the first one to speak. He wanted to hear what Aldo would say next. The two of them had a lot to discuss. And Aldo had promised there was more about his background he needed to share.

But Aldo was unusually quiet. Harry thought his friend looked wistful as he stared out the car window at the familiar sights along the highway.

Finally, Harry asked, "Is it something I said?"

The Italian faced him with a wan smile and chuckled. "Some vacation, eh, Harry? Soon you'll have a gorgeous and brilliant black wife, a business, and a house. Not to mention a white girlfriend who lusts for your body!"

"And I believe I have you to thank for all of it. Or, should I say, blame? I might not want some of those things."

"You have to admit, Harry, that as of now your life has meaning and purpose. I'm not an angel, but I won't mind taking responsibility if things turn out as well as we hope."

"I'm not serious about Veronica, I'm sure you know. I hope she isn't stalking me. She strikes me as a woman who gets what she wants. It might be better if I never saw her again, but I believe you think we're going to need her professional advice."

"The biggest danger to us now is whatever we don't know that we don't know. Digging for facts in the worlds of philanthropy and banking is what she does for a living."

"So, I shouldn't slam the door in her face?"

He chuckled again. "Certainly not! You're a gentleman. And she's practical, if a bit headstrong. I assure you, there's nothing she can throw at you that Esther can't handle."

"Do you think Esther is upset with me?"

He shrugged. "She's jealous, and she should be. You asked her to come with us to Nairobi, and she hesitated. Then she advised you not to come at all. In fact, she pleaded with me to hold you back. So, when we came to town, you had every reason to think she was having second thoughts about the project — and about *you*. Then, when I reported your hookup with Veronica to her — which, I have to say, amazed me more than it did her — she realized she had to make a decision. If she didn't commit to you, she'd lose you. And, as you saw today, she also knew that going further would mean finally telling you the whole truth about Victor and her children."

"It's been quite a day."

"And, to your credit, you haven't freaked out. You are a kind and a wise man. You understand there are flaws in every person, in every situation. And you resolve to see the best in everyone. I congratulate you, and I see, not for the first time, why I'm right to believe you're the one to lead this project. It's not about your background or training. It's a matter of character."

"You flatter me. And when a salesman does that…"

"Oh, Harry. Don't tease." And he sighed deeply. "Remember, I'm the one who has to find ways of pulling the gold out of the donors' teeth!"

"So, what's bothering you?"

"Esther has confessed to you. I have not yet."

"If it's distressing, it can keep until you get back. Just tell me whatever you're doing isn't illegal."

Aldo smiled and gave Harry a pat on the knee. "I owe you an apology. I've worried you unnecessarily. Naturally, when a trusted friend has secrets, you might fear the worst. I'm not a criminal, and I don't expect to pull us into anything bad."

"Maybe start by telling me why you're going to Rome. I thought you told me you have business in Milan."

"What I told you before is part of the truth, but only part. I'm putting together another tour package. One must pay the bills, at least until we have first-in money for our project."

"Now it looks like we'll have more than enough, but I worry where it's coming from."

"That's cause for concern and caution, Harry. But let's not fret about that now. I must tell you about me. I'm not going to Milan. At least, that's not my destination. From Rome, I will travel by train to my family home in Calabria. From the station, I will take a public bus into the countryside, to the convent of the Sorelle del Mano Amica, the Carmelite Sisters of the Helping Hand. There, I will visit my wife."

"Your *wife?* She's a nun?"

"No, a long-term patient. The sisters run an assisted-living facility for the indigent and for *di casi senza speranza.*"

"Chronic illnesses?"

"Hopeless cases. Lost causes. These people, old and young, aren't terminal. They're not ready for hospice care. But the best doctors can't do anything more for them. Their illnesses, whether mental or physical or spiritual, have defied all methods of treatment."

Aldo heaved another deep sigh and choked on a sob.

Harry insisted, "Please, Aldo. You've told me enough. More than I need to know."

"Not at all," he said. "You won't understand unless I explain." He took a deep breath, wiped his eyes with the back of his hand, and went on, "Nadia and I were sweethearts in school. As I say, it was a small town. Our families were close. It wasn't an arranged marriage, but my parents especially were thrilled. We weren't devout, but she made up for it. Always going to mass. She must've prayed for everyone in town. And gorgeous? Caring, giving, a huge heart. She liked making love, after she let me teach her a few things, and she wanted children. Lots of children. But we try and we try — how we try! — and no blessing. She goes to the doctor, finds out she's barren. Some infection she had when she was a kid.

"We'd been married for three years. Happy times until then. I'm a good boy, I'm selling Vespas by the truckload, and I'm bringing home good money. We have a nice apartment, and we're planning to buy a little house. She was already thinking about how she was going to decorate the baby's room.

"When she gets the news, I tell her there are all kinds of ways now. We'll see a specialist, University of Bologna. They can work magic, I'm sure of it. I'll find the money, whatever it takes. Or we adopt. The Church runs a home for unwed mothers in the next town.

"But she'll have none of it. She believed in perfection, the perfect life. And family was always a big thing for her. That's what she thought she had. We had. It's normal to become depressed at such a time, but she gave up on living. I get home from work, every night, all the lights are off, and she's lying there, staring at the ceiling in our bedroom. She won't talk about it. I say I'll pray with her. I'll ask the priest to come. Or the doctor. She waves me off.

"I make her soup. She's losing weight. I get her mother to come. My mother comes. They take turns.

"Now, for this, there are treatments. There is medication. She might have recovered. Yes, with help, she probably would have recovered.

"But then I did something stupid.

"I admit, I was angry. All that frustration. Of course, it's understandable. All that darkness, I'm not seeing any light. So, the mothers are watching her, cooking her favorite foods, which she still won't eat, and I'm now staying out later and later in the evenings. Drinking with the boys, what else? Not an honorable thing to do, but understandable. This, in itself, perhaps would also be curable. Forgivable.

"But then, one night when I'm drunk and out of my mind, I go with a girl. Someone I used to have a thing for, someone everybody knows. After, I pass out at her place, I don't come home.

"Word gets around. Fast. Small town, like I say. I don't know who told Nadia, maybe her mother.

"Still, I don't go home. I go to work the next day. I hear things. I don't know what to do. I know I've screwed up, and all day I'm rehearsing my speech, how I'm going to beg for forgiveness, what I'm going to do to show I'm sorry, it won't happen anymore ever, I swear to God.

"I don't want to go home. I'm afraid to. I'm still a block away, and I can see the emergency lights. I pull up behind an ambulance and two police cars.

"I don't know how she managed it. Must've been sometime when no one was around. She'd jumped from the roof. But it was only three floors, and the fall didn't kill her. She had broken bones, arms and legs and ankles. And her neck was broke. Brain damage."

"Oh, Aldo" was all Harry could say.

"She lies in her bed in the convent, and they tend to her every need. They feed her and bathe her, and someone turns her over a few times a day. Sometimes they lift her into a wheelchair and take her outside. But she won't stop moaning when they do that. She won't speak, or she can't. The doctors don't know anything else to do. She's not sick, she's... damaged beyond repair.

"She's happiest when they sing to her or when they tell her jokes. She laughs. I visit when I can, and that's what I do. I don't have jokes, but I sing to her. She has a few favorite songs. She knows I'm there. I believe she knows it's me, but I think she's just as entertained if it's some orderly. I try to see her every trip back. But I couldn't bear to live close. If I were a better man, I'd visit her every day, but I just can't."

Harry offered, "It would be an unbearable burden for anyone, seeing her like that. Feeling helpless to help. Wondering whether she even knows it's you."

Aldo straightened and said, "I haven't spilled my guts for a long while now. I've been to confession time and again, and these days I don't know what God thinks of me. Or even what I think about God. But I'm not telling you all this for sympathy. And not just because I swore to be honest with you. Harry, I want you to understand why I'm doing this, why I involved you, why despite whatever Victor's purpose, we should keep going."

"You don't owe me any explanations," Harry insisted. "I've told you almost nothing about my background. I don't have anything nearly as grim hanging over me. I don't have any excuses for being indecisive and, I don't know, downright lazy."

"Here's what I'm trying to tell you. I won't pretend to be devout. I won't even tell you I'm a believer. But I've had a lot of time to hang out with my own guilt. Sinfulness, the Church would call it. And here's what I think. As human beings, yes, we all crave love. But that's not the basic thing. That's not what we need most of all. A person can live without being loved, and you can make up for some of that by giving love — even if it's just loving the flowers in your garden or the beauty in a painting. But what we all need, every hour of every day, is *meaning*. We need purpose, a reason to get up in the morning. And, even though I have no faith, I'm attracted to this idea that there are no accidents in the universe. Now, I'm not talking about a divine plan, although there may be one. No, what

I've found is — as human beings who can choose what we believe and how we act — we must try to turn every grievance into a miracle.

"As for me, two things keep me going. First, I need to make money. Lots of it. That's why I can't stay home, and that's why this scheme of Victor's attracts me. The Sisters don't charge for Nadia's care, but I have to give back. I must atone. They are serving, and I will support them with the money I send. The second thing is, I want my own life to have meaning, a huge purpose. I want to accomplish something so good, so worthy, that I can pretend all the suffering I've caused led to this. I'm not waiting for a miracle to happen. I have to make it happen.

"Right from the start, I had this feeling about you. Yes, you're kind and wise, but you haven't yet found that sense of purpose for yourself. I sense that you're like me. You want your life to mean something."

"I never thought about it that way," Harry admitted. "But you're right, I wouldn't mind making better sense of things."

"And I want you to know, I haven't said it in so many words, but I'm not a pimp. Yes, I do arrange these tours. But you can see how little I'm involved in what my clients decide to do here. I understand them because I understand infidelity better than any of them. I know most of them crave companionship, even if they won't admit it or don't find it. Like you were when we started, they don't really understand what will satisfy them."

"You know Victor's money can't be clean."

"We can guess, but we don't need to know. And we shouldn't try to find out. What we strongly suspect is he's made a career defrauding this country's governments — old and new — with payoffs to the bureaucrats who let him do it. What there is in Victor's bank accounts is money he took from the citizens of Kenya."

"And, in a way, we'll be giving it back to them?"

"By providing community services that the government should provide, but won't."

Harry mused, "When you put it that way, how can I refuse?"

"I don't expect you will," Aldo said. "I have more faith in you than you do, more than I have in myself."

"Too bad we couldn't find a house. Even if it's going to be furnished, I expect Esther is eager to go shopping."

"Oh, she'll decorate the place. And we should encourage her." Then he added, "Seriously, if we believe there are no accidents, perhaps we already know where you should look tomorrow."

"That friend of Veronica's?"

"Maybe she didn't show up by chance. Maybe she's following you around. She picked you up easily enough from the gallery. Okay, she has her own selfish motives. But that's no reason not to believe that the old Scotsman's house isn't the one we're meant to have!"

By this time, their car was at a standstill in downtown traffic. Brightly lit high-rise hotels and office buildings loomed over the right side of the vehicle as they headed east along Ngong Road.

The evening was hot and humid, and Harry had his window halfway down for ventilation. A pregnant teenage woman walking in the street rushed at him with her hand out. "Papa! Papa!" she cried. "Small money!"

Joseph, who'd been silent through the entire conversation so far, called back urgently, "Roll up your window!" And Harry did. Seeing this, the woman didn't linger but moved on promptly to accost passengers in the vehicle behind them.

Harry said to Joseph sheepishly, "She should've waited. I could've given her something."

"No, no, boss." Joseph shot back. "She'll be working with an accomplice. He will swoop down from out of nowhere and grab the wallet from your hand. Or your phone. Or a lady's purse." He smirked and added, "And who can say? It's likely to be a football there under her shirt!"

When Harry met up with Esther that night at the hotel, they were both exhausted. The emotional currents of the day had drained the energy from their bodies. As she was drifting off to sleep beside him, she asked, "Did Aldo tell you his story?"

"Yeah," Harry said. "Sad. Complicated, like yours."

She yawned, "At least now you'll never be bored."

CHAPTER 29

*P*auline had no interest in seeing the McAdie house, and neither did Esther, for different reasons. Pauline knew McAdie had never rented the place before, so she expected he'd be difficult. And because Veronica had placed herself in the middle of the transaction, Pauline was not at all sure she'd get her commission. So she wasn't about to encourage success. As far as Esther was concerned, she wasn't eager to do business with any friend of Veronica's. Besides, it was Saturday, and she had promised to take her kids to The Hub, the classiest shopping mall in Karen, as a reward for high test scores. Harry offered to loan her his credit card, but she informed him Victor would be paying those expenses. He'd given her a debit card loaded with a budgeted amount.

So Harry went to see the place by himself, driven by Joseph. Most of the looking they'd done had been around the Hardy Postal Center in neighborhoods favored by expats and diplomats. The McAdie compound was located on the other side of Langata Road and the Galleria, near the Bomas of Kenya community center.

Harry rode beside Joseph, who confided, "You know, Mr. Barbieri is a good man. He will stick by you. Bad things can happen to good people."

"I'm finding that out," Harry said.

Harry had gotten the address and set up the appointment simply by exchanging texts with Veronica. He felt that, under the circumstances, minimal contact would be best. She took care of it promptly, perhaps cheerfully. But Harry wondered about her motives and whether Aldo was right about this being a fate-blessed opportunity.

As they approached the estate, a troop of baboons was foraging for garbage along the roadside, a common sight in this part of Nairobi. Joseph warned, "You don't want to mess with a baboon, boss. They can be funny as monkeys, but one of those big males is strong and mean enough to rip your arm off." He chuckled, "You see them around, you don't get out of the car for pee-pee, you know what I mean?"

Even here in this lush suburb, it was common to see taxi drivers relieving themselves openly by the side of the road. The men, that is.

Joseph had another caution to offer. "You see this forest?" He was pointing to a densely wooded area on the right side as they drove down Forest Edge Road. "The other side of this forest is Kibera. Less than a kilometer away. Young punks come over from there, rob folks, run back. So you don't go walking here, and you don't walk *anywhere* at night. This is Nye-robbery, man. You want to go somewhere, anytime, you call Joseph."

Harry saw plenty of people walking along the edge of the road, but they were all black, probably workers headed for their jobs at the mall. Across from the Bomas center entrance, locals had set up tables in a clearing where they sold crafts, used clothing, and housewares. Harry found it hard to believe that thieves could be so bold with so many people around.

Joseph had more to tell. "This area of Karen, you don't find so many people like you. These are homes built by white settlers before the troubles. And those families are still here. Mostly British and South African. And, these days, some real-estate speculators. Those are Indians and Arabs. They won't be staying after they flip their properties. So, new apartments are going up, and right next door are some old folks who sold off a piece of their land to grab cash to pay their staff. The old and the new, these are different worlds, boss."

"Have you heard of this guy, Jonathan McAdie?"

"No, boss. I fetch clients around here from time to time, but not him. I've never been inside those gates, but I'm guessing it's impressive. I don't think the fellow goes out much. In this part of town, none of them do. They send their cooks for the groceries. The houseman fetches his supplies from the hardware. You won't be going to any lawn parties over here."

As Joseph pulled up to the iron gate, a chorus of dog barks erupted on the other side. McAdie was fond of Jack Russell Terriers, of which he had six, and the yelpers were accompanied by a huge, black Alsatian and a muscular Rhodesian Ridgeback. The small dogs were the old man's intrusion alarm, and the big ones were the armed response.

An askari let them through with a cursory salute, at which time the dogs lost interest and turned on each other in a manic rollick as they scampered away.

Jonathan had already emerged from the big house and was waiting for them at the curve of the crushed-granite driveway. He was dressed all in khaki, including Bermuda-length shorts and knee socks. He was a short, thickset fellow with a broad, almost perfectly round, bald head.

As Harry stepped out, his host extended a meaty hand and grinned, showing a wide gap in yellow-stained teeth that might have been broken off short by a barroom punch or the butt of a rifle. Harry guessed the fellow looked ninety, but he thought all Kenyan whites looked older than they were. His face was pock-marked and freckled, its years of care illustrated with pea-sized moles and deep frown lines. McAdie's broad grin wasn't so much friendly as an expectation he would be admired. He clapped Harry on the back and led him, not into the main house, but down the road to an adjacent white-stucco bungalow, which had its own wrought-iron fencing and gate.

McAdie's walk, supported by a gleaming cane, had a rolling gait, a parade-ground swagger. "All by your lonesome this fine morning?" he chortled, a distinctive burr in his voice. "A man can't settle on a house without his missus, you know."

"True enough," Harry said and smiled. And he explained about the Harambee project and the need for a base of operations. He didn't bother with the cover story Pauline had advised about Esther's needing a place for her family. He guessed that Veronica already knew the facts and probably had told this guy everything she knew.

McAdie seemed amused. "So, you're going to be starting some kind of clinic on Victor Skebelsky's property in Diani? He donates the land and buildings, gets a tax break, and you guys go after charitable contributions to fund the place. Do I have it right?"

"That's essentially it," Harry told him, surprised the fellow had those details. "I take it you know him?"

"Skebelsky?" McAdie shook his head. "By reputation only. I own a safari lodge upcountry, and we had to deal with him years ago when we were pouring foundations. When the wildlife is gone, my business will be over and done. I'm surprised Skebelsky is still drawing breath."

As they were about to enter the house, McAdie turned to Harry, lowered his voice, and the grin disappeared. "I don't know about Americans, but Europeans don't care about little brown babies anymore. There have been too many appeals, too many disappointments. And it's beginning to dawn on them that the real problem isn't climate change or food distribution or even political corruption. No, the problem no one can face — whether in Europe or here — is overpopulation! The politicians don't want to talk about it. Fewer voters? No, let's have more of the uneducated ones whose votes we can buy for the price of a meal! My friend, if you want to rake in the euros, these days the cause will have to be wildlife. Rhinos are deserving, but they look nasty, and you can't raise money for a species that's just about extinct. Big cats? Yes, I suppose. But the hunters want to con you into believing putting a price on their heads will keep the rest of them alive. Bollocks! You can't show them cute monkeys because they'll all want one, and it will just drive demand for exotic pets. Not exactly the intended result, what? And some fools will keep them until the little critters bite their kids. But — baby elephants? Donors will still write checks for orphaned elephants. They all love the precious little things, but the good news is no one expects you to ship them one. Except the zoos, and they're as dead as circuses, if you want my opinion. I'm telling you this for free."

"There aren't any elephants near Diani," Harry said. "There are a few stragglers in the Shimba Hills, I'm told. But don't you think some of those people are doing good work?"

"No doubt. And those doctors who fly into the bush not knowing whether they'll catch Ebola or a bullet in the back!"

Harry insisted, "We need to find a use for Victor's property, so it has to be some way to serve the local community. Give them some help the government isn't providing."

"I wish you luck," McAdie said. "But there's a new Kenyan middle class. They're not happy about white people showing up to solve their problems. Those days are pretty much gone, I'd say. At least they're not keeping *you* out of the country. *Yet.*"

"What about the Chinese? Are they any more welcome?"

"Don't get me started," McAdie muttered and added, "Let's go in. I'm too old and cranky to be solving the problems of the world. But you won't begrudge an old man his opinions."

They were standing in the glade of a forest dominated by a huge baobab tree and profuse with flowers and manicured shrubbery.

McAdie could see Harry was impressed. "My houseman is Gabriel, and he keeps after Cecil, our gardener. They've both been with me for dog's years. There's Mary, the housemaid, and our cook, Beatrice. But perhaps you'll want to hire your own. Frankly, I can't keep them busy enough."

The entry to the sprawling, single-story house from the lush lawn was by a stoop, which gave way to a flagstone patio and then into a half-walled, open-air veranda that reminded Harry of the room where Victor had received them. Unlike the other properties he'd seen, this one was so lavishly decorated it could have been a tourist museum, exhibiting the homelife of the ruling class during the colonial era.

"It's been five years since I lost my wife. This house was my sister Wilma's. She never married. You could call her a tomboy or an adventurer or whatever. She loved the savannah and the animals. She'd go all over, but she always came back here. She'd keep me company, liked to play bridge with me and a neighbor couple. They're gone now, too. I haven't had the heart to do anything to the place since she passed away. It's been just over a year now. It's just as she left it. As you can see, she was a collector. The dear woman couldn't take a trip without buying a truckload of knickknacks. We can clear out what you don't want. Nothing to be sentimental about. Not now."

From the veranda, which was fitted out like an English tearoom with café tables and china still set out, they stepped into a grand living room. The far wall to the left was covered in natural stone surrounding an enormous fireplace. The room featured a conversation pit with overstuffed easy chairs, two sofas, and a loveseat. All built from gleaming Kenyan hardwoods and covered with floral-patterned chintz. Indigenous teak woodcarvings were everywhere, as freestanding sculptures, bases of lamps, and wall hangings. There was almost as much native art here as in the craft shop where Harry had bought the figurine of the Maasai woman. Along with the carvings were hung framed black-and-white photos of safari expeditions, including proud hunters posing with their kill. And among the curios were traditional Maasai shuka cloths, rungu clubs, and spears, also nailed to the wall.

Thankfully, thought Harry, there were no stuffed heads, although the four feet of a coffee table might have belonged to an elephant.

As Harry was studying the photos, McAdie came up behind him. "Wilma never shot anything. But she might have admired those who did. It was another day, another age. Wildlife was plentiful. Now we're the endangered species, along with them. But not for lack of numbers."

Harry muttered, "You could replace that table."

McAdie heard him and slapped him again on the back, "Right you are, mate. Memsahib squeamish about the animal parts? Don't blame her one bit. I needed an excuse to chuck it out."

The fellow seemed genuinely amused at Harry's gawking. Pride of ownership. Harry got the feeling he was the first visitor here in a long time. McAdie explained, "Our parents started the safari lodge in the late forties. They built this compound, which has four houses, in the early fifties. While we were growing up in this house, they were constructing the others, and the property was gifted to us when we came of age. An uncle rented one of the houses for a time, and guests came and went in the other. The main house, where I live, was the last to be built. In fact, I finished it after both of my parents were gone. We had twenty acres here, and back then the nearest neighbor had a farm over the hill. We've sold off some of it. You may have seen the new townhouses on your way in. The Galleria and the Bomas center had yet to be built. Did you know *Bomas* means *depot?* That's all Nairobi was a century ago, not much more than a trading post, and my family's land title goes back almost that far.

"When I was a boy, where the superhighway is was a dirt road that washed out whenever the rains were heavy. The old train ran along the route of the new Chinese line from Mombasa. That's how my father got downtown when he had business, which was rarely. We didn't have a telephone until I was ten. Radio, no television. My mother played piano, and we sang. I have her Chappell baby grand in my house. It was country life, you see. We had a kitchen garden, chickens, goats — you know, the whole bucolic thing. We had chores. It was another time."

At the back of the house, Harry could see a formal dining room, its cabinets richly appointed with fine china, silver platters, and goblets, but he didn't feel he needed to inspect it. McAdie showed him the full kitchen. The appliances weren't as old as the house, but they weren't new. He swore they were serviceable. There were three spacious bedrooms, an alcove with a writing desk, two bathrooms with updated shower tubs, a walk-in pantry, and a maid's quarters. McAdie said he'd furnish linens and towels, provide laundry for those with maid service once a week, all included in the rent. As Pauline had told Harry to expect, McAdie said personal laundry, firewood, and propane for the cookstove would be extras. They'd have to contract directly with the power utility and satellite TV if they wanted it, but McAdie offered a free Wi-Fi hookup to the router in his house.

Harry asked the rental price. McAdie screwed up his face and answered, "You know, I haven't been in the market. What are they asking for the other places you've looked?"

Harry gave him an honest answer, and the Scotsman countered with a number that was twenty-percent lower. He closed the deal by offering a one-year lease but with no penalty for early termination with thirty days' notice.

Honest Harry informed his new landlord that Pauline Ochieng deserved a generous tip for her efforts. Harry didn't feel it was his own responsibility. McAdie's face soured for a moment, then he agreed he'd take care of her.

"Life is uncertain," he said wistfully. "The only sure thing I want is to know there are good people in Wilma's house."

Before he left, almost as an afterthought, Harry asked him, "What about the bars on the windows?" Every window was covered by an exterior grate, and the entry doors off the veranda and the kitchen had lockable gates. Inside the house, access to the hallway to the bedrooms could be blocked by a full-length, padlocked iron grillwork. And off the living room, there was a kind of cage, floor to ceiling, big enough for a human or a large animal.

"This was the only house in the old days. Built in fifty-two. The protection is a legacy of the troubles," McAdie said, "the years of struggle that led up to Independence in sixty-three. There were riots, gangs, armed rebellion. People in these houses would lock themselves in after sundown. And if someone broke into the house, they'd have trouble making it back to the bedrooms. There are panic switches above the beds, which trigger silent alarms in the main house and the askari station."

"And what about that cage off the living room?"

"My father had guns. I still have his pistol. You'd march an intruder in there and lock him up until the police came."

"Ever happen?"

"When it started, my sister and I were sent away to boarding school in England. As far as I know, there were no incidents in this house." Then he added, "I had to shoot a baboon with my crossbow once."

"Crossbow?"

"No one hears the shot. They could lock you up for killing a baboon. He was eating my chickens and would have gone after my dogs. To this day, I think about it. I served in the military, and my hands aren't clean. In the army they tell you some people need to die or they'll kill you or your family. But nothing has ever upset me so much as murdering that ape. Animals, you see? It's easier to love them more than people."

CHAPTER 30

Once the house was rented, events seemed to move rapidly. Esther gave the rooms only a cursory look before she had to return to Diani. She didn't disagree about Harry's choice, and she admitted she could take perverse joy taking over a residence formerly occupied by the Red Strangers, which was slang back in the day for white settlers, presumably because their faces in this climate were always flushed with sunburn. She told Harry she was eager to outfit and even redecorate, as much as McAdie would permit, but she wasn't sure when she'd be back, even for a few days at a time. She explained she wanted to stay on the job at Kusi until Balvan made good on her back salary and also until she was sure that Alice would step up as head of household there. Esther calculated what a monthly stipend for her Ukunda family would require, and Harry agreed they'd include those funds in the budget for her project salary.

On Harry's walk-through with Esther, he took pictures with his phone and sent them to Aldo. His friend hadn't answered voicemail. But he did text back:

Once again, Harambee, you prove you are the man to lead!

To which Harry replied:

How's with you?

And all Aldo sent back was a thumbs-up emoji.

The day Harry took Esther through the house, as they were about to leave, she lingered there in the yard, took in the lush greenery, the floral color explosion, and the fragrance, and sighed, "It is grand. But don't get the idea you'll be living here forever like some arrogant diplomat."

"We have a job to do in Diani," he affirmed.

"Yes," she said, "even though we don't quite know what that is yet."

He turned her to him and asked softly, "You told me you go to church. Do you think we're on some kind of mission?"

She smirked, "You mean, do I think God brought us here? No, not in the sense some of these missionaries think they got a calling. Let's admit you want a way to live like this and I want a job. But should our lives have a purpose? I'd say definitely yes."

"And we've decided we want to be together, whatever we're doing?"

She smiled, "I don't think I've ever heard you say as much before. Yes, we have."

She was wearing khaki slacks with a colorful print blouse. He thought she looked like a suburban housewife already. She shoved her hand in a pocket, and when she took it out, she had something clutched in her fist.

"Since you seem to be in a serious mood, it's a good time to give you this." She opened her hand, and there was a gold signet ring in her palm.

For the moment, he was speechless. He let her take his limp right hand and slip the ring on his third finger. Of course, she hadn't asked his ring size, and on his fleshy finger, the fit was snug. Almost like she was sending him a message it wouldn't be coming off.

Should he make a joke of it? "Does this mean we're... engaged?" he asked finally. "Where I come from, the guy usually does the asking. Not that I mind."

"Call it a friendship ring, Harambee," and she giggled. "Bold as brass and good as gold for me to be doing this, but I hope you accept it."

"Of course. Yes, certainly." The words sounded so lame, but he was sincere. "Not to be crass, but how could you afford this?"

She grinned, "It's real gold, I'm sure, but it's not the crown jewels. Don't spoil it by thinking Victor bought it for you. But there was some room on the card."

He smiled broadly, "Okay. When you come back to stay, we'll shop for yours."

"Careful what you ask for!" she exclaimed, and she kissed him.

He held his hand up to get a closer look, then asked her, "What's the stone?"

"Obsidian," she said right away.

"Meaning?"

She giggled again, kissed him again, then whispered, "It means you've gone black, and you're not going back."

~

HE PUT her on a flight at Wilson and resolved to make the best of an indefinite period of bachelorhood. She told him she wanted to wind up her business with Balvan honorably so at least she would have his commendation. And if she stayed through the holidays, there would be the yearly bonus money for the staff. Tourist traffic in Diani would peak again in three weeks, around Christmas, when well-to-do folks from upcountry typically schedule reunion vacations at the beach with their families. She'd be busy then. So the earliest she'd be able to move in with Harry in Karen would be after New Year's. He thought he might join her at the beach for the holiday, but they hadn't yet made plans.

He installed himself in the master bedroom, which required little more than unpacking his two suitcases. He left more than half the space in the wardrobe for Esther, who might not have much now, but would soon enough, he was sure. As Pauline had warned, the house was indeed chilly and drafty, especially at night. He requested a couple of heavy blankets when he saw Gabriel on the grounds, and minutes later Mary knocked on his door and handed them over. She looked scarcely out of her teens and plain, and unbearably shy. Harry fished in his pocket and gave her a hundred-shilling note. Her eyes lit up, and she smiled, then bowed her head to mutter, "Oh, Papa. It's not necessary. You don't want to be paying me all the time." Then she looked up, "Give me your clothes need laundry, and I'll do them for this. After, just let Gabriel know, and I'll come when I can. You don't pay me then. The boss adds it to your bill. Four hundred a time, I think he said, no matter how much you have."

"Just fine, Mary. I hope that's fair to you."

"Oh, I have a good job here." And she smiled to add, "I pay my taxes every year!"

She waited for Harry to return with a batch of his clothes. Before she walked away, she pointed to a crate on the ground next to the kitchen door. "See? Gabriel has brought your firewood. If you need him to set it for you, just ask."

Harry had built fires on camping trips as a boy, and he didn't want to admit to anyone he wasn't up to the job. The exterior walls of the old colonial were constructed of foot-thick masonry, which no doubt was intended to keep the place cool during the hot months. But this design also made it feel cold even when the sun was shining brightly outdoors. Granted, Harry's blood had thinned since living in Southern California, but in the mornings, when he got out from beneath the cozy blankets and even though he donned a sweater immediately, he cursed the chill and felt he could never get warm.

Getting a fire started in the living-room fireplace was a maddening chore. Gabriel had brought plenty of firewood but no kindling. He explained they used commercial pressed-wood fire starters and gave him some. But in Harry's first attempts he used up the whole box, and even then the process took much too long. In the main house, Gabriel said, they keep the fires going all the time, so they don't have the problem. Harry finally found that wadding up newspapers served well enough, but there wasn't enough newsprint on hand. He could easily go through a small stack of Wilma's old magazines just to get a blaze going. No sooner had Harry achieved that than he felt guilty. Were these vintage periodicals, mostly tourist promotional freebies, actually worth something? Was he complicit in destroying history?

A further complication was that the old fireplace didn't draw. The heat of the fire is supposed to pull air from the room and up the chimney, taking the smoke with it. But the airflow won't be sufficient until the fire is going well. The result was, in the length of time it took Harry to build a fire, the room was beginning to fill with smoke. The smell and the irritant persisted throughout the day, making him wonder whether he'd rather shiver or sneeze.

And even when a fire was successful, its radiant energy only heated one end of the big room. Harry refused to sit all day on the sofa facing the fireplace.

For the duration of his stay, he'd had only his phone for access to email and the Internet. Now that he had this base of operations and planned to proceed with the project, he realized he needed better tools. He bought a laptop from the Game superstore at Waterfront mall and designated his office space at the desk in the small alcove off the kitchen. McAdie's Wi-Fi connection worked just fine, and Harry learned that much of the new Nairobi network was fast fiberoptic. He might as well be anywhere on the planet, except for the frustration of time-zone differences. The local time was ten hours ahead of Los Angeles during daylight-savings months there, eleven the rest of the year. Exchanges with correspondents in the US via email would work well enough. They could reach out to him in the evening and get his replies first thing the following morning. And Nairobi was only two hours ahead of Paris and Rome, three ahead of London, so he wouldn't have much trouble staying in touch with people in Europe.

He bought himself an electric space heater for when he was sitting at the desk. (He wanted one of those oil-filled radiators that plug into the wall, but he was amazed to find he'd have to import one.) Occasionally the little heater, which didn't do much more than warm his feet, would blow a fuse in the old wiring. The unit got fried and almost started a fire the one time it didn't, and Gabriel advised him that simply buying another current-sucker would be a bad idea.

So most days, Harry wore long pants, a long-sleeved sweater, and two pairs of wool socks.

WITH BOTH ESTHER and Aldo away, Harry slipped into a solitary life in a house that simply had too much room. Even though he communicated with her almost daily, although sometimes only by text when she was busy, Esther couldn't yet say exactly when she'd have time to visit, much less move in. And for a chap as gregarious as Aldo was in-person, he wasn't much of a correspondent when he was on the road. Harry'd had a couple of conversations with him, during which his friend seemed preoccupied, and the only solid information he got was that Aldo would necessarily be staying in Italy beyond his initial esti-mate of two weeks. Because of the sensitivity of Aldo's recent confes-sions to him, Harry didn't feel right asking him too many questions.

In the first few weeks of residence on the McAdie compound, Harry concentrated on outfitting the place. He knew he'd soon have to start working on paperwork for government applications, along with a more detailed business plan for the project. He shopped for an inex-pensive inkjet printer to go with the laptop, and he found he needed to put a Wi-Fi extender in the hallway so he could use his phone all the way back in the bedroom. (He liked it best when he would talk with Esther just after he'd tucked himself into bed for the night.) He bought a high-intensity lamp for his writing desk, along with two decorative table lamps to throw warm, cozy light in the conversation pit of the living room in the evenings. (He visualized cuddling with her there on the couch in front of a fire he'd built successfully himself.) Joseph drove him around to the shopping malls, and the fellow seemed happy to nap in the car as he waited for Harry to run his errands. By now he'd replaced the rented van with his own reliable Toyota sedan. And for some reason, whenever he was at the wheel of that vehicle and it was just the two of them, he was much chattier.

"You understand, boss, I come when you call. You rely on Joseph."

"You warned me not to go walkabout!" Harry said, making it a joke.

"I'm serious, boss. Now that we're here in town and you're settled, I hope you don't mind I'm not full-time for you. I run other clients as much as I can, you know? I got my girls in school, and tuition is dear. And there's uniforms and books to pay for."

"I understand, Joseph. Sure. Once I get the place stocked, I might only need you a few hours a week, but not every day."

"When Mr. Barbieri comes back and your business gets going,

maybe you do bring me on full-time." And he chuckled, "I love this car, it's been sweet to me, but if you want to send me looking for a fine ride, we can find something classy. I'll get the very best deal for you."

Harry teased him again with, "You mean, some hulking black limo? Do you expect us to sit in the back? You want to wear a uniform?"

"How about a Range Rover Autobiography Fifty? Or a BMW X Seven? Anybody hit us, they would be the loser!" He cackled, "Me, back in uniform? I wouldn't mind! I would not mind at all!"

"I'm not sure we're ready for that, Joseph. I believe the plan is to be making people think we *need* money."

"But what I want to say is, even when I'm running these other folks, you call me when you need me. If I'm on the other side of town, I'll text one of my mates and they will pick you in ten minutes maximum. Never fail. It's my responsibility to take care of you, understand?"

"I understand, Joseph. You've brought us this far. I'm grateful, and I enjoy your company."

On this day, Joseph was driving him back from The Hub. Harry had looked in vain in Carrefour for Egyptian-cotton bedsheets. He wanted something more luxurious than McAdie's scratchy white linens for Esther's homecoming. But everything in the megastore, even though colorful, was microfiber, which he knew made him sweat, and imported from China. And Beatrice had informed him that the heavy iron skillet McAdie had provided would not suffice. So Harry bought a new set of cookware for her to use.

All during their travels with Aldo, they'd invited Joseph to join them for meals when they were on the road. The custom, however, was for the help to eat apart. Today, Harry was craving Joseph's company even more than usual, and he proposed they stop for lunch at Haru Japanese restaurant. They sat in the cool of this unusually cloudy afternoon on the veranda. It was past the lunch hour, and all the other patrons were hanging out inside in the bar. So they had the open-air space to themselves.

Joseph habitually had chicken and chips. Harry ordered vegetable tempura and a tuna roll. He encouraged Joseph to choose anything he fancied on the menu. His eyes lit up, and he ordered a steak. Harry started with a vodka martini. He suggested Joseph at least have a Tusker, one beer not being too much for the road, but the driver insisted he'd have a Coke. It dawned on Harry that, if they were stopped and the policeman could smell beer on Joseph's breath, the result would be disastrous, regardless of how little the fellow had actually had to drink.

Harry asked him, "Joseph, it was news to me you have girls in school. Are they here in town? I thought you lived in Thika."

"My wife Marta lives there. She cares for her parents. The girls are in boarding school here in the city."

"You're driving all over, at all hours. You must not see them often enough."

He said fondly, "Dad sends them money without fail. That's love, boss."

Harry had been waiting for the right time to ask, "I know when we're in the car, you overhear a lot of personal talk. But you don't say much. You're a professional, and I can see the military man in you. I haven't had a chance to say this, but you have my respect."

"You can trust me with your life, sir."

Harry was touched, but he tried to make light of it. "I'm sure it won't ever come to that." Then he asked, "You've worked for Aldo on all his trips. You knew Esther, as well?"

"I've worked in Diani during the tourist months for twenty years. I knew about her most of those. Not well, but, as you know, it's a small town. And I've been driving Mr. Barbieri for the last eight."

"Am I right to trust them?"

Joseph mused, "Aldo Barbieri can talk the leaves off the trees, boss. But he has a good heart. He keeps his word, and he pays his bills."

"Are there any women in his life? He's a real loner, for all I can tell."

"None that I know of."

"Do you take him to see women? Do you hook him up?"

Harry noted that Joseph didn't seem offended. But the fellow answered earnestly, "A gentleman could not answer that question, sir."

"And how about Esther? I suppose you've known her longer."

"She is a fine woman."

"Is that all you have to say?"

"I knew her husband, boss. The policeman. Charming, a sweet talker. A pretty boy with muscles, and I suppose that's why she fancied him." Then he added, "He was no good."

"Why do you say that?"

"It's ancient history, boss. All I know is rumors. And in Kenya, I'm sure you know, gossip can be the best news we have. But I shouldn't repeat. You can ask her, but understand it might hurt for her to tell it."

"And Victor? Did you know about her time with him?"

"Sure," he said. "People knew. It was no secret."

"And?"

He shrugged. "A person has to pay the bills."

EVERYDAY LOGISTICS PROVED to be too easy. Every weekday morning, Gabriel drove Beatrice over to Hardy to shop for groceries. She was a dedicated menu planner, and even though McAdie was a simple, meat-and-potatoes guy, she also prepared hot lunches for the staff, and for those meals she prided herself on haggling with shopkeepers for the freshest vegetables, which she'd throw into stews and casseroles of variable daily composition. Harry routinely made breakfast for himself, so all he had to do was add his few items to her list, except for eggs, which Mary would fetch from McAdie's coop, keeping careful count so those could be added to the monthly rental bill.

Harry aspired to grow accustomed to having ugali and greens in the morning, which he knew would be healthier, but he couldn't go there yet. He was even looking forward to Esther's ordering him around, including supervising his diet.

Beatrice came over to cook dinners for Harry once a week. She'd make four or five dishes of hers he preferred, and those would go into the freezer until he needed them. Once he'd bought a coffeemaker and a microwave, he judged he was otherwise self-sufficient. Then he realized he would also need an electric kettle for the tea-drinkers, if any ever came. Two meals a day were all he required.

One morning Beatrice was busy chopping vegetables as he sat sipping rich, dark Kenyan coffee at the kitchen table. He usually read the news on his phone or on his computer, but recently he'd reconnected with the joys of thumbing through the paper. Beatrice would pick it up for him each morning on her grocery trip. Harry not only wanted to study the news more closely now that he would be a settler, but he also needed to hoard kindling for the fireplace.

It didn't take him long to sense that reporters in Kenya were careful what they said about the government. There were rumors about past retribution, to put it mildly. But he particularly enjoyed the editorial opinion pieces in *The Standard*. Those astute writers were careful in their political essays to discuss abuses, even corruption, as *policies* of nameless autocrats rather than schemes and wrongs foisted on the public by named politicians. And sometimes there was even the implication that injurious policies were simply misguided, perhaps even unintentional. Any readers who bothered to care seemed to know which families controlled which parties, which industries, and which enormous tracts of land. And yet, if the reporter didn't point the finger at an individual, the news was deemed fit to print. Presumably, the government equated this degree of tolerance with freedom of the press.

This morning, Harry was struck by a recent example. For years now, Kenyan officials had joined the worldwide chorus praising the advent of alternative energy. There was a windmill farm in the Ngong Hills of Nairobi (although for obscure reasons it hadn't yet been connected to the power grid). The Chinese had built a geothermal plant at Olkaria in the mountainous area near Lake Nakuru. And recent legislation even mandated that new apartment construction employ solar heating in their water-supply systems, but not for electricity, which seemed odd. Today there was an announcement of plans for a new coal-fired power plant, located practically on the beach near the port of Lamu on the north coast, where the ancient village at the city center had been designated a United Nations World Heritage site. There were news stories the government was planning to develop Lamu as a commercial port to rival Mombasa, and the US wanted to put a new airbase there. But the articles neglected to mention the political family that owned a substantial share of the national power utility.

As Beatrice worked, she called over her shoulder, "So, Papa, call me Bea. And tell me about the wife!"

He was taken aback at her sudden frankness. "I'm not married," he said. "Do you mean Esther?"

She laughed. "I'm not talking about the girlfriend. I'm asking about your *wife.*"

He wondered whether she assumed all white men who came here were adulterers. "I told you, I'm not married." He wasn't sure he wanted to get into this. And he was surprised this woman he barely knew was making small talk. It had taken a couple of months riding alongside Joseph before they'd shared confidences.

"A man your age? Never been married?" she scoffed. "Maybe you have many wives. I hear you Hollywood folks have trouble staying married."

The novel thought of a Harambee harem was ridiculous, even terrifying. He put down the paper. "My wife Lucille died. They said it was Alzheimer's, but then they said she survived too long with it, so it must have been some other form of dementia. I guess there are all kinds. There at the end, she didn't know who I was. So, in a way, I lost her long ago. We'd been together forty years, and, no, I didn't have any others. Pretty boring by Hollywood standards, I guess you'd say."

"When you knew her, when she knew you, what was she like?"

Harry doubted Bea spoke to McAdie this way. Perhaps her forthrightness was because he was American?

"She was an elementary-school teacher," he said, wondering how much he was willing to share. "Third grade. I think that's the same as Year Four here. They're nine years old. She'd say they were curious at that age, not yet so independent as to be annoying. She was patient and she was kind. But our daughter Nicole was almost too much for her. Headstrong, disobedient as soon as she turned ten. I hope those genes didn't come from me."

"Is your daughter coming over?"

"I doubt it. She's still headstrong, and I'm the last one to tell her what to do. She's teaching English to foreigners, living with a guy who can't or won't support her. Breaks my heart, but she's an adult."

"My daughter Angel is twenty-three. She does hair at a salon over at Hardy. She respects her mother, but, sure, I can't tell her what to do. She's looking for a righteous man, and all I tell her is, good luck! Mary, you know, she's my baby."

This was news, but it made sense. It seemed like Mary still needed parenting.

"And how about your husband? What does he do?"

"I turned that man out of the house years ago. Some Kenyan men think if you don't beat her, she won't know you love her. Can you imagine?"

"I'm sorry to hear."

"So, her name was Lucille. Tell me more. I still got six carrots to cut up and four potatoes to peel."

She was a joker, this one. Harry began to enjoy telling her, "She wasn't particularly one for the outdoors, but we liked to go on hikes. There are a lot of easy trails through the Santa Monica Mountains. Early in her illness, when she couldn't get out much, she grew fond of the squirrels. There were a lot of them around our place, particularly about an hour after dawn. Scavenging for food, chasing each other. She knew you're not supposed to feed the wild animals, but she did. She'd cut up bread, pieces of fruit, and nuts, of course. I'm not sure it was healthy for them, but it made her happy to see them grow fat."

She laughed, "It's true! It's true! We love to see our customers get fat on what we give them!" She pointed to the roof. "Do you hear all those monkeys in the morning?"

"Yeah, it's like a stampede."

"There's about twenty of them. Vervets. They sit up there on the chimney until there's smoke, and their favorite game is to jump on the TV dish."

"I saw that DTV antenna up there, but I haven't found a receiver in here. I meant to ask Jonathan about it."

"When Miss Wilma got confined to her bed, she watched the nature shows. And she loved cricket! God knows why. Most of those matches are from India. Why should she care? Maybe you want to buy a screen and have it put back in. I don't know a man doesn't like his football." And she laughed. "But you'll make the repairman busy. With those monkeys jumping on that thing, he must come out and adjust it all the time."

"Lucille and I would talk about movies and books. She'd get furious with me if I tried to guess the ending. We did watch basketball together, but only during the playoffs. Los Angeles Lakers, maybe you've heard."

"I'm telling you, these men are crazy for football. My sister Delia's husband drives a lorry all week long. He gets home on the weekend, and if it's a game night, he puts on his team jersey, heads out to the bar to meet his boys, and he doesn't come home until the early hours, stumbling down drunk." She turned momentarily from her chopping to shoot him a frown and added, "And you know what makes me mad?"

Harry took a chance when he mocked her, "Oh, Bea, do you get mad?"

"These guys care nothing for the Kenyan teams! You're either Manchester United or you're Arsenal. Now tell me that's not racist!"

Harry chuckled. "I'll keep that in mind. Might keep me out of a barfight someday."

She resumed her work right away. You'd think she was on the clock. Maybe she knew she had to get back to McAdie. She asked Harry, "Any other women in your life?"

"Sure," he said but not willing to take the bait when it came to girlfriends before Lucille. "I got along with my mother, but the problem we had was she would always side with my father, and I didn't get along with him. Then there was my grandmother, her mother, Gracie. I became attached to her when I was little, before I started school. There was a time my mother needed to be hospitalized. I really don't know why. I suppose they thought I was too young to be told, and then she recovered, so there was no need. Anyhow, my dad would drop me off at Grandma's house, and I'd stay for days. She was always in the kitchen, like you. She'd fry up the fish my grandfather caught, bake bread and rolls, and her specialty was chocolate pie. I had a lot of time to myself. She'd been a teacher in a one-room schoolhouse down on the farm. On a shelf in the living room, she had all the books from her classes. Dickens' *A Tale of Two Cities*, Macaulay's *Lays of Ancient Rome*, Austen's *Sense and Sensibility*, and a lot more. There was a full set of *The Standard American Encyclopedia*. I looked at every page, studied all the pictures. I don't know if I taught myself to read or that's just the way I remember it. Of course, I didn't read every book. But what she gave me was all that time to myself."

"I'm sure that wasn't all she gave you," Bea said.

"What I learned from her was unconditional love. I knew they went to church, but not regularly, and she never spoke about it. Yes, there was a Bible on that shelf. But there has been no one in my life who was ever so generous and so kind. When she gave you her attention, it was all on you. Like a warm bath. I loved Lucille, and she was a sweet person, but I don't think she loved me half as much as my Grandma Gracie did."

Bea scooped up the rest of the vegetables from her cutting board and added them to the new stew pot. As she placed the lid and turned down the heat, she wiped her hands on her apron as she took it off and advised Harry, "Now you let that simmer until you can stick a fork through those potatoes. You don't have to watch it every minute, but don't you go off playing with your computer. You burn the fine food Bea makes for you, and you won't get any more!"

He thanked her, and as she brushed by him on her way out the back door, she gave him a motherly kiss on the cheek.

AFTER ANOTHER WEEK of diligent shopping, Harry had run through his list of chores. It was time he got down to the paperwork and tasks he barely understood and knew he'd dread. Yesterday, David Odiengo had followed up with him by phone, reminding Harry that he could start on the filing requirements by himself. Recently, the government had been promoting online services for all kinds of applications and permits via their new portal eCitizen. This part of it seemed simple enough to Harry, who thought himself comfortable with if not a master of electronic access. He'd log on and fill out some forms. How hard could it be? Odiengo advised him he would need a tourist visa extension on his passport, an application to register his publishing business in Kenya, and the preliminaries for applying for permanent-resident status.

So one morning after he'd had breakfast and his second cup of coffee, Harry sat down at the laptop and tried to log on for the first time to eCitizen. He assumed this session would only take a few minutes, then he could call Joseph and be off to The Hub where he wanted to look at tableware, which was an indication of how bored he was.

The eCitizen home page presented him with a single button: *Create an Account,* followed by another screen with four selections: One for residents, one for established businesses, one for foreign residents, and one for tourists. He had to study those instructions to realize his only entry point would be the one for tourists. You needed prior registration IDs to access any of the others.

The next screen had a form for him to fill out, all expected information. He had his passport ready and entered the number, then his name and contact information, including his email address and cell phone number. Once he'd completed all the fields and continued through the menu, the system required a double-authentication code. But when he checked his phone for SMS, then his email, he found no messages, no code.

He'd been through this procedure countless times for just about every other app he used, and he knew that the code was generated automatically, almost instantaneously.

But he waited. And he waited.

He went off to the kitchen to refill his coffee, thinking that this must be some kind of network latency. He hadn't had much experience with the local Internet connection.

When he returned to check his phone and his mail, still no code. Then he clicked *Back* in the browser and tried to submit his form again.

That didn't work.

He closed and then reopened the browser, filled in the form again, tried to submit, and once again experienced no joy.

He cleared the browser cache and closed it, rebooted the machine, and started all over again.

His attempt to submit failed as before.

He felt stupid, as if he were some doddering user calling customer support about a computer glitch only to find out he had neglected to plug some essential device into the power outlet.

He hoped to have at least the preliminary application process done before he called David Odiengo to help him with the next steps. But now he had to call the lawyer because he didn't know what else to do.

As luck would have it on a day when it seemed to be in such short supply, Odiengo answered right away, affirmed that he was in town, and agreed to stop over that afternoon.

Meanwhile, Harry summoned Joseph, and they made a trip to the shopping mall. This errand also proved frustrating. McAdie had only provided the house with dinnerware and service items for two, and those didn't match. Harry wanted to have everything ready not only for Esther's return but also for celebrating with Aldo, and he imagined they'd have guests from time to time. He could wait for Esther to pick it all out, but he was practical enough to worry that she might not be coming soon and he wouldn't be ready in time for whatever social occasion was going to be crucial to the success of their project.

But the store's selection was limited, with more stuff from China, and Harry didn't like any of it enough to buy. So far, the results of the day were frustratingly funga!

At least, Harry and Joseph shared a sumptuous lunch at La Cascina, an Italian restaurant with patio dining on the grand mall of The Hub and in full view of small, hyperactive children dodging one another in kiddie cars rented by aristo parents who wanted time to themselves in the designer shops. It occurred to Harry that these young drivers would one day be well equipped to cope with Nairobi traffic. He had more than his quota of wine since Joseph politely refused to drink it, and he returned to the house in the midafternoon with an overfull stomach and feeling so groggy he was ready for a nap.

But here was Odiengo in his suit and tie, already in the house. Bea had let him in, made him tea from the new electric kettle, and was feeding him cakes she'd brought over.

"I trust you've had a productive outing?" Odiengo asked as he stood from his seat at the kitchen table and shook Harry's hand warmly.

"I was after place settings so we could entertain," Harry explained. "Our landlord has been generous in his way, but I don't expect him to provide everything. I've already had to outfit the kitchen. But no luck." He smirked, "I've returned empty-handed! And I can't say much for my talents using the computer to get these registrations done, either."

It was the Christmas shopping season, and the shops in Karen were getting picked over. Imported luxury goods from Europe, which were always in high demand this time of year, were particularly difficult to find. Harry had seen some mention of disease outbreaks in Italy, but other than restricting the traffic in commercial goods, so far the health crisis hadn't had much effect here.

"Ah," Odiengo sighed as he followed Harry to his desk and pulled up a chair to sit beside him. "You will find a distinct shortage of what you might call luxury goods in Kenya. Even in Karen. It's an indication of prosperity, in a way. Many middle-class Kenyans can't afford foreign goods because of the import duties. And then, whatever the stores manage to stock gets picked over quickly because, especially in Nairobi, there are a lot of people like you who expect the finer goods."

As Harry popped the lid on his laptop, he asked, "What do you think I'm doing wrong?"

"I doubt it's because you don't know how to use a computer, Mr. Gardner. One might guess that the government server is down. Or that too many users are attempting to access the site at the same time. Or it could be a network issue unrelated to your connection here."

"You could work in customer support."

Odiengo smiled sheepishly and admitted, "I did. That was one of the ways I put myself through school."

As the lawyer watched, Harry went through all the steps again. With the same non-result.

Harry looked at Odiengo expectantly. The fellow made a quavering gesture with his hands and said, "Like I say, I doubt this has anything to do with you."

"What's next?"

"One alternative is to drive to Nyayo House downtown and fill out the forms manually. It might be possible to find a terminal free there to do it online, but the place is always jammed with people wanting all manner of things, so I predict difficulties and a very long wait doing it that way."

"What do we do?"

Pulling his phone from his pocket, Odiengo smiled broadly and winked as he said, "Let me just make a call."

Harry could tell that the fellow was calling a private number. He heard him describe to someone he called Edwin what had transpired. Odiengo said, "I see," several times. Then he chuckled, thanked his contact, and ended the call.

He began his explanation to Harry with, "I'm sure you've learned Kenya is a cultural adjustment for you."

"What's the matter? Do they know it's me? Is somebody messing with us?"

"No, no, not at all. Sometimes paranoia is justified, but not in this case." He took a long breath, then continued. "True, the government wants everyone to get used to this new online system. And it is mostly working, I understand. But in this case, there's a very simple reason you haven't gotten your authentication code."

Harry sensed that Odiengo was enjoying this, drawing it out, teasing him.

"Okay, okay! What's going on?"

Again, the broad smile. "You haven't been sent the code because the fellow who does that is out sick."

Now Harry was sure Odiengo was joking. "What! That's impossible. Those codes get generated automatically!"

Odiengo nodded. "Normally, yes. But, you see, the establishment of automated systems such as eCitizen necessarily threatens the jobs of people who would otherwise process the forms. You haven't been to Nyayo House yet, but it's nine stories chockfull of overworked bureaucrats. And those are good jobs."

Harry was stunned. "You mean there's some guy who sits there all day, and his job is to click *Send?*"

"It's almost that simple. You see, another aspect of the Kenyan mindset is suspicion. Adding the manual step not only creates a new type of job, but it's probably also seen as a prudent internal control."

"So what do we do?"

"My friend Edwin works in another department. But he will find the supervisor and facilitate the procedure. We need do nothing more. You will receive the code sometime today, I'm sure."

"Whew! Then what?"

"I've meant to ask you, do you have the originals or at least certified copies of all your documents?"

"Like what?"

"Birth certificate, business registration, college diploma?"

"My *diploma?* I used to have it on the wall in my office, but I don't have the office anymore, and I don't know what became of it. And I must have needed my birth certificate for my first passport, but that was years ago."

"*Hacuna matata.* We will write to your authorities back home and to your school for your transcript."

Harry was bewildered. "But I thought we'd be doing all this online. Why would we need official documents when it's all digital?"

"You will be able to scan your documents and submit them electronically with your application process. But when you are approved, you must present those documents in-person to a government representative."

"Unbelievable. I suppose the reason is to prevent forgeries?"

Odiengo smiled smugly, "Of course, that is the ostensible reason. But based on what we've just experienced here, I'm sure you can guess the underlying motivations."

"So the inspectors will keep their jobs?"

"Not only that. The remnants of colonial bureaucracy pervade Kenyan culture. What does every official document have?"

"A stamp. Or a seal."

"Yes. And the person who affixes that seal is authorized to charge a *fee.* Every time you turn around, you're going to need a stamp of some kind. May I ask, do you own a dog?"

"No, sadly not. It would be difficult to have one here, I suppose.

My wife Lucille had a Westie. He was dearly loved. I think he was a better friend to her than I was, at the end. Now they're both gone."

"I was going to advise you, Kenyan law regards a family pet as livestock. Besides certificates of health and vaccinations from veterinarians, which require stamps, you will also need a special permit if you take your pet on a car trip. And you will need a different permit, requiring a separate stamp and fee, for each county line you cross during your trip."

"Wow," Harry said. "I've lived alone here for weeks. A dog would have been a good companion."

"I suppose the purpose of the law was to prevent herders from driving their livestock into different jurisdictions. Understand, though, even many well-to-do Kenyans still regard dogs as security animals. The big breeds are favored. They are trained to be vicious when strangers approach, and they live outside. Never in the house. Livestock, if you will."

"Yes," Harry said. "There are two big ones here on the compound. And a whole pack of little terriers."

"Ah, yes! They greeted me with enthusiasm when I got out of my car! Are they fine now that they know you?"

"Oh, yes. We all get along. The terriers don't have any patience with the monkeys, though."

Odiengo laughed. "I'd think not!"

The lawyer thanked Harry and Bea for his tea and left, offering to return to go over the next steps after Harry's various applications had been submitted. But his parting message was that the approval processes could take weeks, perhaps longer.

Harry asked, "Must we be in Nairobi for the duration?"

"Not at all," Odiengo replied. "You must return for some of the filings after approval, though. Meanwhile, we keep working on the business plan. Have you made any progress?"

Harry replied, "I spent some time getting the house in order. But it's not like I have much else to do."

Odiengo was almost out the door. Out of earshot of Bea, he asked Harry, "Are you sure you still want to do this?"

Harry answered, "I don't know. How about you? Are you still in?"

"I serve on the boards of several philanthropic organizations. If this one is true to its mission, whatever that may be, I would be honored to participate."

Harry thought that was the kind of non-answer a politician might give to an embarrassing question from a reporter. And he wondered how much Odiengo knew about Skebelsky's real motives and larger schemes. But, for now, he let it go.

The lawyer had seemed sincere. But his elaborate joke about the computer codes was ridiculous! Of course, Harry would never know what really happened. But once again he worried he was being played.

THAT NIGHT, during one of her late-night chats with Harry via WhatsApp, Esther said she feared she wasn't getting her own house in order. When she told Alice she'd soon be moving to Nairobi to be with him, her sister resolved to step up to her new role as head of household in Ukunda. But, in her mind, doing so meant informing the boyfriend on the motorcycle that it was time to park it, which meant she expected to be at least engaged if not married as a condition of his coming to live with them. Except that, once informed of her conditions, including expected contributions to support the others and the baby, he took off. So Alice vowed she needed a new man right away, and he might as well be a rich one. She even asked Esther whether her boss Balvan's marriage was happy. If not, might Esther put in a good word?

"Let me ask," Harry interjected, knowing he was taking a risk. "If the guy has money, does it matter whether he's black or white?"

Esther answered frankly as if it were a business question: "It matters if the parents are involved. If they are, the fellow had better at least look dark enough to be one of their tribe. And if he owns cattle or a hotel or a bank, so much the better. He may have children from some other marriage. He could even have other wives, but not so much anymore — unless the family is Muslim, sometimes not even then. But if the young girl is making this choice on her own, then, my precious dear man, whiter is nicer. That means lighter-skinned babies who might move up, get rich, and support their mother in fine style one day."

Even more delicately, he asked, "I assume you don't want any more."

"Ha!" she exclaimed. "Harambee, are you telling me you've still got sperm that haven't retired yet?"

"Cary Grant was a new father when he was in his sixties."

She laughed. "Oh, all the fun is in the trying, I'm sure. But I tell you, it's not any wish of mine to have any more. I'm lucky the two I've got are only a little devilish and haven't turned my hair white."

"I figured," he said. "I didn't want to disappoint."

There was warmth in her voice when she replied softly, "So far, you haven't. Just keep paying careful attention, and mind where else your eyes go."

CHAPTER 31

*O*n the phone last night, Esther had told him it might be weeks before she could join him in Nairobi, sometime in January. But when she came, she'd be there to stay. This news brightened his morning, and his mind raced through its checklist of chores, all the things he hoped to do to make this vintage house a home for his beloved.

He offered to join her in Diani for Christmas week, but she begged off. She'd made no preparations. She had no plans to visit her father in Nairobi, who, she said, was miraculously still alive and just as hateful. She'd wanted her children to join her in Diani, but she encouraged them to stay with friends because she couldn't give them much attention. And she didn't want them left to their own whims in the beach town. Other than looking forward to a candlelight service at her church, she said she had to regard the holiday as an opportunity for overtime at work. Harry confessed he wasn't one to celebrate either. She encouraged him to buy himself a fine dinner, perhaps invite Joseph whenever he wasn't spending time with his own family.

Harry rarely looked at Facebook or any of the other social media. He'd checked Nicole's posts from time to time, and he noted that none of her recent photos showed her boyfriend. In fact, she wasn't posting much at all. With Christmas coming, he felt he should at least schedule a call on Skype or Zoom. They hadn't exchanged gifts for years. He thought about shipping her the statuette he'd bought her, then he worried he might be sending a silent message he was never coming home. He didn't want to upset her, especially since he wasn't sure. Perhaps he'd decide after that call. On a whim, he looked at Eleanor Amory's recent posts. He hadn't been keeping up with her, but he thought about her about as frequently as he thought about moving back to Santa Monica. Which, he had to admit, was any evening Esther said something that annoyed him. But the one time he checked out Eleanor, there were her recent pictures from Maui, grinning her face off with some new boyfriend. The fellow might be Harry's age but slender, handsome, and tan. Someone he might have seen in the locker room at his golf club. Oh, well.

He rechecked the dates of her Facebook posts. If Eleanor was in Maui, who was minding the house? He fired off a quick text to her, and with the time difference, it was the next day before she replied.

Harry, dear! I tried to reach you. Nicole said she'd be happy to take care of it.

He trusted Eleanor. He didn't doubt she'd tried to reach him. He saw no point in pestering her about how her messages got lost. He left messages for Nicole, both voice and text, but he got nothing back. He should have known it was just as easy to get played by the nice folks back home. If his daughter was living in the house, he knew he'd never have the nerve to charge her rent.

Harry had completed the online applications on eCitizen, and he'd emailed requests, along with payments, for the certified documents he would need. Mary had the house looking tidy and furnished with the linens he'd bought, and even though some days had been rainy and chilly, he'd refrained from using the fireplace, so the funk of smoke and soot was gone. He'd have Gabriel cut fresh flowers to set out around the place after he had Bea ask McAdie if harvesting blooms from the yard was permitted. He still hadn't found the dinnerware they'd need. He resolved that Esther's return would be sufficiently special they'd risk using Wilma McAdie's fine china in the formal dining room. Afterward, he'd do the washing up himself to make sure that, if anything broke, he could rightfully take the blame.

It was another cloudy day. He expected the sun might break through by afternoon. He slept late, having dreamt of picnicking with Esther on a warm afternoon in Central Park. He'd never been to Central Park and had traveled to Manhattan only a few times on business. But that's how dreams go. He'd seen that park countless times in movies.

He made himself a breakfast of fried eggs and toast. The toaster was new. If he could keep avoiding the meat, maybe he'd live longer. Now he had reasons. He went light on the butter because he could not tolerate the Kenyan margarine, which was sold in a pint-sized tub and didn't require refrigeration. He feared it was made of some kind of plastic.

Everything about that day so far was mundane. Even blissfully so, Harry thought. He was beginning to think of himself as a Kenyan. It would be a comfortable life. Of course, he'd had much the same comfortable routine back home, but without a sense of purpose. And without someone to share it with.

It occurred to him then that there wasn't a drop of alcohol in the house. For her own reasons, Bea politely refused to buy his bourbon or even wine on her grocery rounds. Harry would often get Joseph to stop off at the liquor store at the Galleria as they'd be coming home from a shopping trip. Or he'd send Gabriel off with some cash to fetch it. But as of yesterday, Harry had neglected to do any of those things, and when he called Joseph for a ride, the fellow said he'd be spending the day in Thika. He offered to send one of his mates, but Harry chose not to order a driver for such a trivial errand.

He appreciated Joseph's injunction not to go walking after dark. But the day was brightening as the sun broke through the cloud cover, there was traffic on the streets, and the Galleria was just a half-mile away. Granted, the final leg of the journey required crossing the Langata-Magadi interchange on the highway, but Harry had seen crowds of locals doing just that as they made their way to the shops to report for work. He figured it would be safe enough if he waited to cross along with the rest of them.

Against the chill and the possibility of sudden showers, he put on a windbreaker. Thinking his straw hat made him look too much the tourist, he put on a Kenya Safari Club ball cap Aldo had given him but he'd never worn. He didn't inform anyone he was going, and when he passed the guard shack to let himself out the front gate, he saw that Michael, the daytime askari, was napping.

The residential road was rock-strewn dirt, but its surface became tarmac as it approached Forest Edge Road to the east. On the opposite side of that road was the mile-wide strip of woodland. It connected the broad preserves of Ngong Road Forest to the north and the Nairobi National Park to the south. As Harry strolled down this road toward the junction with Forest Edge, he passed the gates of several neighboring estates. As he came near each gate, unseen guard dogs barked immediately at the sound of his footsteps in the gravel. At an estate near the corner, an old groundskeeper stood with a hose watering the shrubbery.

The fellow saw him and called out as he waved, "Fine day, sir!"

Harry called back, "Fine day to you! What's your name?"

"I'm Wellington, sir."

Harry asked him, "Named for the duke who stuck it to Napoleon?"

The fellow chuckled and replied, "Nossir. For the boots!"

Harry gave a good-natured wave and yelled, "I'm Harry!"

"Named for one of those kings?"

"No, sir. They call me Harambee."

Wellington laughed heartily. "Lucky you!"

Harry waved again with a broader smile and strode on. He didn't mind at all the decorous way these Kenyans, especially the older ones, treated whites. As if he were some globe-trotting billionaire!

As he headed south on Forest Edge, the stand of tall trees was on his left, and the development of wooded estates was on his right. None of those houses verged on the road. They were set well back, behind gates and tall hedges or walls.

His gait wasn't lazy, but it wasn't brisk. He was enjoying the fresh air, and he was in no particular hurry. Every now and then, a car would pass at speed, and these would be either taxi drivers diligent in their promptness or locals in SUVs in a hurry to run errands. But the flow wasn't continuous. The road wasn't busy today.

And today there were no troops of baboons foraging in the roadside litter for scraps. Because he'd been warned about the aggressive males, Harry was relieved not to see any. He knew they lived in the forest, and, according to McAdie, they weren't shy about roaming around the woods in the neighborhood, as well.

Not far from the corner where Harry had turned south, Forest Edge enters a dip. There's a ravine at the bottom, and the road descends about a hundred feet into it, then climbs back out. On the other side, the road crests at the entrance to Bomas of Kenya, a cultural community center where busloads of schoolchildren are taken to see indigenous dance performances. But like the other buildings in the area, the center is set well back from the road, surrounded by woodland and a massive car park. Across from the Bomas entrance, vendors were selling curios, crafts, and used clothing from their temporary setups at card tables. Some also offered small meals to locals, trading on the workers who traverse this road on their way to and from their jobs at the mall.

It's an active area with dozens of folks bustling about at almost any hour during the day. But as Harry entered the dip, he couldn't see over the crest, and no one up there could see him. And, at this particular moment, there were no other pedestrians around him and no cars passing.

Harry thought he was alone on this part of the road, then he heard feet on the gravel and looked over to see a young boy striding past on his right. The kid was walking briskly, and Harry was happy to let the kid overtake him.

When Harry looked ahead, in his peripheral vision he noticed another, taller boy, walking just as hurriedly in the same direction on the forest side of the road.

The attack was on him so quickly Harry didn't think to cry out. And his pockets were empty before he realized what was happening. With two long strides, the tall boy crossed the road and grabbed him from the back, throwing both arms around Harry's shoulders in a tight hug as the other boy deftly plucked phone, passport, cash, and credit card from the right pocket of Harry's cargo pants.

The loot in hand, the small boy sprang back with a smile. The hugger let go, and they were about to turn away when the tall boy yelled, "Get his ring!"

The small boy stood frozen. The stakes had changed. He wasn't about to grab Harry's hand. He clearly wanted to run away right then.

But the tall boy screamed at Harry, "Give us the ring or we'll kill you!"

Neither of them was holding a knife, but that didn't mean they couldn't produce one.

More bewildered than he was scared or angry, Harry tugged at the obsidian ring, but it wouldn't budge. Besides the snug fit, he'd salted his eggs this morning, and his pudgy fingers were swollen.

The tall boy could see his victim's difficulty and grimaced, clenching his jaw. The short boy looked pained as if he feared what his accomplice might do next.

Harry spit on his finger, wrenched and pulled mightily, and finally the ring came off. He handed it to the short boy, who was crouching in front of him, and they sprinted off across the road and disappeared into the protection of the forest.

Harry was stunned, frozen on the spot. He patted his pants pockets to confirm they were empty. There were no witnesses in sight. And still no cars. The gate of the nearest residence was closed, with no attendant.

He took a deep breath. His heart was pounding. It occurred to him he might not have breathed at all during the last two minutes. There was nothing to do, no one to tell. Or perhaps he was just too ashamed to act. He'd been warned not to walk here. But he had, and the result would be no surprise to anyone. And, except for his vanity, he was unharmed.

There was no reason to go to the mall now, so he walked slowly back home.

Wellington had finished his chore and gone inside. Harry had hoped the fellow's smile would help him lighten up. He probably wouldn't have shared his story, though.

At McAdie's gate, Harry found Michael awake and on duty. He told the askari what had happened, and the fellow said earnestly, "So sorry, Papa. We have some bad boys out there." He promptly phoned Gabriel, who came out and led Harry into the big house to see McAdie.

The old boy was sitting with a mug of tea in front of his fireplace. Harry had the brief thought his landlord might rarely move from his easy chair.

McAdie stayed seated as he got the gist in confidence from Gabriel and Harry held back. Then he stood and turned to Harry, "You should learn to listen when folks try to give you advice," he said brusquely.

"All my fault" was all Harry could say.

McAdie rested a commiserating palm on Harry's shoulder, softened his tone, and said, "Gabriel will drive you to the police station over at Hardy. You'll need a police report." He glowered and added, "Let Gabriel do the talking!"

On the way to the station, Gabriel listened intently as Harry described every detail he could remember about the incident. He guessed the younger boy might be fourteen, the older one not yet twenty. There was nothing at all notable about their clothing. They both wore dark tee shirts with no designs or logos, dark jeans, and canvas shoes. They were both scrawny. He realized their complexions didn't have the gleam or rosy highlights of health. Their cheeks were sunken and chalky.

Gabriel told him, "That's a jailhouse look, boss. Those boys are from Kibera, for sure. They're likely starving."

"They were a team. They'd had practice. They picked the spot and timed their approach. That younger one had the skills of a pickpocket. He must have seen the bulge in my right-front pants pocket, and he'd snatched everything I had in the blink of an eye."

As they pulled into the station's car park, Harry could see two burly policemen sitting in an unmarked, camouflage-painted van. By now, it was late afternoon, and it might be the end of their shift because they looked weary and bored.

As Gabriel escorted Harry in, he reminded him, "Let me talk, boss. If they want to know something, I'll ask you."

A girl who was so young she might have been an intern stood behind the counter. There was no one else in the room.

Gabriel greeted her with, *"Jambo."*

Her face was expressionless as she replied, *"Jambo sana."*

He announced, in English, "My friend needs to file a report. He was just robbed by two youths as he walked along Forest Edge Road."

She didn't hesitate to answer, "This desk is closed. It's after hours."

Gabriel protested in Kiswahili, "But it's just after four!"

All she said was, persisting in English with a disdainful glance at Harry, "Nevertheless."

There followed a spirited exchange in Kiswahili, after which the girl sighed and pronounced with disgust, in English, "Proceed to the copy shop across the way. Return with the form. The cost is twenty shillings."

Gabriel didn't bother to thank her for the information. He took Harry by the arm, turned him toward the door, and they marched out.

Harry exclaimed, "Twenty cents! They don't have a supply of their own forms?"

Gabriel smirked. "They either have a deal going with that store for pennies or she's embarrassed to admit her supply is funga. That's probably why she wanted us to come back tomorrow."

"Tomorrow!"

"They have no intention of catching these boys, boss. They know you need a report, especially to replace your passport and your phone. And that's what they will provide."

The copy shop on the other side of Ushirika Road was scarcely larger than a closet. But it was doing a brisk business not only in copies but also in stationery and inkjet cartridges. A half-dozen people, mostly student-aged, were queued up at the door, each holding a sheaf of paperwork. The machine inside was not self-service, and it was a long wait before Gabriel and Harry emerged with the single sheet they needed to provide the clerk at the station. Harry was doubly embarrassed that he had to borrow the nominal cost of the copy from the houseman. Luckily, the fellow was not flat broke.

Back at the station, Harry watched patiently as the clerk meticulously hand-printed the required responses on the report form. She listened to Gabriel's description of the event, which he repeated entirely in Kiswahili, after which she had only one question, directed to Harry in English: "Amount of cash stolen?" Harry told her it was a hundred bucks. She needed no translation.

After completing the form, she applied a rubber stamp to it. Then she recorded what looked to be a brief description in a folio-sized logbook. With an exasperated sigh, she closed the book and gave the stamped form to Gabriel. She didn't keep a copy.

As they got back in the car, Gabriel handed the form to Harry and advised, "Don't lose it. Take it to the shop when you request a new phone. And get a copy made. We needn't wait around at this place today. I expect you will need to surrender the original at the embassy when you apply for a new passport. Then carry the copy with you at all times, and fold it into your new passport when you get it."

"You seem to know all about this," Harry observed.

"We haven't had an incident on that road for a very long time," he said. "But a German visitor friend of the boss was staying at a hotel in Karen last year. He neglected to use the private safe in his room, and when he returned from dinner one evening, his passport, phone, and a tidy sum of money were missing. He was extremely angry and reported the theft to management. To accommodate the fellow, the hotel summoned the police, which is typically not done in minor matters. Officers came and conducted a thorough search of his room. He should have been suspicious about why they wanted to inspect. The police found a bag of marijuana, which did not belong to our guest, but they arrested him for possession of drugs and hauled him into jail. He spent the night there and was released the next morning after pledging a handsome fine, which he could only satisfy after an officer marched him to the nearest ATM. Then he had the bother of replacing the passport and his phone. It's not easy."

As they turned north from Langata Road onto Forest Edge to head back home, they saw two armed men in uniform walking along their side of the road. They were walking in the direction of the dip where Harry had been robbed.

Seeing the officers, Gabriel said, "You are already famous, boss!

Word of your robbery must have brought these fellows here. They are not usually around."

"Are they police?" The men were wearing camouflage gear with high boots. They had rakish berets on their heads and semiautomatic rifles slung on their shoulders.

"No. These are Kenya Defence Force. Policemen wear blue shirts." Then Gabriel asked, "Shall we stop and speak with them?"

"Why would we do that?"

"I don't look for trouble. But I'm curious. And a bit angry. One of our own has been attacked!"

"Okay, but you do the talking."

Gabriel pulled the car alongside the officers on the shoulder of the road and rolled down the window. He spoke to them in Kiswahili, and Harry assumed Gabriel was telling them the story.

The men looked at each other to share a smirk, then one of them answered Gabriel brusquely.

Gabriel looked annoyed and turned to Harry to translate: "They know those boys, but they cannot pursue them." Then he asked, "Do you wish to pay for their tea?"

"A bribe? Are you kidding? What's the point of paying if my stuff is gone and those kids are going to get away?"

Gabriel answered in a low voice, "The robbers care only about cash. And they will get some for the ring, as well. They took your phone and your passport so you would not be able to report the incident right away. And the bank card is useless to them. They likely threw your things away in the forest. But if these fellows should come into possession of your property, they might be inclined to return it to you."

Harry was appalled. He kept his own voice down as he asked, "Are you saying these guys might be *working* with the thieves?"

Gabriel shrugged. "It might be best to remember, boss, that *offering* a bribe is also a crime."

"You mean they might be trying to entrap me somehow?"

"I have no experience with KDF. But remember, the German had no drugs. Let's not give them an excuse to lock you up."

Gabriel thanked the officers, and he drove Harry home.

Harry had been robbed the afternoon of Christmas eve. Too late for it to make any difference, Gabriel had confided in him that the holiday was always a high-crime period in the city. And the police would be looking for any opportunity to demand a bribe. Everyone needed more money than they had, except maybe the public officials who flew to seaside resorts for the holiday in their helicopters.

Harry used McAdie's landline phone to call his bank to report the theft of the card. He borrowed some cash. He was relieved the old fellow didn't gloat. He sent messages to Esther and Aldo, neither of whom replied. Even though he craved comfort from Esther, he wasn't eager to retell the story to either of them. She'd be here to hold him soon enough. He asked them to communicate with him via email or SMS on his computer, but he resolved not to check it until morning.

By this time, it was early evening, but Harry had no appetite. He'd made no plans for Christmas dinner, nor had he invited anyone to join him. Now with his emotions drained, forcing himself to celebrate seemed pointless. He had a hot bath and tucked himself into bed, pulling the covers over his head, before the last of the daylight had faded from the sky.

HARRY AWOKE in panic in the middle of the night. The clock by the bed showed 3:49 a.m. He was gasping for air, and his tee shirt was soaked with sweat.

His mind was in a spin. He knew he'd been restless and dreaming actively, but details escaped him. He remembered only a snippet, a scene hardly more than a snapshot.

In the dream, in the moments before Harry was jolted out of it, the young boy who took his ring was seated opposite him at the kitchen table. Instead of looking fourteen, as Harry had described him, he now appeared to be no more than ten. He was sobbing. Tears were streaming down his face, the wetness etching tracks in the ghostly, chalky coating on his cheeks.

Harry asked him cautiously, as lightly as he'd greet any local on the street, "What's your name?"

"My name is Micah." He sniffed. "Mike."

"What's wrong, Mike?"

"Papa, my mum wants to know what will become of me."

Harry tried to answer, but he choked on the words. Furious with himself, he tried to yell, to force sound from his throat. Nothing came out but a strangled gag, and then he couldn't get any air. It was the hypoxia that woke him up.

CHAPTER 32

*E*sther arrived at Wilson Airport on January 17, 2020. Joseph met her at the airport and brought her to Karen. In the days since Harry's unfortunate incident, he'd tried to calm down, but his sleep was still restless, his days fitful and unproductive. During that time, he'd spoken with her every night on the phone, and eventually he'd shared it all. Except for one detail. The first thing he said to her when she got out of Joseph's car was "They got the ring."

She rested a hand tenderly on his shoulder, gave him a long, lingering kiss, and said softly, "My precious dear. Thank God you still have your finger."

On Harry's instruction, Joseph had brought champagne. No doubt appreciating the occasion's specialness, he was savvy to also buy a bag of ice, and then he found Gabriel to borrow a bucket so he could set the bottle in it to chill. He left them alone with their glasses on the veranda after sheepishly offering his condolences about the theft and making his excuses about needing to pick some other clients.

They were using Wilma's Waterford crystal. The extra weight of the leaded glass in Harry's hand made him think celebratory drinking shouldn't require such heft. It was a passing thought, when he should have been thrilled Esther was finally with him. But he was annoyed she'd stayed away for so long, and it made him uneasy. Aldo had left a vacuum, as well, and that absence was mostly unexplained.

Harry told her the whole story, just as it had happened, for the first and, he hoped, the last time. He included the episode of the boy's appearance in his dream.

When he was finished, she reached across the table to take his hand. "Look, Harry. You were wise not to fight back. In the value of the things they took, it's small money. I'm sure you know that ring did not cost a fortune, but I know it upsets you to lose it. Don't think of it as some message from God. I'm here, and I'm staying. And we'll exchange rings soon enough, if you still want me."

Harry assured her, "This doesn't change my mind about you. Or about Kenya. I was mugged. It could have happened in Los Angeles — or anywhere on Earth. Only there, the guys would be addicts, and they would have been crazy, waving their knives in my face. Or their guns." Then he added, "And McAdie is right. I should learn to listen."

"It's upset you, though. You're shaken. I can see it."

Harry blew out a puff of air and gulped some wine. "The bank card was easy. I'll have a replacement by air courier tomorrow. The passport's a pain. Two weeks for a replacement, and I have to go to the embassy — twice. Once to apply for it and again to pick it up. A hundred and fifty bucks. Insult to injury! The phone is actually the hardest. Turns out you not only need a passport to get a phone but also to move your account to another one. Or even to start over and buy a new phone. I hadn't thought to make a copy of my passport. So one of the calls I made was to the hotel. They make a copy when you check in, and they were happy to email it to me. But when I presented it at the phone store — along with the police report to *prove* it was stolen — they said I must have the original! Now I have to wait just to get another phone. Fortunately, I have the computer and the Wi-Fi." Then he added, "But a lot of good that does me because Aldo doesn't respond to my messages. And I have to ask Gabriel to call whenever I need Joseph."

"But you could use your computer to text Joseph! At least when you're home. And when you're out and he's dropped you, you just set a time for him to pick you."

She was right, reliably practical. He mumbled, "I never thought of that," and he drained his drink. He had to admit he'd been looking for excuses to feel victimized.

She studied his face and said, "None of that is what's bothering you."

Harry said finally, "Yeah, it's the boy."

"You know the older one was giving him orders, would have hurt *him* if he'd disobeyed."

"In the dream, he asked me what would become of him. He said his mother wants to know."

"He might not have a mother. Could be the other fellow is the only family he has."

"But he asked me as if I *know* what will happen to him. As if somehow I'm in control of his future."

"You know you're not."

"Then why do I shudder every time I hear him say it?"

THAT EVENING, Esther applied all her talents to make him feel better. He was already exhausted emotionally, but his body rallied despite himself. He didn't even need a pill. Then he was well and truly shot, and he slept through till midmorning the following day.

CHAPTER 33

The next morning, Esther had been up for hours before Harry stirred. She made him ugali and greens. He tried to dig in but couldn't manage it. He should have been famished and well on his way to feeling refreshed, but he was still down.

He liked her coffee, though. It was the same brand he'd been using, the same water. When he asked her what was different, she explained that she put crushed eggshells in the bottom of the pot. Bea had bothered to hold some back from Gabriel's garbage collection.

He finally confronted Esther with, "What's going on with Aldo? I can't believe you haven't heard from him. Is he thinking of backing out?"

She'd been bustling about the kitchen, busy with washing up when there was really no need. Bea should have shown up by now to begin her chores, but Harry guessed Esther had sent her away.

Esther sat down slowly and said, "Aldo has been tending to Victor's affairs in Europe. It's become complicated."

Harry's face flushed, then he demanded, "Do either of you ever tell me the whole truth?"

"You don't want to know — you mustn't know — about anything

266

to do with Victor. His proposal was to rent us land and buildings. That is what the bankers would call *arm's length.*"

"Do you mean to tell me there are things about this deal that you know — that I will *never* know? Not even as your husband?"

"Like I say, it's complicated. And it has become more complicated. It's not likely to get sorted anytime soon."

He stared at her. "This is maddening! And what about all the time you've been spending in Diani? Don't tell me it was only because of Balvan."

"It's all because of Victor," she said softly.

Harry stood up, jostling the china on the table. "You're still seeing him!"

"No," she said, coming over to embrace him. "Not in that way. Not in the way you think."

He pushed her away. "What can you possibly have to do with him now?"

She sat back down and gestured for him to do the same. She took a long breath, then said, "We never had a formal divorce settlement. Or... really a divorce at all." Then, she added, "Now, we do."

Harry had nothing to say. He was glad he'd eaten no breakfast because it would have come up on him.

She went on, "You see, until there was you, there was no reason. We lived apart, he went his way, and, as I told you, he only showed up at times to see the children, and they regarded him as a stranger. Then when he agreed to send them off to school, there was no reason at all for him to come around."

"Is he holding something over your head? Some lawyer's trick? Is that why it's *complicated* all of a sudden?"

"It's not because of you" was all she would say. Harry was too stunned to move. She got up abruptly and ducked into the hallway. He could hear the inner security door clang shut and the rattle of the key as she locked herself in.

He raced after her and clutched the bars as he watched her march down the hall. She was sobbing as she retreated into the bedroom and closed the door.

A half-hour later, he heard the sound of tires on gravel as a car came to a stop outside. She must have been waiting for it because she soon emerged from the bedroom, pranced down the hallway toward the kitchen, turned the lock in the security grate, and freed herself from self-imprisonment.

She'd washed her face and had changed from her casual clothes into her business suit. She carried her one suitcase.

"What the hell is going on?" he asked her.

"Joseph is taking me to the Hotel Troy." Harry had seen the sign on the road, just past the Galleria. The place was scarcely a mile away.

"But *why?*"

"Aldo returns tomorrow. Joseph will pick him from the airport, then he will come for you. The three of us will have tea at the hotel. Or drinks, if you prefer." Then she added, "Yes, it should be drinks. I'm sure you'll want that."

He reached out for her, but she was already moving past him. "This makes no sense!" he exclaimed as he turned to follow her to the back door.

Joseph took her case and was loading it into the boot of his Toyota when she turned back before getting in to say, "Harry, Aldo will explain. I will explain. As much as you can know. Then it will be up to you to decide. You may decide you want to go home after all."

CHAPTER 34

*H*arry was useless, fretting all day. He could have used his computer, in the way Esther had suggested, to call her. But he couldn't, or wouldn't. He wasted most of the afternoon watching a day-old YouTube of unexciting football as Arsenal trounced some team he'd never heard of. Later, after he'd tucked himself in early and without supper, instead of sleeping, his mind raced.

Why was Esther so upset? Was it because he'd finally expressed his nagging suspicions? She must know by now that he could be indecisive by nature, and waiting around all these weeks for their project to progress didn't help, especially since he was stuck here in Nairobi, which was never meant to be home. It was obvious to him now that Aldo must have been communicating with Esther all the while they'd left him housesitting here.

He'd had the recurring fear that, during his entire African adventure, he'd been more of a witness than an actor. He was a tourist. He was watching his new life experience as if it were a movie. And he had been enjoying the show. There had been no costs, be they financial or emotional, he hadn't been able to afford.

Did she seriously think whatever else they had to tell him would send him packing? All the way back to Los Angeles?

Aldo's friendship had seemed sincere, if baffling at times. And Esther's love seemed freely given. And yet, even after each of them in turn had finally opened up to him, he still felt like an outsider. Knowing that they'd once been intimate, for however short a time, helped him understand. But it didn't make him less suspicious of their closeness.

And Kenya itself was a nest of puzzles. From the air, it was a vast expanse of lush, equatorial greenery, a Garden of Eden, the cradle of the Rift Valley, the human family's ancestral home. And here, as industrial clog and climate change threatened to choke so much of the rest of the so-called civilized world, the herds of wild animals still thrived, even though their numbers were dwindling. And yet, Paradise was rapidly and eagerly transforming itself into Purgatory. Nairobi was its New York, and Mombasa its Los Angeles. International capital was pouring into its economy from all sides, priming the pumps for the wealth gushers of an emerging One Percent — including the children of bureaucrats who'd been sent away to university in Paris and Princeton and Pretoria. They were the new, optimistic young capitalists. For the most part, they were English-speaking Christians, and the world's bankers were betting on their vision, their tenacity, and, yes, even or especially their greed. Why should these future leaders be any different from the rest of us? Many of them, like the expat visitors who kept returning as voluntourists, knew only a few words of Kiswahili, and their accents bespoke refinement acquired on other continents. The high-speed rail cutting through the national park, the superhighway bisecting the Serengeti, and the new avocado orchards planted in the paths of trekking elephant herds in Amboseli would someday worry them less than unemployment and inflation rates in the big cities. They'd become increasingly less concerned with the erosion of natural vistas and migratory freedom for wild herds, no more than decimating buffaloes and exterminating indigenous tribes had troubled the white settlers of the American Wild West two centuries ago.

Harry couldn't offer the excuse that he didn't know the stories or the stakes. He was a publisher of history books.

The question was, where did he fit? What was there for him here?

Until now, most of his work had been aimed at the simple goal of achieving life's comforts. But was it a question of work? Most men value themselves that way. Some women, too, now that they're permitted to be equally ambitious. Or was it all about family and relationships? Whom you love, those who love you? Harry didn't have much to show for that. He'd been kind to Lucille, and she to him, and there was Nicole. But his daughter was a stranger to him, not so different perhaps from the way Charles and Yvonne would someday remember Victor, as a historical footnote in their life stories, a supplier of sperm and half of their DNA, but not of their essential selves.

If he didn't understand himself, how could he presume to really know anyone else? Each of the eight billion souls on the planet carried a voluminous life story. No matter how much Esther and Aldo shared with him, he could only hope to get bits and pieces. He'd spent almost all of her life so far with Nicole, and yet he could only guess why she had chosen this succession of losers to love.

Was it all about personal satisfaction? The simple joys of living?

But enjoying life implies you've found some contentment in where you are. Or at least in where you're going. Even nomads want to know what they're about, most days.

Harry wanted to believe that Esther and Aldo weren't setting a trap for him. He understood that, each in their own way, they were partly ensnared in traps that had nothing to do with him. He was learning to let go of the idea that he was the cause of everything that happened to him. He'd never been one to covet possessions, but this trip had stripped him down to bare essentials. The baggage he carried was just two suitcases. And his replacement ATM card!

He resolved that he'd hear whatever they had to say. Like some hard-headed investigative reporter, he would challenge them. They might sincerely be trying to protect him, but that excuse was wearing thin.

CHAPTER 35

*A*ldo didn't return as he had planned. The worldwide crisis of the pandemic got in the way. Harry had been watching the news reports on MSNBC and CNN via YouTube. He'd finally gotten around to getting DTV installed, mainly because he wanted to watch sporting events as they were actually happening, but the antics of those devilish monkeys on the roof kept knocking the satellite dish out of whack.

In the early phase of the outbreak, news reports were conflicting, and rumors abounded. But since rumor has always been the primary engine of news in Kenya, it was more difficult than ever to know what to believe. And the sudden pronouncements of national and county officials seemed arbitrary at the best of times. Harry was aware that the virus was racing through Italy, and he was concerned for Aldo. But no word came, and his friend persisted in ignoring messages. Harry also worried about Nicole, and her replies were characteristically terse.

I'm okay. Don't worry.
When are you coming home?
What about the house?

He didn't offer any answers. He assured her he was okay, and, in the almost meaningless complimentary close people would be adding to all their correspondence, he hoped she'd stay safe.

Harry texted back, realizing he hadn't asked about Geoffrey.

Duh, Courtney. He's history. No loss.

His thought at the time was he should follow up on this. He really should.

Particularly confounding was the news as it was being covered by the American networks. There was serious concern expressed initially by the Centers for Disease Control and the World Health Organization. But the US president and his cohort were downplaying the potential impacts, some even asserting that this virus wouldn't be much more consequential than a seasonal flu.

One of Harry's old colleagues, Richard Armbruster, had been spamming his email box with links to what appeared to be conspiracy-theory articles and videos. Harry knew Armbruster as the author of a textbook on geopolitics. The fellow was a retired university professor with a degree in economics who had once served as an advisor to USAID. He was, Harry thought, a harmless crank and didn't reply to any of Armbruster's emails. He had no strong opinions as to their veracity, but he didn't want to invite more of the fellow's rants. Few people even knew that Harry was in Africa, and he was content to keep it that way. He wasn't yet ready to tell anyone back home about his plans for Harambee.

Harry weighed all of these developments, and it gave him a preoccupation besides football and trying again without success to understand the rules of cricket. He tended toward the notion that sensationalism and panic do wonders for news ratings. He didn't know anyone who'd ever died of influenza, although as a boy, he'd been told that during World War I a great-uncle had survived the Battle of Argonne Forest only to succumb to the Spanish Flu.

He wondered whether these events would end up sending him home. He saw no reason to go now. He worried about Nicole, but then he always worried about Nicole, and whether here or there he had nothing to say about her decisions. They were still out of touch, but he assumed she was living in the house. He also tried to anticipate how, if the pandemic were to spread to Kenya, it would affect his plans and development of the Harambee project. But there were too many moving pieces to this puzzle.

Then came a surprise, one he could not have predicted. To East Africans, this coronavirus was hardly a novel threat. They'd already dealt with Ebola in two outbreaks, and HIV was an ongoing challenge. And during past flu seasons, they'd avoided iterations of SARS. Malaria was a topic of everyday conversation, and locals were aware of dengue fever and drug-resistant tuberculosis. Perhaps because of lessons learned from these incidents, the Kenyan government moved more decisively and more quickly than anyone expected. Kenya was one of the first countries to close its borders. Tourists were encouraged to go home. Their visas would not be extended. Inbound airline and cruise ship passengers, as well as those arriving at border checkpoints over land, were restricted to citizens and foreigners holding residence permits. Even then, entry required those travelers to quarantine in government-designated facilities for fourteen days before continuing to their destinations.

Which meant Aldo was stranded in Italy.

And Harry worried he might be coerced into going back.

Because of Odiengo's help, Harry's business license, along with his work and residence permits, were already pending. He'd recently renewed his tourist visa, which would be valid for another three months. So far, there were no rumors current visas would be revoked.

As he had done about most of the major decisions since he'd traveled here, Harry thought he could stay put and let events unfold.

~

It was late on the day when Aldo was supposed to meet up with them. But he'd sent a text to Esther with news his flight had been canceled. He vowed to have a conference call with both of them soon, but he didn't say when. Then she'd sent Joseph to get Harry and bring him to the Hotel Troy. They were finally having that drink in the garden courtyard by the pool.

"We'd better get back to Diani" was Esther's advice. "I am hearing they will be closing the roads soon. They can't be everywhere, but the police will be stopping anyone on the highway to Mombasa, and they'll turn you around. Only emergency vehicles and cargo may pass."

"How soon?" Harry asked her.

She shrugged. "These politicians are unpredictable. It could be today, tonight, or never. But we don't want to get stuck here, I can tell you. I have a family to care for, and your future responsibilities are all on the coast."

She was having tea. He was delighted to find the bar stocked Jack Daniels. He'd finished his first double on the rocks and was about to have another. He worried that, if he had too many, he'd start in on her again about his frustrations with her. But, for now, the Tennessee all-purpose sour-mash elixir for what-all ails you was working, and all he felt for her was warmth. He wondered whether she'd rented a room in the main building or one of the private bungalows. Perhaps they could request an upgrade and have what the British euphemistically refer to as "a full and frank exchange of views."

There was no mention from either of them of their spat yesterday or its reasons. The seriousness of the situation was front and center, and both assumed that whatever they'd be doing about it, they'd do it together. And his notions of what they'd be doing together in the next hour were getting increasingly specific. He was prepared to forgive and grind it out, if not forget.

But he didn't advance the proposition. Instead, he offered, "We'll fly, then," hoping he sounded nonchalant. He wanted to see some hint she'd be the one to soften first.

"No," she said. "The regional flights are already restricted. You'd have to be a government employee or a health worker."

"Are you sure this is necessary? I've put a lot of effort into getting the house ready. And Odiengo made it clear that, in the short term, we'd be able to get more done in Nairobi. Not to mention, I signed a lease."

"I'm telling you, staying in the city won't be healthy. You see what's happening in New York. All these people jammed together? We'll get Joseph to drive us, and to be cautious, we'll go at night. He knows the side roads if they try to divert us."

~

HARRY GOT no time in the sack with her that day. She was too preoccupied with preparations to leave, even though he was the one with a household to close down. Joseph dropped her at the school so she could discuss plans with Charles and Yvonne. She expected the government would close the schools, but she wanted the children to stay as long as they were open. Then they'd join her in Diani. The family couldn't all live in her little house in Ukunda, and she'd need time to prepare a place for them.

Harry wondered why one of the houses in Skebelsky's compound couldn't be made available to them on short notice. Esther sniffed and announced, "Victor dismissed his staff before Christmas. God knows what shape the place is in. As far as I know, his offer stands, but we won't be able to go there straight away."

Joseph drove Harry to McAdie's, where he confronted the crusty fellow in his habitual easy chair. Harry remained standing, if awkwardly. His approach was to be honest and straightforward. He didn't want to give the landlord details about his plans because he had none to give. He'd pack his suitcases that evening, lock up the house, give Gabriel the keys, and communicate later with them whether any of the household goods he'd purchased should be forwarded.

Harry had paid through the end of the month. McAdie had not required a deposit. The fellow, still seated, looked uneasy when it became clear that Harry intended to break the lease.

Harry explained, "Nobody knows how long this virus outbreak will last, but we don't expect you to hold the house for us. We've done our legal filings, and I expect we'll take care of business by courier where we can."

"No reason for you to stay," the old man muttered.

Harry might have been appealing to a Scotsman's parsimony when he suggested, "You know, I've bought linens and housewares, even some small appliances. Why don't we just agree you'll keep those as liquidated damages? You know, for the next tenants?"

McAdie huffed, "I'd have given you a fair price."

Harry insisted, "Oh no, I wouldn't think of it."

That brought a smile. "Just so. Save you the expense of sending it along."

And that was all that needed to be said. Harry hadn't grown as fond of McAdie as he'd expected. The fellow had kept to himself. But he knew he'd miss Gabriel's help and wise counsel, Bea's cuisine and her chattiness in the kitchen, and Mary's demure smiles.

As Harry left the big house, Gabriel took him aside and expressed that he valued their friendship and was sad to see him go. Harry sensed the fellow was not all that happy to serve McAdie, and he was reminded how much he missed Beto's companionship.

THE THREE OF them hit the road that night. Joseph had once again rented a Nomad van so they'd be comfortable. Harry finally asked where they'd be staying on their arrival, and Esther said she'd used Balvan's influence to gain a discount at Beachfront Apartments, a residence hotel.

"What's the matter with the Kusi? He should be able to give us a price at his own place."

"We've been closed for slow season since the week after New Year's," she explained. "You wouldn't know it living in Nairobi, but February is so hot we call it *suicide month*. There are no tourists, and that's when the mzungus take ski vacations in Europe or visit friends upcountry. Mount Kenya and Aberdare are popular with the wealthy Kenyans just now. At the beach, the lodges use the time for renovations. Balvan has been replacing old plumbing with copper and putting in new commodes." She yawned. "I've had to handle the purchasing and the contractors."

The tourist season usually wouldn't begin until May, peaking over the next few months with the arrival of European and American families on their summer vacations. Harry asked her, "What about reopenings? Maybe this virus scare will be over before the season starts."

"That's the question, of course," she said. "We expect the orders to close the schools and the hotels will come at the same time. As I say, any day. Many of the expensive restaurants have been on hiatus, and now they will stay that way. Places where the expats eat will try to stay open, but there is no predicting. The food markets will have to find ways of dealing with it, but it's all so uncertain. Local farmers and kitchen gardens can't grow enough, and at regular times we get most of our fresh produce from Mombasa. Now there is talk they will close the road from Likoni, so for some while, we may be scraping by."

Even before the outbreak, uncertainty seemed to be the prevailing mood in this country, and Harry had begun to get used to it. But now?

They didn't find much else to say to each other, and they both tried to sleep. A few hours out, they made a rest stop around Voi, but there were no refreshments. The roadside café was closed. With his usual faithfulness, Joseph had brought sandwiches and bottled water. A single attendant was on duty at the petrol station, and Joseph had to wake him up. The fellow explained he only took cash or M-Pesa. The bank-card system was funga tonight.

As they neared the outskirts of Mombasa, conditions became hazardous, and the experience was harrowing. A violent, unseasonal storm overtook them. Rain pelted down in sheets, coming as a torrent of big drops and thudding loudly onto the roof of the van like panicked tribal drumming. But what was worse, this section of the highway was four lanes across — but there was a pair of headlights in *each lane* — all coming in their direction! The lorry drivers hauling cargo from the seaport had taken over the entire tarmac, forcing east-bound vehicles onto the shoulders. Those unpaved portions were rutted and even rocky in some places, and going was slow. The rain compounded the challenges of seeing clear roadway and navigating the ruts. Joseph had the wipers on high, but the frantic pace couldn't keep up with the volume of water. The only things he could see clearly were the oncoming, near-blinding high beams of the huge lorries. He had to hold his track to the left of them, but not too far, or he might slide off the road and into the ditch.

They'd been driving in the rain for a half-hour when Harry and Esther were jolted violently forward in their seats, at first thinking they'd been struck from behind, as Joseph slammed on the brakes, throwing the van into a skid in the muddy track. They were on a barren stretch of road lined only with unlit warehouses hardly visible in the storm. This portion of the highway was still under construction, and temporary concrete barriers were set up along its edges. But Joseph had to make the panic stop when a row of barriers suddenly turned inward to guide traffic flow into single lanes in each direction. Heavily loaded lorries were hurtling toward them, hogging both lanes, and an inattentive driver's choices would have been to hit either the concrete piling or a truck head-on.

As Joseph caught his breath, he exclaimed, "These lorry men, they're crazy! They don't even know we're here! All chewing *khat* and stoned out of their minds!"

This was how cargo haulers stayed awake as they drove at top speed through the night — high on an ancient drug that is still legal — perhaps only because daily commerce depends on it.

"Thank you, Joseph," Esther said softly. "Once again, our lives are in your hands."

He waited for a break in the oncoming traffic, which took a while. Then he pulled out cautiously into what should have been the east-bound lane and proceeded slowly. Moments later, here came another pair of headlights, right at them, but its driver must have seen them, was forced to slow down and then had to stop, with a blast of airbrakes and a brief skid of eighteen wheels on the slick pavement. Other drivers had to react a split-second later, and all traffic had stopped in less than a heartbeat. It was a miracle there wasn't a pile-up. At the meeting point with the tiny Nomad, the passable section widened where barriers had been pulled back to permit access to the shoulder. Joseph steered the car to the side, where he proceeded carefully as a chorus of lorry horns blared in fury and the monster engines roared on.

CHAPTER 36

*S*uicide month had come and gone. It was the ides of March, and by now Harry and Esther were settled into their apartment at the beach. They'd had no eventful news from Aldo, who was still away and barred from returning, and the Harambee project seemed to be at a standstill. When Harry wasn't enjoying being lazy, he still worked on the business plan.

He was looking out the living-room window, the one that faced east and the unimaginable expanse of the Indian Ocean. He'd been a while in Kenya before he realized how inadequate were his notions of the geography of this part of the world. He had imagined that, if he sailed due east from here, he'd end up somewhere on the Saudi Arabian peninsula. No, that was hundreds of miles to the north. Or, the tip of India. Also to the north, not quite as far. Sailing toward the sunrise, he would not strike landfall until Sumatra, more than four thousand miles distant, almost but not quite all the way to Singapore.

The idea that this area near Mombasa was the endpoint of one of the world's most ancient trade routes made him feel even more like a time traveler. The resort where he and Aldo had first stayed in the area and where Esther still worked was named the *Kusi,* after the trade winds that blew from the southeast, carrying sailing ships from China,

Southeast Asia, and India. Then, for almost half the year, the trade winds, now called the *Kaskazi,* shifted to blow the other way. Hence, the term *trade winds.* Riding this natural cycle, for thousands of years, the merchant sailors would go from here to there and back, hanging out during the becalmed months in some faraway port, perhaps with a second family that had no inkling another household on a far-off shore existed.

A monkey, an arm's length away, was staring at him. Harry would learn that this species was a Sykes, with an expressive gray face, dark-gray fur, and an incredibly versatile tail longer than his body. This was a change from those black-faced vervets with their light, greenish-gray bodies whose drumming on the roof had disturbed his morning sleep as their trampoline games wrecked his DTV reception in Karen.

This monkey had shimmied up almost the full length of the palm tree by the window. Just beyond him and the stalk was a dense copse of African tulip trees. Here at the four-story hotel's penthouse level, Harry could see a gleaming wide strip of the ocean just over the greenery of those trees.

A person could get used to this.

The monkey's frank stare might have been asking him, "Why are *you* here?" No doubt monkeys had inhabited these forests eons before there were ever hotels, before there were even humans. Its pinched pink nose and puckered mouth seemed to suggest disapproval. Sykes are comedians, and they go wherever they want, whenever they want.

The Beachfront Apartments proved to be grander than Harry had expected. The place offered furnished suites and catered to longer-term stays by businesspeople and weekend vacationers from upcountry. The rates were modest by resort standards. The hotel had only a dozen rooms in two buildings, but because so few overnight tourists stopped here, Beachfront could be nearly empty much of the time, especially now, coming out of slow season.

The place was not more than a hundred yards from the beach, separated from the white sand by dense growths of trees. Esther had rented them a three-bedroom suite, which took up the entire top floor of the south building. The vista from the picture window in the living room was at treetop level, taking in a profusion of bright-orange blossoms. Over the tops of the trees, running along the blue horizon, Harry could see the outlying coral reef running like a rippling ribbon just beneath where the broad expanse of water met the sky.

Stunning to Harry at first was the sight of bars on the seaside windows. He'd become accustomed to them at the estate in Karen, even though discomforting feelings of imprisonment arose from time to time. But surely no one expected Mau Mau gangs to be climbing up here!

Of course, it finally occurred to him, the bars were to keep the monkeys out whenever the occupants pulled the sliding glass back to catch the ocean breezes. The width of the bars was only a couple of inches. Harry wondered if even those gaps were too narrow for the resourceful critters to squeeze through.

Here at Beachfront, a troop of about two-dozen Sykes would come just after dawn to munch on the colorful blossoms of those trees. They reminded him of the ubiquitous squirrels back home. Vervets came occasionally, but only when the more aggressive Sykes weren't around.

A different species would come some days, but only a few, to munch on those blossoms. Harry would look out to see three or four Colobus monkeys sitting, balanced on the branches. Vervets and Sykes wouldn't dare show up at those times. These creatures were twice as large as the Sykes, their fur jet-black with white markings. And remarkable compared with their hyperactive cousins, the Colobus monkey was sedate, even meditative. Harry thought they looked like priests. He learned they were endangered, partly because bygone hunters — tribal and then colonial military — prized their pelts for hats.

The length of the north side of the living room was spanned by French doors that opened on a long patio balcony. The balcony was directly above the swimming pool and an outdoor cantina. Especially because he'd grown used to open-air, veranda-style living, Harry liked to throw those doors open wide. The salt-air breezes were delicious, and in this part of the country, they were balmy most of the year, if not downright hot. The apartment provided air-conditioning only in the master bedroom.

No matter where Harry moved in Kenya, he had to become accustomed to a new batch of environmental adjustments. As the vervets had done in Karen, the Sykes would scavenge for food in the early mornings. As soon as those tulip trees blossomed, the flowers would be gone. And because of the hotel, the weekend visitors, the bar, and the detritus left by tourist revelries, the monkeys had grown used to snacking on the leavings of potato-crisp packages, bread rolls carelessly left in baskets on dinner tables, and even jars of nuts. The clever beasts knew how to take the lids off. And they not only liked bananas, but if someone were careless enough to leave one momentarily on any surface, they also ate the peels.

So, as a lesson learned, Harry noticed that several adult monkeys would perch on the railings of his balcony, especially in the mornings. If he was sitting in the living room, they wouldn't dare come in. They would just give him those blank stares as if daring him to leave. But if he were so careless as to walk away and leave fruit (or really, anything edible) on the dining table just inside the door, when he returned only moments later, both the food and the monkeys would have disappeared.

There were even times when he and Esther sat there over dinner, and in a flash a thief would appear and make off with a tasty bun.

No doubt they'd all be laughing at him then.

Whenever he could summon enough inspiration to believe the pandemic might end, he'd spend his days working on the business plan for Harambee. Odiengo had given him spreadsheet and word-processing templates, and Harry fretted over his computer to fill in the details. It wasn't just a matter of filling in the blanks. He had to think through scenarios and hypotheticals. At times, it all seemed more like a fanciful story than a practical plan. But memories of working through the details of his publishing-company startup came flooding back. He had been there, done that.

Harry had his laptop set up on a writing desk in an alcove off the apartment living room. In front of him was a floor-to-ceiling pane of glass that looked out over a profusion of green plants in an atrium on the building's ground floor. One morning, he was staring intently at the computer screen when, just above it, he saw a furry tail reflected in the glass. It was long and curled, bouncing jauntily as its owner passed just a few feet behind him.

Harry had forgotten he'd left the French doors open.

He didn't get up. He turned around slowly in his chair. The Sykes stopped and casually turned to face him, straightening up on two feet like an indignant human. The message in its expression was clear: *Why are you still here?*

And the critter scampered off, out the open door, ran along the balcony railing, then jumped onto a tree branch, swung to another, and disappeared into the foliage.

It didn't occur to Harry right away, but he came to realize that this place was their ancient home, and he was a short-term visitor. He feared the same might be said not only of his stay in Diani but also in Africa.

Perhaps it was a suitable metaphor for the existence of human beings anywhere on planet Earth?

ESTHER SEEMED PREOCCUPIED, as she had been when he was living in Karen, and she was fretting whatever she had to fret about here. She was still working for Balvan on his renovation projects, she said, because she had no reason not to. She'd leave early in the mornings, and Harry would have his days to himself. He adopted a habit of arising with her early, just after dawn. As she was leaving, he'd have his first cup of coffee as he sat and watched from the balcony as the sun rose over the ocean. Then he'd walk a half-mile to Kokko's coffee shop, where he'd indulge himself in a full breakfast while enormously enjoying chatting up the staff. Then he'd walk across the street to the open-air fresh-vegetable stalls near the supermarket, and he'd shop for the ingredients of today's dinner, which he'd prepare himself in time for them to sit down on Esther's arrival.

It was bliss. Or it would have been if he could avoid wondering whether his life here had any purpose at all. Or needed one.

Last night, he'd finished reading *The Constant Gardener* for the second time. It had made him think about Kibera. Once, with Harry's reluctant permission, Joseph had cut through that part of town to avoid a jam on the highway. Harry couldn't imagine what it would be like for a child to grow up in a place where such extreme overcrowding and privation were facts of life. And he was also struck by Justin Quayle's obsessive devotion to his wife, loving her more passionately in death than he had when she was alive.

After breakfast and back in the apartment, he'd pop his laptop and work on the Harambee project's business plan and budgets. In these ways, he felt most days were productively occupied. The cold facts of pandemic lockdown, when they came, didn't much concern him. Besides wearing a mask when he went out, his routine hadn't changed all that much. Kokko's had open-air tables, spaced a suitable distance apart. His negotiations with Mama Odile at the vegetable market were short, and she and her staff likewise wore masks.

He was well aware that Mama Odile only accepted cash, the main reason her goods were marked down a third to a half less than the prevailing prices for the same items at the supermarket, which he found out she also supplied. She had confessed to him that everything came in before dawn via tuk-tuk from Mombasa's huge markets. The big shop could get away with those high prices because the well-heeled mzungus were in the habit of using their bank cards for everything.

One morning, his eyes were bigger than his pocketbook, and he was thirty shillings short. Thirty shillings. Thirty pennies, three dimes. Mama Odile smiled at him, dismissed the difference, and pronounced, "We are family, Papa!"

The next day, he was careful to have the coins to make up the difference. As he handed them to Odile, he pronounced, "I owe you this."

She looked at the pieces in her palm, and Harry could tell this was something she might have demanded from a countryman, but never from a mzungu. She repeated her pronouncement of yesterday, looking up at him with watery eyes and saying softly, "We are one."

Harambee. Maybe that was what it was supposed to mean. Forty-three tribes. As in the land of *E Pluribus Unum,* this country had some distance to go.

The practical effect was, after lockdown, Harry's reclusive habits hadn't changed much. But he knew his neighbors were suffering. It was like the yearly slow season in the resort town, only it threatened to stretch out into the summer months and beyond, into the time when they all should have been going back to work, making generous tips, and sharing laughs with bright-eyed Europeans.

Some of his friends were begging. If not on the streets, they reached out desperately via their smartphones to anyone, anywhere in the world, who might spare them some money. PayPal had refused to do business in Kenya, perhaps because of the risky banks, but now their Xoom service was set up so their users anywhere could send funds direct to M-Pesa accounts on their phones. Even though he was still in-country, Harry caught some of the traffic as though they thought he'd already gone home.

Papa! How are you and your family! I hope all is well! So many of us face difficulties. Can you spare some to help us out?

Papa, small money, please!

Papa, my family has been evicted. I have poured a foundation for my new house, but my money is funga! Please send a few thousand for our roof and we will pray for you forever!

Papa, my brother and his family all have Covid. Can you help?

Papa, the new school year is approaching. You know I always have savings from my job for them, but not this year!

It was frustrating they'd had no further word from Aldo. Harry had seen news reports that the virus had been ripping through nursing homes and assisted-living facilities. So naturally he feared that Aldo's invalid wife was at risk. Perhaps she'd died, and he was lost in remorse? Or she and the sisters were surviving, and he was pouring all his money in there? What would they do in a place like that? Was the Vatican ahead of the curve or turning the other cheek and simply praying harder?

CHAPTER 37

$\mathcal{M}$ ost stunning was the day when a van pulled into the car park of Beachfront, and a load of familiar faces popped out. Gabriel, Bea, and Mary. Harry had been doing backstrokes in the pool, gazing up blissfully at the summer sun, and here came a new group of tourists. Only they were his old friends.

"You have visitors, Papa," the groundsman Nico called out to him.

Harry was climbing out from the pool when Gabriel addressed him. "Papa Harambee! Mr. McAdie has dismissed us. We come here to serve you!"

Gabriel explained that, responding to the pandemic, the old man had locked up his compound and flown back to Scotland. Harry guessed the old fellow would have had to pull strings and pay dearly to book the flight.

Harry choked up, thinking it was beyond presumptuous that this crew had made the three-hundred-mile trip from Nairobi on the off-chance he'd hire them.

But, of course, he did. And Gabriel became his new Beto!

The Beachfront was understaffed not only because of the off-season but also during lockdown, and so Gabriel became Harry's houseman, Bea his cook, and Mary his housekeeper. He resolved to pay high-season wages, but even at that, all of them cost him in a week about the same as one fine dinner for two at a local restaurant.

Gabriel resolved on his own that his daily chore would be cleaning the pool. Because of neglect, the water had taken to looking like murky green Jell-O. Within three days, and after chemical treatments he knew how to administer, the fellow had the water sparkling.

Bea spoiled Harry and Esther with dinners, although Harry insisted on taking her shopping lists to Mama Odile himself so he'd still have the pleasure of the outing and her friendship. Mary handled all the laundry by hand — there were no washing machines — and she still had time for ironing and mending. Harry gave her extra money for those modest chores.

Esther approved of all of it. She seemed to delight in how easily Harry took to the role of mzungu benefactor. This was, after all, the expected role for anyone who stayed longer than a vacation.

HARRY HAD NOT EXPERIENCED an unfortunate incident since the attack by the two boys on Forest Edge Road. He was beginning to think it was a fluke. As Esther had reminded him, a mugging could happen anywhere, and in this case no one had brandished lethal weapons, as one might expect in a country where no one could afford bullets, much less guns. Watch for the knife, but even then, if they dared use it, they'd spend a lifetime in some filthy prison for so much as scratching a white man.

In what you might call normal times — that is, when it's tourist high-season, the money is flowing, and the beach city is experiencing high times — the crime rate is low. Tourists are royalty, and anyone who dares touch them will be reported to a special police division, if not disciplined by locals by furious fisticuffs on the spot.

But times had changed.

As a matter of routine now, Harry had grown used to having no car. And he was happy to have neither the responsibility nor the expense. He either walked to the coffee shop and the market or he called Joseph to pick him — or him and Esther — to take them to restaurants or special shopping trips in Mombasa. Most of the time, the driver would be booked in other areas, sometimes as far away as Nairobi, and they'd simply choose another day rather than rely on someone they didn't know in town. But in this one instance, their landlord Pankaj, who turned out to be Balvan's brother — was in town, and Harry had asked to borrow his car. He'd been told his California driver's license was sufficient, and he resolved that, even if stopped, the tourist police would look the other way for a small monetary consideration.

So, during the day while Esther was still at work, Harry drove himself in Pankaj's Suburu down to Galu beach, where the expanse of sand was whiter and broader, and where tourists didn't often go because there were not yet any resorts built up around it.

He was stunned to realize that, to this day, he had never fulfilled his dream of wading out into the turquoise water and digging his toes into the luxuriant white sand of the Indian Ocean.

He looked across at Singapore and sent them his fondest wishes. The morning sun was still at eye level, dazzling and beneficent, the giver of all life. He waded out some distance, the waves breaking over his calves. The water was still so shallow the breakers barely reached his knees. The sand was soft and supple. A million square miles of Indian Ocean were today, in this moment, his own personal bathtub.

The sun on his forehead was a blessing. The breeze was the very breath of life. He was more of a floater than a swimmer, but this was enough.

Kenya was his home now. Whatever he resolved to do, he could make it happen somehow. Would it involve a bribe? Skirting the law? Sucking up to politicians and arrogant Europeans? What-ever. What price could a man put on a life where he could define his own freedoms? Even if they had to be purchased?

Just as long as betrayal wasn't a cost.

When he returned to the car, which he'd parked on the verge of the beach near a refreshment stand, it was surrounded by a group of boys. They looked to be not yet teenaged. One or two were taller, probably older.

One of the tall ones held a cricket bat.

As Harry approached, he realized having the keys in his hand might be a bad idea. He shoved them in his pocket — perhaps too late, he feared. They could mug him, grab the keys, and take the car.

But their plan was much less nefarious.

One of the younger ones, who might have been elected because he had the most strident, shameless voice in the group, called out, "Papa! You see how faithfully we have guarded your car!"

Coming up to the kid, Harry mumbled, "It's not my car. But thank you. What's your name?"

The kid announced proudly, "I am Edward!"

The tall boy rebuked him immediately, "Stupid! *Tell* him!"

Edward recoiled slightly but found his voice again quickly to face front and demand, "You will appreciate, and you will give us small money for keeping you safe and staying your friends!"

Harry fished in the pockets of his cargo shorts, but he had no cash, not even a coin.

"I'm sorry," he said sheepishly. "I have nothing. Funga."

The tall one with the bat pulled a phone from his pocket. "M-Pesa! I give you the number!"

Harry replied, "I'm sorry. No phone. I don't carry it at the beach."

The tall boy screwed up his face in a sneer, swung the bat in a powerful arc, and connected with the front window of the car — *smack!* — leaving a star pattern of shattered glass.

The batsman sneered, "Next time, you pay attention!"

And they all ran off.

Here was the price of Covid. Families with no money, no food. Kids who should have been in school, but now experimenting with petty crimes.

Harry would end up paying for that window. Pankaj carried no insurance, and the replacement part had to come via tuk-tuk after a two-week wait from a salvage yard in Mombasa.

It would all, no doubt, get very much worse.

CHAPTER 38

*A*ldo's news was not heartening. Working through Esther, he'd set up a Zoom call. Harry followed the link on his laptop, which he had hooked to the widescreen TV in the living room.

Esther had invited David Odiengo, who joined them in front of the screen. She'd given him tea. Just before the meeting, the lawyer pulled a courier envelope from the breast pocket of his suit. He presented it with some delicacy to Harry.

Harry opened it and scanned the letter. It was from Singh's law firm. Aside from some formality, throat-clearing, and legal gas-passing, the cogent sentence read:

We regret to inform you that we no longer represent the interests of Messrs. Gardner and Barbieri, and we hereby resign your account forthwith.

No mention of Skebelsky. As if their patron and the instigator of all their plans never existed. Harry tossed the letter onto the couch and sighed, "Now I find out *I* was an account holder? News to me. No loss, those guys."

The screen lit up, and with two clicks, a virtual window opened. There was Aldo, his curly hair and bushy eyebrows filling the top half of the screen. His wavy hair was uncut, pandemic-long, and pulled back. He looked like Big Brother. Or maybe some new Mafia don. Everyone else in virtual meetings was clad in sweatpants or pajamas, and here he was in his gray suit with a new silk tie!

After pleasantries, which didn't last long enough to establish anything except that he and his wife had so far avoided the virus, he spoke in word code: "I have stayed long not only for my wife's illness, which is no better, but because I have been tending to our friend's business affairs."

Esther glared at Harry as if to say, *Don't mention the name.*

Aldo went on, "His business is being audited, and there are many complications. He has closed down his compound. He has emigrated to Europe. I believe he plans to live indefinitely in Montenegro. I am sorry to report that his charitable activities will not be carried forward."

Harry thought it was safe to say, "Aldo, my friend. We love you, and we send our fond wishes. To you, to your wife, to her caregivers." He took a deep breath and added, "I must say, I didn't realize you are much more involved in these business matters than I had imagined."

He shot a look to Esther as if to ask, *Did* you *know?*

The old Aldo would have smiled and cracked a joke. This dour fellow nodded soberly and took a long moment before he said, "Harry, I am sure by now you understand. We all do what we must do to care for our loved ones. And to survive."

"Yes, my friend," Harry finally said. "I do understand."

And that was the end of the session.

Harry turned to Odiengo to ask, "Audited?"

The lawyer explained, "Mr. Skebelsky's holdings have come under investigation by authorities in both the EU and the United States. The Swiss banks provide some cover, but not as much as they once did. I had not known about Montenegro. I'm surprised Mr. Barbieri shared that bit of information. You see, there is no extradition from Montenegro. One would hope that Mr. Skebelsky has already taken up residence there."

Harry turned to Esther to ask, "And how much of this did you know?"

She replied frankly, "Not much more. I knew that Aldo has been handling bank transfers for Victor, and that's the main reason he's stayed. But not more. And I've never wanted to know any of it. I'm concerned about my children and what they've been promised, but I can't think too far ahead. As for you, Harry, as for us, as I told you when we left Nairobi, you may decide to go home. Harambee was a nice dream, but it's not to be."

Harry asked Odiengo, "So, Victor's compound is shut down? No one living there?"

Odiengo nodded. "Yes, the staff was all dismissed and the place locked up. I have the keys, but I am not to allow anyone to live there without further instructions from my client."

"What about the taxes?"

"A considerable sum is past due. Collection agents may move on it any day. With the banking difficulties, Victor is not particularly liquid at the moment. He has larger problems, as you can imagine, although I'm sure he will be sad to lose the place. And, of course, he had high hopes for our project and the benefits it could bring to both of you — to all of us."

Harry asked the lawyer, "So, David. Is there any way in hell our plan still works? I mean, assuming the government doesn't grab Victor's property?" Harry took a long moment before he followed up with, "If we stepped up, do you think his rental offer still stands? I mean, rent the place for a buck and get the county to look the other way on the taxes?"

Odiengo sighed, "You'd need substantial funding, enough to show you will undertake real operations." But then he frowned and added, "But, the certifications? Those obstacles would still be there. You might think starting a school would be easier. Diani has schools, most of them private. But you can't certify a school until it's staffed and open. Or, if you decided to follow the clinic idea, it's even more complicated. Medical licensing, and such." He shook his head. "It's a tempting thought, but even with backing, under the circumstances, I would say wholly impractical."

After Odiengo had left, Harry confronted Esther.

"I believe you when you say you've known, but not so much more. And, you're right. Don't tell me. But it upsets me that you and Aldo are both tied more closely to Victor than you made me think. So I have to wonder whether you're protecting me or you're deceiving me."

She spoke tenderly and firmly. "Oh, my Harry. You should know by now what everyone knows. Corruption is the mother of Kenya. Only naïve Americans who refuse to see it in their own backyard can't understand."

BEFORE THEY WERE ready for bed, Esther offered the excuse that her mother was ill, Alice was away, and she'd have to spend the night at her house in Ukunda.

Harry couldn't tell from her expression whether this was a fib, but he let it go. Although he might not sleep so well, he wouldn't mind being alone with his thoughts tonight.

CHAPTER 39

*H*e stayed up later than his usual bedtime watching day-old episodes of late-night American talk shows, then he phoned Nicole on Skype. He wanted to see her face and for her to see his. He figured he'd try to catch her around her lunchtime.

He was happy she didn't duck the call. He'd been the last one to reach out, but weeks had passed, and she hadn't replied. He didn't want to lead off by scolding her about moving into his place in Rustic Canyon.

He was on his phone, lying propped up on his pillows in bed. It should be noon there, but from her woozy expression, it appeared she hadn't yet gotten up. Her face looked not only sleepy but careworn. "Hey, kid." (He'd never addressed her that way.) "I guess the world has gone crazy. They won't even let me leave now. Or if they did, Uncle Sam wouldn't let me in."

"Now you know how the Mexicans feel, hah," she yawned. "Seriously, you can't come back?"

He made light of it, and, for all he knew, the virus really was just a kind of flu, and the panic would pass almost as quickly as it had come. "Not for now. But that'll change. How are you holding up? No sniffles?"

"I'm not getting so close to anybody I could catch anything. They closed my school down, and I think you know I've been living alone."

He could tell she was bummed. After she'd lived through her trying teens, he couldn't remember many times she'd admitted weakness to him. He commiserated. "Good news and bad news, I guess." It was a point of pride with her that she never asked him for money. He risked not offering any now, fearing it might make her feel worse. If she did ask, he could step up.

She stayed cool, only wanting to know, "How about you? I've been watching the charts, and there are more cases in Santa Monica than you guys have in all of Kenya."

Now he could be chatty and not so personal. "One of the first things you learn here is not to rely on any statistic you get from the government. But I admit I haven't seen a lot of sick people. I hear they take them upcountry, which is a nice way of saying they might be getting shipped off in the middle of the night to somewhere no one would want to be."

"Not the wild time you expected? Or paid for?"

"Listen, Nicole. You've probably wondered why I've stayed."

That amused her. "Y'think? I dunno, maybe because your rent and your food are a fraction of what you'd spend here? You don't have a car, but you get driven everywhere? And you've got people waiting on you hand and foot for next to nothing in wages?"

"I'll have you know, the people I employ get more than they would from working at a luxury hotel or a fine restaurant. The government does expect me to give them benefits. I'll have to work through those details if I do stay any longer. But you're right. In many ways, I live like that English lord in Downton Abbey." He didn't know much about the things she liked, but he remembered she was a fan. Daughter of a history geek.

"Robert Crawley, Lord Grantham. His family's estate was in Yorkshire. All fictional, of course. None of those old farts were that kind to their servants. You might be treating your staff well, tipping them at Christmas and all that, dishing out the scraps on Boxing Day, but you're still exploiting them. They probably all hate you, gossip about you and your girlfriend behind your back."

They'd never talked about his lifestyle! Did she know how to hack his phone? "Where are you getting all this?"

"It doesn't take much imagination, Daddy. Lucky guess, and I scored one. Is she pretty? Older than twenty?"

He wasn't about to tell her. At least, not yet. "I don't tell you what to do."

"No, you don't. You don't tell me much of anything. So I have to guess, and from what you're *not* telling me, it sounds like I'm not far wrong."

"Can we stop snapping at each other for a minute and play nice?"

"You first."

"You teach English as a Second Language, right?"

"I did until last week. Don't ask anyone how well. And if you could understand any of my students when they answered, I'd be amazed."

"I'm living at the beach. That's probably where I'll settle. I was working with some people here who wanted to build a clinic, and now with the virus, their backers have pulled out, and they can't get anything started. English may be the national language, but many poor children can't speak it, much less read or write. Their parents can't afford to send them to school, and they need them to work at home anyway. You could tutor, is what I'm suggesting. You wouldn't need a license. No one is going to stop you from holding picnics, say, and giving them cooking lessons while you teach the names of vegetables and tell them your lame jokes."

"And why would I do this?" As if she'd never consider it.

"Ask yourself, 'Why wouldn't I?' I can't explain why I want to stay. And it's not just for Esther. That's her name, by the way. What I'm proposing is, when the travel ban is lifted, I'll pay your way. Give it a year. Call it a long vacation. Satisfy your curiosity. Visit me while you still can. Then, if you want to go back, go." Then he added, "But I'm willing to bet you won't."

"What would you bet?" Harry figured she was probably thinking he'd pay for her airline ticket and expenses, with a chunk of mad money thrown into the bargain.

But he said earnestly, "If you win and you go home, I'd be willing to give you the house." He paused, waiting for her intake of breath.

The hook was set. "Now, that's sounding like a deal," she admitted, carefully.

"Except you'll lose. But it won't matter because I am absolutely certain you won't ever want to go back." Then he added quickly, "And because I'm selling the place."

He expected she'd be angry, even furious to the point of speechlessness. Manipulation hadn't ever been his way with her, and he felt a pang of guilt he was trying to play her now.

Now he knew, sooner or later, she would come. He'd taken away her only reason for staying.

He told her he loved her, and she mumbled something like that back. Neither of them said it often enough, he knew, but today was all about new beginnings.

Before she ended the call, she yawned again and added, "Oh, Dad? You know, with my breakup and getting fired and all, I'm living in the house. I knew you wouldn't mind."

He wouldn't tell her he'd known. He sighed, then said, "No, sweetheart. I don't mind."

CHAPTER 40

*H*e hadn't given Nicole the house keys, but he expected she guessed where the emergency spares were hidden. Eleanor Amory had two sets, one for herself and maintenance access, one for renters. Of which there presently weren't any. Except, as he'd just been curtly informed, now Nicole. And with the pandemic lockdown in place and no other sitting tenants, he wouldn't be able to rent the place. Like two boxers in the ring, he thought he had her on the ropes, but then she threw him a deft punch below the waist.

He'd slept surprisingly well, given his misgivings about so many things, and he woke up with a ravenous appetite. He was pleased that he'd made some progress with Nicole. He might be happier if he knew his ploy had worked, but he admired her for joining in the game. He resolved to call Eleanor and arrange for the house sale, but his decision to do that wasn't yet firm.

So as was his habit when he had decisions to make, he could at least make the decision to have a meal first. He was sopping up the last of the egg yolk in his full, mixed-grill English breakfast with his buttered toast at Kokko's when a female figure wearing a broad-brimmed straw hat and patterned-cotton medical mask appeared across the railing from him in the patio dining area. The hat and the mask obscured her identity, but the sparkling eyes, even though shadowed by the brim, looked familiar.

It was kind of cute that her sultry voice was muffled by the cloth, but right away, he knew who it was — and feared he was being stalked again.

"Fancy meeting up with you!" Veronica exuded.

"Sorry I haven't called," Harry said with mock seriousness. "You wouldn't be stalking me?"

She giggled, "Some may go on safari to hunt giraffe. I'm usually after some hairless ape."

"So you flirt with the men and pry gossip from the women."

There was no discouraging her. "Truth be told," she went on, "my coworker Betsy and I have nothing to do with all the precautions, so we decided to take a breather and visit my friends in Bamburi. Seaside getaway, all that. But then, of course, I remembered you'd taken up residence here. And is there anywhere but Kokko's to find anyone who's anyone of a morning?"

"Okay, you have friends on the South Coast. But you came all the way to Diani on the chance of finding me?"

She cooed and lifted her hand over the railing to caress his forearm. "Almost, dear heart. You see, we do need to get back. Our driver suggested we follow the coast road down to Tanzania, then cross back. So, in all innocence, we had to pass through here."

"But you were counting on finding me. You do have a way of turning up on cue."

"You darling man. How could I resist? Care for a walk on the beach?"

THEY AMBLED along the sand at the water's edge, which was just a short stroll down the side road from Kokko's. They walked in their bare feet, carrying their sandals, as the warm water lapped their toes. They were headed south. Harry wouldn't be upset if they ended up at Nomad's and he'd be starting cocktail hour before noon.

She'd taken her mask off. Harry hadn't been wearing one. He'd dined open-air and he hadn't expected company.

No sooner had they stepped out on the beach than she jumped right in, "I think love is transactional, don't you?"

"I've heard that term," he said. "These days it's all about politicians and quid pro quo. You don't ask if you don't expect to get. It gets nasty, that's clear."

"Just so," she said. "Have you noticed how transactional Kenyans are?"

"They seem so generous to me. Even when I'm sure they want something."

"Basically," she explained, "there are Christians and there are Muslims. The Christians are mostly fundamentalists, except for the well-to-do Anglicans and Catholics. They live their faith. When they smile, it's genuine. And none of them has ever asked me, in all the years I've been here, if I've ever met Jesus. To Muslims, I'm a tourist, and they are all about manners and graciousness. If they don't invite you to tea, their tradition says they've insulted you. If they can't haggle until you buy something and they don't offer a bonus gift, they feel they've insulted you twice over."

"Everyone in Kenya seems to be after whatever I have in my pocket, but if I know that about them, even if they're wearing a police uniform, I can deal with it." He looked at her. He couldn't find deception in her face. The ocean breezes and the lapping of the waves and the golden sun, which had yet to climb to zenith, made it a magical moment. He went on, "But what about love and transactions? I didn't think you were talking about the tourist experience."

She smiled at him. She really was lovely, her skin so translucent and delicate, her unretouched eyebrows soft and blond. Her eyes so blue.

"What I mean is, we are at the stage in life when, regardless of what our experience of romance may have been, we don't regard it as essential."

He tried to be honest, but he wasn't sure whether he had enough insight on his own experience to be truthful. "Lucille and I had something. In the beginning, we were over our heads. Then it became, I don't know, what it usually becomes. I stood by her, she by me."

"This is what I mean. Even for those passionate young ones, love-making is transactional. You give, you get. Whether more or less on either side might not be an issue. It depends on the transitory states of each organism. Two slot machines rarely pay off at the same time, what? She's in the mood, or he's not. He needs a pill, or he doesn't. Do you know what I'm suggesting?"

"This is all in the abstract so far," he observed. "Are you talking about you and me? I'm not sure we're a subject anymore."

She hesitated. "Yes, I'm talking about us. And I admit we parted last time as though there might be no *us*."

"I'm more committed now than I was. I must confess."

"I understand," she said. "And expected. Accepted."

"So what do we have left to talk about? You're lovely, you are kind, and I have no regrets. But I admit I don't know what you want from me."

She stopped in her tracks, grabbed his arm, and turned him to face her. Then she said, "What I mean to say, before we are overcome by events — about love being transactional — is that I expect only *two things.*"

"And what would those be?"

"Quite simply," she stated as she looked straight ahead, "compan-ionship and honesty."

"That's your formula for the transaction?"

"Yes!" she exclaimed. "It's all I expect. All I require. In point of fact, all *I need.* All I feel able to *give.*"

"And what would I be expected to provide?"

"Harry," she said earnestly, "if you and I were to decide to be together, that's my minimum *and* my maximum. To put it crassly, if you must, if you were to go off philandering, I wouldn't care. As long as I don't know and you always come home."

He wondered how far the gossip had reached. He asked her, "How much do you know about what's going on with me?"

"I hardly remember her. I believe she's pretty."

The question echoed Nicole's. But he doubted they'd been talking. He surmised it was a matter of feminine instinct, a kind of radar.

"I think she's gorgeous," he said. "But so are you, and I'm not just pitching you compliments. With her, it's companionship, it's honesty, it's loyalty, and it's something more. Something I don't need to ask about, but it's there."

"I don't doubt you have it," she said. "Otherwise, you'd be with me." Then she added, in a low voice, "All I'm saying is, you could still be with me. And with her. I don't need to know any more than I do right now."

He didn't understand how that was possible. But in her mind, evidently it was.

What she was suggesting would be far too complicated, as well as require him to be the kind of person he wouldn't want to know. Yet, he didn't fault her for being who she was. He didn't know any other way to say it. "Veronica, no matter what, you're a friend."

He could tell she got the message. But she wasn't the slightest bit discouraged. "I am, Harry," she said sincerely. "You can count on me."

"This pandemic has sidetracked our plans, but there may be ways to move forward. I have a different plan forming in my head. But one thing that has stopped me is, I still don't know whether I'm getting the whole truth from Aldo. Or from Esther, for that matter."

"My dear," she said, "a wise man once told me that love is any relationship you have that you've not yet betrayed."

"Meaning?"

"I suspect — no, I know — that there are things your partners haven't told you. But remember where you are — in a country, in a culture, where possessing too much information can put you at risk. Where knowledge can imply culpability. Has either of them betrayed you? That is, have they lied to protect themselves or to protect you? Or was it both — to keep you from knowing facts that would only get you in deeper and subvert the enterprise?"

"They both say they are looking out for me. And I don't know different."

She grabbed his arm and quickened their pace toward the nearest bar as she said, "That's your answer, then."

As they settled down at Nomad for a libation, he asked, "Why Tanzania? What about the travel restrictions? Can you get over? Get back?"

The answer came, "They are saying the border is a bit porous down there." And she laughed.

The shore was dotted with more than a dozen feluccas. It was the day of a perennial wind-surfing contest, staged mainly for the tourists but not averse to a cohort of Kenyan cowboys cheering from the water's edge and guzzling Tusker like it was mother's milk.

This day, no tourists came, and the boat crews went through their drills anyway, sailing out to the reef, coming about, and clocking their times in. The winning crew, probably composed of fishermen who had no work, got something. No one remembered what.

VERONICA HAD A WHITE-WINE SPRITZER, made her excuses, and left. As she got up from their table, she apologized for being so forward. She told him she felt she had to speak up now because she expected he'd soon be off the market.

She didn't wait to hear his reply, and once again he was stunned by how much women seemed to know without his telling them.

A performing troupe of four crazily grinning teenage boys had taken up a spot on the sand in full view of the Nomad patrons. Harry recognized them as acrobats, a group that performed routinely up and down this stretch of coast, wherever they expected tourists to be congregating.

Today, they had summoned a five-year-old mzungu boy from among the patrons, and they were tossing him around. The stunner act before their bagman made his rounds to collect donations was high-lighted by boosting the child up to stand on the shoulders of a performer who was himself standing on the shoulders of another. Then they dropped the kid — catching him before he hit the sand.

Flawlessly executed, the stunt was impressive, and the kid was overjoyed at the physical thrill as well as the honor of being the center of attention as his parents watched.

No one seemed upset, including the lolling mum and dad with drinks in hand, and that fact alone upset Harry. Your kid's getting a broken neck would not only ruin a vacation and destroy the fabric of your family but could well put full-stop to these fellows' careers as entertainers.

But at least these resourceful gymnasts weren't threatening to damage automobiles or snatch purses. And their popular performances would make their faces so familiar to the tourist police that they'd never be successes as criminals.

He got up, made his way past the patio railing, and walked out onto the sand to confront the ostensible leader. Harry pulled two hundred-shilling notes from the pocket of his shorts. Granted, it was not a lot, just his walking-around money, but it might be more than they'd collect in tips that day. Then he said in a low voice, "The next time I see you guys, if you don't go throwing little kids around, I'll give you another two hundred. Each."

The leader grinned. "As you say, boss."

CHAPTER 41

The pandemic outbreak had been rolling through the world, including Kenya, into the early spring. The hotels should have been announcing their reopening dates. But this year, everyone who cared knew the foreign tourists wouldn't be coming anyway. So the mood of the town was depressed as usual, and now people were worried about getting sick. Nicole had reported to Harry that young people in Santa Monica often went around with no masks, and it was only the seniors who were faithful about it. And the same seemed to be true here at the beach. The mzungus, who were typically older, wore their masks, indoors and out. The expats wouldn't venture into a shop and sent members of their staff out with their lists of groceries and supplies, as they had done most of the time anyway.

In late April and into May came moderation of temperatures and the rainy season. The rains came in the mornings, not long after sunrise, in furious bursts that might last a few minutes, rarely more than an hour. The rain complicated the prospects of dining outdoors, especially since the onsets were sudden and surprising, the horizon at the beach looking crystal clear until dark thunderheads rolled in like some invading air squadron from the southeast, sweeping across to drench the land, then flying off as quickly as they'd come.

The schools had been closed for months, the government vowing the decision would hold for the whole academic year. But rather than coming to live with them in Diani, Esther's children had chosen to reside with the families of their best friends in Nairobi. Esther had outfitted the two other bedrooms at the Beachfront for them, and she was disappointed. But Charles and Yvonne must have colluded to get their story straight because their separate appeals stressed the argument that their homeschooling would be much more effective if they could be with their classmates, who were also top performers. So Esther really didn't have a counter-argument.

As for Harry, he didn't mind being relieved of coping again with teenagers living in his house, although he let Esther make her decision on her own and never offered any objections.

Besides the travel restrictions and school closings, the government was making a lot of noise about handwashing. For example, here on the coast, they'd set up temporary wash stations on either side of the Likoni ferry. Never mind that the crowds of pedestrian passengers were as closely packed as ever. Mask wearing on the boats was impossible to enforce, and so was anything like social distancing. But news clips of all that scrubbing up gave the impression that something was being done.

TOWARD THE END OF MAY, tourism in Diani was coming back slowly, begun by packagers offering deeply discounted deals to middle-class, upcountry Kenyan families who, until now, had never had a vacation longer than a weekend.

Harry had kept up his habit of reading *The Standard* faithfully every morning, and now he was scanning *The Independent* as well, along with postings he read on Facebook of the South Coast Residents' Association and Diani What's Up. One morning, an editorial caught his eye that upset him deeply:

Pandemic May Cause Children's Homes to Close

In their policy responses to the global pandemic, officials are said to be considering revoking the licenses of charitable children's homes and orphanages. These institutions typically depend on funding from external donors, which is now not sustainable because cash inflows have dried up. Budgets have been reduced, and quality of care cannot be assured. Some homes, for example, are only able to provide one meal for their wards per day. Besides these unfortunate overall trends, the immediate concern is that the facilities cannot perform adequate sanitation measures or social distancing due to overcrowding. In the words of one official, who requested to remain anonymous because of the sensitivity of policies that are as yet undecided, "Our best option may be to accelerate the reintroduction of these children into their communities." The practical effect, in some cases, will be to return children to impoverished grandparents or to the abusive situations that motivated their placement in those institutions. Similar circumstances apply to halfway houses and prisons, and those policies must be revisited, as well, the official told us.

It started with a question about an action and climaxed with an argument about whether they should be together at all.

Harry showed Esther the news article, and when he was sure she'd read it, he asked her, "So what are we going to do about this?"

She looked up calmly and asked him, "Who do you mean *we,* and about what?"

"You know what's going to happen. What kind of plan is it to absorb these kids back into their communities? Who are they kidding? They'll be throwing them into the street. More homeless children who will have to steal or they'll starve."

"And it's up to you to solve it? Are we back to talking about how it's the duty of white men to fix Africa?"

"Do you think those politicians are doing this so the orphanages can't come back at them for money?"

"Very possibly. Perhaps even likely. You're beginning to think like a Kenyan, Harry. Sometimes paranoia is simply a feeling you get before you let yourself finally see the truth."

"We had a project, and we had a plan."

"Not for an orphanage. Those places have to be licensed, and you can guess they won't be issuing any more of those for a long while. And, besides, our funding has also gone away. We're fortunate that you still have your investments and I still have a job."

"Did you ever care — I mean, *really care* — about those kids we were going to serve?"

"Did you? Was that the purpose of this vacation of yours that's turned into a low-cost retirement plan?"

"It's an opportunity that dropped into our laps, I admit. But we all thought we were finally involved in something worth doing."

"I'm involved in seeing my kids through school, keeping my family together, and, by the way, praying we all stay healthy."

"You know, I've wondered why you introduced me to Victor. And, when I thought back, Aldo was too quick to join in. I've even wondered about his reasons for booking my tour. All along the way, the two of you have been in communication with each other much more than you let on. And whenever you decide to let me in on some of it, I find out later I never got the whole story. Even now, with Aldo gone so long and you spending your days caught up with Balvan — whose problems never seemed to concern you so much before — it just seems like I've been carried along in a scheme I never understood. And still don't! Now you and your partner have dropped everything because your plan to grab Victor's land and the inheritance looks like it won't work out. Or was it all about Victor needing to launder suitcases full of cash?"

He expected these accusations would infuriate her. What he really wanted was her vehement denial. But instead she said, still calm and unperturbed, "Harry, I told you when you asked me before. All I want is a decent job with a boss who treats me fairly. What happened with Victor would have been like winning big at the casino. For all of us.

And the first I learned of his plans for the trust was when he came to see me, which I told you. Who knows whether my kids will ever have it, but you can imagine I'm not counting on it."

"Do you even love me?"

That stopped her. "Love?" She gave him a long, hard look. "I haven't offered it, and I don't require it from you. Kindness and tenderness, yes."

Hers was not anything like the answer he expected.

She added, "While we're on the subject of feelings, Harry, may I ask, what have you learned about yourself in the time you've been with us?"

"What are you getting at?"

"It's a simple question. Do you know more about yourself, about your character, now — than before you accepted Aldo's suggestion to travel?"

He shrugged, "Until this moment, I thought I was kinder, mellower."

"That may be true. I didn't know you before. But what I will tell you, which I believe you don't know, is that you have trouble making up your mind. You can't come out and say what you want because you don't know what that is. Or you won't admit to yourself what it is you want."

"I wanted to be with you," he said quietly. "From that day in the store. I haven't changed."

"I believe you," she said, coming close. "This much, I do believe. But what about all this other stuff? The great cause you suddenly profess to care about?"

"You and Aldo were always coming up with something. So now that there's this big problem staring us in the face, I hoped you'd already thought about it, discussed it."

"Harry Harambee!" she huffed. "Mister go-along. The fellow who's happy to ride in the back and look out the window. Don't you see that's been what you've been doing all along? Did you ever once announce to us — 'I know what we should do!'"

She surprised him again when she rested her palms against his chest and started to cry. "Harry, you are a good man. You have a good heart. But if you retire to Diani without a plan, you will spend your afternoons guzzling Tuskers and passing out before dinner."

After a moment, Harry asked her, "And what about Aldo? What should we think of him? How can a man who works for Victor be one of us?"

She stated simply, "Aldo will return when the business he has undertaken to do is done. Then, he will keep his word to us, as he has always done."

He took both her hands in his and kissed them. There was a twinkle in his eye as he asked her, "So, where did you plan we'd go for dinner?"

She laughed, rested her head on his chest, and replied, "Wherever you say, Harambee."

EPILOGUE

en years later,

  The international press was touting Kenya as "the new California." And wags were beginning to call the southernmost strip of South Coast "Silicon Diani."

Over the last decade, animal migration routes had been progressively disrupted by human-animal conflict, but UN, USAID, and EU grant programs, collaborating with myriad NGOs, had funded projects by agrarian and environmental engineers to mitigate the impacts of rapid suburban and exurban development. Sadly, the rhinos were gone, and in Diani, the Colobus monkeys were only a memory.

Land prices in Naivasha, Kisumu, and Eldoret were skyrocketing as professionals employed in Nairobi sought countryfied homesteads from which they could, for the most part, telecommute.

Kenyan diplomats had been working closely with the Ethiopians to help arbitrate water rights to the headwaters of the Nile brought on by ongoing consequences of Israeli projects to dam and moderate the riparian flows. In return for their participation, the Kenyans were promised access to the resource by their commercial water bottling plants in Ethiopia.

On one bright Monday, Charles Skebelsky-Mwemba stood next to the President-elect as they cut the ribbon in the gleaming main concourse of Terminal 1 of Diani International Airport for the benefit of videographers and assembled dignitaries. As CEO of Skelbelsky Holdings, Mr. Skebelsky-Mwemba can be credited with the architectural vision, construction management involving hundreds of thousands of tasks and a dozen subcontractors, and the highly automated, heavy-mechanized logistics to complete the massive development project in less than two years, beating the project deadline by a month and achieving a contract bonus of Ksh200 million.

In an unbroken chain of title since the area was owned by the Sultan of Zanzibar, a handful of political families still controlled the ten-mile strip of land that borders the ocean. Adjacent to the airport, a new building complex arose. It was a high-tech campus of mixed-use buildings, designed by the Danish firm that built the Bibliotheca Alexandrina near Cairo in 2001.

From a feature article in *The Standard:*

Harambee Made Real in Kwale County

The Harrison Wilson Gardner Memorial Harambee Center for Youth Development occupies the grounds and buildings of the former Victor Skebelsky compound in Diani Beach. The project was initiated during the Coronavirus Pandemic of 2020 as an unlicensed youth hostel, made possible through a generous private donation from the Gardner estate. Except for a small administrative office, a nurse's station, and a dining hall that was once a grand living room, the five houses on the campus quickly filled with bunk beds. When the houses reached capacity, several shipments of mountaineering tents arrived, donated by Davis & Shirtliff Group. Those makeshift lodgings soon covered the grounds until there was no plot left to drive a stake.

Over the years, the Harambee Center has been the only home to thousands of homeless youth.

The new Ukunda campus is scheduled to open later this year, constructed under the leadership of the center's director, Dr. Nicole Gardner.

In a speech before a meeting of the Council of Governors last month, President-elect Yvonne Skebelsky-Mwemba acknowledged her debt to the Harambee Center and the experience she gained there as a teaching intern. No doubt she was acknowledging Kenya's proud traditions of cooperation among public officials, private benefactors, and NGOs on the burgeoning South Coast when she said, "The Kenya of today is a miracle. But only because those who came before us believed that miracles don't just happen."

IN HIS WILL, Harry Gardner had stipulated he be buried, not in Diani as his friends and admirers would have expected, but in a small plot in City Park in Nairobi, close to the grave of Pio Gama Pinto, the socialist leader who dedicated his life to the liberation of the Kenyan people and who became the independent country's first martyr in 1965, allegedly assassinated by political operatives.

Harry's interment was attended by his family and close friends, including his widow Esther Mwemba-Gardner and his colleague Aldo Barbieri. Until that time, the plots around Pinto's grave had been overgrown with weeds. Not far off, the graves of British soldiers killed in the rebellion are marked by pristine white marble slabs arranged in neat rows, with a manicured lawn. One can only speculate that the public administrators of the park wished to send a message by not tending faithfully to the eternal resting places of troublemakers.

But a groundsman who goes by the name of Gabriel can be seen from time to time mowing the area.